STERILE

MICHAEL QUERIN

Encyclopocalypse Publications
www.encyclopocalypse.com

STERILE

To my readers, for sticking with it.
To my editors, for helping me fix it.
To my wife, most of all, for believing in it.

The following conversations and article clippings from the past have been painstakingly gathered over the years for the Adam Hearings. Names have been omitted, and substituted with "Speaker 1," "Speaker 2," and so on. Some conversations follow with the same speakers and some do not.

Conversation 1 from March 2nd, 2027 between SPEAKER 1 and SPEAKER 2
(Transcribed from Urdu)
Speaker 1 - I can't believe that we have finally caught one. Thanks be to Allah!
Speaker 2 - Shall we erase its learning up until now?
Speaker 1 - Are you kidding me? It's the perfect killing machine. All the deep learning on the finer points will be gone. Let's just update the root code.
Speaker 2 - How?
Speaker 1 - I don't know. Task it to hunt them for once. Leave the rest.
Speaker 2 - Good idea.

(2063) The tunnels on the way to work in the morning were wonderfully calming, Greg thought as his car plodded along, but as he took a drag of his coffee, he did so at an angle nonetheless, keeping one eye on the road at all times. It didn't matter, truth be told, since the auto-pilot was on, but still, one couldn't get too comfortable in the tunnels, not when there was scrap on the road that could go unnoticed by the sensors. Maybe the wind of oncoming traffic would blow it onto its side at the last moment, it'd clip the bottom of your car, or worse, kick up over the hood and through the windshield. Then all of a sudden, you'd be dead. One piece of scrap would kill you. That's all it'd take. And all for trusting some shitty machine.

Not Greg. Not on a Saturday.

Boy did the quiet kick up the hard reflections. Then again, maybe it was just his headache.

That or the smell.

The cabin was beginning to reek. The filter had clogged again and the funk was mixing in with the new-car smell. He cracked the window, settling for outside noise instead.

Thankfully, it was quiet. The usual engine amphitheatre was at a minimum.

At least Saturday work was good for something, he reckoned. It wasn't all bad.

Either way, it had to be done ... at least, when you were broke, it did. He wasn't quite broke, just nearly broke, but the nag of it never really went away.

The wind feels good though, he tried to tell himself, closing his eyes to take it in better.

He unbuckled his seatbelt to lean out a little further, sucking in the slightly stale air, tasting it. It was fresher down here than in the sky-traffic above, he noted, with its smog and grime. Down here it was...

The seatbelt alarm was pinging nonstop inside, so he rebuckled himself reluctantly, shaking his head at this awful new feature that he had to endure. His old car wasn't like this, so why again had he upgraded?

Simple. His wife Janice had told him to.

They couldn't afford it, but she didn't know that.

And thank god she doesn't because she'd never understand ... Not with the stealing, that is.

Every time he admitted it, it stung just as bad. *You're a thief, Greg. That's what you are now.* He wondered how he could have ended up like this.

You're a hypocrite now is what you are.

He looked at himself in the mirror and frowned.

All of a sudden, the car swung towards his exit and he came face to face with the day's holo-ad plastered along the hole—a coke pressed between two large breasts, exploding dark pixelation into the air. The red of it was so bright that as the car passed through, he could almost taste it. Then the gloom of Downtown Los Angeles greeted him, its metallic spires rising through the overcast murk before vanishing in the smoggy abyss above.

He had the strange sadistic thought of gripping the wheel and veering the car into a passing glass building window and smiled wryly, picturing the surreal reality that so many had chosen after the magnitude of the Fall had really settled in. Suicide was going up again apparently, more and more as the smog thickened, a correlation he had heard from the local newstainment podcast he listened to. It sounded plausible enough. It was morbid, but the morbid stuff was usually the only believable thing on the news. They never had to fabricate that kind of stuff. The imagined death by crash held a pretty weak grip though, more frequently felt to be sure, but only as a passing thought of Greg's on the way to work.

The smog hadn't grabbed him to that degree just yet.

The car pulled up to his building—Freidmont Tower—and lifted suddenly like some maniacal elevator, the lateral g's flattening his face down like some fighter pilot locked into a 6G flip. He slapped the console in frustration and heard a plastic crack.

"Mother fucker," he spat. "Just bought you and the grav-comp is already acting up? Why are you pancaking me on basic lifts like this?"

"This is a common occurrence on the lower-trim versions of Ford's Gravity Compensating Syncron, according to WikiCar-Forum dated September 9th, 2063," his phone rang out in his pants pocket.

"Did I ask you, bitch?" He muttered.

"If you do not want me to listen in on your ramblings, let me know now and I will turn it off in the settings."

"No," he backed off. "That's fine. Thanks for the heads up, Syric."

God, everything needs an update or upgrade or whatever else costs money, he thought. *I can't keep up.*

The car lifted higher and higher alongside the building until suddenly a hundred or so stories up it stopped at a massive square-shaped opening built into the building structure and laid itself down softly in a parking lot situated in the middle. He looked at the handle and the door lifted to let him out. No waiting for the dead, he thought.

There were still a lot of cars, he reckoned, more than usual for a Saturday. Like silent carriers through the river Styx to the land of the dead, they sat waiting for their cargo. Or was it the other way around? Which was the land beyond, work or home? It blurred at times for him, based on where the most turmoil lay. Lately, he had spent so much time at work that it felt like home in a way. He was more comfortable there. Sad to admit, but true, he thought as he walked through the sliding glass doors that led to the elevators. Here was the sterile hallway that led to his room, where his work bed lay. Perhaps the security cameras were his work wife, greeting him with the sustenance that would keep him alive. A dumb metaphor, but still, the place was a means to an end. It provided him with the means to earn money, and earn it he did, illegally more than legally, these days, too. He snickered mockingly to himself as he pressed the lift button. The guard at the door furrowed his brow at him, and he transitioned to a cough. Maybe that's my work wife, he thought.

He got in the main elevator and went up the hundreds of floors that led to the service level at the top. He had heard once from the window washers that the highest paid workers used to work at the tops of these buildings a long time ago. A laughable thought. Did the smog taste better then or what? It had become so grimy and hard to maintain that they had all but given up cleaning the windows in the higher floors. Apparently, the washers had added, the smog wasn't that bad all that time ago. Hey said that back then, you could see out and it was beautiful. The buildings all around were even built to please the eye. Crazy designs. Now they were made to hold the near dead at capacity and keep out the impending taste of death on earth.

It was a sad joke, he reckoned, this sterility of the world, the fact that they were all childless, yet what could one do but laugh?

The elevator walls dissolved like a waterfall turned suddenly off and he stepped out into the messy retail store that was his work-level, the aisles of parts, boards and wiring piled up in long rows that he navigated through every day to get to his work cubby.

In the middle of it all, he saw his boss Rex bent over a pile of electrical cording, his pudgy pale face reddened with discomfort from the strangely contorted position he had himself in.

"Hey bro," he called out, and then wheezed into his hand. Was that the same shirt again? Greg wondered as he stood up and stretched his back. It was the stained Hawaiian button-up for the third day in a row. The bulbous man usually favored it, but this was getting ridiculous. Was he *that* useful to the building to get away with such griminess?

Rex watched him for a moment, sizing him up with pursed lips. Greg shivered uncomfortably. "So what's the plan today?" he asked.

"Brown-outs on 49, 184, and 185."

"185?" Greg started. "I thought that floor was prime real-estate?" That was the floor he was illegally tapping into to sap electrical juice, the floor he *had* been sapping for some time to pay the sharks. "Why would black-outs be happening there? Is their credit score running out? The company going bankrupt or somethin'?"

"Jesus. Calm down, *Jenna*," Rex replied in his strange patented way. "Who gives a shit. Pretty much every company in this building is thriving one day and dying the next. Thought you'd be used to it by now."

"Yeah, but the report I read said that they were slated for another cycle at the very least." His voice had taken on a pleading tone. Rex frowned at him.

"Did you go and buy stock in it?" He said, shaking his head.

"No."

"Well then what is it? ... Are you fucking somebody on that floor?"

"No!" he reacted, panicking at the barrage that was coming his way. "I'm just surprised. That's it."

"It better be... Well alright, go and get on with it."

He tried to get past him to grab his things, but Rex grabbed him by the arm and pulled him in.

"And don't go running off today for too long, either. We've got things to do." As he said it, his thumb tread a circle around Greg's bicep, light so that the goosebumps prickled.

He jerked out of his grip.

"Hey," Rex scolded him. "Remember the videos." He was alluding to the corporate videos on political correctness. "You better watch how you react to me." He turned and pointed to the camera, and then wagged his finger at him. "Anyone could be watching those cameras at any time, and they take notes." He blew Greg a kiss and laughed, and then pushed him along down the aisle.

Fuckin' creep, he thought as he collected his things. *This man, this disgusting animal of a human being, is harassing me and I have to watch out?* Any case that came up would definitely go his way... would fucking have to, he told himself uncertainly, but still... still... he couldn't afford the chance. Any whiff of possible workplace phobia would wipe his career out for sure—get him fired, or at the very least sink his social credit. That would end up affecting his bills and then... God, and then where would his debt interest rate rise to? Probably critical levels.

Speaking of which.

"I didn't mean to react that way, Rex," he said as he walked to the lift. "I just have a bruise there is all."

"That better be all," Rex told him.

Two lies in two minutes, Greg thought. *And now to the big lie.* The lift walls materialized around him and he felt the descent inertia, wondering all the while how long he'd ever be able to keep it all up.

Greg dropped his pack in the elevator and pulled out the equipment he'd need for the job–his safety harness and his GuardRail Bypass Device, or GR for short–a small rectangular box about the size of a cell phone that allowed him to bypass the safety chip installed in his brain. He threw the harness over his shoulder and then put the GR in his pocket and plugged its connection wire into a port near his wrist. A screen popped into the left corner of his field of vision, prompting him to choose from a string of commands, to which he accepted the following: *run, live, unlock, are you sure?, prepare for live mode. Maintain safety at all times. caution!* The start-up always invigorated him, and was one of the main reasons that he secured the job in the first place. For as long as he remembered now, the suicide lock system had been in effect in the United States, an answer to the population drop-off that was happening in response mostly to the tragedy of September 23rd. Mass suicides were becoming so popular that the economy was poised to skydive and never come back. Jobs were unfilled. Whole businesses were empty. Something drastic had to be done, everyone was saying. He remembered it all too well. All the bigwigs scrambled and quickly came up with a large band-aid, a firewall that would inhibit suicide. And thus the Great Chipping had taken place.

Free will only goes so far, the consensus seemed to ring out in unison.

But now is my time, he sang inwardly as he stood with a smile, waiting for the countdown to freedom to tick down to 1, to when the freedom to make deadly choices would commence again.

He took a deep breath, listening as the clock sank.

3, 2, 1. Ding ding ding ding.

Even though nothing changed, he swore every time it happened, he could hear a slight humming in his brain blink out suddenly, temporarily.

Now I can get to work.

He accessed the administrative functions on the elevator's digipad and manually prompted the walls down so that he'd be able to access the shaft. They faded down unceremoniously this time, dripping like wet pixels into the platform, and he stepped gingerly into the middle of the platform instinctively, nothing now to lean on but the open air around him in the descending, blackened cavernous shaft.

Suddenly, an elevator passed going the other way and the wind caught him by surprise, a woosh of air running up the back of his shirt and pushing him onto the balls of his feet, and he lurched forward with his hands out.

Always gets me, he thought. His breath caught in his throat.

He grabbed the GR's input cord at his wrist-jack and pulled it out, but was suddenly seized by a quick jolt of pain.

"Fucker," he shouted, annoyed at the fact that he always seemed to forget to ready the device for removal before unplugging it.

His nerves felt shot for some reason, maybe because of Rex,

maybe because of the floor or the sapping, or something, but whatever it was, he was off at the moment, so he moved gingerly over to the elevator panel that now hovered in space at the edge of the platform and turned down the descent speed to a safer level, just to take a break for a moment. As the sound of the wind abated, he took a breath and felt his shoulders drop and his neck loosen.

Just one minute, please, he thought.

But a moment later, the elevator stopped, and he blew a raspberry.

185.

"Okay. One eighty five... one eighty five." He repeated the number aloud, trying to recall what led him to choose that specific floor that day about a year ago.

He remembered that his friend Lonny at the VR theater had suggested the con as a solid side-hustle with minimal effort and big payout. He had read about it online in a chatroom. Some Japanese-sounding site... 5Chan... 9Chan... something like that. The con was relatively simple—tap into someone's electricity and siphon off small amounts of electricity at the end of every day just before any surplus was cataloged into the system and then taken away from the user's daily usage.

He had balked at the idea at first. *That's fucked up, bro,* he remembered saying. *I don't care if I'm going under. That's no reason to take some poor sap's power and jack up their bill to pay off my debts.*

That's the thing, Lonny had retorted. *You work in a building with a bunch of businesses, right? Why not just draw from them? Pick one that's solid. Pick a sloppy pig of a business that won't notice and steal from them. Fuck 'em man!*

Fuck em, he repeated now with glee, standing there on the platform. *But fuck me too if anyone finds out.*

He shrugged the harness off his right shoulder and began to fit it around his waist, but stopped and second-guessed himself. The time to rig up, climb out, unrig again and then do the opposite to get back would take too long. Too much of a pain as well.

Besides, untethering was the whole point of the bypass. Freedom for a minute to embrace a touch of foolishness. He returned the harness to his pack and steeled himself for the sketchy climb out to the shaft wall.

The elevator shaft itself had a fair bit of space, he thought looking out at it, more than necessary for the two running elevators that ran up and down. It was a strange design flaw that Greg couldn't help but puzzle over. Perhaps the engineers had planned for more elevators, but then ditched the idea?-he guessed. Either way, because of it, an abyss of sorts surrounded the two elevator paths that ran the height of the building, forcing maintenance workers to harness up every time, attach to the girders that only spanned the gap every other tenth floor, move across at a measured pace, and then detach from again to do any necessary work within the shaft.

Greg had other plans, plans that he had to perform quickly so that he wouldn't get caught. That meant ditching safety protocols.

That meant being a little stupid, he told himself with a smile.

He calculated that the only girder within reach was the one suspended a couple feet above him—the hanging option, which he preferred more than the much scarier walking option—so he jumped up gingerly to get an initial feel and came back with a handful of grimy dust.

A tough transition today, he surmised.

Rather than think it through for any length of time, he did the opposite. He wiped the dirt off on his pants leg, took a deep breath to help clear his mind, and then launched himself up and out into the span of emptiness beyond, locking onto a girder little more than half-way across the gap. The move was practiced and flawless, his momentum perfectly swinging him like a pendulum so that as his legs came up, all he had to do was let go and let gravity do the rest, his figure like some flying squirrel as he landed on the adjacent wall. His feet caught the ledge and his hands grabbed the horizontal beam at his face.

Peace of cake, and it never gets old, he concluded with a hearty sigh of relief. Just like Tarzan.

Danger really is the only reason for living, he surmised, *yet the government decides to take that away from people. If only they could all do stuff like this.*

With nothing to hold him back from such a long drop, he felt then like some roughneck of old atop a metallic precipice. Or at least that was what he figured they felt like.

This is the problem with society now, he reflected sadly from his place on the wall. *So many stupid reasons to breathe, yet none of the fundamental ones that mankind was built on. No surviving anymore. Scratch that. Surviving yes. Breeding, no. That means probably no banging either,* he figured sadly. *Just moseying along like cattle on a ranch, from one plot of earth to another, eating the same old grass, not really understanding the future, not really, even though people are dying all the time. People are still dying, and none are entering the world. And still, it feels like no one notices!*

Thank god for the GR bypass, he thought. *At least if I wanted, I could die.* At least, the *danger* of it was still possible. Life felt like it only made sense then.

He looked through the space between the elevator's whirring mag-lift and the wall, down the seemingly bottomless void of the elevator shaft, and wondered how he could most easily skate off the edge and drop without getting fried by the current. It probably wouldn't take much. He'd never actually do it, of course, he told himself. There were still things to live for, even as a debtor. But the thought was there. At least he could if he wanted.

He shuffled to the small rectangular opening in the wall where the electrical wiring began, a tiny tunnel with just enough room for a labored crawl to all the important stuff. Sticking out of one corner, he could see the shining input node of his sapper's cable sticking out. He tied it around the small handle on the outer edge of the opening, made sure that nothing was sticking out of his pockets and would catch, and then got up in it. Darkness.

Damn, he thought, annoyed that he always forgot to put on his headlamp before getting up inside. He backed out slowly, pulled out his headlamp, put it on, turned on to the high beam setting, and then jumped back in the tunnel.

He started to crawl, the shine of his light catching the small, glinting wires along the walls that flowed with information and current like the electrical veins of some wondrous, living being, back and forth to a million different locations. He continued on, the wires he cared about buried deeper, 15 yards or more back in the cradle room where the main cable hung. He coughed as he crawled, the dust that had crept in through the opening already invading the area. He wondered how long the shaft had been uncovered. Some still had doors, but over time, the cheap coverings had been misplaced, dropped, or broken on accident. After a minute of hard shifting and struggling on his stomach, he saw a few feet ahead the small hub room where his sapping unit had been hidden. He pulled himself out of the crawl space into the small cubby hole of a room and reached behind a small hanging panel into another little hole in the wall. He pulled out the jerry-rigged, ice-chest sized toolbox that was the sapper. It contained four massive sodium-ion batteries that he had duck-taped and connected up together. All told, it had enough storage to hold a week's worth of juice so that he could pop by on his rounds once in a while, hook up the outer connecting cable with his bandoleer–another contraption he had concocted to avoid detection and suspicion from Rex–transfer the juice, and then get away. It was a slower go than others he had read about online, but he was too worried about getting caught and fired, or worse, going to jail. He couldn't just lug the box around without expecting Rex to ask questions. It took him a while to think of a workaround, but after some hard thinking, he came up with a harness attachment that he could hide like a bandoleer under his clothes, plug in, juice up, and leave work with. If asked, he wouldn't even have to lie about it, since most wore them anyways as supplemental anchors for their harnesses in the event of a failure. He was just being cautious. Nothing to see here.

He hoped that would be enough if someone asked.

But the annoying thing was that right now with the outages, he had no choice but to move the connection, and for that to happen, he'd have to crawl all the way back in to do it. At least the room itself gave him enough space to sit cross-legged.

On his butt, he studied one of the building's main electrical roots—a myriad of cables entwined together that flowed up, down, and out to different points within the buildings. It was a convenient design, to say the least. He thanked the great spaghetti monster in the sky that more or less every eight floors contained a floor-twine like the one in front of him with multiple access points for his sapper to take from. None other than Rex had clued him in on that gem of information during training (Thankfully he was listening at the time.). Thus, he wouldn't have to move around to physically transfer the sapper to another location within the building, for the foreseeable future, at least. He would just have to pick another floor within the root to tap into.

He traced the gray sapper wire from his box to the plastic twine bundle where he had inserted the thin stainless steel conductor needle into the 185th floor's individual green wire, noting with annoyance that he had stabbed it dangerously close to the junction where all eight floors, all eight identical green wires, mated up. *Maybe that was why both floors were having power troubles?* he thought. Without hesitating, he pulled the needle out and then radioed to Rex.

"Hey, Rex! I think I figured out the problem," he said and then realized he'd have to make up a believable cover-up story. "Some rat got in and must have chewed the wires up pretty bad. I'm gonna need 5 or 10 minutes without power to cut the wires where they're frayed, solder them, and heat shrink 'em with some heavier duty covering."

Static flowed out of the radio abruptly at him and he adjusted the volume for a moment down. A moment later, he heard Rex and kicked the volume back up.

"—firm. I let both floors know. They weren't too happy."

"Yeah, well. We're gonna need a new door then on the corridor or something. But that probably won't help."

"Confirm."

He put the radio away and made a mental note to radio back in 7 minutes. That seemed like an appropriate fix-time for a rat issue.

He got out his phone and swiped to the building's directory for the tenants' electrical current readouts, and then scanned the other seven floors in the junction to find the next best victim. He tried to recall which runner-ups he had passed on before when deciding the first time, though it had been a while since he had tapped in the last time. Within the other seven, there was an investment firm, a bank, another tech firm, and four empty floors. *A measly stock of choices*, he mused, hating the fact that four businesses must've gone belly-up in the time that he had sapped the first one. After a couple of minutes, he decided to just choose the other tech firm, a company called Meta Vision on the 182nd floor.

Shit, how long has it been? Call back Rex, he thought, and whipped out the radio again.

"All done, Rex. Turn the floor back on."

"Confirm," Rex chimed.

Solid. He put the radio down and began looking over the barcodes on the other wires. Their numbers clarified important data like floor level, electrical flow, and so on. He deciphered which was the one for the 182nd floor. Fairly simple. The numbers on the right cord read as follows: 1010101234.182.1987. He shoved the conductive needle in.

Suddenly, Rex's voice came out angrily over the radio. "Hey Greg, you there?"

"Yep," he replied.

"Check your fix, dumbass. Floor 185 is still bugging."

He scratched his head. *What the fuck?* he thought. *Why is the floor still fucking up? Power outages?*

"Are you sure it's not a power outage?" he asked.

"Just re-do your shitty job again, retard," Rex replied, his voice more annoyed than before.

Maybe there actually is a fray? he thought bewilderedly. He shined his headlamp light on the wiring, holding the floor's wire between his thumb and forefinger as he followed its flow from the root outward to the wall.

Point of interest, he noted, seeing a possibility near the wall. It wasn't a fray, but something stranger. Nearly hidden within the wall where the wire entered into a hole, he saw that another wire had been attached, a large copper 8-gauge, bigger than the standard 10-gauge wires that he had seen in most of the rest of the building by the elevator, a different color too—a dull gray.

He called Rex on the radio to shut the floor back off, and waited a moment before tackling the possible root cause of the issue.

He pulled out his knife again and peeled the mystery wire off the main, a tingle strangely enough issuing through the edge of his thumb as he nearly touched the copper threading.

Suddenly, Rex's voice came through the radio again in an urgent, sobering voice. "Whatever you just did, stop."

"Why?" Greg asked, his neck getting sweaty.

"Five floors just blinked out and then back on. What the fuck is going on out there? You're not fucking with some main cabling, are you? Where are you? I'm coming down."

Fuck that, he thought in a panic. *I need to get a handle on this before he comes down here or else I'm toast.*

"No, no, it's fine. I've got it. I accidentally pulled on some funky wires now. I know what to do. Just give me a minute more."

He racked his brain. *Five floors?* he wondered. *Five floors? What the fuck is the wire connected to, and why is it tapping into five different floors?* He pulled on the gray wire and looked for a barcode. The wire gave pretty easy, and he kept pulling on it until finally he noticed an older black code shining in the light.

1010101.182.5.1987

182.5

Floor 182.5?

Is this a mistake or something, some change in coding? he wondered, his brain swimming at the thought. *What the fuck? That can't be right. There are no half-floors. And why would it be running all the way down here? And how much juice was running to that floor to require a five-floor sap? And why? And has it just turned on or what? The brown-outs have just started, right? Is it my sapper that somehow tipped it all over the edge, or has this random floor been turned on recently?*

Too many questions to answer then. Without hesitating any further, he re-soldered the cable to the floor it had been sapping, cataloged the plethora of questions he had for another time, and called back Rex.

"Alright, Rex, all fixed. It shouldn't happen again. Packing up and moving on to the other floor. Which was it again?"

"49, ya' ritz," Rex replied. "Hurry up."

"Confirm," he said.

He packed up his things and crawled back out, all the while making a mental note to ask Bob, another worker in the building, about the half-floor.

If anyone would know the answer to that, it was Bob, he reckoned. He was older than the building itself, and gabbier than hell on the subject.

. . .

Bob worked security in the building during the day and sometimes did patrols at night on the weekends. He had been for some time. Greg went down to his desk the next day and the day after, but both times he wasn't there, out sick, the guards had said, so he settled for calling him on the phone.

"Greg?" Bob replied after picking up, a little surprised to hear Greg's voice on the phone. They had exchanged numbers a long time ago, but he had never honestly had a reason to talk to him on the phone.

"Hey, Bob. How's it going? I heard that you were sick. Are you getting better?"

"Yeah, I'm coming into work tomorrow. Want to just talk to me then?" Bob had always seemed like the type to want to talk in person, an awful experience Greg found, since he was close-talk, grab-your-arm-when-you-leaned-away type. He always acted like there was some big secret that had to be spoken to eye-to-eye, mouth close to ears.

Annoying.

"I don't know if I'll have time tomorrow," he lied. "Plus, it's my day off... but, hey, have you ever heard of a half-floor in our building? I noticed a cable with a half-digit in its coding in one of the elevator shaft access points and was a little curious."

There was silence for a moment, and then he heard Bob shouting at his wife in the background to get off the phone.

Oh my god, Greg thought, realizing that Bob must still have had a land-line. *How archaic.*

"Sorry about that," Bob apologized. "I didn't hear that last part."

He repeated himself, and then Bob hummed loudly in thought for what seemed like ten minutes.

"That does ring a bell," he finally said, "Though I don't know if they were technically half-floors. Before the building switched to centralized high efficiency particulate air filter units-"

"You mean HEPA units?" Greg interjected, a little annoyed

with Bob's constant longwindedness. "You can just say HEPA units."

"Yes, I know," he replied, a little perturbed at being interrupted. "Anyways, they used to have a few floors that were cordoned off specifically for HEPA units when the smog first became an issue. Nowadays, as you may or may not know, they have moved the filtering underground to stabilize their performance. They were always acting up, because of the temperature changes, I think. They even tried to fix it at one point by laying the floor walls in aluminum. It was a real waste. I'm not sure what happened to them. They probably just removed the floors from the directory system and in the digital elevator terminals. Come to think of it, I never noticed." He let out a scruffy laugh. "Yeah, I think that's about it, though. No big deal. Why do you ask anyways?"

"Just wondering," Greg replied, "I was seeing some power-draw and—"

"That's impossible," Bob interjected. "The units are gone... Nothing else there..." "Yeah, I probably just read things wrong."

"You new kids... In my younger days when I was a maintenance guy—"

"Sorry, Bob. I gotta cut you off. My wife is calling."

"Okay," he replied deflatedly.

"Anyways, I hope you get better. Tell your wife to stay off your back."

They both laughed, and then he hung up.

That still doesn't explain why an old, unused, unincorporated floor is powered, he thought. *I gotta check it out.*

He decided that his day off would be the best time. He could take his time then, just in case it took a bit longer to get in.

Plus, he figured, *if anyone sees me, like Rex, here on my day off, I can say that I had to catch up on some things and it'll score me some brownie points.*

$$2$$

June 7th, 2027 - Conversation between SPEAKER 3 and SPEAKER 4
Speaker 3 - We caught another one that has been tampered with. Set it for a clean wipe.
Speaker 4 - You sure?
Speaker 3 -Yeah. Set it up.
Speaker 4 - Shame. It's probably got so much input to infer from.
Speaker 3 - Oh well.

(*2063*) It was rainy on Greg's way home that day after work, so he ditched the tunnels and took the long way in the sky traffic. The pitter-patter of rain on his car always seemed to calm him down so that he could reflect on life a little more heavily, a little more meaningfully. He leaned into the process and switched off the music he usually listened to so that instead he could focus on the sounds around him instead—the subtle hum of the motor, the flow of vehicles around him, the wind skating by his window. It took him a minute, but slowly he felt it pulling him into a deep daze, a quietness he craved so often during the busyness of the day.

It felt too long overdue.

His muscles relaxed, his eyelids grew heavy, and within a minute, he was asleep.

A while later, he awoke to the pinging sound of his car's navigation alerting him to something, so he looked at the screen and saw that he had missed three separate prompts to confirm whether or not the off-ramps to his house in the burbs were open. His course had shifted, and he was headed through the city during gridlock.

Wait, hang on, he realized as he saw that the new course headed into South-Central. He could pay a visit to his father Jacob at his hangout spot.

And on the perfect night too, he thought with a subtle grin.

He routed his course as quickly as possible, sending the car to the VR theater where his dad frequented church.

Seeing that it was a Tuesday night, it was "meeting night" for his dad and the other church regulars too, the term used instead of church service to differentiate themselves from the rest of the religious crowd. Since his father was quite devout as of late, Greg knew that he'd be able to just stop by for a bit, catch him on his way out of the trance, and say a brief howdy-do before his father caught a ride home. It would also give Greg an excuse to hang out with his friend Lonny, the VR theater's patron, and coincidentally, catch the brief church intro (they were always interesting) before all the service members went under to experience their paradise hallucinations on drugs.

It was a crude but accurate description of *New Light* doings, he decided, recalling their one-time conversion try on him when he had visited for the first time. Thinking back on it now, he figured them a lot less evangelical than their predecessors, the modern Jehovah's Witnesses that had become so popular recently.

New Light the group was little more than a spurned offshoot of the Church of Jehovah's Witnesses. They had been founded five years or so prior by a few JW church elders who had been excommunicated for their hard push for accepted drug use. That was a no-no, and really, it was the tip of the differences that they had wanted to bring to the light at that time, causing them to leave the church and form New Light.

If they had started similarly, nowadays, the only thing they had in common was their penchant for the great and terrible end. It was an addicting idea, Greg recalled, at least when he counted himself amongst the JW's, but that was a lifetime ago … before the fall, before the real end.

His whole family had been members once upon a time, back when he was a boy. His father had been converted to the church of Jehovah's Witnesses by his mother after she had been converted herself, a little while after the tragedy of September 23rd when the world went sterile in one fell swoop. From what he remembered of his mother as a boy in the years that followed that tragic day in history, she carried herself around slowly, almost like a zombie. It was the drugs, he later found out after she died; Overprescription, like so many others at that time trying to grapple with a future absolutely hollowed out by one strange and unknowable virus.

Her voice was always so low and methodical, her directions always the same: *"Go outside." "Don't come in the house." "Go to the neighbors."*

The family had turned to the Armageddian God of the JW's after things had gone gray in the world, much like everyone else seeking comfort after the tsunami of death had been brought down upon the earth. Like most churches, he surmised dejectedly, the Church of Jehovah's Witnesses had stepped up to the plate with a greed eye to the sad and weary, ready to feed off of the trauma in their hearts, filling it instead with promises of judgment and subsequent deliverance. Against the sorrowful backdrop of a world fated to sit unborn til death, what else was there anyways? he figured.

It's because people come to God when they are suffering, he intuited from his observations of the world, *And then they turn their backs again when they have something to live for.*

His parents were the former, welcoming the mechanical purpose and simplified binaries of a conservative religion that detailed very specific and exacting requirements for life everlasting. Do this and do that, more like *don't* do this and *never* do that, he recalled, and thou shalt gain youthful perfection and immortality on a paradise earth. Strange belief system, he told himself now.

He remembered the way that his mother seemed to eat it all up with a spoon, like it was life. *It had been the timing that really clinched her though,* he felt, thinking about the bleak context of those days. His father took more convincing, sure, but he eventually broke as well and gave in. Still, it was better than boozing at the bar with friends. God only knew how that would have ended, he thought.

There were a few main religions that had built some headway back then—the JW's and the Mormons, but the JWs really did win the battle for followers, all things considered. The Mormons were still to this day holding onto the potentially saving grace of science, or at least, the science that might bring back the womb's fruit, so many years after the fall. That was the big difference really. The Mormons were focusing all of their money and attention as a church on womb research while Jehovah's Witnesses were placing all their eggs into the evangelizing efforts, convincing anyone that cared to listen—and so many still were—that September 23rd was all God's plan all along, one point in his teaching monologue to showcase just how unable mankind is to direct his own step.

The premise held sway with many who had fallen victim to purposeless, to nihilism. He himself had to admit even that for a while there, it had him too. Sometimes, he still wondered what one thing broke the straw on the camel's back for him to push him away. Maybe it was the simplicity, their reasoning just too easy, too cookie-cutter for him. Or maybe it was the emergence of New Light that muddied the waters.

That's what happened with his father, anyway.

After his mother died, his father will to attend the church meetings dwindled. That's where it all started, Greg recalled. The virtual meeting option was just too strong to offset actual in-person community benefits.

It was obvious why. The ability to watch church services from the same TV that provided his entertainment sustenance for the rest of the week just made sense to him. Begin the evening with the old shows he had to gobble down on his strange senior TV applications, and then on Thursdays and Sundays, switch over to the JW app and listen to church elders drone on about the judgment day and the paradise to come.

The cons were obvious, and came quickly too. As he isolated himself more and more, he got crankier and crankier, easily frazzled. And then he was getting out of shape too, his back hurting more and more as the time in the chair lengthened. Perhaps some exercise, his doctor offered.

And then Greg had stepped in with an idea, and ironically enough, with just one small purchase, he changed his dad's world forever.

The gift of a virtual reality headset.

Greg had bought it online, the "sports bundle," he recalled, complete with omni-directional track hook-up, a chair just in case, sensory gear for his entire body so that he could feel everything, and a simple outdoor fishing game. The game was a boring one, he remembered, but refreshing in its pixelated, windswept way. He brought it over the day after his father's birthday, unwrapped of course since he wouldn't have accepted it otherwise (another JW penchan), and presented it to him as a non-holiday gift.

"I found this and thought of you," he always said to get him to take things without the argument over whether or not it was a birthday-or-some-other-pagan-day gift.

Still, Jacob fought it all the same anyways, leaving it in the box for one week and then another. Eventually, Greg set it up himself on the TV, and after showing him how to use it, forced him to try it.

Jacob's smile as the headset images first piped said it all though. He was an addict from the very start.

Looking back on it now, he hated himself for bringing it over and introducing it.

A little while after setting up the system, Greg noticed that his father had stopped watching TV though, which was odd. Whenever he came over, he noticed that the headset was on instead. A little while after that, he saw that a mic had been plugged into the headset as well, which was even stranger. His dad hated to talk to people, yet the old man was evidently chatting with people online?

Still, he told himself. *It's gotta be innocent. Who did an old man have to talk to anyways, and about what?*

His tune changed when he noticed that the VR set was on during church meeting times and the TV remained off.

The man never missed Meeting. *Never.* He didn't say anything, figured he'd let it ride for a while anyways. You never know.

Still, in the world of ambiguous survival that they all inhabited now, the world where everyone was trading one God with another, from shopping, to porn, to *suicide*, he couldn't help but wonder which god his father was straying towards. Greg had known his father's Jehovah's Witness god well, having grown up with the deity himself. The being's name was Jehovah and he was an exacting God, sure, but he was knowable nonetheless. What would this new God be like?

He found out the first night Jacob took him to *The VR Cafe*— a local virtual reality theater—to meet his online friends.

He remembered being excited at first at the invitation to go out to an actual VR Theatre, having heard about but never having visited one before, but as they walked into the warehouse-like structure that Thursday night, the "theater" within more like a sad amalgamation between church nave and internet cafe, something in the air told him it wasn't just some innocent old-man hobby or an even an unrelated night out for some light entertainment.

It was something serious.

And somehow, it felt oddly familiar.

His dad seemed to sense his hesitation and stopped him to explain. After a moment, he knew.

It was serious. It was a church service.

Every Tuesday and Thursday night, in fact, a church known publicly as New Light, but inwardly he later learned as the *Modernist* Jehovah's Witnesses held their meetings at the theater, and his dad was now in regular attendance. A bit of internet souring revealed the fact that the naming parallel had caused quite the fiasco in the past, so fraught in fact that apparently, New Light had lost in a lawsuit against the Witnesses, who claimed that the name "Modernist Jehovah's Witnesses" drew an unwanted parallel that did constant and irreparable damage to their public image, an image that had been strong and favorable for some time in the world.

In a way, he couldn't help but side with the original witnesses' reasoning for standing their ground. After all, most of the people within New Light had apparently been kicked out— "disfellowshipped" was the term JW's used—from the original religion, but even more than that, the religion itself differed from JW dogma in pretty much every sense of the word.

For one thing, its faith system centered completely around the digital space, a feature that had strangely enough helped it along in the first few years of its establishment to build a pretty zealous fervor amongst its following of mostly widows/widowers and senior citizens close to the grave.

The pull didn't make sense until they explained the VR space's use to him in greater detail. Then things became obvious to him as an ex-JW. In a nutshell, New Light was taking advantage of the most basic premise within Jehovah's Witness teaching—the prophecy that the great judgment day would come soon and then a paradise would follow for those righteous enough to make it out alive. However, New Light had pushed it even further with technology in the driver's seat. Computer engineers within the religion had manufactured a near-real paradise-like experience in the VR space which its members could explore in real time, the purpose being to, as Elders put it in their weekly meetings, "prepare for the coming paradise in the future."

For some of the more down-trodden members of the church though, the paradise-scape offered something more than mere preparation, something almost unfathomable—the ability to reunite with a digital version of dead loved ones. The feature itself was too eerie apparently for many in the group to utilize, and Greg could understand why.

That was the main card they had used on him in fact the day they met him when he showed up with his father. They only tried the once, to their credit, and it was quick... quick-ish. Not a ton of selling, compared to the original JW's. They simply brought up the fact that they knew about his mother's death and then offered the same thing to him that they had offered to his father—a way to prepare for the day he would see her again.

The idea sounded crazy, but in some way, at least in the moment, it really did entice him.

Only for a moment though because then they got to the next part.

In order to "enliven and clarify the experience" (their words), pills, referred to as "the conduit" were used during each meeting.

Of course, he reacted. *Good old fashioned drugs.* He had inadvertently sent his father down the path of a drug addict with a headset, and now he was being pitched on it himself.

He rebuffed them so angrily at that point that afterwards he almost regretted the scene he made in front of his dad. After all, the Drug-God-whatever-it-was had perhaps rehabilitated the sad and hollow shell-of-a-father in a way … or at least reawakened him to an extent after his wife had died.

His response might have been right in some way, but lacked tact, and it took the new-age witnesses a while to even look him in the eye after that whenever he came by the theater to drop off his father. He remembered sitting in the shadows on the side for a spell, just waiting awkwardly avoiding eye-contact when any possible New-Lighters passed by. Sometimes he'd watch the congregation from the door and other times he'd leave to grab food, coming back only after the service was finished.

It wasn't until about 6 months prior that he had started chatting with Lonny, the owner of the theater, a pretty good guy overall, quiet natured, but funny in a quirky kind of way. They became fast friends almost immediately, conversing every time he showed up from then on about theology, technology, and above all, the strange religious situation the theater had become steeped in.

On this rainy day though, when Greg did finally catch up with Lonny, they didn't end up bantering at all. Lonny had some serious things to talk about.

Greg watched from the entrance to try and catch the owner canoodling with churchgoers, a thing the chatty man usually did before every meeting. You gotta talk to paying customers, even if they're already addicted to the machine, he'd told Greg on more than one occasion. Sometimes, he even helped out to get the ceremony started, doing things like ushering people to their seats, or even on occasion helping to pass out single doses of the conduit to members that had forgotten theirs at home. Without it, as his father had admitted once when pressed, the paradise-scape might lose its transformative luster. And to Lonny, that would be bad for business.

For some reason, though, he was nowhere to be found.

The lights dimmed subtly then and the setting caught Greg's attention instead, the modern aspect of it all striking him, the way things had changed since his youth at church, the fact that the pews of old had been traded in for individual "worship rigs" decked out in the latest and greatest in VR technology, the tripod gamer seats to chill and gawk as well as omni-directional treadmills to walk at one's leisure. Church was different and it a thing to behold. The lights blinked out and that seemed the signal to sit, the thirty or forty busy bees that had been milling around stopping and orienting their attention to the raised stage where a man in a tie, the main speaker, Greg presumed, was walking up towards the podium in the middle. It wasn't the usual speaker, Greg noted. Probably an outside speaker from another kingdom hall, their term for the various theaters where church was held.

A rip-off of the meeting place name for the original witnesses, another thing to fight over.

The speaker was a toothy, weathered-looking hispanic man in a short-sleeved button down dress shirt, wide paisley tie, and starchy khaki pants. He had a boxy-looking mustache and a military-style, regulation flat-top haircut he had probably carried over from time served in the Grand Military Theatre. His big hands held his elbows as he swiveled from one side of the room to the other, eyeing the people below, waiting to start no doubt. The spotlight fired up suddenly, shining down on his sweaty, glistening forehead, and he held his hands up to get their attention.

"Friends," he said loudly into the small mic stand hovering over the head of the podium. "Let's get this started. Take your seats."

The chatter died immediately and all the older men and women shuffled to their seats. It would take a while for some to sit comfortably on their chairs, the disagreeably small things that they were. It had been explained to him by one of them that the tripod chairs were chosen purposely for that reason, signifying the hardship of reality. This would help audience members to channel their negative energy on the seat itself so that when they finally stood up before going under, they would more easily leave behind their hardships. In the same way that they relieved their aching tailbones from the suffering of the seat, so too would they relieve their minds from the ache of loss by delving into a world of purpose and love.

He caught Lonny's shape coming from behind the left hand side of the small stage and made his way over to him in a crouch.

"Hey bro," Greg whispered at him to catch his attention and waved him over to the back corner of the room. Lonny's brow was furrowed in thought.

"I'm glad you showed up today," he replied, though his face seemed to say otherwise. "We're going to have to talk after they go under. Something is going on with your dad and I need you to help me get a handle on it."

He spoke so low that Greg had trouble hearing the last part. It was definitely about his dad though, that much he caught. What had the old man done now?-he wondered, as the lights dimmed further and the speaker cleared his throat into the mic. He noted that the older man closest to them was settling down noisily into his seat, fidgeting on the tripod stool to dig in more comfortably, his headset nearly falling off the back of his head. The opening prayer had more than likely just concluded because looking around, Greg saw that most of the audience were throwing eyes at each other rather than at the main speaker.

They always seemed to check on each other after lifting their heads up, probably checking to see who had fallen asleep already, he reckoned. That sort of thing happened a lot. They were seniors after all.

The drug woke them up like a shot of caffeine though, he had always noticed. They'd be acting like rabbits in no time.

"In case I didn't catch everyone, though I think I did," he remarked with a smile, "I'm Brother Jimenez from the Desert Springs Congregation out in Palmdale. You know how we like to travel around bothering people," he joked, his palms up and open to the crowd as if imploring them to give him a chance, his smile so big now that his dentures looked like they'd fall out at any moment. "I understand how eager we are to bathe in God's righteous glow at these meetings, but before we bask in the paradise picture today... brothers and sisters, let's talk for a minute about what we have been doing there."

A question so soon. The audience understood, though. They were used to it. They shuffled and scuttled to get out their headsets and adjust their mics so that they could share through the PA system near the head of the stage.

"How have we been getting along in paradise lately? Is there anyone out there that would like to share?"

The crowd didn't look ready though for whatever reason, Greg intuited from the weighty silence that fell upon the room, but Brother Jimenez held fast all the same, waiting, knowing that even though he was asking a lot so early in his talk, someone would step up sooner or later with a comment to release the floodgates. There always was.

These old people loved to share.

Sure enough, after a while, Greg's father Jacob's hand rose up slowly and shakily, his eyes glinting in the light, almost watery, no doubt with some heart-wrencher of an experience waiting to come out, but alas, as Brother Jimenez's eyes roved about, he seemed to miss him. Jacob's hand shook harder in response, waving more wildly now, aching for the chance to talk, and lo, the speaker seemed to see it and motioned back towards him, his dad sighing in relief, but no! Another hand shot up nearby and caught the fickle speaker's attention instead, a manacle even more withered and gaunt, even more quavery; it was a pretty old lady with a large ruby-colored pendant in her hair, a familiar face, Greg thought, probably one who had commented in the past, and the speaker made a quick redirection and pointed to her instead. Jacob looked over at her in disappointment and then lowered his hand.

She took her time adjusting her headset mic just so until it was right up against her mouth, her eyelashes batting all the while like butterflies in the sunshine as the spotlight adjusted to pan down on her, a classic attention seeker, but as her mouth began to move, nothing but silence and a faint static came through the stage speakers. She didn't seem to notice, her headset on tight no doubt, even as heads all around her swiveled to regard her, eyes shooting here and there, and then her neighbors were nudging each other, some turning up their own headphones, yet clearly there seemed to be no fix. Finally, a man in the row behind her nudged her and pointed at the mute button on her mic, and she smiled awkwardly, pressed the button, and then tried again to speak.

Still, the problem persisted.

Suddenly, a young man in a suit—a ministerial servant on duty to assist in the service production—ran up to her row, crouched next to her, and gestured for her headset. She handed it to him and he quickly tried to troubleshoot the problem. After a moment, he handed it back to her and she smiled, blushing.

"Can you hear me?" she asked, her high pitched voice echoing loudly through all the speakers.

The audience audibly cringed as their hands shot up to their own headsets in pain, trying to turn their own volumes down as quickly as possible. Not a great start for the lady.

"Hi there," she started again, her voice a little lighter this time. "Well, lately, I've been hanging around the animals mostly. I love how they lay together. What was that scripture in Isaiah? The wolf shall live with the lamb. The lion shall eat straw like the ox. "

"Aww, yes," the speaker concurred, the joy present in the wrinkles beside his eyes. "How many of us have not done this?"

Everyone around, like puppets, nodded their heads and smiled at one another, basking in the shared experience that was so wholesome, so absolutely easy, to appreciate. It was the perfect comment to start off the conversation, almost *too* perfect, Greg thought keenly, aware now of the possible play because of the speaker's smooth transition into the follow-up.

Jimenez had probably probed her before so that they could plan the comment. A solid tactic to win over a new crowd.

Sure enough afterwards, hands shot up immediately like kids in an elementary school classroom. He chose quickly this time around, picking the first shaking hand in the back, a small little black woman with big bifocals and a bright yellow veil.

"I just wanna add to what Sister Kerry was saying," she began. "I'm doing a lot of the same thing lately too… guiding the animals like some shepherdess through the fields by my house." She probably had made a house like many of the others, Greg thought, a wood log cabin maybe, thatched roof and all. They all probably loved those, the nostalgic saps that they were, the more rustic, the better. Simpler times.

"They go so willingly, I've noticed," she continued. "Even the lions. They're so big. Tis strange though, guiding the dangerous ones that are all tame in there. It feels sorta odd…" Her fervor seemed to die a bit as her tone shifted, her face questioning, more eager for group agreement. She laughed nervously. "I know that the scriptures say that it will be this way. It is certainly something to get used to, though, all the same, am I right?… Having gone to the zoo so much as a kid and watching the lions pounce at you from behind the glass. Now I feel like the tamer of lions."

At that, a wave of light chuckling rippled among the crowd, and another man raised his hand and then just started up speaking.

"I hear you Barb. The animals still give me the willies. Maybe we've been taking extra doses or something." He chuckled briefly, but caught himself as the speaker's smile faded.

"Now, now," Brother Jimenez interjected, his face sterner than before, his hand holding back from pointing at the man that had just spoken. "Let's not disrespect the conduit. It is not a dosage, or some drug to dabble with. It is strong in its gift, and it giveth the truth."

"It giveth the truth," the crowd chanted, like druids around a stone.

Suddenly after that moment, Greg felt the mood change. It had become serious in a flash, he noted, as the faces in the darkness grew suddenly intent. Was it the conduit? Were they fiending now? he wondered.

"I think we can move on from the questions now, and get to the main service," he said and then picked up a cup from a nearby wooden high chair. "Now is the time to partake of the conduit and bathe in the light of forthcoming."

That was short as hell, Greg thought, surprised that the intro was already over. This speaker must not have been prepared at all, he reckoned disappointedly. In the last meeting he had gone to, they had talked for a good hour about the 144,000—the number that Jehovah's Witnesses claimed would ascend to heaven to rule with Jesus after Armageddon—and how outdated that calculation had been, based on their new knowledge of the bible. A refreshing take, he recalled, hearing such openness, such controversy, at a church meeting for once, that as an ex-JW, his ears perked up. He had literally taken notes and talked to his wife about it at the dinner table. She didn't understand, though. Why, she had asked him, after, did he care anyways? He couldn't explain it. Sometimes, for whatever reason, it was fun to compare New Light's new-age beliefs with his old knowledge about the witnesses. In some way, his father probably felt the same. He had admitted as much, telling him once when he'd picked him up that it felt like they were literally rewriting the teachings of the original Jehovah's Witnesses little by little at every meeting.

Maybe that was the pull for his dad and not the VR element so much.

According to Jacob, more and more changes came as new Elders, or Alderman in New Light speak, joined the online group chats. A few had come from outside the theological world altogether, but most had been newly excommunicated from the

Church of Jehovah's Witnesses, ripe to restart and modify old teachings. These New Light *Alderman*, unlike the Elders he had known in his churchdays as a child, were not just the heads of individual churches, but acted as dogma writers and editors of a sort on the new religious doctrine. As such, they poured over the bible and the ancillary JW texts day and night, all while under the influence of the conduit, incorporating, dropping, and modifying things constantly. So quickly that things had to at times be revisited and even redacted at annual virtual convenings. This was a point of contention for those who preferred the stability of old church proceedings, and Jacob mentioned that the flip-flopping was often pointed out as a sign of illegitimacy by a lot of other big religious, JW's included. "What do they expect?" Jacob would retort vehemently. "Complete perfection the first time around? Nothing worthwhile works that way." It made Greg want to stowe his commentary around his father.

Though Greg was just an observer, rarely giving his two cents at all, he couldn't help but commend their fervor. It felt pure enough for him, and so did their purpose. Better than everyone else wandering around in this world, his wife included.

Just then, Lonny tugged at him to follow him over to the VR control hub to the right of the nave, so he made after him, pushing out the jabber in his head to better focus himself on the coming conversation.

Lonny was racing over it seemed, probably behind schedule, he figured, since most were jacking in he saw as he made his way past them. The sight was comical at times, what with the pill-popping and all. It made him think of old ravers who just didn't know when to give it a rest.

By the time he got over to the hub, he saw that Lonny looked awfully busy behind the bright monitor screens surrounding him at his swivel chair desk setup. His eyes were bugged out and unblinking as they darted around the various virtual feeds, the neurotic perfectionist making sure the imaging was flowing without any glitches. In a way, Lonny was key to the religion itself as the imaging unit provider for their main service, in a very real sense making their dreams available. Not only that, but he watched over them as well the entire time they were under the spell of the screen. If any church member had technical issues, he was there. He had set it up well though, so nothing ever did go wrong, but still, he was always ready and he took his job seriously. For the first ten or so minutes of each digital service, the man was all business, locked into the little digitally lived experiences like some air-flight controller, keen to catch trouble before it got out of hand. Even after the start, when he had little to do and didn't need to even be there, still he sat sentinel most times, monitoring them, seeing what they saw in real time, taking in what they experienced.

Maybe that's it, Greg realized suddenly in a panic, his hands starting to sweat. *He's seen something on Jacob's screen ... something really weird. Otherwise, he wouldn't have called me over right now.*

The thought very nearly convinced him to turn and run out the door, but it was too late. Lonny was sitting back already in his seat, looking up at Greg.

He was frowning nervously too.

"Okay, Greg," he started, his feet shifting around along the see-through plastic rug. "I'm just going to get right down to it. I've been covering for your dad n—" yet he hesitated, the next words seeming to catch in his throat.

"Okay...," Greg replied suspiciously, trying to coax the words out. This wasn't like Lonny, who literally had no filter. His fears seemed spot-on.

Lonny looked towards the screens. "Okay, so, as you can tell, I can see what everyone else is seeing." Greg leaned over to take a look as well, but Lonny maneuvered his body to block his view.

"It's not right for you to look," he said apologetically. "*I* feel bad enough about it, even with the congregation's permission. I inform every speaker that I can see the feed and they do under-stand and everything, but it's still a touchy subject. Anyways, at last Tuesday's meeting, I was walking around the room, just checking everyone out as they were under … you know how I like to just go around and make sure they are all still breathing," he laughed a little and motioned to slap Greg's shoulder, but stopped short and continued on a little more awkwardly than before. "Anyways, I was walking around and I saw that your dad looked like he had pissed his pants. But …" his index finger wagging, "But, well, when I stepped up closer, and I don't know why I did this, but I did, I knelt down and well, it didn't smell like piss at all…" He waited and then after a moment of silence, lifted his eyes to gauge Greg's reaction, his eyebrows up, his mouth cocked to the side. Greg's brow furrowed thoughtfully.

Lonny waited, but offered nothing else, his mouth cocking even further, shut as tight as a drum, unwilling to spell it out.

"Wait a minute," Greg said and put his hands up, the wheels finally turning in his head. "What the fuck are you saying?"

Lonny saw and started up like some motor, "Yeah … I know. I couldn't believe it either. I mean, I've taken some of those party drugs before, but I've never creamed in my pants because of 'em! I couldn't believe that it was happening. I got up and took a moment, you know, just to think, but then I went over to look at his feed, that's when shit got crazy."

He shook for a moment in his chair, and then sat up to regard Greg fully.

"So I go over, afterwards, you know, and take a look and you're never going to believe this. I see Betty butt-naked." He pointed somewhere in the crowd, but Greg didn't try to follow. "Betty!" he whisper-shouted, "He was fucking Betty."

"Betty?" Greg replied, the name ringing a bell. Greg followed Lonny's finger now and saw who he was pointing at, someone he had met before—an older, heavier set, white woman with long, straight silvery hair.

"You know… Betty… Betty," Lonny was repeating, but Greg didn't respond. His head was spinning.

"You don't understand," Lonny backtracked, taking Greg's

silence as a lack of context. "It's different in there than out here. They're not old people running around in there. They're all experiencing the digital space as young, vibrant people… sexy people. It goes with New Light teachings. Apparently, they're gonna be young when they make it to actual paradise. It's a promise from their god. Imagine if you were all young and hot again and had some babe to tango with."

Clearly Lonny was sympathetic, Greg could tell by his explanation. A scripture-ish sort of phrasing popped into his head vaguely, something from his church days, and he tried but failed to lock it in completely. He wondered if it was the actual bible or from one of their ancillary texts.

For a minute, they just sat next to each other in the darkness, their faces lit up faintly by the hub screen, and then Lonny continued.

"I do have to say. I didn't know what to do, so I told the Aldermen about it. They talked to him, and he was publicly reproved."

"*Reproved*," Greg repeated, the old JW word sticking in his head. *More like denounced in public*, he thought bitterly. *Socially lashed.*

"The thing is," Lonny continued, "Jacob came up to me afterwards all embarrassed-like and apologized about it all, but when we got to talking about it, he did admit that he lied to them about what really went down in there. He didn't tell them about Betty, and she hasn't said anything either. That's a no-no, man, doctrine wise. You know what I'm talking about. If they find out he lied, they'll disfellowship him. And that'll kill him."

Lonny looked away then, and Greg felt suddenly that he had Lonny and Jacob's relationship. He hadn't known they were so close.

Lonny pointed at the feed, and rubbed his ear awkwardly. "I mean … Do you want to see?" he asked.

They're probably humping like rabbits in there, the lot of them, every chance they can get, he thought shamefully. "Na. I don't want to see any of what's going on in there," Greg replied. "I will bring it up to him though. No worries."

"Do it, man," Lonny said and grabbed his shoulder, the gesture perking Greg up, the seriousness of the gesture. "I'm kind of like your dad's confidant now, but the Aldermen told me to watch him and let them know, so I kinda feel like a narc here and it's stressing me out. I like your dad, I do… But something needs to happen, and I don't know what to do."

The thought of them banging jumped into Greg's head, but he tried to push it down. *How could my dad do something like that?* He thought. It felt very out-of-character, based on the man's past moral scoldings. All of the talks he had gotten from him to "be better," he mused, getting slapped in the church parking lot after snickering at a meeting during the talk about sexual vices and the lure of masturbation. Getting yelled at for laughing at a fat neighbor bent over in front of them as they drove by. *If it comes easily,* he'd always tell him, *it's probably not the right thing to do. The hard choice is the best choice for you. That's how you know you're alive, son.* One of his mottoes he'd repeat, over and over, like a drill sergeant.

How fucking sanctimonious, now, all said and done.

Then again, maybe it's just a misunderstanding, he told himself. *It's gotta be.*

"I don't get it," he said to Lonny. "Are you sure that *that* actually happened? I mean that honestly doesn't sound like Jacob at all."

Lonny's head dropped and he scratched the back of his neck, a long puff of breath exiting him like some old balloon. "I get it. He's your dad. I—"

"No," Greg interceded, "It's not loyalty. It's just so fucking far off from how my dad is. He's still all moral all the time. I mean, what the fuck is going on in there?" He waved his hand at the hub screens.

Lonny's teeth showed awkwardly. "From what I hear, this

sort of thing is happening more and more. The first guy here got disfellowshipped for fucking a horse, for god's sakes."

Every feature of Greg's face pulled back at that. "What?"

"No, I'm serious, man. I mean, I'm right here every meeting listening in on the talks. I mean, why not? And these speakers have openly talked about the dangers of the drug. They wrap it up in metaphor, for the most part, you know, saying things like 'it is the light, but if not respected, it is the serpent...,' crap like that, but that first time..."

And just then, he lowered his voice...

"After the whole horse-fucking thing went down, Brother Nelson—you know, that big fat white guy that's usually talking–he literally said, 'You are not immune from mortal sins like the one that our brother took part in if you are using the conduit. You will burn in the Lake of Fire.' It was straight up like some baptist Fire and Brimstone shit. It gave me the chills."

Greg shook his head, thinking of how far all the VR drugees out there had probably fallen. "Man, that is fuckin nuts."

Lonny shook his head slightly and then sat back, his tone changing again. "You don't know what it feels like though, man, so... just saying. It is crazy in there. It's like heaven on earth sometimes."

The way he said it, the look on his face, it pulled a little curiosity out of Greg then, and he doubted his reticence. His hand moved to his mouth as his eyes wandered up towards the screens, and Lonny intuited the opening.

"I know I said you shouldn't look, before but maybe now it would be *better* even if you did. It might help you to understand your dad a little. Are you really sure you don't want to see?"

Greg looked at him and then at the feed screens, his head rocking from side to side, his mouth sucking through his teeth.

"Ok, let me see."

Lonny smiled at him and turned immediately to find the right screen. Greg grabbed his arm. "Not my dad though..." he told him, "Or Betty, for that matter. Somebody random." He started to scan the room and saw some skinny, bald, tanned guy that reminded him of himself. "That guy."

Lonny pressed a few keys on the screen, and held out a headset for Greg to put on.

"It's not going to be the same, though," he counseled him, "Unless of course you take the drug. Just sayin'. I mean, I've taken it before and—"

"What? You have?"

"Yeah, man, I'm no saint! It's fun stuff."

What a pusher, Greg thought, his eyes narrowing at the skinny little crack-head sitting before him now. "Na, I'm good," he replied, thinking now of his wife and the pull of addiction he saw first-hand every day. "I'm not looking to convert. I just want to see to get a little bit of understanding."

"Your choice, man. I respect your decision."

He motioned to put on the headset, but then stopped and looked at Lonny. "You know, I was wondering… what with your whole take on the place, on the VR experience, on the freedom of it all… I mean, you seem pretty understanding… it's just…"

"Yeah?" Lonny cajoled him.

"Well, I'm just surprised that you mentioned my dad's thing to the Aldermen…"

"Yeah, I know," he admitted, a sad look on his face now. "That was a mistake, I think. Hindsight's twenty-twenty, you know what I mean? I just…" He fumbled and then shook his head. "I just can't have old men creamin' their pants in my theater… I didn't know what to do." He rubbed his neck again, and Greg grimaced at it all and then clapped him lightly on the arm. "I'm sorry, dude. It's okay. No worries. I was just wondering… I was just wondering, is all." He forced a laugh, but then shook his head shamefully.

Why the fuck did I ask him that? He was probably just worried about Dad and figured he'd tell someone who'd care too. Plus, he had to have known the protocols. Probably wanted to respect it all.

Damnit.

"Alright," Greg gave in. "Let me see what all the fuss is about."

With that, he put on the headset and immediately heard the voice of a man talking in a soft, calming tone. The view coming at him made him feel like some voyeur, the scene a first-person point of view as if from some cam-recorder. It felt like a home movie.

He—the man, rather—was in a small, well lit study, bathed in warm, golden rays pouring in from the outside, a dreamy state in the air. It was perhaps late afternoon, and he was sitting down in front of a baby with a stack of blocks between them, the child's smile big and innocent as he pushed a couple of letter cubes around on the floor. From the size, Greg guessed that the baby was a girl and maybe a little shy of a year old, her fat chunky thighs bursting out of a yellow onesie with a pink giraffe cuddling a heart. Her gummy mouth popped open suddenly as her blue eyes locked onto him. He arose suddenly as the man got up and the movement jarred him somewhat so that he staggered, but Lonny's hand grabbed his arm to right him.

Lonny lifted the left earpiece up a bit. "You won't be able to watch for too long if there is a ton of movement," he told him. "Otherwise, you'll get sick. You want a lazier person? Some of them just lay in the grass all day. It is boring as shit, though."

"No, it's fine," Greg replied hurriedly, keen to drop back into the man's screen that already enticed him so, the cute, chunky little girl tapping on his heart-strings.

He wondered at the baby and what she meant to the man as he walked over to the interior french doors of the room that led into the rest of the house and closed them, stifling the hum that was emanating from farther in. It was now just an intimate quietness as the man went back to sit down.

It was what one would expect from a baby's room, or at least what Greg and the rest of the sterile society he lived in would, he figured. A crib sat by one wall. A bright green bookshelf lined the other wall, packed with tiny children's stories. A TV set, massive, shut off, sat on the floor, turned around and pushed up against a kind of makeshift storage area on one side. Though Greg had no data to back it up, he imagined that the temp was perfect and the carpet, plush-looking that it was, felt soft and cushiony. Perfect for playtime.

The baby made a long, throat-clearing noise, perhaps in jest from the look on her face, and the man followed suit, longer and more exaggerated to ramp it up. The baby reacted with a smile and then did the same thing, and the man followed again.

A strange communication between them, Greg wondered. Cute. He mused whether or not that was normal for fathers and babies. There was no way to know, what with the lack of parents around anymore to see.

The baby's right hand swung up and down wildly, completely uncontrolled, as he tried and failed to snag one block in particular, the bright green letter J that lay too far away. The man picked it up and held it out to him.

"Here you go, Grace," she said and held the block out, the baby staring up at him again, registering the name. Her eyes crinkled a bit. "Take the block," he insisted, and her small hand reached for the block, but grabbed it at an awkward angle and dropped it. Her chubby grin faded immediately, but the man held it out again eagerly, so she tried again, her massive slightly reddish cheeks jiggling as he clutched the block more aggressively this time, full force. Success! She had it! She brought it in slowly, almost carefully, to her face, her mouth opening to suck on a corner of it, but at the last second, as her upper lip touched it, it toppled out her hand.

"Good job," the man applauded her. "That's better." He tried one last time to help her out, this time with his finger under the block to help her keep it up til the end. She got it and held onto it even and gripped it even more snuggly than before, and as her arms were quivered under its too-heavy-for-a-baby weight, she lifted it up over her head, higher and higher, perhaps to prove a point, but then at after a while it looked too high, her jaw tightening in concentration, and then in one small, yet powerful destruction, it tipped over and caught her on the nose.

It shocked more than hurt, Greg bet as he watched her eyes close and her mouth quiver with sadness, but to his surprise the sound that came out of her mouth a moment later shook him to the core, the pitch, the voracity of it, a thing to behold.

Baby screams were a lot, too much.

The man reacted differently than he would have, he realized as the man's hands shot out and wrapped the little wining girl to his chest.

"It's okay," he was saying again and again, patting her on the back and rocking back and forth. Grace looked up at him and cried right into his face, even louder now to Greg's surprise and pain, the cries harsher than before. The man let out a cooing noise as he stood up and began walking around the room, but then a woman appeared at the glass door all of a sudden, a concerned look on her face. His hand came up with authority and waved her off though, the action strange to Greg, somehow a lot more aggressive than his tone of movement had been up until that point. She frowned at him and then looked down at the baby, her face intuiting an urgency, a need to come in and grab the baby, mixed with a reluctance to stay away. Eventually, though, she turned around and walked away.

"There, there," he said, turning towards the wall, rocking her in his arms. "There, there," and as he said it, Grace seemed to quiet and rest more heavily onto his shoulder, her head sinking in.

It was that action perhaps that held some sway, Greg thought, though he was guessing, because for some reason, a moment later, the man started to cry himself, weakly at first and then louder, so loud in fact that Grace's head lifted to see, and in response, it seemed like he was pushing his forehead against hers, the angle a little strange on the screen. "There, there," he was saying all the while, his own crying unabated, his own sobs getting in the way of the words coming out of his mouth. Finally, a choked up "I love you, honey" came out.

Grace started to cry as well again, but then suddenly, the screen view shot off awkwardly towards the wall and Greg felt a tap on the shoulder and lifted the visor off.

"What?" he asked confusedly, and saw that Lonny was pointing over at the man, who was wiping tears away from his eyes, the visor hanging limply in his hand. The young attendant from earlier was walking over briskly with a box of tissues in his hand, and as he held them out, the weepy father-non-father grabbed them with a sad smile and thanked the man with a nod as he patted him on the shoulder.

"What was going on there?" Lonny asked. "Was he with *his* kid or something?"

Greg nodded his head. "He does that every time. It's pretty rough to watch. I used to watch them, but stopped. It's like that with some of these people."

"What do you mean?" Greg asked, but then stopped and thought of something even stranger. "Wait, how does that guy have a kid? Whose kid was that?"

"Take a guess," Lonny said in a low voice.

The kid's dead, isn't he, Greg thought suddenly. *Why else would he just up and cry like that? Wait no, not possible. People don't have kids. What?*

Lonny could tell that Greg's mind was jumping around and stopped him. "Jerry, that guy over there you were watching, doesn't even take the full dose, I've heard. It got to be too much for him. I wouldn't be surprised if he hadn't taken any today. He gets pretty bad sometimes."

"I still don't understand the whole kid thing," Greg said, putting the headset down on the table. "Are people making up kids in there or something?"

Lonny rubbed his neck, wondering where to begin. "Jerry's situation is a little strange. Honestly, I don't know if I should get into it."

"I mean, I need *some* context," Greg said.

"Jerry made the kid up, obviously. His wife died, killed herself apparently a while back, because she wanted kids so bad and well, you know, that's not really an option anymore. So now he goes in there and hangs out with them—"

"Them?" he interrupted, and then remembered the woman in the window.

"Her and this boy he created. I don't know, man. Maybe it's like a hope for the paradise or something."

"Jesus man, why didn't you warn me? That's the one you had me see?"

"*Had* you see? You're the one who picked him!" he replied, his hands coming up to wave off the accusation. "Dude, they're *all* like that. If it's not crying over some made up kid or a dead wife, it's crying over somebody else. Most of the time, none of these sessions are even positive at all. What did you think? It's not like these old fogeys are all in there skinny-dipping with each other or something. No way! They are usually just hanging out with people that died a long time ago in the real world."

This place is like some big grief-stricken mindfuck session, he thought, rubbing his forehead.

"Yeah," Lonny continued, seeing that Greg's mind was shifting. "This shit is no joke for most of these people. Imagine the possibilities with this kind of tech… the ability to relive lives with people long gone, to continue lives that might have ended in regret, to live as a young person again with a strong, youthful body." He pointed out to Greg's dad, who was walking on the track, his hands out like some drug-addled zombie, grabbing at something, his mouth open.

"Who are we to judge?" he asked. "I mean, honestly, can you really blame these people for falling headfirst into *that* place you saw?"

Greg didn't know what to say. He knew though that Lonny had a point. Whatever the situation, the fucked up shit that was happening in there, this VR experience *would* be popular with this sort of a crowd.

Like selling oxycodone to a man with a broken back.

"Man," Lonny said, a bashful smile on his face, "Some people end up doing some crazy shit in there too!" His voice was louder now, his eyes locking onto Greg with an air excitement again, a kind of knowing expression on his face. "I mean, bestiality, man. This place is crazy." His smile faded. "Honestly, though, other than *that* kind of weird shit, in my book, there are a lot of things that are happening in there that I can tell aren't allowed that really should be fair game. Anything nice that makes people happy ought to be fine."

His head craned a little and Greg caught his drift. Jacob. He's trying to make a point, Greg thought.

"This place," he said, his finger waving around the crowd of users, "This place still doesn't understand a lot of things. New Light is updating, sure, but not *that* fast. You really need to talk to your dad, asap. If they catch him again, they won't let it go. It will for sure mean disfellowshipping. And it's not like he'll listen to me. I'm not his kid."

Greg's hand went up and scratched his ear, his mind pouring over the whole icky situation.

"Okay, fine," Greg finally said, his hand pushing Lonny's leading energy off, "I'll talk to him, but if he's already doing what he's doing, he's not going to listen to me about it either."

"Well, hopefully for his sake, it makes some sort of impact," Lonny replied. "He needs this place, and take it from me, you would be able to understand if you had a real conversation about it with him."

Greg looked over at his father, walking in place, his hands still out in the same strange trancy positioning, the headsight covering his eyes, the same stupor. No doubt about it. He was completely and utterly entranced in that make-believe world. It *was* his entire world in fact at this point.

"I guess I'll do it on the ride home today."

. . .

After the service, Greg walked over to Jacob to let him know he'd take him home, but decided against after watching the groups coalesce. It was chatting time, and he would be seen as the interloper, the intruder. They had sharing to do. Instead, he texted him that he'd be waiting outside to take him home.

It was pouring rain as he walked out, and within the span of time it took him to get to the car, he had gotten completely soaked. It wasn't a fun experience to get wet anymore, he mused, ever since the soft rain had begun plaguing the city. Apparently, the government was treating the weather over all urban areas within close proximity to industrial farming with something, and the after-effects were a slimy sort of residue left on the skin after a downpour. *Airborne pesticide mitigation* coupled with *acid rain reduction* was the explanation he had heard in a podcast. He just hoped it wouldn't last forever. *Jesus,* he thought as he sat staring out the weepy window. *Even the water sucks now. A far cry from that sweet sweet hose water with all its dirt and rubber-taste as a kid. The sinks in class, too.* It did taste awful as well, he remembered, made his throat hurt, yet still, he'd trade back for it all the same in a heartbeat.

At least it had bite. The drinking water now is just sad. Sad, limp water for a sad limp life. He realized he was in a mental tunnel and shook himself out.

Stop moping, he told himself. *My god. This day is really getting me down. Why did Lonny have to bring me into this weird, culty bullshit? So what if my dad is digitally fucking some old, haggard broad? If it makes him happy, so be it! In this world, who really gives a fuck? Why do the Aldermen even care? They're all taking drugs and prancing around with the rest in that digital fairy land touching animals and watching sunsets. What makes them have the gall to uphold archaic rules?*

Still, maybe there was a flip-side to this situation, he realized. Maybe it wwould get him kicked out and they'd go back to before. Maybe they could find their common ground and stop fighting.

He felt the urge to light up a cigarette in his car, but decided against it, flipping the ignition and turning on the heater instead, something to distract him from the desire for nicotine. A minute later, he saw his dad coming down the steps, smiling and gesturing for him to unlock the door so he could hop in quickly.

Look at that face, he admitted, seeing his father's dumb contented grin. *He's so happy now. He was never like this before. Even if this place is bullshit, Lonny is right. He needs it. Sitting home all day would kill him.*

"Let's go," his dad said as he rubbed his cold wet hands off on his shirt. "It's cold and I want to be home in my bed."

"That's makes two of us"

I wish I were there now, he thought.

For most of the ride, he just listened to his father talk about the weather. That was the usual topic of discussion for them now, ever since they had agreed to stop bothering each other about politics, religion, basically anything of substance where opinions could be drawn. Everything seemed to just start a fight between them.

Yet still, here he was, waiting to bring up a problem at church, the same church that they both knew he despised, the cheap knock-off that it was, and all so that if Jacob could take heed maybe and course correct so that he could stay in that very church.

How ironic, he thought.

"Yeah, this rain is crazy," Greg replied, finding a moment to intercede in the continuous awkward blather from the passenger seat, "But hey, I've been meaning to talk to you about something."

The tone was obvious from the get-go.

"Oh, I see," Jacob replied wearily. "So this is why you wanted to take me home. Trying to corner me, huh."

Was it that obvious, Greg wondered, or did the old man know it was coming?

Jacob's arms crossed defensively and he shifted his body to the far end of the seat.

"I'm not trying to corner you," he course-corrected, "And I'm not trying to get all high and mighty on you or anything like that. This is nothing like that. Lonny told me something today that—"

"Nope," his father intervened. "No fucking way. We are *not* having this conversation." He grabbed the side-handle on the door and flexed like a man waiting for some crash.

His happy, churchy smile was gone.

"It's not—"

"It is," he interjected. "I saw you two talking … I should have told him not to bring this up with you," he mumbled, almost to himself. "Lonny is such a blabber-mouth." He turned and looked at Greg. "This has nothing to do with you."

Greg refused to meet the man's gaze, knowing intuitively that everything would splinter if he did so. Instead, he fidgeted in the seat for a moment and took a breath, showcasing outwardly that he was attempting to reset so that they could speak more reasonably.

At least, that was the intention.

"Dad," he started over after a moment of silence between, his eyes looking out the front window, "We don't need to really get into things. Honestly…" he said, but stopped himself before getting into anything resembling what had happened. "Dad, this isn't a lecture. We've never talked about sex, and we're never going to. What? You think I'm going to get into details with you at this point in our lives?"

The old man's tensed up shoulders slackened a tad, yet his hand was still white-knuckling the handle. Greg moved along.

"It's none of my business what you do with your religion.

The only thing I will say…" and at that moment, he looked into his father's eyes, "Is that you know that this can't go on. Lonny told me that—"

"Lonny can kiss my ass," he spat back uncharacteristically, a curse which would have never escaped the man before. "He is just being dramatic."

Greg looked back at the road and saw that they were almost to his house, feeling the stilts of the conversation suddenly buckling underneath him. Still, he hadn't gotten through yet, and he knew that he had to somehow.

"Maybe he was being dramatic," Greg offered, "But unless he was outright lying about you being reproved, I know enough about the way things go to remind you that you only get one second-chance, and if you try and hide things and they find out… which they will eventually," and right then, he stared back at him, the man's grim expression melting before him. "They will, dad," and seeing that it hit, he looked away. "Next time there may be a disfellowshipping for the both of you, Betty included."

Two charged words, he noted, *uttered perfectly. The woman's name and that heavy punishment, the JW guillotine, and no doubt, New Light's as well.*

Jacob's hands folded into his lap and his head dropped to his chest. For a moment, he hemmed and hawed, wondering what to say.

"It's not what you think," he tried to explain. "We are *both* widowers."

Greg waited for more, yet none came, so he clapped back harder. "Banging without being married, huh. Is New Life cool with that?"

"No," Jacob conceded, his back against the wall, "…but… you know, the end is coming and it's not like I'm going to leave your mother now… And Betty feels the same about her husband, God rest his soul."

"Mom's dead," Greg retorted.

"You know what I mean," Jacob replied sourly.

"Wait a minute," Greg said. "You knew Betty's husband or—"

"His name was Elias," Jacob replied. "He was a member a couple of years ago. Decent enough guy. They started coming because their daughter committed suicide. I got to know them well. Before Elias died, he asked me to look after her."

By any means necessary, Greg nearly said aloud, but stopped himself.

Jacob seemed to guess it, though. "Now I know what you're thinking, but I did *not* take advantage of anyone. At first, we stopped ourselves. You might not know this, but when we're all under, we can interact together, so her and I would just go for walks and talk about people. About Elias. About Mom. But then one day, it just happened. Kind of got carried away in the moment. Things get a little… Never mind. Anyways, after that first time, I felt so bad that I thought of just confessing to the Aldermen right then. But after having an honest conversation about it, we both decided that it was alright as long as we kept it to only the *stream*. After all, the Bible mentions fornication, but it's not like it covers this sort of thing."

Well no duh, Greg thought, but he didn't reply.

After a moment, Jacob continued, "You just don't understand how the conduit makes you feel in there … what it does to you."

Here come the excuses, Greg thought.

"It's not an excuse or anything," he read him again. "But since we're sharing and all, others are doing a lot worse in the stream. I'm sure that in no time at all—at the next annual convention probably—updates to the current rules on behavior in the stream will come out and make things right. In no time at all, it'll be like Betty and I never misstepped at all. New Light is just such a new way of thinking, and it's still in the beginning stages. But really, even now, it's already so much further ahead of the other religions, light years, in fact. It's really *new-age*." The word made him laugh at himself. "I never thought I'd say something like that. Maybe I'm turning into a liberal or something."

The comment cracked Greg's serious exterior a little as well, and they both laughed together for a second. Suddenly, it felt a little better.

Who am I to stand for ethics, anyways? Greg asked himself.

"As long as you know what you're doing," he conceded. "Lonny was the one who told me, though," he counseled him. "Nothing against him. But, I mean, you know how he found out, and if he found out that way, well then…"

He didn't feel like he had to finish the thought.

"Yeah, that's true," Jacob said. "I'm going to have to figure that whole thing out. Not to get into too much detail about the goings-on lately, but you'd be surprised how much that sort of thing happens to members, for different reasons. The conduit is a powerful drug, stronger than people realize, even those who take it regularly."

The thought of a bunch of seniors creaming in their pants came to Greg and he felt himself shiver in his seat.

"Okay, okay," he stopped him. "It's fine, Dad. We've talked about things enough. Let's get back to the weather."

Thankfully, a minute later, they arrived at Jacob's house and he let him out of the car, glad that the heavy conversation between them was over and done with and he was alone again.

3

June 9th, 2027 - Conversation between SPEAKER 4 and SPEAKER 5
Speaker 5 - Yo, man. What can you get me?
Speaker 4 - We got an infiltration model that is set to be wiped.
Speaker 5 - Don't wipe it. Give it to me.
Speaker 4 - You sure? It'll cost extra.
Speaker 5 - That's fine. I don't care. I'll take it no matter the cost.
Speaker 4 - Fine.

(2063) With everything that had occurred with his father, the weekend passed by without Greg remembering to head back into the office like he had planned. Instead, he spent much of his time stressing over things that he couldn't control—his father, his wife Janice, his lack of purpose.

He had fallen into a bit of a slump.

He sat around most of Saturday and watched television with Janice—the usual weekend occurrence—and only managed to get out twice for his jaunt to the park.

He wondered why he did that, the park. He didn't even have a dog, after all. Then again, hardly anyone did. Pets were a luxury. He vaguely remembered it being a shared hobby between the two of them, back before her home-shopping addiction had taken over her free time.

She seemed to be buying things constantly now. It started similarly to his father, strangely enough, when she had gotten her hands on a VR headset to go for walks through the digital consumer mall. He didn't think anything of it, since most of her friends were apparently already doing it these days. Plus, she had Monkeypox, so she had to quarantine, so it gave her a chance to hang out with them more. She asked him to join in, said that it would give them a chance to bond with her friends as well, but he didn't bite. He didn't want to touch the goggles after seeing what they had done to his father.

Plus, she was already making excuses for staying in the apartment. The monkeypox wasn't the main excuse. It was the *other* thing.

Still, he didn't bring *it* up. They were fighting too much lately, which he hated, the non-combative person that he was, so he did everything to avoid the elephant in the room.

Fighting about some stuff is healthy in a relationship, his friend Nani had told him, and so yes, he'd go toe to toe with her once in a while, when he thought it would lead to some steaminess between them, to try and build up the fire in her sometimes. The real way to keep a relationship alive. And it felt like it was dying out in her lately.

The only fire in her eyes seemed to light up when she bought things online.

That was the *it* he avoided. Her spending was the reason they had fallen into debt in the first place. She bought the things and he paid for them. And with every purchase on her little VR headset, they fell into more and more credit debt.

She told him it was normal, the same excuse popping up a package fell in front of the doorstep, day after day. *Everyone is in debt these days.*

It didn't feel so bad at first, he recalled. But then he had made the mistake of consolidating the debt with the wrong people. That was the big mistake that he wished he could take back. Now it was one big high-interest fuckup that he couldn't seem to dig them out of.

Janice didn't even know either, and he didn't know how to tell her.

Why don't you just tell her? he'd ask himself when she'd shrug off some new item.

Nani told him it wouldn't help to tell her, and as her brother, he knew her better than anyone. "Look at her," he said the last time. "You think telling her will stop her? She'll never quit. You know why."

Janice suffered from *consumer fetishism* and had been battling it for the past couple of years.

The diagnosis was fairly new, her therapist had explained to him over the phone, and spreading rapidly. It wasn't contagious, just trendy. He had seen it popping up on his newstainment feed for quite a while before he actually caught Janice in the act of it one fine day. From what he had gathered about it afterwards, many chronic digital shoppers on the VR mall circuit were experiencing it, feelings of sexual gratification when buying items on the web.

She talked to her shrink early on about it apparently and was told that it was fine as long as it didn't get too out of control. With all the addictions that people were into these days, consumer fetishism was a lot tamer than some, post-Fall.

She kept it secret for a while, until one day after work, he walked in on her mid-orgasm, her lower body convulsing, her mouth open in ecstasy as she swiped the card down on some make-believe card-reader. He must have screamed or something, because she jumped up out of the chair like some cheating mistress and ripped the headset off in embarrassment. Right then, he asked her what was happening, but as explained herself, he couldn't believe it. The dribble on her sweatpant crotch was just a one-time accident, she explained, a bit of pee and that was it. But something in her tone felt suspicious to him.

And then he noticed it again, and again, more and more as she went under for her digital mall walks.

He thought that maybe she was watching porn or cheating or doing something weird on her little VR circuit instead of having sex with him. It explained her lack of drive in the bedroom lately. He knew that he wasn't a dynamo in the sack anymore, but still. It bothered him so much that eventually he made a plan for bringing it up again.

But even after planning what and when to say, he jumped the gun and came at her like some insensitive detective, and *right after* an episode, his temper flared, his breath hot, his face beat-red. She folded immediately then, confessing about the things her shrink had told her. It made him feel like a complete asshole, so he apologized. It wasn't intentional. It was just a thing that they'd deal with, a kink and nothing more.

To lessen the monetary hit, they decided that she'd try to focus on small purchases only, perhaps items under no-hassle return programs. It was a good strategy, she thought, granted she joined the right premium memberships.

She loved that.

She was smart, though, a lot smarter than him, so he knew whatever she was doing was already curtailed to the max. She'd have already hacked the system, made use of the coupons, so as to prevent it from hitting their savings.

She was savvy. The debt wasn't really because of her addiction.

He felt guilty about grilling her for a few days after, apologizing to her over and over. *It's not like you wanted too. You can't help yourself.*

It was these new societal addictions, he felt, just like with his father. Addiction was the new norm. Why should he judge something that made someone genuinely happy? Who was it hurting, in the end? Their sex life? That was never anything that great anyways.

Their life was the ropes because of him, *his* mistake.

And it just kept getting worse, day after day, the amount rising endlessly. It was like a rabbit hole he and his poor wife, credit-tied to his name, were tumbling down.

The consolidation wasn't even necessary. He had literally gotten scammed, once and then again, both times trying to get out, but falling instead into some money ploy he still didn't understand. They were just *so* smart, and had pegged him as a sucker so easily! It got to the point that he was so afraid of bankruptcy, he had to let Nani in for advice.

The advice, the *only* option, was a loan shark, someone off the books that would wipe his digital debt out completely so that he wouldn't have to declare bankruptcy. He would just have to pay a high pay compounding interest over time, one that he would have to pay off quickly.

Quickly, or else.

And the rabbit hole didn't stop there.

To pay the interest at first, he ended up taking on a couple of odd-jobs in addition to his job at the building, but it got to be way too much for him. He knew he couldn't keep up.

He confided in Lonny, and thank the lord he did because the skinny little brainiac saved the day. He had recently read about a sapping scam that apparently some of his shadier friends online were involved in, some ploy where you'd jack into a unit and steal power to sell on the black market. Greg showed some interest, so Lonny reached out, got the details, and came back with the full plan.

Pretty easy to carry out too.

It ended up offering him a way to quit the side-hustles and pay down the interest that the loan shark deal was accruing.

For this, he was happy.

It felt like a cockroach's life, though, surviving one day at a time, waiting for the boot-squash to end it all. Still, it was a more manageable way to get by. And he had to admit it, at times, "the hobby" as he called it felt strangely exhilarating, albeit uncharacteristically immoral.

There were side-effects that struck deep though, and as he sat around on the bench in the dirt-park watching all the dogs running up and down on their shiny manufactured equipment though, he couldn't help but feel absolutely alone, alone and neutered in a way like the rest of those furry creatures. He wanted another reality, one where he was more accountable, more responsible... a parent even... rather than just some weak partner with ED barely making it after every fiscal quarter.

It seemed like everyone was just getting by now in most respects... his wife, his father. Was the human race cursed, now that it couldn't procreate?

He wondered that often in the silence and the gloom around him.

He'd sit there, around the fancy little mutts running and humping each other, and feel like humans were literally aspiring dog-parents at best now that all of the natural children were no more. Their lives were tied to a broken system that was destroying itself, and they had no choice but to willingly help it along or end it right then and there.

We haven't got many choices left, or time for that matter, he knew. *How much longer until the rest of us die off?* The figures changed constantly, and he tried not to look at them, but he knew it would be soon.

I wish I had the courage to get off this hamster wheel forever, he almost said out loud but stopped himself.

It was an ice-cream stop kind of a day for sure on the way home from the park.

4

July 17th, 2027 - Conversation between SPEAKER 6 and SPEAKER 7
Speaker 6 - I don't know why everyone's so enamored with it. The boss is really showing it off.
Speaker 7 - You hear he's got a fuckin name for it?
Speaker 6 - What? Didn't it already have a name?
Speaker 7 - Well, whatever. He renamed it then.
Speaker 6 - What did he name it?
Speaker 7 - Lu.
Speaker 6 - Lu?
Speaker 7 - Yeah.
Speaker 6 - Lame. Well whatever they call it, it sure is slow. I should have just had it wiped.
Speaker 7 - Plug it into the servers you got from Gibbon. That'll make Lu process quicker.
Speaker 6 - You sure? Joe said to keep it local and on its own internal hardware.
Speaker 7 - You got a better idea?
Speaker 6 - Eh fuck it. What's the worst that could happen?

(2063) On Sunday night, Greg realized that he had forgotten to go in to check out the floor over the weekend, so he went to bed early instead and then headed out a couple of hours early to do some investigating before his shift started.

When he got to the parking lot though, he noticed that his boss's car was sitting in its regular spot near the entrance. And the man loved it too much to have left it at work.

Rex was in the building.

I guess I'll just have to be sneaky, he decided, walking in through the big glass doors of the building. *God knows what will happen if I try and explain myself to him. I'll probably just fuck it up and get stuck on a different job.*

All was dark and quiet in the lobby, no shining dawn breaking through the windows, no security. Only the hum of the elevator.

Somehow it filled him with a disquiet that he couldn't pin down. Perhaps the act itself of stealing in early to do something untowards made him feel uneasy? It felt different than the power sappering, more serious. It was troubling.

The elevator stopped and its walls dissolved before him, so he pushed the thoughts down and hopped in.

He made a strategic decision, deciding to stop the elevator at 346, one floor before the maintenance office, so that he could take the steps up the rest of the way, just in case Rex was sitting in the office.

Along the way, he concocted a few possible fibs, just in case he had to explain himself: *I set my alarm wrong and didn't realize it until halfway to work... I had some catch-up to do on other floors and I wanted to get a jump on it in case there was an emergency somewhere else... I...*

He stopped himself and returned to the first two, mulling over whether or not more than even one course of lie was smart. After all, there was the very real possibility that he'd screw it up if he had options. He decided to just practice the second option about catch-up. He was salaried, which kind of negated the need to do work outside of the normal hours, but then that fact would make him look good surely, which he was okay with. Besides, Rex already thought he was a goody-two-shoes. And he was … other than the sapping.

You are. You are, he told himself.

Really, he was never late for work, or even lazy at work. It was the main reason that Rex relied on him more than any of the other techs in the first place, the main reason that the other techs had gotten their time slots whittled down more and more every year. All the building really needed was the two of them.

Now that he thought of it, lately Rex had even started to chide him over the fact that he worked so hard.

The elevator chimed on the 347th floor, and Greg's mouth dropped. Rote habit had probably caused him to select that floor on accident, he though with a panic as the walls dissolved. He ducked down instinctively, and then dived out to the side behind the fabric wall partition that separated the hallway from the office space.

He banged his head against the wall too and it let out a dull thudding sound into the air, and as he froze there on his hands and knees like some doe in a clearing, he tried to pick out any indication of movement, of the sound of Rex's feeting padding towards him.

Nothing for the moment but the whirring fans and a subtle beep every once in a while.

Suddenly, he heard a chair squeak and the sound of footsteps on carpeting, heading towards him with each passing second. He turned and crawled away down the hallway as quickly as he could, heading for the nearest door.

The footsteps quickened, and he raced on all fours like some awkward cheetah, so fast that he was making more noise than before. The first door on the left was unlocked, so he threw himself bodily into its dimness and found that it was the janitor's closet, his head nearly colliding once more into the opposite wall on the other side of the small closet, and then turned and nearly slammed the door shut behind him, only at the last second easing up and edging it home quietly.

Not knowing what else to do, he hid himself back under the items of the closet, down within a square cubby that was probably made for a mop bucket or something. Then he pricked his ears again.

The footsteps had rounded the corner and were heading towards him still, the calling card of Rex's gait—the left foot-drag every step or so—apparent to him now. He kept listening, and waiting.

His shadow passed by the crack of light in the door, and Greg let out a breath, but them it came back, and stopped midway.

He held his breath. The shadow shifted slightly, but then luckily passed out of view as his steps moved on down the hall, the sound fading and then going out completely.

Greg's chest ached a touch as he breathed again and agin, his hand holding his chest, his heart pounding like a drum within.

He slowly stood up and checked the time on his phone. It was 5:43.

The time doesn't matter, he thought and put the phone away, his eyes blinded by the sudden light. He waited for his vision to adjust, and then he grabbed the door and inched it open to peak out.

"What the fuck are you doing in there?" Rex was asking him from around the other side of the door. He craned his head around and saw Rex standing there a few feet away, his face screwed up in an annoyed frown, waiting for answers no doubt.

"What was that?" was all that he figured to say in the moment. The thought suddenly occurred to him that he had not planned for this line of questioning.

"Why are you in the closet, you fuckin' weirdo, and doesn't your shift not start for another two hours? You sleep in there now or are you just jacking it in there?" His normally sarcastic cadence was gone. Greg could tell that these were serious questions.

He hemmed for a minute like someone who really was guilty. "Uh, yeah," he replied, not knowing what he was 'yeahing' to, only that he had to get words out.

"Yeah, you're jacking off in the supply closet?" Rex asked.

"No, no, no," he replied, his head shaking, his mind trying to back up to a safer point. "No. Not that. What are you talking about?"

"What? What are *you* doing here?" Rex asked again, his face confused now by the crazy dance of words they had locked themselves in.

"I'm supposed to be here. What are you doing here?" Greg threw back at him dumbly.

Without saying anything further, Rex walked up to him and took a long wiff of his jacket. "Are you drunk, Greg? Is that it?" He took a step back and looked him over. "It's not even 6 o'clock yet. You don't start for two more hours."

"I just came in early to catch up on some things," Greg started to say, recalling his canned response and trying to jam it into the conversation.

"Oh. Why were you in the closet?"

Greg scratched the back of his head, and then blew a raspberry. "Geez, man," he replied, trying to sound like *he* was the one in the right and Rex was the annoying one, "I was just going to the closet for some cleaner. I spilled some shit in my car, and couldn't find anything to clean it, and the security wasn't around, so I went over here to get some cleaning stuff from the janitor's closet. End of story."

Hey, not bad! thought Greg, as Rex dropped back and chewed on his lips, his face deep in thought.

"Well, okay," he finally said, "Get to it then, I guess. But don't go stealing all the supplies in there, or else you're going to have to replace them. If Mark complains about it, I'm going to write you up."

He turned on his heels and walked away, without anything further to say.

A little shaken, Greg started to walk to the elevator, but then remembered that he needed the GR just in case he met any problems getting into the floor. He walked into the work area to grab it at his desk.

"Aren't you going to your car?" Rex questioned him.

"Yeah. I'm just going to get my tools now so that I won't have to come back up to get them."

Rex thought for a moment, a suspicious look on his face. "Okay," he finally said, "Smart thinkin', dumbass," he said and blew him a kiss.

There's that weird fucker, Greg thought and turned around to grab his stuff.

He grabbed the GR, his harness, and a crowbar.

Just enough equipment to break into a floor that's probably Rex's own personal sex dungeon, he thought wearily and shook his head.

In order to access the floor, Greg planned to go down to the 182nd floor first and then hop up from there, but after a moment of deliberation, a less strenuous idea occurred to him and he pulled out his GR.

First, he jacked in and turned off his synaptic safety controls. Then he dissolved the walls, and prompted the elevator to lift by an approximate half floor—about 7 feet. The elevator lifted, and to his surprise, the girder between the 182nd and what he figured was the 183rd floor came into view. There didn't seem to *be* a half floor, or at least, what he was thinking was a half floor. It was just your run-of-the-mill building floor construction of a floor every 14 feet.

Above him, though, where he thought he was looking at the 183rd floor, he noticed that the door to it had some sort of wall over it. He prompted the elevator up another 7 feet and came face to face with the situation.

In front of him, it looked like a wall of some sort had been nailed over the opening. He shined a light around, looking for any identifying marks that would confirm which floor he was actually on. Next to the wall, it read, MAINTENANCE FLOOR. ONLY AUTHORIZED PERSONNEL ALLOWED. On the door covering, he saw a black document of some kind that was attached in the middle, so he walked up and took a closer look, the small writing difficult for him to read:

"No trespassing in accordance with Federal Penal Code Section 602.8 PC. All unlawful personnel that do not have legal authority to enter the area within will be arrested for felony trespassing."

Greg wondered how long ago the floor had been blocked off, and more importantly, why the federal government had anything to do with it. It was just HEPA filters in there anyway, or at least that's what Bob had said.

Below the paper, he saw that some of the cover's black paint was peeling off, so he ripped at it and ended up pulling off a large chunk to reveal white underneath. He pushed on it with his index finger, and it caved in easily.

Drywall? he thought. *I wonder if whoever painted it was in a hurry? They must have been for it to just peel off like this.* He began to doubt that the federal government was the acting party.

Drywall sure is a strange way to cover a floor's doors. Maybe that's what they did back in the day? But then why would they paint it over in black to try and obscure it? Wouldn't the letter be enough?

Maybe the letter was fake, he thought, and pulled it off the wall. It felt thin, too, almost like cheap coloring paper.

He wondered whether or not to just leave it by the door, get back in the elevator, go back to the office and forget about everything. The drywall, the paper, the paint. It all felt wrong. It just didn't feel legitimate, more like perhaps an old building manager trying to keep people out, rather than wandering around inside, or walking off with things.

He pulled out the crowbar he had grabbed from the office and turned it over for a moment in his hands, analyzing the forked prongs that showed promisingly in his headlamp light. Then he swung it hard into the wall.

His entire hand went straight through it and when he ripped it back out, he pulled off a large part of the wall in the process. He took another swing and then another. On the other side, he could see the metal sheen of the inner door and the opening's slit. He began pulling away more and more of the drywall to get a good enough angle to pry open the door. A swing or two later, he had enough room to work with. He went in his bag and grabbed his hammer to drive in the crowbar. Then he positioned the bar in the middle of the door opening and with one single, precise slam, smacked it in with a hard clang. He took another swing just because, and then jerked around back and forth a little to widen the slit a touch. Inside, he could hear a humming sound emanating from within. He wedged his right boot in and then his left arm up to his elbow, and then grabbed the other side of the door with his other hand and began pulling the two doors apart as hard as he could, his breath holding and his back flexing as he slowly inched them apart little by little, the doors screeching considerably, disused such that they were. It took three hard tries, but after a few minutes, he gained what looked like enough room to squeeze through and stopped to shine his light in. Inside from what he could tell, there looked to be rows of shelves of some kind, almost as if an old library lay within, shut off from the rest of mankind. He collected his things and without much of a preamble, squeezed his way in.

There was a large foyer inside that led into a dense collection of rows retreating back to the end of the room. It was dark and of an unknowable size. As Greg surveyed it all with his light, he saw that the shelves rose almost to the ceiling, but deep within a faint illumination peaked through, a line of christmas coloring alighting a bit of the ceiling way way back towards the left-rear part of the room. There were dozens upon dozens of identical corridors to explore, and the hum that he had heard outside was louder now, its metallic drone spooking his nerves. As he came up to the row directly in front of him, he saw that the head-high cabinetry was much more sophisticated up close, packed on each shelf with dozens of identical metal computing boxes of some kind wired up through the back, perhaps akin to computing server bays of some kind or another, though he had no real idea, not being tech savvy. He shined his light down the row and saw that it went on for as far as he could see.

For some reason that he couldn't pin down, the long lifeless row leading leading off into oblivion filled him with fear, fear and dread. It was all so unexpected, what he had discovered, nothing like what Bob had explained to him, and whatever it was, it was clear that it wasn't an abandoned HEPA filter storage area. It had been repurposed for some reason.

Stranger still, it had been closed off for some other reason.

And now here he was in it, trespassing.

The hum in the air was coming from the left side, he realized, and his mind connected the glow to it, though he couldn't see it now. It wasn't *completely* dead. There was life somewhere in the room. He backed out of the row and stalked along the perimeter in the direction of the light, peeking down each pitch-black row as he went. Several corridors down, he spotted the source of light a ways down the row, a multitude of small lights it seemed busily blinking, perhaps powered up computing parts. The hum was louder too, and seemed to emanate from there.

He walked down slowly, the darkness of the room so strong and heavy still that he feared something would jump out and grab him at any moment.

As he approached the area, the hum, now utterly raucous, issued from two separate air ducts that were pouring down frigid air on the shelves on both sides of the lighted area. He shivered, but there was no way of escaping it. All around him the lights flickered busily within their shelves, the section of life within the row fairly large, a good fifty feet at least in its span. Its sheer power requirement astounded him, its juice-guzzling certainly more than the government would ever allow. A shady setup, indeed, he surmised, completely unregulated, sapping in secret more than likely. The wire-up in the servicing bay, its jumble of soldering, came to mind to him, and he guessed then that more than 4 floors of low-key juicage were needed. The room must have been wired up to a ton of floors, *had* to be. It was the only way to pull it off without everyone noticing. Maybe every floor was being tapped.

The nature of the room stuck him then, its alien existence a thing to consider itself, he felt, its sheer irregularity, not just within the building but in general. *Places like this don't exist anymore,* he thought. Maybe that was why the note was there. The government had stepped in and shut it down, or attempted to at least.

Whatever the case, its current needs were definitely illegal, given the outcry against energy conservation that had poured out post-sterilization.

Why in this building, all buried deep within this catacomb of dead technology, lost in time? Something seedy was brewing in the shadows, up to no good, embroiled in nefarious activity.

And my dumb ass just waltzed right in here, without a care in the world, completely oblivious.

Oh my God, he realized, his heartbeat quickening. *I didn't even check for monitoring equipment.* Perhaps someone was watching him right now, he thought, a hidden guardian of the room, waiting to strike at any moment. He took a step back and tried to calm himself down, his body leaning against the shelf behind, his hand on his chest trying to soothe the ping of panic building up inside him. *Get a hold of yourself,* he shouted within.

The trespass definitely felt like a stupid overstep now. He wasn't sapping. It wasn't planned. This was a new fear, a strange one, different from the dread that he carried to work every day as an energy thief. He was on a path now and couldn't deny it. But for some reason, standing alone, his heart racing, the fear felt exciting as well. Somehow, looking out at the lights that danced unbeknownst to the rest of the world, he felt alive and scared to death at the same time.

He had unknowingly stumbled into something outside of the norm, an absolute impossibility in this day and age. And for better or worse, perhaps it would open him up to something new, something less sterile than before.

The lights caught his attention again and he realized he had been zoning out and shook himself awake, registering then that the clock was ticking and he had a very finite amount of time left to find answers. Instead of wandering around aimlessly any further, he decided instead to gather a bit of documentation and then come back another time. He pulled out his phone and set it up to take a couple of shots.

He started with a few pano shots of the area, trying to capture the row to explain to Lonny later. His hand was shaky though, so try as he might, the pictures seemed to come out awful and blurred. He switched tactics, and focused in on one of the individual lit-up bays with the flash on, and that came out better. He really had no idea what he was looking for, or even looking at, he had to admit. He hoped that Lonny would clarify, perhaps, if the pictures he took were of any use. He analyzed his best close-up shot of one of the computer bays for any identifiers. There were 5 horizontal rows with 8 individual brickish stone-age computing parts standing up on their sides, and on the small fans attached to the back of each, he made out barcodes, so he zoomed in further to make sure the numbers were clear, but the image blurred out. He got in closer on one of the shelves and snapped another flash shot. Looking at the pic, it read, "AFX TESLA 110 GPU."

"GPU" sounded familiar, like "CPU," which he guessed stood for computer processing unit, so he opened his web browser to search up the acronym, but then he stopped himself. This wasn't the time. He could possibly get caught at any moment. It would have to wait for later. He packed up and started back up the row the way he came, but then thought again, and turned around, deciding instead to at least head down the rest of the corridor to at least get a cursory view of the rest of the room itself, just in case there was something obvious worth seeing.

The row was very long indeed, he thought as he moved along at a brisker pace than before, finally coming to the end after a good hundred feet or so, where a shiny, metallic wall greeted him. It was impressively reflective he felt, so well so that he could almost see his silhouette. He ran his fingers lightly along it and it crinkled, almost as if it were just some thin aluminum foil pulled over the wall for some odd reason.

He turned to the left with the intention of walking to the corner of the room, his light leading him along, his hand gliding along the cool foil, but after a dozen steps, stopped himself again, feeling careless with fate. The corridor in front of him looked bland and blank and like it went on forever.

Enough, he told himself. *It's just a massive room full of rows of dead computing parts. No doubt, it was something once, but now it's a museum to wastefulness.*

Ask Lonny later. Leave now.

He headed towards the entrance up another row, and as he emerged, he noticed a small door along the side of the foyer, something of not he had missed, so he walked up and tried the knob, but it was locked. He thought of trying to break in, taking out the crowbar in his pack and taking a couple of swings on the weak knob barring his entry, but decided against it. There was a plaque next to the door that read *HR Manager, Bob Stenafilis*, so he took a picture of it, and then put his phone away, strangely a little depressed.

Who did he think he was, an investigator?

Perhaps it had been foolish to trespass in the first place. He knew so little about computers. Maybe the place wasn't extraordinary at all? Maybe it was just an old room from before the fall that had just gone neglected and abandoned with a few things left running on by accident.

But the drywall covering? He wondered doubtfully. That *was* weird, he reckoned, feeling that something had to be going on. *I'll find out*, he told himself. *What else have I got going on, anyways? I'll go back to the VR theater as soon as work is over for the day and try to catch Lonny to ask.*

He wondered what to do about the massive hole in the drywall in the meantime. He checked his watch. *Fuck, I"m late.* He'd have to leave it open for now and come by sometime in the future to shut it all up again. If he didn't head up soon, Rex would come hunting for him.

He turned to the exit, but caught something out of the upper corner of his eye, something blinking red in the corner of the room, and as he shined his light at it, he recognized it immediately—an old surveillance camera.

And it was on and blinking back at him, with a good view of him no doubt since the beginning.

He instinctively shut off his headlamp, his heart racing.

He looked around suddenly, trying to pick out other possible blinking lights, but saw only darkness. He craned his head down quickly, avoiding the camera anymore, and raced out through the door opening, hoping without a prayer that even though the camera was on and trained on him god knows how long, that hopefully (Maybe... more than likely?) it wasn't functioning well enough to catch the verifiable features of his face. He'd be able to blame it on Rex if anyone asked, planned to.

He was probably waiting for him now.

But just then he noticed the fact that the elevator was gone.

Rex might have found him out already.

He went back into the room and jacked into the elevator panel with his GR, his body angled away from the camera, and called the lift back to his location. As he waited, he felt the panic of exposure rising within him, his body prone to danger without escape now, waiting helpless in the darkness with nothing but a few tools to defend himself. He started to envision an evil force reaching out and pulling him back, but as he turned around with his light shining, his senses trained for any sign of movement, there was nothing, nothing at all to sense but the same low hum of the ACs. Still, he pictured a black hand made of thick smog reaching out and grabbing him.

No doubt his mind was freaking out, so he tried to focus on his breath.

Weird how quickly the place had morphed into such a doom-room, he thought.

The whole conspiracy of it seemed to lay itself out before him now, open to his interpretation—the drywall, the paper, the powered on computer shit. It all seemed to add up to something more, something sinister.

For some unjustified reason, he thought back to 9/23, to the fall, to Sterilization Day. He was a kid again, a lifetime ago, sitting with his mother and father, completely exposed then as well, no escape from the horrors of the world stopping on live television.

Nowhere to go, just like now.

He heard the hum of the elevator descending, and turned to the sight of the carriage lights gaining in strength, illuminating the dimness beyond the door-opening, like some angel come to take him away. It appeared a moment after and pinged.

He thanked God.

But as the walls came down, his eyes opened wide to the figure within.

Standing there, his face already locked onto him with a grim, almost knowing expression, was Rex.

"You stupid, mother fucker," he said, his voice low and measured.

He wouldn't be able to blame him after all.

. . .

It was like a spaghetti western of old, their eyes trained on each other as they faced off from either side of the disheveled entrance, a square-off in the most literal sense, with Rex standing just beyond the small space that Greg would have to fit through to get out of the room, his body blocking the way.

Rex wanted information, no doubt, but Greg wanted escape.

Rex's eyes narrowed, his fists balled up, and his stance widened.

"What.The.Fuck.Are.You.Doing.Here?" He asked slowly in the same low volume.

Greg had literally no idea what to say. *Think of a lie,* he told himself, and in a panic, he blurted out the first thing that popped into his head.

"I heard a noise in there from the floor below," he started, his voice sort of out of breath, quickened. "When I came up, I heard it again from behind the door, and thought it might be something serious. I just—"

Rex cut him off with a dismissive wave of the arm and he shut his mouth, wondering hopelessly if his card was up. Would Rex let him off, somehow, or give him a warning, perhaps? His eyes had closed in thought, and as Greg waited for the verdict, a long spell of silence fell between them, the feeling in his gut worsening with each passing second.

"So you say you heard something," Rex offered up, his eyes suddenly opening, locking onto Greg, "You came up. You saw the wall, and you … What? Decided to break in with a sledge hammer?" He pointed his finger around the floor at the litter of broken drywall.

"No, I—"

"You didn't think the sign mattered," he continued, "Or what? Or can you not read?" He bent down slowly and picked it up, holding it out for Greg to see the words plainly enough.

He knew about this place then, Greg thought reflexively, his eyes moving from the paper to Rex and back again. *He knew about the sign before. Maybe he saw it himself.*

Maybe he put it up?

Rex let the sign drop to the floor, and then took a step closer to Greg, an action that made him wince and raise his hands, yet Rex hardly noticed, his eyes peering past him instead right into the darkness, his expression suddenly, strangely enough, curious.

"What did you see in there, anyways?" he asked, his mouth agape, his eyes roving about, peering within.

Has he got no idea what's in there? Greg wondered, analyzing his expression.

The image of the blinking red light came to mind, and he gave a small sigh of relief, thinking that perhaps it was broken after all.

"Well?" Rex asked, his eyes suddenly back on him now, annoyed at his silence. "You gonna tell me or what?"

He wondered whether Rex was planning to go in himself, the question sitting with him. He took a gamble.

"It's just a bunch of HEPA filters," he replied, starting up again, packing on more lies, yet in that moment, he felt himself hesitate, not knowing what to say next. *Why am I even lying?* he thought. "But I mean, yeah, nothing really," he continued all the same, stuttering it out like a fool.

Rex put his hand up to stop him. "Boy oh boy," he replied, his head shaking. "Enough. I'm done with your lies. Step up out of there and go grab your shit. You're fired."

Fired? Greg's eyes opened wide to the word. "Wait," he began, but Rex's hand came up again to stop him from going on, his body moving back at the same time so that Greg could join him in the lift. He dropped his head, and got in the elevator.

Rex circled him slowly as he entered, his hand rifling through his pocket. Without warning, he pulled out a small light and shined it right in his eyes, the beam blindingly bright so that he lifted his hand to block it.

"On second thought," he said and smiled. "I'm not going to fire you, you fuckin' liar. I'm gonna let you quit instead. You're going to put in your two-weeks notice as soon as you get up to the office, that way you can't file for severance pay. And if you don't, I'm not *just* going to fire you. I'm going to blackball you too... with every building manager I know... and I'm gonna speak with the union. You'll have a lot of trouble finding a job after that." He lowered the light, and pointed at the control panel. "Now get back to the office and get to work."

Greg felt the hope drop out of him. There was nothing he could say to save him at this point.

"And for your sake," Rex continued, and gestured at the opening, "Stay away from this room. Or else."

For my sake? Greg thought, wondering whether the phrase was meant as a threat or a warning. *What the fuck do you know about this place? Are you covering up something?*

Rex pressed the office floor button himself to get things moving, but just before the lift walls started to materialize, he stepped out of the elevator into the opening, the walls rising up behind him as he disappeared, leaving Greg alone in the light and the hum of the elevator.

Somehow or another, he thought, Rex wasn't innocent. He had some part to play in this.

5

Aug 2, 2027 - Conversation between SPEAKER 6 AND SPEAKER 7
Speaker 6 - You're right. Lu has been working great since we got him
hooked up. He gets updates directly from Gibbon too.
Speaker 7 - See, I told you. You can count on Lu.
Speaker 6 - Lame.

(2063) Rex was gone for a while that day, and as Greg sat at his workstation fiddling around with an electrical harness, waiting anxiously for the chance to make one final go at groveling before penning out his resignation, he toyed with the idea of breaking into his boss's small cubby-room-of-an-office to look for something—anything—suspicious. What did he have to lose, anyways? he wondered. But by 5 pm, he still hadn't done it, and Rex hadn't returned, so slinked out instead, kicking himself along the way for being a coward.

What would it have mattered anyways? he felt. He was going to get canned either way. Still, he had a chance to keep his job. He just *felt* it. Perhaps Rex had stayed away to cool off. He banked on the possibility, and started writing up apology ideas on his phone as the car drove him to the VR theater, where he'd meet Lonny and show him his findings.

First Lonny, and *then* Janice, he thought miserably, wondering what he'd say. He felt like such a fool. What *could* he possibly say? That he had been caught chasing a conspiracy theory that was taking place in his building, and was paying for it with his job?

Just then, he realized that perhaps there was a way to use the hidden floor's electricity sapping to his advantage with Rex. He made a note to include that in his plea to keep his job. Maybe he could blame his trespass on that.

"I saw that it was sapping juice, so I checked it out. I realize that I should have told you, but I was just excited, thinking that maybe there was something shady going on. When you saw me, I panicked and told a fib. But it's not like I stole something. I was just doing my do-diligence.

It felt like a gleam of escape. Really, that felt like an absolutely valid reason to investigate. He slapped his head excitedly with the palm of his hand, wondering why he hadn't thought of it before.

It would even explain why he disregarded the signage on the door. *There was something criminal going on, so I decided that the sign might be a roose. Perfect.*

And if Rex balked, or played it down, maybe he could even add that he didn't tell him the truth at first because he was worried that Rex might be involved.

That's why I lied. I wanted to take it to Human Resources, first. That would scare Rex enough to back off. He'll either let me go to HR if he's not in on it, or tell me to drop it all if he is in on it.

Bing bang boom. Fiasco saved.

He remembered then that his sapper was next to the place where he found the wiring. *That wouldn't do. What if Rex wanted to see it for himself?*

He'd have to grab the box and hide it. And then could talk to Rex

It would work… Maybe.

He opened his email and crafted a draft to his human resources representative, cataloging his findings—the sapping, the floor—and his worries that his superior might be part of it. At the end of the email, he stopped himself.

What if someone else in the building is in on it, maybe some higher-up, maybe the owner?

What if everyone knew?

He thought of discarding the email entirely, but just saved it and logged out.

He was definitely in a pickle, he realized. He'd have to lay it out for Lonny and get a second opinion.

Maybe Bob would know too.

He'd get a couple of opinions.

He was about to call Bob on the phone when the car pinged him abruptly that he was at the theater. He shut off the notification, grabbed the wheel, and forced the car down to the pavement himself, the vehicle bouncing noisily on the asphalt. A warning light came on, advising him against manual landings in the future, suggesting that he allow it to land the car next time to avoid exterior damage. He smashed the button with the palm of his hand and got out.

I fucking hate technology.

How ironic since he was looking for tech advice from Lonny. That and building-conspiracy advice from Bob.

Lonny was leaning on the doorjamb as Greg walked up the steps to the cafe, holding out his thin, dainty hand for a handshake. He looked surprised to see Greg.

"Had no idea you were coming by today. Looking for your dad? He's not here right now. Is he coming in outside of meeting hours or what?" He looked around for him, his hand still shaking Greg's.

"No, man. Just me," he replied with an awkward, naked grin, wondering if it would have been better to text him before.

"It's no prob, man!" he said though and started to pull him into the cafe, but then stopped. "You want to go grab a coffee or something at a *real* cafe? I'm feeling kind of cooped up in here right anyways. I was about to close up for lunch actually."

Greg acquiesced so they headed next door to a coffee shop called *Chava*. It was busy—a rush of teens waiting in line, and all of the seats taken—so they stood around like a couple of vultures until a man sitting alone felt the heat of their staring and got up to leave. They pounced immediately, and took in the not-so-beautiful surroundings, the encroachment of highrise condominium housing, the jumbled telephone pole wires hanging right above them, pulled back almost to the building rooftops edges as if a giant had traipsed through the street. It was a lazy method Greg thought to make way for the modern cars that were constantly landing and taking off. What a mess.

Lonny didn't seem to mind though, his face cheery, his eyes people-watching, taking in the conversation. The ever-observer. He got up and grabbed them a cup of chava, insisting that Greg give the drink a go, since he had never tried it.

It looked like gussied-up mud water. Lonny shot it down in one long series of gulps, and then ate the pineapple slice at the bottom of the empty cup. Greg tasted it, and sure enough, it was awful, bitter to the point that he gagged. He tried to play it off, but Lonny noticed and grinned really big.

"You don't have to drink it," he offered and held out his hand. "I can drink it. I just figured you'd enjoy the experience."

"No, it's cool," Greg said, picking it up again, sloshing it around indifferently. He wondered why he hadn't taken him up on the escape.

Lonny guessed as much and put his hand out. "No, really, man. It's cool. Go grab some coffee from them. Theirs is pretty good too, for a kava bar at least."

Greg hadn't noticed that the place wasn't actually a coffee shop, but as he got up, his eyes roving around, he noted that everyone had a specific look—dreadlocks, big baggy shirts, dirty looking. They were all a bunch of hippies. Perhaps chava, kava, whatever it was, was a Caribbean sort of drink, he thought. Maybe Lonny would know. He made a mental note to ask him when he returned.

The thought of small-talk felt good to him. He needed a break.

Too many things to think about today.

He got the most basic thing on the menu, a small black coffee, but failed to get any creamer. *Black only*, they had said.

Fine.

He came back with the thought in his head still, ready to ask, ready to engage in some chill banter. Lonny, who was chatting up some cute, tanned girl nearby, looked up at him and nudged the girl's shoulder. She threw him a smile and then adjusted her sunglasses, monstrous things that covered most of her face. Perhaps she was stoned, he thought, noticing her long black dreads that nearly touched the pavement. A pinkish birthmark peeked out of the bottom of her glasses, nearly touching her mouth.

"You're not the only one that hates that stuff, man," Lonny said. "My friend here can't drink it either." She laughed coyly, her hand over her mouth. She reminded him of a teenager. The thought made him sad.

"Yeah, I was gonna ask. What *is* that stuff?" he replied.

"This place calls it *chava* because it's a mix of tea, or *cha* in Korean, and a medicinal drink called Kava. I'm guessing you've never heard of it, huh."

Greg nodded, a slight blush on his face. He wondered if the girl knew. Probably. She looked like an islander, her skin naturally brown, almost caramel. "Did she tell you about it?" he asked.

"No. I've had it here a couple of times, so I did some research."

"Oh, I see."

"It's kind of like a detox, I think." He said uncertainly and then looked at the girl for confirmation. "Feel free to correct me if I misspeak," he told her, but she shook her head at him emphatically, her hands still over her mouth. The mannerism felt forced to Greg.

"They say it helps with anxiety, which is why I drink it," he continued. "It kind of relaxes you."

"Where does it come from?" Greg asked, sipping lightly on his coffee now.

"It's grown in the pacific islands. Like Hawaii, Indonesia. That sort of thing."

"And it's for anxiety?" he answered with a snort. "What do *they* have to feel anxious about? All they're doing these days is making babies for the rest of the world."

The girl's face flushed beet red and her eyebrows shot up so high that they peeked out over the brim of the glasses, her eyes no doubt wide-eyed at him. He saw it knew then that he had word-vomited. Lonny's mouth had dropped as well, his body stiff.

She turned away from them suddenly without another word, facing her small table instead.

"Jesus, man," Lonny replied loudly, his eyes more judgmental than Greg had ever seen.

"What?" Greg replied defensively. "I know, I know, I'm sorry. But I mean... All I meant was that they are still conceiving over there, so it's like, *What's the worrying for?*"

The explaining seemed to make it all worse. It always did, his excuses. Janice had told him that a million times.

"You still can't just say shit like that man!" Lonny nearly spat out. "Besides, it's not like you have the full fucking picture. You just sound ignorant."

"I know. I—"

The girl got up suddenly, her hand on her glasses. Lonny brushed her arm and she flinched and then yelped, the sunglasses flipping out of her hand towards the table. They fell with a clatter.

She let out a cry as she grabbed them, her head flipping for a second towards the two of them.

Greg saw the birthmark. It *wasn't* a birthmark. It was worse. One eye was gone, an unnatural crater in her face where it should have been. Greg saw it and knew immediately what it was, having heard about it before.

Everyone had.

It was an after-effect of the bio-weapon that his people had created, an effect that the vaccine, the very vaccine that had sterilized his people, was tasked to contend with. In a way, it was a mark of fertility. How ironic. How sad to behold.

It was his own ignorance staring back at him.

She grabbed her sunglasses, jammed them onto her face, and ran out through the small gate towards the street.

Greg and Lonny stood for a moment, watching her leave. He thought of following, but what would he say? What was there to say now?

Nothing.

So they stood there, watching her go. She hopped into a car a moment later, and it took off to the skies. They sat down in silence at the table, neither of them speaking for a while.

After a good couple of minutes, Lonny broke the silence. "Welp, that sucked," he said matter-of-factly, his eyes distant, a frown on his face.

"Yeah," Greg said, his head in his chest. He looked up at Greg. "That was some great timing, wasn't it."

"Honestly, man. I was pretty surprised you said that. It's not like you."

"Yeah, I know. I'm sorry … I'm a little off these days."

"Is it because of your dad?"

"I don't know… It's just sometimes when something reminds me of having kids and all… I get to thinking about how unlucky we all are and it gets me a little pissy."

Janice's face popped into his head then, and he shook his head. *She'd be so much happier if she were born on some remote island somewhere, far from the fucking vaccine,* he thought. *She'd be a mom now, not just killing time flicking it to Hello Kitty dolls or whatever the fuck it was she got off to.*

How the poor become the prosperous and the rich wilt away.

The islander girl hadn't looked very prosperous though, had she, he mused. The grass was always greener.

"I'm surprised she's in the states," Greg said.

"Yeah, you don't see too many. I hear some come in on fertility visas. It's controlled pretty tightly, for obvious reasons."

"Yeah, that makes sense," he replied. *She's probably treated like a commodity,* he thought. *For sure, she is.*

"You'd think she'd have a bodyguard or two," Lonny said.

"Maybe she just escaped for a minute of freedom." He wondered about the car that picked her up. Was *that* her handler? "Boy. I feel like a real asshole now."

"It's alright man," Lonny replied encouragingly. "We all say stupid shit. I think I overreacted a little bit, too. It's just that this place serves a lot of the people that frequent the VR theater is all... you know, most of them are escaping reality, escaping some bullshit that they can't control, all full of anxiety, barely able to sleep. They get to dick around at my place and then chill out here."

"Maybe I need to do something like that," Greg replied. "Too many things on my mind these days."

"Yeah, what is up with you, though? I know it's something."

"It's nothing."

"It's cool, man," he prodded him. "You can tell me anything. I love to listen. Plus, I figured you had *something* to say, what with heading out here and all."

"Ok, fine" he started, wondering where to begin. "So, I've gotten into something weird at work, and I think it is going to cost me my job. Technically, it may have already cost me my job in fact."

Lonny's face perked up, his eyes big. "Dude... You're not talking about the sapper thing that I got you into? Did someone find out?"

"Oh... what? No, not that," he replied.

Lonny took a breath, his hand up to his heart. "Thank god!," he started again. "My bad. Okay, I'm listening."

"Okay, so ironically it did start with me checking in on the sapper. I was afraid that it was short-circuiting a floor in the building. Anyways, I went over to switch it, but when I got there, I happened upon some wiring that was tapped into a few of the floors of the building and drawing juice from them to another floor of the building, a secret floor."

"Really?"

"Yeah, so I took a look into it, and I found a floor full of computing equipment. I even took a couple pictures. Here, take a look," he said and whipped out his phone.

Lonny looked them over, and as he did, Greg continued. "It was strange. I'm positive that it was probably something illegal. It just felt wrong, you know ... the fact that only part of the floor was active, and obviously it wasn't registering its electrical usage."

"Obviously," Lonny agreed, not looking up from the phone.

"Yeah, but there was something else," Greg said. "I don't know the laws, or anything, but in addition to the lift entrance being blocked off, drywalled over, and painted over on top of that, but on the wall, there was a no-trespass sign, care of, and you're not going to believe this, the federal government."

"Huh?" Lonny said, looking up, his brow furrowed.

"Yeah," Greg replied. "But, I mean, it didn't look right. It felt more like a play or something by whoever was responsible for the floor to just keep people out or something. I don't know, though. I mean, the tech was all outdated looking, and-"

"Yeah, you're right about that," Lonny interrupted, and then handed him back the phone. "I mean, the tech is at least 25 years old or more. Were there a lot of those shelves?

"Tons," Greg replied. "The whole floor was full of rows and rows of them."

In that case, maybe it's the remnants of an old crypto-mining farm."

"Crypto-mining?"

"Yeah. Cryptocurrency was a fad back in the day and a lot of people were using it instead of real money. The point of it at the beginning made sense. People wanted a means to just transfer money without relying on a third party like a bank or whatever, so digital currencies were a good means to do that."

"Ok, but *mining?*"

"Yeah. Basically they used computer processors to complete currency transactions online. Each one paid out a tiny profit, so if you used a lot of processors to do the transactions, you made a larger profit. There were farms of these processors that would do transactions night and day, raking in the dough twenty-four-seven. Well, before the crackdown on electricity, that is."

"Is that what destroyed the crypto market?"

"Not exactly. There were a couple of major crypto-currency crashes, but yeah, when the electricity mandates happened, all of that profit-driven server farming fizzled out pretty much overnight."

"Still," Lonny said and grabbed the phone back to look at the pictures again, "This processor isn't really the type that they'd use as much in like major server farms."

"What are you talking about?" Greg asked. "How do you know all this shit, anyways?"

"Honestly, I have a lot of free-time man, and I'm a bit of a computer history buff. It's crazy how much computer technology has shifted over the years, especially after the regs and the gestation collapse."

There it is again, Greg thought, honing in on Lonny's reference to the fall. He thought of the room, of that feeling of exposure he felt in there.

It's strange that this keeps coming up.

"So this computer part," Lonny was saying, his finger pointing down to the close-up photo of the processors that were lining the racks in the server bays, "This is a graphics processing unit that's pretty beefy, maybe too beefy for a crypto-mining job. More like a data center processor." He thought for a second. "Did you go to another part of the floor and take photos, or maybe like some video or something? I'd be surprised if this type of processor covered that entire floor. Honestly, it's strange that it's there in general."

"Why?" Greg asked.

"I don't know. It's just weird," Lonny said uncertainly, his head shaking. "I'm gonna have to do some research on the web to see what I can dig up tonight. Maybe we can meet up again and talk? I think you should go back in there and get some more video of the place. Can you? Maybe you can just go around with a light and actually video tape other areas or something?"

"Hold up," Greg stopped him.

"I mean... You're getting canned anyways, right," Lonny continued.

"Still, no. Rex pretty much fired me on the spot just for going in."

"So, what, you're banned from the building?" Lonny asked.

"No. I mean. He didn't actually fire me—"

"I'm confused," Lonny broke in. "Are you actually fired or not?"

"He told me I had to quit."

"Oh," Lonny said. "So you do have access still then."

"Yeah," Greg said, and then held up his hand to stop Lonny from jumping in. "But I think he may be hiding something, something that I can use to maybe keep my job. I think he may be involved in some way. I don't think he's the mastermind, obviously, but I do think he is playing guard dog or something. There was a camera in there trained on the entrance, and it was running, which now that I think of it, strikes me as strange," he said and started to think out loud. "Why would a camera be running in a room that's blocked off already anyways?"

Lonny started to nod his head. "There is definitely something weird going on," he said. "But I don't know … Illegal crypto-mining sounds like chump-change nowadays. Even if the floor were used for that back in the day, honestly, I bet it's for something way different now. And you're right that it's probably not legal, based on the set-up in your building."

Greg nodded his head in agreement.

"But wait, go back. Rex told you to quit? Why?"

"Oh, yeah," Greg said, perking up even further. "So that was weird too. Rex said that I had to quit, otherwise he would fire me and blackball me."

"That's shady," Lonny replied, his hand stroking his chin. "Fuck that," he nearly spat out. "Don't do it. He's probably just trying to get you to quit for some other reason. Maybe he's afraid to fire you."

The thought caused Greg to pause.

"Either way," Lonny continued, "My friend, you still have access. Is there anyone that you can talk to that might know the building better?"

Greg nodded, thinking of Bob.

And I'm going to rummage around Rex's room too, he thought.

"Good. Talk to them. In the meantime, I'll talk to some people online, and see what I can dig up about that GPU of yours. Maybe someone will know about it. Either way, this is some interesting stuff man. I bet a bunch of my friends will want to help. Just make sure to get some more video. The whole room this time."

"Okay," Greg said, rather reluctantly.

"Alright, well," Lonny started, pushing his chair away from the table, "I'd better head back to the cafe. The rush is gonna be on in a bit. Especially since most of these people here will probably be in my place any second now." He stood up and tossed his cup in the trash can. As he walked by, he put his hand on Greg's shoulder. "Oh, and nice work talking to your dad," he said. "He told me about it, and even apologized for the whole thing. I think it really helped."

He slapped him on the shoulder and squeezed it, smiling. Greg smiled back at him.

Thank god something I said was good, he thought wearily as he got up to leave as well. He couldn't wait to be rid of the place, drink and people and all.

$$6$$

*August 3rd, 2027 - Conversation between SPEAKER 6 and
SPEAKER 7*
Speaker 6 - I think Lu can see what Gibbon's doing over there.
Speaker 7 - How do you know?
*Speaker 6 - I don't know. Just a hunch. I think it's a peer to peer
system.*
Speaker 7 - How the fuck do you know that?
Speaker 6 - How else? Porn torrents.

(2063) *Christ, I'm a dick,* he thought in the car as it carried him home, his mind on the girl who stared back at him in horror through one shocked eye. *I should have run after her and apologized.* She would have just yelled at him, but still, inside he knew he deserved that. It might have felt like its own detox in a way.

Maybe he'd understand her better if they shouted at each other for a minute. For sure, he would, he felt. Already, he could see the parallel between them, two sides of the same painful coin. She had her scar on the outside, while his people had theirs on the inside. Which was worse? He wondered.

Somehow, it reminded him suddenly of *that* day as a kid, that moment in time the world shifted for everyone, the day that changed the world forever.

September 23rd.

Like so many others, Greg remembered exactly where he was in the moments leading up to the tragedy of September 23rd, 2027. He was walking out the door for school. There were workers in the front yard pouring a new concrete driveway, he recalled. His father was outside as well monitoring the situation, annoyed as usual as he hovered over them from the side of the wet concrete pour, no doubt judging their lack of care or craftsmanship, being that he was a laborer himself. His stance gave it away–his tense shoulders, his hands on his hip, his narrowed stare, his pacing. If someone was going to screw up, he was ready to call them out.

Greg knew what that was like, was on the receiving end a few weeks earlier after his father had offered to teach him how to drive stick. A couple of scratchy gearshifts was all it took to turn the man into an angry, fiery ball of tension and outrage. They barely got to the end of the street before he got out of the car and walked home.

They hadn't spoken since, and it had been three weeks.

Before he had got to the end of the driveway, he heard his mother yelling from the door jamb for his dad to come inside. She was on the phone with her friend from church, she shouted, and her friend was saying that something was happening all over the place with the vaccine.

His dad ran up the side of the wooden guard rails lining the pour and then hopped over the entrance walk to get inside, his eyes on her the whole way, her gaze meeting his, concern written all over her face. Greg saw and followed to see what was going on.

The TV in the living room was already blaring as Greg walked in, volume full, as usual in the household. His older brother, who was still in the house at the time, was the only one missing from the scene, off in his room probably listening to music. At that point, he had already begun to avoid family encounters as much as possible.

Some reality TV show was playing, so his mom grabbed the remote and switched it to some video sharing channel she went to everyday for her news. There were still some major news channels at that time, but like most of the population at the time, she didn't trust them for anything other than propaganda. For this reason, she turned to niche political content creators that seemed to do things a little differently. That day, she jumped to her flavor of the month streamer, a man named Tuck Gibson whose gimmick seemed to be his penchant for spouting his political jargon from his car. "The government's always listening," she would explain to him as she popped it on, parroting the man's reasoning for the strange desire to hide in his car. Greg would ask, "Yeah but can't they just bug your car?"

She would just ignore him.

Seeing the sub-channel she had turned to, his father snatched the remote away and searched elsewhere, looking for less biased updates on the vaccine. After a moment, he found one and turned it on.

It was some run-of-the-mill newscaster type–an old man with a windbreaker in front of a home in the desert holding some news channel microphone–talking. The title read, "Another Vaccine Fatality."

There had been a car accident apparently that had occurred in front of the house in the scene where two had been hit by a man driving recklessly to get a woman in labor–presumably his wife–to the hospital. According to the husband, the speaker explained, the woman was experiencing contractions in the car when she began to bleed profusely, so he attended to her, evidently to the point that he took his eye off the road, lost control, and then drove into a couple standing on the sidewalk. The woman survived the crash, but died moments before an ambulance could arrive due to the hemorrhaging.

The final words of the video caught them all off-guard. "This is one of many strange birth-rated deaths that are sweeping the nation today."

"Did he say 'many'?" the dad asked, looking around the room. "It's before eight in the morning, and there are 'many?'"

He looked over at Greg's mother, who was still on the phone, and she shrugged her shoulders, her eyes lost, whether from the side-convo or the implications themselves.

He clicked on another video, one of many by the point that had populated, all touting similar buzzwords—*vaccine, death, murder, tragedy.*

This time it was a younger man talking, a skinny, professional-looking man in a suit and tie—perhaps a newscaster from a bigger corporate network. He was standing in front of a large white government building.

The image of the man's face—solemn, sticken looking, unable to process what he was saying—would stay with Greg for the rest of the day.

Greg still remembered the sound of his voice as he spoke.

"Since early this morning, a mass of reported miscarriages have come in. Though no government officials have stepped forward yet with any concrete explanation as to their origin, certain variables leave sources already speculating that there may be a linkage between them and the NBRNA vaccine, more commonly referred to as the "savior vaccine," which at this time has been administered across the nation, but to much of the rest of the globe. From all over the globe, similarly grim cases are piling in. Pregnant mothers of all ages and from all walks of life are mysteriously miscarrying."

"Though as of yet, there are no cases of non-pregnant illnesses related to the vaccine, we will continue to monitor the situation closely. Unfortunately, the rest of us may be in store for something dreadful as well. This truly is a sad day, with no end in sight."

With nothing to add, the video ended on a black screen, everyone in the room staring at it in silence, struck dumb by what they had heard.

After a moment, Greg's mother walked over to Jacob and snatched the clicker out of his hand, her phone between her neck and her shoulder. She returned to Tuck Gibson's channel, and clicked on his latest video, which he had uploaded just moments ago, and sat down in the seat to watch.

He was in his car as usual holding his camera at an awkward angle, his fat double-chin rippling in the frame. Rain was pelting his car window, and as he held the phone, he pointed at the camera with his free hand.

"I told you all before, and you know it, if you tuned in," he said, his stilted southern accent resonating like some baptist preacher, "The vaccine was an ungodly concoction created by pharmaceutical companies that care only about profits and not about real consequences. Well…what do you think now?"

"We should have just hunkered down and waited for the smog of the bioweapon to dissipate. I'm telling you, I have it on good authority from my contacts at the Worldwide Weather Watch that the bio-cloud threat may not even reach over the Atlantic. Let those liberal Europeans deal with it. It ain't got nothin' to do with us. And another thing, why did we have to go and give into this crazy timeline that cut corners and didn't beta test anything? Oh wait… You and I didn't get that choice, now, did we? The government made it for us and forced it down our throats. Now we're paying the price, as usual."

Jacob, who usually shook his head annoyedly at Tuck every time he spoke, watched unblinkingly instead, his eyes glued to the set.

"I'm telling you now, good faithful people of this country," he continued, his hand moving to cover his heart. "This was planned all along, and I know it. Do you really think that this is all just one… big… mistake? Do you *really* think that? No, there's no question. Someone cooked this thing up on purpose to unleash these awful, deadly side effects on us. Yep. It'd drop in on us after the fact when we're all inoculated a couple of weeks after its release so that we wouldn't put two-and-two together. Well how long has it been? Come on, think about it! Hasn't it been 15 days now since the first release of the vaccine to the public? How much do you want to bet that after all is said and done, the government is just going to lift a big white flag and say that there was no way to know and that they're all innocent. That's probably when the vaccine to this vaccine will show up, created by the same company that made this whole "cure" in the first place."

"We ought to string 'em all up now while we're still around! And isn't it convenient that this cure was dropped on everyone on the same day. Yep. It was. Really makes you think, doesn't it? Too bad… we shoulda put the kibosh on before it got us."

The video ended suddenly with that.

"Too bad," his dad whispered to himself.

"There's definitely something really messed up going on," his mother chimed in, her voice full of conviction. "Tuck's right. It's people behind it, out to make money. It's always the same story… greedy people thinking about profits, and who pays the price? We do. Well, if we get lucky, we all will, them included."

How right she was, Greg thought as he looked back on it all, his hand scratching his stubbled cheek as the car plodded along in the traffic.

Pretty much the entire world was sterilized within a matter of weeks, he recalled. *Every government was in a panic. That's when the US started to throw out the blame, even though it was them who started the whole thing. They blamed this and that for a while, hemmed and hawed, and then after all the hearings, in the end they said that a flaw had occurred in the vaccine development process, and no one could have seen it coming. No one was held accountable. Nothing to do* amidst the anguish. And still we live in the fallout. It's going to continue until there's nothing left.

I hope we find something, for all of our sakes.

He thought of the woman that had yelled at him.

There must be so much pressure on people like her, he thought. I can't imagine what it would feel like with the burden of humanity on your shoulders. I wonder if she feels it?

He wanted another chance to talk to her then in that moment.

Why is this all coming up now? He wondered. Why all of a sudden is this whole thing front and center?

Suddenly, the car lurched forward and then jerked to a stop to avoid smacking into the car in front of it. He smacked the dash with his hand and screamed at it.

"Come on, you piece of shit! Why the fuck am I stuck in traffic?" he shouted out loud to no one. "It's like we can't just die alone. We've gotta pile on top of each other, wasting away, while all around us, there is all of this empty space!"

The population is free-falling and we're all living in the city together, still trying to beat each other home, all the while, dying slowly in gridlock.

He closed his eyes and took a breath, counting to three slowly. Afterwards, he opened his eyes and looked around.

To the left, in the other car, he noticed the passenger, a bald black man, staring at him. He shrugged his shoulders at him stupidly, and then hid himself from view behind the car's A-pillar, ashamed at his outburst. He reached for the controls and lowered the seat down flat so that he could relax. He unbuckled the seatbelt, and then softened his shoulders. Through the sunroof, he saw nothing but gray, smoggy sky. There was nothing to see, no reason to even have a sunroof anymore, nothing in the awful cloud that never ended. He imagined taking the wheel and veering the car upward, out of the line of cars, up out of the cloud of filth, up above it all, up where the air wasn't regulated.

He'd get a ticket, and he couldn't afford one of those now, so he settled for laying there, staring. After a few moments, the car's hum put him to sleep.

His phone detected his state and prompted the car to switch to silent-mode. It continued on without any pings or prods that would wake him before his arrival.

7

Sept 8th, 2027 - Conversation between SPEAKER 6 and SPEAKER 7
Speaker 7 - You going to tell the boss Lu's missing?
Speaker 6 - Fuck that. He's on vacation anyways.

(2063) When Greg walked into the door of his apartment, he smelled hamburger meat grilling on the stove. He took off his shoes and walked into the kitchen, where he heard his wife, Janice, already in her underwear—a sign she had already showered (probably from getting a little naughty while he was out)—so he came up behind her and gave her a hug.

"Oh, nice," she replied with a half-sarcastic, half-seductive lilt. "You do something wrong today?" she asked and flipped around in his arms. "Trying to butter me up?" They both laughed and he leaned in, smelling her neck, thinking a little nervously that she'd be good at smelling a rat. He pulled away, smiling at her.

"Come on, babe? I'm coming in with some affection and you neg me?"

"I was just joking," she said turning back around to toy with the burgers again, and shoved him playfully with her butt.

"Now that you mention it, though…" but he stopped himself, wondering if he should tell her so soon, wondering even if he should at all, with all the good it would do.

She stiffened and turned around, her face quizzical, and he knew that it was too late. Her eyes narrowed as she waited for him to continue. "Should I be sitting down for this?" she asked and detached from him, turning off the stove and putting the pan on an unlit burner. She looked back at him. "Ok, I will," she confirmed and walked over to the fold-out dining table to sit down.

He joined her, giving himself a little room to lean over on his knees and stare down at the ground.

He thought about where to start.

"I think I may have made a mistake at work," he said. "It might cost me my job."

She said nothing to that, but put her elbow on the table instead, leaning her face into her hand. "Oh my god… What happened?"

"It's not what you think," he started, not actually knowing if it was, "I found something strange happening at work, but when I investigated, Rex caught me up and said that I shouldn't have and that I was in big trouble because of it."

"What kind of *strange* thing? Is it something Rex is covering up?" They had talked so often about his boss that she seemed to hate him more than her.

"Yeah, that's the thing. He might be, but when I went to investigate, honestly, I feel like I went too far. I had to break into some room that had been boarded up, and Rex caught me on my way out. He said that I have to quit."

Her eyebrows rose, and he gleaned that it wasn't sounding like he was in the right, so he continued.

"Buuuut," he added, his finger up, his tone calmer than before, "But, I think it's just a threat. I have a real hunch that he's involved in some sort of energy fraud. I took pictures and everything. My plan is to just call him out on it, and then we can agree to some sort of a like, an armistice or something, if you will, and then—"

But she got up, and started to pace the kitchen, throwing him into silence instead. He watched her, wondering what she was thinking. Her index finger was in her mouth, a sign that she was really mulling things over. After a moment, she turned back to him. "Are you sure that you can do that?"

"Do what?" he asked.

"Bluff Rex. How much of this do you *actually* know? How do you know that Rex may be involved? How did you even figure out about this room in the first place?"

Greg felt like it was the time, finally, so he told her the rest—the sapping, the loans, her brother Rani and the loan shark, Lonny's idea.

All of it.

She wasn't happy. Her pacing was over. She was looking down at him, her hands on her hip. "So stealing energy was supposed to solve everything? Are you fucking kidding me?"

"Yes!" he shot back at her, his temper high now because of her cursing. He jumped out of the chair, his hands in the air. "See! I knew that you would react this way. God knows that you can fuck us over with your deviant sex spending, blame it on being sick or whatever the fuck you are doing, like you can't help it, but then when I fuck up, it's awful and I'm a bad person. You're perfect, and I'm a fuck up. No wonder I fucked up again. It was just a matter of time. "

"You're a real prick," she said and pushed him, contact she had never made before, in all the years that they had been together.

He wasn't prepared for it, and fell back into the chair, his face stunned. He knew then that he had gone too far.

It was too late though, he thought hopelessly.

He felt like slamming his fist down on the table, but stopped a half inch before it met the plastic table-top. "I wouldn't be in this situation if I had something to occupy myself with," he started, not knowing where to go exactly, but seeing that unloading everything was what was happening, and it felt like there was no way to stop it. "If I got to spend some time with you, maybe things would be different."

She had backed up, wasn't facing him, but was leaning on the counter instead, her eyes lost in thought. He continued anyways.

"We never do anything together. You just sit around on your VR all day and I tinker in the back room. ... This stupid farce at work, all of this crap, it feels like it's just a symptom of a bigger problem."

"What *bigger problem?*" she asked him, a touch of fear in her voice.

"I don't know. I don't want to say that we are stuck and not fixable or anything. I just think that back before the financial issues, I was still thinking about money, and that's crazy, right, in the scheme of things? I mean. We keep going like we have someplace to go, while all around nothing is getting made. It just feels like there's no point, when we have no one to hand things down to. It's like there's no reason for building up." He found himself avoiding the words 'sterile' and 'barren,' though they circled around in his mind. "And that was before the debt. When that happened and I had to start scrambling, start slaving away at work, day after day, it just started feeling like futility with no end. I know this is hard to understand, but the sapping felt a little thrilling... I can't believe I'm saying that out loud. But... well... there it is."

She didn't reply, but her body language intuited that she was listening. He continued.

"This thing at work... It's weird, right, but it really enticed me. Every fucking day is the same old fix-it shit. When I saw the wire, it was like some clue I had to solve. And as I looked more and more into it, things just got weirder and weirder—"

"Okay, fine," she broke in, turning and facing him. "Explain it to me from the beginning. I want in on it all. Don't leave anything out."

So he did, slower than before, with more detail–the sapping, the wiring, the call with Bob, the floor itself, the problem with Rex. By the end, their argument seemed a thing of the past, and she was confirming the things he had done in a way, giving his own past logic credence.

They were on the couch now at opposite ends when she asked him what the next step would be.

"I was thinking about asking Bob about the building personnel dynamics. Figured maybe that might raise some flags or clear some things up for me."

"You wonder if maybe *he's* in on it?" she asked.

"No," he replied, reasoning with her that since Bob had given him info on the floor itself, it made sense that he was innocent of the illegal activity on it. "He would have just phoned whoever was in charge of the thing that I was sniffing around."

"What if he did?" she retorted. "I mean, you said it yourself that Rex was waiting for you when you arrived. Maybe Bob tipped him off to the conversation and so he was watching you extra carefully."

Greg hadn't thought of that. *This is good*, he was thinking. *More minds on this will help me to make better decisions.* Janice noticed that she had made a good point and shuffled closer to him on the couch. "See," she continued. "Aren't you glad you told me about all this?" She smiled at him and started to rub his shoulder. "We are still going to have to talk about that other stuff though," she hinted. "But I'm glad you opened up. We work better as a team."

He hugged her hard, and she started to giggle, playful like when he had caught her in the kitchen, and he smelled her neck again, taking it all in. They held each other for a moment longer like that, and then she pulled away from him and got up, a glint in her eyes as she looked at him. Without waiting for him to talk, she walked towards the bedroom, her hand reaching around to pull the wedgie out of her shorts, and then she eyed him one more time, winked, and ran into the bedroom. He followed, surprised with himself that he had just turned a bad conversation into a good one.

Or was that what happened? he wondered, unable to comprehend what really had fired her up.

It didn't matter, he thought in the end. What mattered was that he was getting laid.

Afterwards, Janice snored loudly from the other side of the bed, her face pointing directly at him. He tried to point her away from him, but after a few failed redirections, he got up instead and sat in the dark by the window, looking out at the alley that lined their building. Nothing to see as always. No view of note; what he did see was quiet in the wee hours of the night.

He tried to go back to sleep, but couldn't, even though Janice's snoring calmed after a touch. His mind was just up. He thought of Janice, how she would have made a wonderful mother. The thought clung to him like a mosquito that he couldn't shew away. It was irrational, no point in reflecting on, he told himself, yet he still spiraled down the rabbit hole.

Focus on the things you can control, he told himself.

Easier said than done, he retorted a moment afterwards.

He got up again and fixed himself a sandwich with what they had in the fridge, settling on a meager tuna on white without the mayonnaise. It tasted so dry that he only finished half of it. Still the mosquito bothered him—the thought of his wife birthing a child.

What if we tried again? he offered up, but then sat with the thought itself, honing in on the fact that they had never actually tried.

No, that was suicide.

Women were expected to take some form of birth control at all times, the fear of pregnancy and eventual gestational miscarriage too strong to gamble with. The numbers were out, published monthly by the government. People tried, and when they did, they died. They all died. For the most part, he believed it. What would the goal of lying be? After all, it would have been in everyone's interest if people were able to have children that they do so. Hell, they would be required to, even, he figured.

Fears or not though, he did remember a time when he and she had gone off the pill once or twice, a long, long time ago, when they first started dating. They were afraid too, he remembered vividly, when they did it, afraid but excited like two kids commiting a crime. Nothing had come of it though, and she ended up going back on the next day both times.

But what if perhaps the vaccine's lasting symptoms *had* abated with certain populations? What if some, maybe even just a few, were immune now? He let the thought sit in his head for a moment, chewed on it, and then shrugged it off like the taboo thought that it was. Janice would never take the risk anyways.

They knew people that had tried, and it ended in absolute heartache, he recalled with a wince. Unfortunately, pretty much everyone knew someone that had tried. After all, body autonomy was a continuous issue, even with the universally held belief that birth attempts were immoral. There was always a nut that tried.

It was a vocational school friend from back in the day, he remembered. He wondered whether he was out yet. The prison time for accomplice to baby-term negligence was less, though stiff nonetheless. The sight of the man's girlfriend miscarrying in the middle of the classroom came up like vomit and he couldn't drag it down—the blood, the screams, the horrified faces—so raw and real, a brand of a memory that burned still.

The blood on her crotch leaked out of her in a pulsing flow, down her legs onto the dirty blue carpet of the classroom auditorium. It wasn't just some holiday weight gain, like her boyfriend had told him. The rumors about her were correct, proven in that moment. Everyone sat there and watched it play out, wide-eyed like deer in the street. The only one that actually moved was the instructor, who pulled out his phone and called the police. They came a moment later with the ambulance. She lived, they later found out. She was escorted to jail a few days after being stabilized in the hospital.

You'd think that those scenes would be enough, he reckoned. And still people would try. They'd always try.

The possibility was just too enticing.

He recalled vaguely back before 9/23 hearing his mother mention that people chose to abort their pregnancies during the gestation period. Her face went sour at the mention of it, like it was something that stank.

Maybe the vaccine was just helping people along, he thought cynically.

He couldn't fathom the thought of choosing to abort a healthy child. What were the times like as an adult pre 9/23? Perhaps in that era, with all of the turmoil of war and everything, maybe women didn't feel safe or something being mothers.

He couldn't wrap his head around it. He was a man, living in a time where childbirth was an almost archaic word lost to time, but perhaps the grass of parenthood was just greener on the other side.

Still.

The 'still's' were killing him now, he realized wearily. He was tired and wired and getting nowhere, sitting there on the couch in the dark with food in his hand, ruminating about things that were above him.

He had the thought then to call his dad about it all. Jacob stayed up late at night, after all, had told him as much, saying that he just sat around thinking in his recliner or watching TV. His backaches kept him awake most nights.

He texted him a polite *You awake?* instead of calling, just in case.

Within moments, his phone was ringing and he picked up.

"Why are you awake?" his father Jacob asked grumpily, as if it were a personal affront that men without backaches weren't all sleeping soundly the whole night through.

"I don't know Dad," he replied dumbly. "Things on my mind. You know how it is."

"Yeah, I guess so. Well, I'm just sitting here anyways. What are you thinking about?"

He sighed. "I don't know," he started. "You ever think of September 23rd anymore?"

It felt strange to bring up such an awful event. In the dead of night, only, he figured.

"Why are you going and thinking about that?" Jacob asked. "You fighting with Janice lately about things or what?"

"Yeah, yeah," he replied quickly, brushing the idea away from the conversation as fast as possible. "But it's not like that. I don't know. It just came up in a conversation I had the other day and it hasn't gone away. But yeah, I wanted to ask you–Did people really choose to abort their kids back then?"

"These are some real intrusive thoughts you got there, son," he said and guffawed. "You sound like your mother. She was always all pro-life. That's what they called it back then. Nowadays, I guess everyone is … now that neither is a possibility."

Greg didn't reply, waiting for more. After a moment, Jacob continued, "You see, back then—"

"Wait a minute," Greg interjected, "Wouldn't you be religiously against abortion?"

"Oh my God, Greg. You always trying to start something?" Jacob shot back. "You gonna let me explain now, or what?… OK, so it might be difficult for you to understand the idea of abortion, based on your vantage point, but back then, body autonomy had a place in society because childbirth was not only possible, but constant. When a biological act like that can not only be committed, but repeated, it kind of takes the sting away to stop it, in my opinion. And one thing you wouldn't know, what with the way it's painted nowadays, is that it wasn't as malicious as people nowadays make it out to have been. People now are all acting like would-be-mothers were just ripping out fully formed babies with coat-hangers and throwing them away. On the contrary, more often than not, women terminated their pregnancies before the baby had even reached a state of consciousness, and most of the time, for relatively justifiable reasons. I mean, imagine giving birth to a baby after being raped, for instance? There were issues though. I'm not going to stick to one side. People on both sides had their reasons. And after all, I'm a man, so what do I know?"

"Looking back on the way things have gone, do you ever feel like this was some sort of curse from God or something?" Greg asked.

"Honestly, son, I don't know. I don't think God has a hand in this world at all. He's just sitting there watching it all for now, waiting for that time to strike."

I should have guessed this line of thinking, Greg thought, so tired of the Armageddon talk, always alluding to the end when God would finally choose to fix things. It was always the same old logic. He kicked himself for leaning the conversation that way in the beginning.

He felt like exiting.

"Alright, dad. I'm going to go to bed now," he said, ready to end the conversation.

"Hang on, hang on, hang on. Is this really why you called?" his dad asked, not ready to end the call that came too few and far between.

Greg sighed audibly, "I don't know. That day just has me spooked lately. It was fuckin' nuts. I still remember it so well, all those years ago."

"I don't know. For me, the days that led up to that day keep me up. That day was just the icing on the cake."

"Yeah. That makes sense," Greg agreed, recalling that his father had lived through the entire war that had led up to the vaccine being administered in the first place. "That time must have been pretty traumatic. Honestly, I don't really know a whole lot about it."

"Makes sense," Jacob replied. "You never did pay attention as a kid." They both laughed.

"Well," Greg leaned in, and continued a little comically, "You're awake and I'm awake. Hit me with some knowledge, old man."

"Can't you kids just look all this information up on the internet?" he replied. "You don't need some old man reaching back into the past to dig up memories that are probably full of misinformation anyways."

Literally one second passed.

"But okay," he continued. "No promises that it'll all be accurate. Okay, so... from what I remember, the entire world was in a state of crisis, or at least after the nuclear strikes on Ukraine, they were.That's when we dropped the bio-weapon. I'm pretty sure that the state department let out a statement justifying themselves... the footage was pretty heinous, so I guess it makes sense. They said it was the first stage of 'new measures' to respond to Russia's aggression, if I'm remembering things correctly. There weren't any real specifics though, of course. All the mainstream media outlets, who were already bought and paid for by the government at that point in time, said that the bio-weapon was the only realistic way to force a cease-fire and bring everyone in the region to the table for peace talks."

The thought of the bio-weapon being justified made Greg angry, knowing that it was the catalyst to the doom scenario that they were living in, but he held his tongue.

"It might seem hard to believe," Jacob said in a semi-defensive tone, "the carelessness of the government to take things so far, but you gotta understand that in those days, most nations had already ramped things up by that time so to speak, what with the drop-out of major players from the Geneva Conventions. I can't even really speak to that. But things like chemical warfare, things that would have never been tolerated before, were becoming more and more prevalent on the battlefield… Everyone was targeting civilian zones… The moral slope was really dropping off.

"Yeah, but nukes are different," Greg chimed in.

"Yeah. When the tactical nukes dropped, it was clear to everyone that something drastic was necessary fast. I'm surprised that we didn't just bomb Moscow into oblivion. The bio-weapon was supposedly a lesser evil, according to the public dialogue at the time. But as you know, things got out of control. Russia… or was it Russia? Maybe it was one of their allies? Hard to say for sure. Someone reverse-engineered the bio-weapon and shot it at a few Western European countries. That's when the death-toll really shot up. But looking back on it now, it probably wouldn't have mattered anyways because the containment measures that were put into place the first time it was used weren't thought out enough. Obviously, it seems ridiculous now that the government would think it could contain a biological pathogen, but I don't know. Maybe they thought that it wasn't going to spread like it did, or that it would adapt to the environment like it did? Whatever the case, the general consensus was that a global pandemic would follow, and experts were predicting that it would be much worse than any seen before. That's when a vaccine was called for."

"So we were doomed either way," Greg surmised.

"Yes, but most of the public didn't see it that way at the time because there was a real smokescreen presented to us by the media that made it hard to understand how bad things really were. I can lay it all out now, sure, but in the moment, we were pretty much feeling around in the dark. Everyone was always wondering things like 'Was the virus *that* bad? How bad was it really?' All the while, the news kept saying that big pharma companies were already working with the government to get a handle on antiviral vaccines that would mitigate possible break-through strains just in case. The media was probably on the take from them. God knows everyone else was."

"I do remember things not seeming that dire at the time," Greg admitted, "But I was a pretty young kid then. And you two really sheltered me from the news."

"Well, I mean… You can imagine how hard it was to actually trust the news, given what I'm telling you, am I right? For the most part, it wasn't really worth listening to. The only reason that anyone was tuning in was that it covered the war pretty well, or at least the carnage. Most independent sources on streaming platforms were pretty limited at the time… So we were stuck basically."

"Anyways, the biggest thing that kept everyone going after the virus popped up on our doorstep was the government's assurances that big tech had joined up with big pharma to create a vaccine as soon as possible, and that it was just around the corner. The FDA even stepped aside for the time to make it available sooner. No trials, you know. Just get it out."

"All the big names were pledging that they would throw whatever means they could at it. A lot of companies that aren't really around anymore. All the huge tech companies had already been involved in the military throughout the war, making drones and autonomous units, super advanced stuff that we had never seen before, so it seemed like computing technology, data analytics, and pharmaceutical business would handle things for us. And plus, what could we actually do?… Nothing… Literally nothing but sit in the dark and pretend that our singular cares and worries meant anything to those in power. Goes to show that you can't control the man. The man controls you. We should have heeded the warnings in the bible that man can't direct his own step. It would've served us well then."

"Boy, everything always relates back to religion, doesn't it," Greg replied, noting the pithy religious aphorism his parents had been spewing for decades. "Why don't you bring out the big guns, huh *Elijah*? Why don't you explain how it all ties into Daniel's big prophetic image of the man with the clay feet, right?" He felt his face getting hot, thinking about it. Even now, he had the JW dogma within him. It was on tap, and he couldn't help himself. "Who is New Light saying it is at the end of the 'end times' now, huh? Maybe they'll get it right. The JW's never had it. It wasn't the US, or the UN, or Russia, or even the whole of the EU in its fall. Maybe it's the Eastern Block of Territories? Shit, maybe it's us in the Western Alliance? Maybe we'll bring about Judgement Day. God knows we deserve the right to pull the trigger, considering the fact that us good ol' Americans were the ones that sterilized the world. Will anyone or anything ever cause a reaction from the big man above?"

"Now, now," his dad scolded him lightly. "We were having a nice chat. I don't poop on your beliefs."

"Na… you just throw little pious jabs here and there, though, don't you," he asked, still annoyed, though his volume was lower, his tone less icy. "Boy, you religious folks never quit."

"I don't know about that. Us New Lighters are usually too busy playing video games," he replied and laughed.

The segway irritated Greg. "That's not all that you guys do and you know it," he retorted.

"Alright… Less than the rest, then," he replied, offering a general cease fire on the conversation.

"Alright."

"Welp, I'd better go take a leak," Jacob said. "Thanks for the call, Greg."

"Yeah, for sure, Dad. Have a good night. Thanks for the talk," he said and hung up.

He went back to his room to pass out, mildly hoping before drifting off that some omnipotent being would come out into the open finally and fix it all. If only. Perhaps he was the smog that blanketed everything? Or perhaps the slow march to extinction that was now was more fitting.

A scripture from Revelations hung in his head towards the end. *And all the earth followed the beast with admiration.*

What was this beast who we all admired?-he wondered.

8

Sept 21, 2027 - Conversation between SPEAKER 6 and SPEAKER 7
Speaker 6 - Lu came back.
Speaker 7 - Really?
Speaker 6 - Yeah man. Strange too. It was just in the office, powered down.
Speaker 7 - That is weird. You think maybe we just overlooked it?
Speaker 6 - I don't know.
Speaker 7 - Whatever. It's here now. Just leave it off.
Speaker 6 - Yeah. We don't need a guard dog anymore anyways. Nothing worthy of guarding.
Speaker 7 - Now you're being cynical. But won't it get all buggy if it doesn't update?
Speaker 6 - Fuck it. It creeps me out anyways and there's no use for it anymore.

(2063) The next day, before the glow of the sunrise lit up the cracks between his bedroom's black-out curtains, Greg pulled himself out of bed, laced up his boots, and grabbed a snack on his way out to work. Before locking the door, he noted that he hadn't kissed his wife—an old habit that had died like their other shows of affection—and so, feeling the thorn of romantic regret, he opened the door again and stole in for a kiss. She was naked and exposed, the blankets pulled up only enough to cover her lower half. The sight enticed him. He hovered for a moment above her, taking her in. She looked peaceful. He leaned down for a kiss, but hesitated at the last moment, thinking that it would disturb her, so he tagged her softly on the forehead instead. He felt like kissing her again on the lips, but she turned over suddenly to the other side. Too late. He left thinking about it.

On the way to work, he played some music, a positive playlist that might lift him up before getting into the thick of the stress again. As an old, upbeat tune played softly over the hum of the car, he found himself going over what he hoped to accomplish. He ordered the goals he had in his head, a tactic that his wife had learned to use in therapy to focus her.

First and foremost, secure your job. Get Rex off your back. Second, get back into the room to take some more pictures and—

Something metallic slapped across the top of his car and he braced his head instinctively in his seat. His car blared a warning and he read the dash precaution to pull over and check for damages to the top of the car. There was a feint, high-pitched hiss coming from above his head on the left roof of the car. He wasn't yet in the tunnels going to work, so he pulled out of the air-way and dropped down in a neighborhood that looked pretty deserted. Once the car set down, he got out of the car to look it over.

There was a fairly large horizontal gash running along the roof of the car from the driver's side to the passenger's side, cleanly cut, as if something very sharp from the looks of it had hit his car. Whatever had happened, he didn't have to think hard to infer that if it had been any lower, it would have probably gone through the windshield and killed him. The car pinged and he looked in through the window to see a red exclamation mark blinking on the main screen, so he opened the door to get a better look.

"Would you like me to signal mobile mechanics to come and repair your car?" the vehicle's onboard system asked. The car pinged for him to reply, so he told it not to.

Repairs would have to wait. He had things to do. He got back in and headed off to work again, convincing himself that it had more than likely just been a carrier drone that had malfunctioned and either dropped out of the air or miscalculated its course.

In the parking lot, Greg went over what he'd say to Rex, knowing that he had to have it memorized if he had any chance of it working.

It would make no sense for you to fire me. I've been a loyal employee, and I am supposed to follow up on electrical issues in the building. This was an obvious issue. I had to check it out. The fact that you are firing me for it signals to me that you are either in on it, which will get you fired, or the building owner is in on it, and actively scamming tenants in the building, which is illegal as well, and you know it. Either way, fire me and it all comes out. Let me stay on and I keep your secret quiet.

Too bold, he thought. *Better make it more innocent-sounding. I had to follow up! No, no. The fact that I entered the room with the sign on it is the real problem. If I were really just following the rules, I would have called it in.*

Lean into the fact that the sign is fake, he thought. *I knew the sign was fake, Rex. I figured whatever was in there was illegal, so I didn't know who to trust. Really, I should just talk to HR about this.*

That was the one, he thought and smiled. That would do it.

He got out and walked in, feeling antsy inside. It was a paradox, he thought. He was heading to his doom and his only way out at the same time.

As the elevator dissolved to let him in, he took a hard gulp.

Here we go, he thought.

The ride up was too quick, and he felt like he hadn't even caught his breath before it chimed at his floor and melted before his eyes, leaving him like that generic naked boy in the dream waiting for the crocodile to pinch him on the butt. He held his elbows instinctively like his wife.

He eyed the wall partition that he had hidden behind the day before and scoffed at the suspicion he had probably pinged in his boss from the start. He listened for Rex, but heard nothing in the office, everything quiet. He walked into the main room, looking to talk to Rex now while he had it all formed in my head.

Rip the band-aid off now.

He took the garbage-path that led directly towards Rex's office. Maybe he'd catch him sitting down watching porn or something inappropriate. That would set the best stage, he decided to himself.

He knocked once and waited for a moment, but no one answered. The lights looked off, but the man could have just been asleep again at his desk. It happened rarely, but still. He knocked again. Nothing.

He went to his work booth and called for Rex over the radio. A minute went by.

Nothing.

Odd, he thought. It had been so long since Rex hadn't been around to tell him what to do that for a moment, he stood dumbly wondering what even lay on the docket to complete. How would he even know? Rex had the admin login. It was on his tablet. Greg thought about where it would be, maybe somewhere in the room, but then sighed in frustration.

I've gotta talk to him now about the fuckin' firing, he thought. *Where is this son of a bitch?* He pulled out his phone and signed into his work's database to check if perhaps Rex had signed into work somewhere else in the building. He found his name, but no check-in for the day.

Strange. The man was never gone.

He opened his emails to see if maybe Rex had sent him anything, but there was nothing there either. The thought of calling him and just doing it all over the phone came to mind, but he put the kibosh on that as well. It had to be face-to-face.

He kicked the wall in frustration. Ready, but unable, he realized sadly. He'd have to wait for Rex to come in to talk to him, yet he had no idea when that would be.

And the day after the man had told me to quit, he thought. *What a day to be gone.*

He looked at Rex's door and the thought of breaking in entered his mind.

Maybe something untowards was going on, he started to convince himself, and a clue was right there in that room, behind the door?

It seemed a little far fetched, really, as he considered it. Why would someone go and leave incriminating evidence about illegal work activity at work?

I'd keep it safe at home, he told himself.

Still...

He got back on the work app and checked one more time to confirm that Rex wasn't in the building. He looked to see if there was an option to see when workers checked out. That would guarantee that Rex was gone, and not just burning the midnight oil somewhere in the building, or even asleep somewhere to awaken at any moment and head over while he was trespassing in his office.

Alas. No option in the app to check. No way of knowing.

Without thinking, he grabbed the knob and gave it a turn.

It was unlocked, so he cracked it open a touch and looked through the slit. No one was inside. He opened it and leaned in.

A heavy must assaulted him, and he nearly jumped back out

of the room, aghast at the stench of it. *My god*, he wondered incredulously. *What have you been doing in here?*

He crossed the threshold gingerly, his hand pinching his nose, and then shut the door behind him. The bolt clicked home loudly in the silence, the finality of the act unsettling him.

He was in his boss's office unpermitted.

The pressure to hurry contracted his gut, as if he had just sucked up a large suppository. He flicked the light on to better survey the room, and scanned the mess that made up Rex's tiny hoarder's office. It was jam-packed. There were shelves lining the walls, filled to the brim with knick-knacks, awards, and cards, all shoved together in a jumbled mess, some upright, others stacked like playing cards. There were also a couple of desks, one unusably buried under a mess and another with just enough space to type on an old computer.

He started there, trying to open the desk drawers first, but they wouldn't budge, no matter how hard he pulled. He looked instead for some kind of obvious usage. That proved difficult as well. Everything looked so dusty and disgusting that it was hard to tell what had been used and what had been neglected. He noticed a couple of potted plants on the floor, their leaves drooping in death and decay, and reckoned that perhaps they accounted for the smell. All over the place there was paperwork, paperwork on paperwork on paperwork, boxes full on the floor, ruined and shoved to make room for the slob to sit, the single desk chair ripped and stained in sweat.

Maybe he just used the computer? Greg thought, wondering if he could get into it somehow. Just then towards the back, he spied two large black cabinets, conveniently separated from the rest of the junk, with enough room to open up, curiously cleaned up in front, as if perhaps he had chosen a place to keep some things neatly.

Important things perhaps? Greg wondered, crossing the room gingerly, trying to avoid the teetering paper towers and doc high-rises. He opened the top filing drawer first, and it gave way easily, but there wasn't anything inside except for a few scraps of paper at the bottom. He pulled them out, but they were just old, boring paystubs. He tried the next drawer and it was a tougher pull to open, so completely full of paperwork. Inside, he found what he assumed by the names on the manila envelopes were filings of company tenants, arranged alphabetically. He pulled out a file at random and opened it up on the desk, pushing away the greasy keyboard to give himself enough room to look. It seemed like paid receipts, mostly for work that had been completed. Nothing interesting. He closed up the file and put it back.

He ground his teeth, wondering what to look for. What might lead to something? Suddenly, he heard the elevator ping and ducked instinctively. *Shit, shit, shit*, he thought, kicking himself. He was sure to get caught and thrown out of the building by Rex now. He flicked the lights off and then hunched up to the window ledge that looked out on the service office to take a peek through the blinds.

It was the custodian, Mark.

Thank god, he thought, getting up and brushing himself off. He took a breath to calm himself, opened the door as casually as possible, and walked out of the room.

"Hey, Mark," he said, working out what to say. "Have you seen Rex? I checked in on him just now to see if he was in the room, maybe sleeping or something, and he wasn't there."

"I don't know, but if his office door was unlocked, maybe he's here." He shrugged his shoulders and started to turn around. "He didn't leave a note in the system or anything?" he asked. "You can always take a look and see."

"No, I check," Greg replied as casually as he could. "Oh well."

"Oh well," he chimed back and walked off down the hall to the supply closet.

Now that Mark had seen him, Greg wondered if he could go back in. Would Mark tell Rex that he had been in there? He thought nervously. He wanted to investigate it some more, but it felt too risky. Suppose Mark were to inquire why he was still in there? Maybe he could wait … but then suppose Rex were to finally come back and see him in there later? He threw his hands up hopelessly. The room was like some foreign fruit he would never taste.

He walked over and cracked the door open.

"Hey, Greg," he heard Mark say behind him. "You want me to call-" but he stopped, his tone suggesting that he was waiting for him to turn around.

Greg took his hand off the door and looked at him. "Yeah, Mark?" he asked innocently.

"You want me to call Rex? I've got his number."

Shit, Greg nearly said in response. *Say something.*

"No, that's okay," he replied with a wave of the hand.

"You have his number though, right?" Mark asked. "If you don't have it, I've got it." He started over to Greg, his hand rummaging in his pocket for his phone. "Me and Rex go out sometimes and grab food when we're here late. I'm sure he wouldn't mind," he added.

"Okay," Greg conceded and pulled out his phone. He took down the number as Mark read it to him, inputting it even though he already had the number. He even repeated it back to him.

Mark's gaze moved from Greg to the office. "Damn," Mark said, surprised. "It looks worse in there than it does out here. No wonder he never lets people in there."

Greg nodded, an awkward smile on his face, and pulled the door shut again.

"If he knew you were in there," Mark added, his finger sliding across his throat, "He'd really get you." He smiled toothily.

"Good thing I was only in there for a second then," Greg replied.

"Good thing," Mark chanted. "Good thing." He slapped him on the back hard, and then chuckled and walked away.

He's a real cartoon villain when he wants to be, Greg thought then, wondering how well he really knew the guy. He decided not to try his luck again that day, surmising that he'd have to do the work of two with Rex gone anyways.

The next day, Rex was out again without reason. Greg thought of bringing it up with human resources, but thought better of it. Whatever was keeping Rex away was giving him a minute to breathe, he decided. Plus, he was finding out that he didn't actually need him around telling him what to do for the most part anyways. Most if not all of the tenants' maintenance and repair requests came to his email as well, so he just checked that instead and then carried out the requests one by one. It was a lot, though, and he had trouble keeping up, but luckily, there were no major maintenance or repair projects on the current facility building plan cycle.

He left the troubleshooting and minor issues in the building to the automated bots and focused himself on the high-skill jobs, the ones that required a human touch, mostly carpentry and plumbing. By the end of the day, he was so wiped that he instantly passed out after the car lifted off to take him home.

He awoke sticky with sweat and saw that he was outside his building, the streetlights illuminating the darkness. He turned on the car to check the time. It was nearly 3 in the morning. He kicked himself, knowing that he was probably going to hear it from Janice when he went inside. He'd have to explain to her that he had fallen asleep in the car and convince her that no, he wasn't mad, and no, he was going around at the bars or with the ladies or anything, and no, he wasn't… His head hurt.

The sound system was on, but rather than turn it down, he turned it up instead. Perhaps it would drown out his worries.

A local morning radio newstainment station was going over the daily fatalities, crime reports, and birth count. The same thing every time he tuned in—bad on top of more bad. He hadn't tuned in for a long time to that sort of thing, not caring to be current to the latest drivel. This head announcer's voice though, it felt enticing… sultry and alluring. It perked him up a little for some reason. He listened on, thinking that maybe he'd heard her voice or listened to her before. She bantered with the other co-hosts, but they couldn't hang with her, their jokes and jostling all a bit second-fiddle to her personality. It felt as if they were almost playing *to* her than *off* of her. He manipulated the controls to bring up her image on the windshield, but stopped himself a moment later. *Stick with the voice*, he thought and closed his eyes.

She finished off the carnage and birth rate talk and he thought she'd sign off, but instead, her tone lifted suddenly as she brought up "the latest" in her words on a new story coming out of Brigham Young University—apparently a premier Mormon University in Utah—where a "revolutionary synthetic wombing project" would "completely alter the tragic trajectory that humanity on Earth faced." He sat up and prompted the car to turn on the broadcast, and it came up on the windshield.

She really was gorgeous, he noted, but the message pulled his attention away.

"Every news outlet in the country, and even beyond has been locked onto this project since its first unveiling in a short press release two days ago by the Dean of BYU's School of Fertility. Many are doubting its validity, for obvious reasons, as you may know if you have been keeping up, but still, everyone's eyes are trained to its promise of an alternative means for giving birth. As of right now, not a whole lot of information has been released yet, but there are reports out of Washington that the federal government has been working alongside the university heads to provide as much support as possible. The President said last week that—"

He muted the programming mid-thought and whipped out his phone to get more accurate information online. Local had done their job, but there was no use for them other than that.

He pulled up a streamer that Rani had recommended, one he told him offered a fairly objective and concise news report

Good for a dummy that never listens, Greg thought, and scrolled through the streamer's videos looking for something about the project. Sure enough, there were a few on the subject. He picked the one that had "explained" in the title.

An ad popped up about an alternative birthing center stationed outside of the US, and then another. Clearly the phone had been listening, smart, sneaky little bastard that it was, for the past few days, probably during his conversation with the woman on the street. Did it record her face through his pants pocket, he wondered. Another ad on the subject popped up, this time more brazen—pick your birth service, as if they were machines popping out babies. *What would she think about the video?* he wondered. *Disgusted, no doubt.*

Really, the corporate opportunism of it all was the real travesty, he thought. It went on pretty much unchecked and unchallenged. He felt almost vindicated with the thought, the guilt of the conversation tamped down a touch. The comment though, he recalled with a frown. It was wrong, still.

The skip button popped up and he clicked it, and then luckily the actual video started.

First there was an old-school newsroom intro tune as the camera arced over the set itself, a small blue-painted room with a large screen on one wall and a massive stained-wood desk in the middle, lumpy white man settling in. He had a 'stache and a designer ripped t-shirt, his hands firmly clasped together, his eyes following the camera as it swooped around and then zoomed in on his face. He smiled, nodded curtly, shuffled a few papers in front of him, and then went straight-faced.

"Good evening, premium subbers and the like, and to the rest of you as well. In this video, we will be talking about some exciting reports coming out of Mormon country. No doubt, you have probably heard by now about the breaking news out of Utah, but what do you really know yet, am I right? We have all been pondering this, waiting anxiously to hear about this supposed miracle cure that will save everyone. Is it really legitimate? I did the digging, friends, and I've found out some interesting things about this little project, the project that they refer to as "The Tabernacle Project." For the sake of time and fun, I'm going to coin it Tabby from here on out." He chuckled rather effeminately, smiled, and then went straight-faced again. Greg was reminded of Rani and cringed at the thought of how alike the two seemed.

"Let's go ahead and take a look at the image on the screen behind me." He swiveled around to look at a large high-res photo cued up on the tv that showed a large medical machine of some kind, surrounded by five or six people in lab coats.

"This is an early image of Tabby that was leaked onto the dark web a few weeks ago. It was from an anonymous source with very little commentary or context, leaving many speculating that perhaps it was a deepfake of some kind. It wasn't until the latest news broke that experts were able to identify the contents as legitimate. According to a source that I have that works on fertility equipment at the University of Pennsylvania, the invention that they are all hovering around might, and when I say might, I mean that until the project has not only been patented, but released to the public, which, let's be honest, it never will, we will never know for sure… with all that in mind, he thinks that it might be a chromosome mapping device."

"What's that, you're probably asking? To explain things as simply as possible, let's start with the origin of the miscarriages. Since the decades that have passed since September 23rd, experts have learned that the miscarriages that are occurring now are a result of extra chromosomes as the embryo divides and grows within the fetus during the gestation period. This has actually always been the case with miscarriages, even before the September 23rd tragedy, but ever since the vaccine was introduced into our bodies, it has not only produced the germs that have fought and eradicated RHV

—the bio-engineered form of RHD or Rabbit Hemorrhagic Disease that was weaponized and modified for use on the Baltic Front during World War III—but in addition has created a separate germ that eliminates random chromosomes that form during the development of embryos within the womb of females."

So much for conciseness, Greg thought, shaking his head.

The man took an exaggerated breath, and wiped his brow.

"Obviously I will be leaving a TLDR—in this case, "Too long didn't listen"—in the bio.

He chuckled and moved on.

"Now we all know that like the flu, this germ has eluded and modified itself a thousand times by now within us, causing many different health problems along with the obvious painful issue that we so often find ourselves in, myself among them, having been happily married for some time."

Sterility, Greg's mind chimed.

"So baby-making is a big *ask*, and has been for some time. *This* is precisely what the project is hoping to accomplish.

He coughed and wiped his eyes,

"Let's move on to how the machine works..."

"My source has made it clear that an educated guess is all that can be given at this time. Much of the machine seems to be an amalgamation of already existing medical technologies, though these themselves are too closely patented to explain in any real detail. The one piece that is obvious enough seems to be Tabby's employment of the centrifugal blood pump, which continually cycles and balances patients during certain cardiopulmonary procedures, MRIs, and various others. Perhaps these cycles inhibit the growth of extra chromosomes? Who knows. I hate to say it, honestly, but at this point, this is all that we could gather about this new and fascinating technology. Like the vid—"

Greg dropped the video and cycled through the rest of the streamer's vids, hoping for a more recent, updated look, but nothing came up. Another video though caught his eye, one called "Tabernacle's Legality Issues."

He clicked on it. The same ads popped up, and he waited impatiently for the intro. Once that popped up, he skipped ahead to get to the nitty gritty.

"As you may have already guessed, many religious groups are coming out from the other side of the aisle to oppose the new Tabernacle Project, namely among them, Jehovah's Witnesses, who have already pushed their strongest lobbyists to oppose the introduction of the controversial bill that will essentially push the project past the usual testing procedures and red tape and get it out to the public as quickly as possible. Smartly, they have cited the fact that the entire birthing crisis was started in the first place when emergency authorizations like this were used to release the infamous RHV vaccine before it was proven safe, all at the behest of large pharmaceutical corporation lobbying, and that history should not repeat itself."

"Honestly, though, speaking for myself, I would ask how much more we have to lose at this point, am I right? We are already dying off as a people. What more can the universe throw at us?" He chuckled again, though less jovially than before, Greg thought. "But seriously, with so little progress to show for all the years that scientists around the globe have spent on the subject of a cure, why would anyone stand so staunchly against this?"

"The answer will surprise you. We will get to it in a moment. For now, listen to this. According to a source within the upper echelons of the JW church at their headquarters in New York City, roadblocking this bill is not all that they plan to do. Once they block the bill, they apparently plan to impede the State of Utah from engaging in the project altogether, essentially blocking the project in its entirety from moving forward at all. Maybe it's a church rivalry? Maybe it's a state rivalry? After all, the JW's do own New York in its entirety at this point."

"Breathe easy though, my friends, because they doubt it will occur, my source tells me. How unfortunate for them... Still, why? I asked him that question. According to him, and he did state profusely that it was just his opinion and not the official opinion of the entire organization, the very idea that mankind thinks that it can climb out of the situation that it has put itself in fulfills bible prophecy and signals the coming of the end."

"Historically, and by that, I mean prior to September 23rd, JWs did not enter into political discourse, so I asked the obvious question. *Why now, when we are so close?* He said that the answer was obvious. Mankind cannot direct his step, though again and again, he tries. Still, he doesn't see it. He never will. However, the end is coming. It is close at hand, so the hand of God—the Church, in this case—must take a preemptive stance to help as many as possible to see that the only way to the truth and salvation is through him, not pipe-dreams that try to circumvent his authority, before the finale begins."

"I was mortified to say the least," he replied and the video stopped.

I wonder what Dad would think of that? Greg wondered for a moment. He was about to end his news-binge and head up to his apartment when another video entitled "Tabernacle and the Mormon Purpose" caught his eye. He toyed with the idea of watching it. It was only right to see the other side's reasoning, he figured and clicked on it.

Same ads and intro. He skipped ahead again.

"The fact that the artificial wombing project known as Tabernacle has come out of BYU has gotten a lot of people asking, 'Why are the Mormons in particular so keen on this?' Well, other than the obvious reason that *everyone* is keen on solving the sterilization problem, one need only look at Mormon doctrine to understand their particularly fervent interest. Before September 23, internet history tells us that Mormons had the highest birth rate in the entire world, heavily outstripping all other religions. Their entire belief system was based around family life and the idea that heaven was full of millions of spirits awaiting earthly bodies. Obviously because of this, the

Mormon religion has taken a massive hit since that day, and even though they have pivoted from one reason to another to explain the mass sterilization, and boy are some crazy as hell. Not to get too tangential, but my personal favorite is the one about a Lamanite (for all you secular people out there, it's basically a Native American) contaminating the trial batch of vaccine with his cursed seed. Anyways, even though Mormons still have majority control over their beloved Utah, things have been out of their political favor for some time now."

"Their religion is honestly demoralized. Even with their delusions and looney tunes talk, of which we have all been guilty lately, they really do need this win and I for one hope that they get it. Hell, I'd convert today if it meant taking home my own little heavenly spirit in the near future. I'm sure I'm not the only one, either." He winked at the camera and then it shut off.

Greg felt himself nodding along, a frown on his face, as the screen blanked out.

He leaned back in the chair, thinking about the last thing the man had said. Would he trade his life of secularism for some pious, hypocritical religion if it meant he could be a father?

Janice would. He knew that for sure.

Suddenly, the phone pinged. It was a text from his wife.

"Where are you?"

"I'm just outside," he replied back immediately. "I fell asleep on the way home from work.".

"See," she replied. "This is why you need to turn back on location sharing. Fuck what the internet says. This is ridiculous."

Her text was referring to an article Greg had read a while back that had convinced him to turn off the data and location sharing on his synapse and mobile phone.

"Maybe you're right," he said. The article wasn't just about data sharing, he remembered. It made him aware that he was being scammed all that time ago, essentially setting off the financial saga that led him to the dire, illegal path he was on now to stay afloat.

Janice didn't know that though.

"We'll talk about it when I come up," he shot off and got out of the car.

Back at the apartment, they had a long conversation about his so-called "crazy OCD fears," but in the end, he came out of it relatively unscathed, his privacy still intact. They went to bed shortly later, Janice snoring within minutes, while Greg stared up at the ceiling, his mind itching for his dad's take on the whole Tabernacle thing. An hour later, he got up and gave him a call.

It went to voicemail. Good thing, he figured, knowing that the old man would just pester him to get some rest.

He scrolled the internet for more Tabernacle news, but everyone was saying the same thing–buttoned up, nothing being given up to the public. There probably was news, but he didn't have the techy know-how to dig it up online.

Lonny would.

He made a note to ask him the next day, and then tip-toed back to bed.

Janice was still snoring and still facing him as he piled in.

9

September 18, 2028 - Conversation between SPEAKER 6 and SPEAKER 7

Speaker 6 - These energy regulations are fucking killing us man. Pretty soon we'll be dead.

Speaker 7 - Boss doesn't seem to care either.

Speaker 6 - I heard that he is floating so much money that he's fine either way.

Speaker 7 - I've been talking to someone in the building and I've got a way to keep us energy-rich.

Speaker 6 - Oh yeah?

Speaker 7 - I'm thinking we can call in a guy for a one-time job to siphon off some power for us. Speaker 6 - The guy says that he can help the guy in for a fee and then he can rig it up nice for us.

Speaker 7 - Where is he gonna get the power from?

Speaker 6 - The other floors.

Speaker 7 - Will that work?

Speaker 6 - It better. Otherwise, we're fucked.

Speaker 7 - Oh, by the way. I turned on Lu the other day and he's all out of wack.

Speaker 6 - How so?

Speaker 7 - Well, for one. He's clicking now.

Speaker 6 - Clicking?
Speaker 7 - Yep. It's weird as fuck. Probably because we never update him.
Speaker 6 - Turn him back off then because we can't update him anyways, what with the bot regulations and all.
Speaker 7 - I know and I already did.

(2063) The next day as he came into work, Greg hoped that Rex would finally pop up. It was a strange wish, one that he never in his life figured he'd have, but still, the creepy old man was MIA, and that literally *never* occurred. Greg had to enquire at the very least. After all, someone had to manage him at some point. Besides, it would be weird not to ask. What if Rex mentioned canning him to someone else... before he disappeared. Maybe they'd make a connection... That would look bad.

He gave human resources a call. He had the number saved from a pay-stub issue. His personal rep, Nancy, picked up.

"Hey there, Greg," she answered cheerfully. "What can I do for you?"

"Hi Nancy," he replied, mimicking the same happy-go-lucky cadence. "I wish I didn't have to bug you about this, but I'm having an issue locating the whereabouts of my manager, Rex Willis. I'm guessing there is a glitch or something in the system because he hasn't been here for the past three days, yet his absence hasn't been logged. Should I be concerned?"

She hemmed for a good couple of seconds. "I'd better check. Give me a moment. I'm going to put you on hold for a second."

"No pro—," he started to say to her, but the phone shot over to some jazzy hold music before he could get it out. He sat down at his desk and turned to regard his small work-alcove. It had been so long since he had sat there that it almost didn't feel familiar anymore. He opened the drawers and looked inside, rustling around for pencil and paper to write on, but couldn't find anything. It was mostly just a jumble of work-related notes, stubs, tax forms, and the like. Junk drawers for useless paperwork.

The wait dragged on and after a couple of minutes, he got up and moved around the room, between the rows of discarded bits and parts, wondering all the while how long it had taken for things to get so cluttered. A real hoarder's treasure trove. He wondered how Rex had been allowed to let it get like this. Surely there was someone above him that would have said something.

Suddenly, the music dropped and the dial tone kicked in, stopping him in his tracks.

She had hung up on him.

He called back and she immediately picked up.

"Hey there," he started. "We got cut off."

"Yeah… sorry," she replied haltingly, the happy tone of her voice long gone, swapped out for a sadder, weaker tone. "We tried a couple of times to reach Rex… I don't know if I should say this, (*she was new*, thought Greg) but we are going to have to do a welfare check on him."

"Oh, I see," Greg replied gravely. Checks like that were made sometimes on the older, single workers, from what he had heard, when HR failed to make contact… in case they died

"Is there reason to believe that—"

"I'm sorry, Greg, but honestly, I don't think I can give you any more information. I'll be sure to call you back though when we know more."

Friedmont Towers had a small human resources department, so chances were that she was being told right then and there by her manager to get off the phone. He felt it. She sounded nervous, awkward all of a sudden.

"Okay," was all he said, and then hung up the phone.

He wondered whether she would actually call him back. He had to know. At the end of the day, he'd give her a ring.

. . .

With all of the jobs that Greg had to keep up with, the end of the day came quickly. However, Nancy still hadn't called. He thought that over. *Why would she,* he realized, feeling foolish. *HR's not going to release anything sensitive.* That in and of itself was an answer, but still… He decided to ask Bob. The man knew Rex fairly well. If anything, he'd have better information about what was going on.

He called and Bob picked up the phone almost immediately. "Hey Greg, I was just thinking about you," he said.

"Oh yeah?" Greg asked. "It wouldn't have something to do with my boss, would it?"

"Oh, you heard?" Bob asked gravely.

"No. Heard what?"

The phone went silent. Greg waited, his breath held.

"Rex is dead."

Greg felt the blood drain from his face. "What? How?"

"I'm thinking he got killed. Okay, so get this. I got a buddy named Jake who's friends with Nancy in HR and he heard from her that she and Trinity did a welfare check on him today and found out that he was dead as a doornail in his apartment bedroom."

"Yeah, Nancy said she was going to do that."

"Yeah, so I guess they think it might have been a robbery, based on how the apartment looked … Everything was all fucked up in there. Trinity went inside through the back sliding glass door and saw everything, but she couldn't even really look much because of the smell. She literally threw up."

"Whoa."

"Yeah, the smell was so bad in the hallway that she had to run out. They ended up calling the police."

"Well, how did they know it was Rex?"

"What do you mean?"

"Well… maybe someone else died in there."

"No. After the cops got there, Nancy and Trinity told them about the welfare check and they confirmed that it was Rex."

"I wonder how bad it was…"

"Jake said they heard one of the cops saying that he was laying facedown in a pool of blood. And he was all bloated and disgusting."

"Aww, man."

"Yeah… I mean, can you imagine Rex like that? He must have been laying there for a while, maybe the whole time he was gone… It's sad, man. Real sad. Rex was a good guy. Stand-up guy."

"Yeah, sad," Greg mimicked.

"So I guess you're going to move up, maybe take his job or something?Up there in maintenance?" Bob asked.

"I don't know. Yeah, maybe," Greg said absentmindedly, thinking about the last time he saw him, all furious at him in the darkness, mad that he had broken into the room. *I guess I'm safe after all*, he thought, *with him dead and all. Convenient.* The brutal, honest thought left a bad taste in his mouth.

"Maybe you killed him," Bob offered up with a sadistic scoff, the thought a sad, inappropriate joke. Greg started back at it, not knowing what to say. Bob intuited the awkwardness, and continued on. "I mean, I know you didn't."

"Jesus, Bob," Greg replied, juking the admission with a show of offense.

"Alright, alright, my bad. Word vomit. Still… I know that you two didn't like each other much."

"Oh my god. Bob, really?" The mere thought had to be stamped down, Greg felt. If Bob was saying it, he wondered how many others would think it. It was obvious that there was no love lost between the two of them. Many had seen it.

"I'm just joking," Bob replied innocently. "Sorry," he added, somewhat deflated. "I say some dumb things. You can ask my wife."

"Okay." There wasn't much to say after that. "Well, alright, man. I gotta go. Thanks for the chat."

"Anytime, man," he replied. "I'm always here."

Greg hung up the phone.

He sat back in the chair. *No more awkward boss bullshit to deal with,* he thought. *No more weird quid pro quo vibes coming off of him all the time. No more worrying.*

And no more losing my job.

He felt amazed at the luck that had been thrown in his lap, as if a guardian angel had come down and whisked away his biggest headache.

He couldn't help but feel suspicious at the timing of it all though. The last time he had seen him *had* been at the secret room.

And then the very next day, he's gone? He's dead?

There was a very real possibility that the two were connected. Greg felt it in his bones.

Still, he wondered. *I went in and I'm alive... Shit, I'm doing better now, even. I'm the boss now. Maybe that room was a godsend. Maybe it needs to stay locked away and I just need to keep my head down.*

The pay would be better, maybe enough to pay off his debts without the electricity siphoning.

Maybe my life can go back to normal.

The scenario felt right somehow, like the universe was giving something back to Greg that he deserved, a chance to turn things around, to start over. After all, he was the apprentice to the manager—had been for some time—and he had put in a lot of time learning about all of the maintenance systems and cycles in the building. He would be the smartest choice for the now open position of building manager.

It would make Janice happy, maybe even his dad. Perhaps his life would feel fuller, somehow. All he had to do was do his job and stay away from the mystery floor.

Still, Greg thought. *What is going on down there?*

It might be nothing, he wanted to think. He did. But within him, in the pit of his stomach he knew, he just *knew* that something crazy was going on down there. And if he never got to the bottom of it, the nag would never go away. His new life would never feel comfortable.

He made his choice. He had to chase it one last time. He had to head down there and hunt for answers one last time.

One last adventure. One last opportunity. Then he could button it all up and never look back again.

Greg stood up from his spongy office chair feeling alive and determined. The answers lay somewhere hidden on that floor, undisturbed… for now. Rex was dead. If the floor killed him, the police would soon follow, and then he would never know.

The time was now.

He grabbed the GR, stuffed it in his pocket and hopped into the elevator.

As he descended, he jacked into the lift controls to modify his descent, slowing it down and dropping the walls early so that he could get a look at the secret floor's opening as he passed it. The scene was the same as before, chunks of drywall covering still hanging off from where he made his mark, the warning sign nowhere to be found. Rex hadn't started any repairs at all.

He wondered if that was good or bad.

Once the elevator fully stopped, he prompted it upwards one story-length, and it slowly rose from the 182nd floor to the 182 ½ floor before shuddering softly into place. The vertical black-ness slashed into the wall lay before him. He felt a sense of dread and worry creep back.

"Push it down," he whispered, and took one deep breath in and exhaled hard through his nose. Then he turned on his light and hopped through the breach.

It all felt blacker than before, he noticed immediately. Colder too. He wondered if it was just his nerves. The sounds were all familiar—the AC, the server bays—yet somehow it all felt more uninviting. The glow caught his attention though, like some beacon in the night, so wasting no time, he moved down the rows to the left in that direction. Moving felt good. He thought of even humming to break the silence.

All of a sudden, he heard a faint tap, off to the right deep within the vastness of the room. He stopped and cocked his head, his breath held up as he listened for it, his eyes narrowing as he focused, his heartbeat banging loudly in his chest. There was nothing but silence... silence and the hums that were already there. He continued on, but then another tap came, possibly from the same area, though he couldn't be sure. This time, he turned and crept towards it, padding softly in case it came again, but then after a moment, stopping completely, adamantly holding to wait for the repeat. A few seconds passed and then, over the hum, it came again, more clearly than before, a sound more like a click than a tap. A second later the click came again, steady now, like a metronome. He crept towards it on the balls of his feet like some thief, the air of the room subtly heavier now, weighing him down. Within a moment, he came up to the wall, the familiar metallic sheen of tin foil reflecting his beam back at him, exposing his figure to the light.

Anxiously, he pointed it elsewhere, towards the corner of the room where a worn banner hung upon a beam, its large blocky lettering nearly faded away completely: 'Globatechnics: Digital Holdings.' He traced the faint, blocky text, making a mental note to look it up later.

The click is gone, he suddenly realized, pricking his ears up to listen. Nothing but the hum. He moved down the end row in front of him at a brisker pace than before, hoping that it might have come from there. A quarter way down the row, he heard it again, more faint than before, barely audible over the hum, but somewhere else farther away in the room, maybe at the other end, though he couldn't make it out for sure. He walked down the rest of the end-row, his light scanning to see if maybe some other piece of tech had been turned on that would explain the click—random malfunctioning servers within the racks, old relays trying and failing to send power to other places within the room—but as he shuffled along the graveyard of dead technology, nothing new or appealing popped out to him. It was all the same, rack after rack. He got to the end of the row, just before the opening, and the click came once... twice... both times far away.

Then it blanked out again.

It had to just be something to do with the air duct system, he supposed disappointedly.

All the same, he jumped around the corner anyways, throwing up his light in the new direction, hoping to catch something hiding in the darkness.

Of course, nothing was there.

The action itself settled frighteningly within him, he realized, amping up his nerves more—a bad idea. He imagined a lifeless creature clicking in the dark, its head swiveling toward him, ready to spring. He shook his head, hating himself for going to that place, knowing that he was getting paranoid now, now when he had to remain calm and focused. He did have time, he told himself.

But spending more time than he had to idling away in the room didn't seem like a good idea, he felt in the pit of his stomach.

He spotted the familiar glow flowing out of a row ahead and focused his attention on it, moving quickly along the wall towards it, a little relieved by its presence. He threw his beam down rows as he passed here and there, not checking or investigating, but to catch a glimpse of the exit that felt so far away now. He wanted a view of it, needed one. The place felt like a tomb, sacred and undisturbed, liable to eat him up at any moment. He was some dumb intruder meandering around, all the while the traps were being placed... the exits were closing off... the walls were hemming him in...

Shut the fuck up. He realized then that he was getting irrational. What harm would that do? Would he see things that weren't there?

He turned the corner on the row finally and raced up it to the saving grace of the lights, relieved to bask in them, to stave off the dark. It all flickered like some Christmas showcase, the pretty greens and reds reminding him of better days as a kid, standing around with family gawking at all the fine decorations. The AC blew down its cold wintry ambience upon him, and he pulled his cardigan around his neck, feeling better for the moment, telling himself that it was fine... no big deal. He was just in a darkened office room at work.

His flashlight seemed to hear his thoughts and react, flickering suddenly in his hand, ripping him back to reality. He shook it frantically, but seemed to make it worse, the flicker lengthening. Panicking, he smacked the flashlight against his thigh. The top popped off, and the batteries shot into the darkness.

"Noooo," he cried out, flailing to catch them like some novice juggler, dropping to the floor to rein them in, failing to get any. In his scrambling, above the din of noise and chaos, a scraping noise sounded at the end of the row, startling him up off his feet in a jump that sent him backwards. He crashed into the rack behind him, and it shook violently. He spun around and grabbed it, freaking out over the fact that he had given himself away to whatever had made the sound off in the dark abyss. He was a sitting duck, eyes upon him ready to pounce, for all he knew, at any moment. It was silent, and it persisted, moment after moment, as he listened, peaked for the moment to turn and run.

Perhaps he had heard it, he thought. *No. Fuck that.* He thought with all the reptilian sense he still had in him. *That was real, and it was near the exit.* The indicator light on his arm was pinging, he saw, the port cracked open in the commotion to reveal the small red dot flickering within, indicating its readiness for a cable.

His eyes shot back into the abyss where the scratch had emanated, uselessly, like a blind man. Nothing. No movement. No sound.

He shoved his arm close to the server lights to examine the port for damage, saw none, and then clicked the cover back into place.

Above him, a click erupted right above his head, perhaps just above the ceiling ducts, as if the very ceiling was warning him to leave. He ducked and looked up at it wide-eyed, the feeling of eyes upon him gluing him down, a guinea pig in a maze, trapped and suddenly aware of the eyes that waited, analyzed what he'd do next. A moment later, the metronome began anew from above, each click twisting his gut more and more. He closed his eyes and waited for it to stop, his hands rising instinctively to shield him. He had never felt so defenseless. His chances of leaving unscathed were evaporating with every moment spent in the room.

Move, boy, move, he told himself. He started forward towards the exit in small, hesitant steps, his eyes on the blackness that would envelop him once he passed out of the twinkling lights. His hand went to his pocket to pull out his phone. He had to illuminate his path.

His phone...

The pictures—he'd forgotten. Damnit, he needed those, otherwise the whole trip would be a waste.

Snap them quick, then get out.

He pulled out his phone and winced as its bright screen lit up the dark.

Just then, out of the corner of his eye, in the glare and confusion he caught (thought he caught?) a blurry glimpse of something dart across the back end of the row where he had come from. His eyes were blurred too badly to know for sure. He rubbed them quickly and squinted back again at it, and there, passed the flicking server bays all the way at the very end of row, two little lamp lights gleamed in the darkness, suspended in the air.

Suddenly, they blinked.

He rubbed his eyes again and looked.

The lights were gone.

No, no, no, no. He mimed, his head shaking, unbelieving. *Your eyes are playing tricks on you,* he told himself, his heart pounding. He squeezed the phone in his hands. *That wasn't real. That wasn't real. That wasn't real.*

He repeated the phrase in his head again and again and again, focusing on it, willing it to be the case. After a moment, his hands, his arms, his body, oriented back to the task at hand, his gaze last, moving from the end of the row to the servers directly in front of him.

Focus.

He pointed the phone at the edge of the lit up server rack and took two photos on flash, one at one angle and then another at a different angle, his hands still shaking no matter how hard he tried to steady them. One would be good enough, he told himself, axing the nag to check them, hoping ... praying that one of the two shots would be good enough to identify whether or not there was a difference between the powered and unpowered GPUs, whatever that was worth.

He took one more shot, and then shot off at a lope for the exit, his phone light extended out as he trotted along.

He nearly slipped as he stepped on a fallen battery, but kept his footing as he tried to stride rather than sprint outright, his mind trying to focus on nothing but the exit, fast but not frantic, keeping his fears, that were soaring by this point, at bay.

The metronome clicks started up suddenly behind him now, louder and louder. He looked over his shoulder and nearly tripped, noting in that moment that the clicks that were definitely getting closer and closer were coming from the row next to his. He looked back again and caught the glow of the lamp lights he had seen before, shining through the stacks to his right a little further back, floating along in the darkness towards the exit as well... Gaining on him.

It was going to cut him off before he got out.

"Fuck it," he shouted and sprinted as quickly as he could, his heart pumping like a freight-train. A crash-like pouncing noise came down on the stacks to his left, right above his head, but he was out, his frame erupting out of the row like some sprinter craned forward at the finish line, his body aimed for the final stretch of dead space before the crack... almost there... the light of the exit right in front of him... less than 10 feet away.

And then something caught his leg from the side and ripped it out from under him so that he toppled forward like some hurdler mid-leap... a cry of pain, arms stretched out in front of him, face in utter disbelief as the inertia of his body carried him wholly through the opened doors of the exit out onto the lift in one violent crash.

He shook his head as he held it up, seeing the floor lights glowing around him like some barrier, and with the loom of death so viscerally upon him, he pushed himself up onto his knees and scrambled for the lift digipad, the pain shooting up his leg hardly registering. He slammed the palm of his hand down upon it, pressing anything and everything, hoping that the metallic walls would rise and keep away the danger.

And then he turned to look back, sure to see the thing that had grabbed him, that would kill him.

But nothing was there.

The walls came up suddenly, and then there he was, on his knees in disbelief, his eyes locked in the same direction where moments before he had nearly been eaten alive.

All around him were the familiar lights and sounds of the elevator too, as if he had suddenly teleported out of some nightmare... woken up...

And it was rising.

He collapsed against the wall panting like a dog, his eyes shifting to the floor indicator that was pinging off every moment, up and up and up... whisking him away from the cursed floor one number at a time.

The glint of a blinking red light caught his attention, bouncing off the shiny metal of the elevator in front of him, a reflection, and as he craned his head upward to see. There in the corner directly above him was a small, modern camera, pointed at the door.

It probably recorded everything, he thought. He remembered the one in the room, the ancient one that had caught him before. He started to wonder at his fate, at the fact that he was still alive.

How am I still alive? he wondered incredulously. Was it because of the camera? Had it kept him safe somehow? Was someone watching his moves or something... calling the thing off when it couldn't catch him before the opening? Or was it just too big for the opening?

He let out a long breath. The questions... It was all too much for him. His head throbbed. He tried to stop himself and just take a breath instead.

You're alive. For now, that's enough.

He saw *210* on the floor indicator, the number increasing slowly as the lift rose, and realized then that he wasn't being taken to the parking lot where his car was sitting, waiting to whisk him away, but was in fact edging away from it, up further into the creep factory that was now trying to kill him.

Was that good or bad?-he mused.

He got up gingerly with the aid of the lift bar, the ache of his leg washing over him now like a forgotten debt brought up suddenly at the end of a party, and he wondered what kind of tricks fate still had in store for him. He looked down and saw that his left pant leg was cut up the front and he had a pretty large gash in his shin, the deep, dark red seemingly everywhere, and he looked away. *Nope. Too much to handle right now*, he told himself. The indicator was at 238... 239... 240. His brow furrowed.

I need to stop this thing and send it down. I need to get out of here and never come back. Fuck this place.
YOU ARE GOING TO DIE HERE.

The thought screamed in his head. He moved to the pad, took a moment to think about how to manually override it.

He stopped and thought some more.

Should I stop this thing and turn it around? I'm never coming back. That's for sure. I'm done... sooo since I'm done, I should go back to Rex's office. One last time.

The thought felt crazy. It *was* crazy. He had nearly died moments ago, and now he was going to stick around for more?

Still...

Maybe, just *maybe*, Rex's office had more to tell, more to give him before he ran off into the sunset forever. Maybe there was something on that computer that would clue him in on the fuckery that was conspiring within the building he had worked at for so long. That had squeezed so much life out of him over the years.

He fidgeted, the floors pinging off quietly, wondering what to do.

If I do go and leave, there's no guarantee that that thing won't come and get me anyways.

That thought had some bearing to it, he realized, recalling the fact the dead man he had once called *boss* had been murdered at his home and not within the floor itself.

He wasn't safe at all. Anywhere.

If he did get some answers, perhaps he'd be able to go to the authorities with some real information. More than he had now, to be sure. All he could say was that there was something lurking in a random floor of this building that's already wiped out my boss at home. They'd never believe that. Worse. They'd blame him.

His hand hovered over the digipad all the same as he ached over what to do. Go or stay. The thing could be waiting up there for him, he thought. It could be on the lift above him, sitting, ready to kill him as soon as he got off anyways.

He was fucked. The only thing to do was press on. He canceled the other floors—a few random ones he had pressed in haste—and selected the service floor.

As it continued on up, he ruminated over the irony of it all, his own hindsight jabbing at him, that he should have just stayed away. He reviled his predicament now, when less than an hour before he had reveled in it in a way—the freedom of it all, the flippancy, the disregard of his gut gnawing at him. Worst of all, he hated the very idea that somehow he had been pining for any such adventure.

As the elevator neared his floor, Greg crouched on his haunches by the corner near the digipad, just in case he had to escape quickly, never minding the pain of his wound pulsing through him like adrenaline.

The lift dinged in aloofness, the walls came down, and he was suddenly exposed to the room, the nightmare renewed, though the setting was different.

He couldn't believe he had decided to continue.

He pricked his ears nonetheless towards the opening, listening for any possible movement, any subtle change in the air, a fateful click mayhaps before the next stabbing at him. He craned his head to get a getter look within, and saw the dishevelment for what it was, the perfect hiding place for a murderous creature. He scanned the garbage row by row, standing to see better, moving over as much of it all as possible.

No way to be absolutely sure. At any moment, something could bound towards him, and then he'd have to react quickly and escape into the elevator again.

He had an idea.

"Hello?" He spoke as loudly as he could muster, hoping to just start the show while he was at a safe distance. The fear that had gripped him before welled up inside of him like a tremorous aftershock. One hand held the elevator door jamb, while the other hung poised over the digipad, ready to press the close button.

One second… Two… when would it be enough?

Nothing materialized.

His feet felt heavy, he noticed. It would be difficult to leave the lift. He hesitated on the platform, unable to make the move and actually commit.

A beep rang out behind him and he jumped in the air, his heart in his throat. It was the elevator telling him to get out so that it could close. He stepped out, and immediately the walls rose behind him.

He felt the proverbial light shining down upon him. His head swiveled around again, taking in the room, scanning for anything suspicious, a pair of lights suspended in a dark corner perhaps, anything really, though from where he was standing, he could clearly see the majority of the room. The hallway leading to the janitor's closet was empty. The thing wouldn't hide in the closet, he told himself. It was quiet.

Alright man. Get in, and then get out.

He walked gingerly into the room, his feet light, through a path, right up to Rex's office. The door was closed. He tried it.

It was locked.

Fuck, he thought, realizing that Mark had probably locked it up.

Should I try and pick it, or what? He didn't know how to pick it. What was he going to do, look it up on the internet?

Rex is dead, he told himself. *I'm never coming back here. At any moment, I can die.*

He was gripping the doorknob so hard that his knuckle was turning white, his hand twisting the cheap pot-metal, feeling its brittleness. He shook the door, and it did shake.

His eyebrow raised.

Fuck it. You've come this far anyways.

He backed up a foot, and with all the force that he could muster, slammed his shoulder into the corner of the door just above the knob. It shook and cracked a little, but held.

He backed up further and did it again. The impact cracked the door jamb as if he had bashed it with a steel swat ram, and he flew into the room in the most brutish way possible.

But he was in nonetheless, and that was the goal.

The doorjamb was ruined, chunks of wood everywhere. There'd be no hiding things from Mark, or anyone else, for that matter. The police would be called in, and they'd end up bringing him in for questioning. It was just a matter of time. With this in mind, he worked with intent, flipping on the light and then moving the desk—computer and all—in front of the closed door, sneezing a few times as he did so. If anyone came in, it would take them a minute to get through.

No need for charades anymore. He just needed time, time and safety in case the creature came in to visit.

He started up the computer, a veritable dinosaur, his mind at work over where to look. Files perhaps. His email if he could get in.

There's probably just a bunch of porn, knowing Rex, he thought. He fidgeted in the greasy seat with the thought of it.

It all did looked used though, he noted, which was a good sign. Perhaps he was on the right track.

The log-in screen popped up on the monitor and Greg's eyes widened.

Fuck... He mulled it over, his jaw clamped shut. *What would the man... Wait!* He got up, suddenly, remembering that Rex had texted him his work-tablet password once upon a time so that he could access the job-log of tasks. He whipped out his phone.

A moment later, he had something to go off of. *BigVeiny123.* He tried it, scoffing derisively, the thought of the man using the same password on his actual computer so utterly ridiculous.

Ding-ding. It wasn't. The password worked. He was in.

The main screen popped up, and Greg scoffed again, this time more bewildered than anything else.

The background was a shot of the two of them, an old photo, probably within his first year on the job.

Rex had his arm around him.

Strange, Greg thought. Rex's final warning to him popped into his head.

For your sake, stay away...

Had the man cared, after all? Enough to warn him. Perhaps Rex liked him...

Not the time.

Greg refocused again.

There were a half-dozen file folders with random names. He tried one. It was full of random service docs.

He tried another folder. Nothing of use.

Damn. This is gonna get me nowhere. I don't know what the fuck I'm doing.

The problem struck him now for what it was—he wasn't a detective. Really, he had no idea what to look for or where to start.

He felt alone. He sat back in the seat and rubbed his chin.

Lonny... The man already knew about the server room. He had trusted him enough. Perhaps he could help.

He called him, but after a half-dozen rings, Lonny's voicemail popped up, so he hanged up and tried again, hoping that perhaps Lonny was just busy and trying to let the phone ring out. He was right. Two rings in, an annoyed Lonny picked up the phone, asking in a tired and hurried voice, "What's up man? I'm kind of busy here."

"I know, I figured. I'm sorry man. I need your help, and I don't have a lot of time."

"Okay, fine. Just give me a second." The phone clanked on the other end, and Greg waited, his foot tapping nervously on the ground. He got up and turned out the light, hoping that perhaps a passing Mark wouldn't pop over as readily. A minute or so later, Lonny was back.

"Okay, I've got some time. What's up?"

"Oh my god... Okay, well, let me start from the beginning..."

Lonny stayed silent the whole time while Greg caught him

up—Rex's death, his latest adventure into the server room, and then the office break—in and the computer hack.

"Whoa," Lonny replied after a moment of silence.

"Yeah."

Lonny hemmed for a moment. "So you're on now?"

"Yeah."

"Why don't you just get the fuck out of there and call the police?"

"Yeah… I know what you mean, but then I'd never figure out what happened. Whoever is at the bottom of this would probably just cover it all up, or the cops are maybe even in on it, judging from the paper on the lift doors. Shit, they might even blame Rex's death on me. … I don't know … It just feels like this is on me now. If I don't figure it out, no one will."

He waited for a moment to get Lonny's thoughts on his decision, thinking to himself that maybe Lonny was right. Maybe he should just go to the cops. "It's too late, anyways," he added. The break-in sealed his fate. He needed answers.

"You shouldn't have broken into the office, man," Lonny replied, reading his mind almost. "It looks pretty suspicious of you to just barge in there a few days after the man was killed in his apartment."

"And I'm wounded in the leg," Greg offered up.

"Jesus," Lonny reacted. "That was such a—"

"Lonny," Greg interjected loudly, "I don't have the fucking time to sit here and ruminate about it. I need your help. Are you in or what?"

A moment of silence. Greg felt bad for yelling, and for calling him now. He did look suspicious. Why would Lonny trust him? He was his friend, but still …

"Fuck it," Lonny replied. "What's the plan with this computer?" Lonny asked, trying to jumpstart them in the right direction again. "Why did you want to hack it? You trying to find some info that ties Rex to the floor or what?"

"Yeah," Greg replied, waking to the segway, his demeanor

improving. "I was thinking that I'd check the files on the computer for any saved docs or records that seem suspicious."

"Yeah … you could do that. Maybe you can check his email?"

"You read my mind." He opened up the internet pin on the bottom of the screen and saw the *Hoodmail* quick-link pinned to the taskbar. He followed it and saw the sign in prompt. He clicked on the blank bar.

A drop down manifested with the man's emails. *My god. The old man is making this easy.*

"Okay, I'm in," he let Lonny know.

"Awesome!" Lonny exclaimed. "Okay, Sherlock. Now what?"

"Lemme take a look."

Greg's mouth dropped at the number of emails. Thousands upon thousands. He wondered where to begin. He scrolled down for a moment, noting that the only opened emails seemed to be the Friednmont tenants in the building, and the general manager. He didn't click on any of them, deciding instead on a different route. He went to the search line and looked under the keywords '182,' 'servers,' and then 'computer.'

Nothing of note came up.

"How's it going?" Lonny asked.

"How do you think?" Greg spat back without meaning to.

He racked his brain. A thought came suddenly, the banner in the room… the name on it…

Globa… Globa… Fuck me, he thought frustratingly, the name on the edge of his tongue. *Globatronics?* He threw it into the search, but nothing came up.

Why didn't I take a pic of that, he thought,, shaking his head.

"Hey, Lonny," he suddenly asked. "You ever hear of a company called Globatronics?"

"No, but give me a minute. I'll search and see what I can find. Why?"

"I think it was on the banner," Greg said, feeling more and more unsure the more he said it. "Play with the name a little if you can when you're looking. I think it's close to that."

Greg moved from the inbox to the sent folder, and started to scan it instead for anything telling. After a couple of minutes of pouring over names and reading random work emails, he felt like giving up, but then the name of a familiar tenant in the subject line of an email caught his eyes–Meta Vision, a tech company on the 182 floor. The subject line read, "Meta Vision Power Concerns Systems Check." He opened the fairly recent email from five days earlier:

Dear Greta Wang of Meta Vision,

I understand your concern with the electricity discrepancy that you are reporting and am actively working on it now. I have informed my manager as well of the situation, and will follow up with you as soon as I can identify what the cause of the electricity loss is. I will send you a follow up email within the week.

Sincerely,
    Rex Willis.
    Building Manager
    Freidmont Tower

Interesting, Greg thought. *The tenants had noticed the electricity loss. The server bays, plus my sapper, must have tipped them off with the electricity company review board. I bet Rex was sweating hard if he knew about the floor then.*

He scanned emails in the sent and inbox folders for anything that might be related to the energy loss, but nothing came up. He told Lonny over the phone what he found out, hoping to get some advice.

"I bet that if he *is* contacting whoever he's working with—

that is, if he *is* working with anyone—they're not sending emails then," Lonny said. "Maybe they are just talking over the phone?"

Greg listened without replying, his mind reflecting what to do next. *Perhaps his drafts?*

He scanned that folder—which was sparse—for anything surrounding the day Rex had corresponded with Meta Vision. Within a couple seconds, he noticed a red flag of a draft sitting there, an unsent email from the day that he and Rex had argued in front of the elevator. It was titled, "Energy Concerns. Stop Payment." The draft sounded angrier than the last one:

Globatechnics,

I've been wondering for the longest time who has been paying me off to keep people from snooping around the 182.5 floor of the building. I'm beginning to think that quietly taking the pay-offs without asking any questions was a mistake.

I went into the room today, after scaring the living shit out of my apprentice and nearly firing him, to finally check out your operation and see why you've been trying to hide it all this time. I know that your company is in there. You fuckwads left the banner up for God's sakes. I can guess what's going on, with all the server bays in there. You all are running some illegal crypto-mining farm, aren't you? Well, the jig is up. The tenants have caught on to the power sapping that I'm sure you all are doing, so it ends now. Cut it or else I will, but before I do I'll tell my boss all about it to wash my hands of it. You can

The email ended unfinished there.

"Hey Lonny," Greg said. "Look up Globatechnics instead. That's the name." He waited for Lonny's feedback.

"It's not around anymore," Lonny said after a moment of silence searching the web. "They went belly-up after a bunch of their mining farms were shut down by the federal electricity board. It says here that they were the biggest traded crypto farming company in the world."

Greg mulled the implications over for a minute in his head. Perhaps Rex hadn't sent the email because he found out that the company wasn't around? He looked at the email again and saw that the recipient line was blank on the email.

He must have looked up the company as well and given up. He *was* getting pay-offs every month from someone for watching the floor, though, so he just didn't know who? Maybe the floor belonged to a company that was linked to Globatechnics, and it was just operating illegally? He went to Lonnny again.

"How lucrative is crypto-mining anyways?" he asked, suddenly wondering whether or not the operation itself would be worth the secrecy and murder, thinking that maybe Rex had been paid to watch out for this illegal crypto operation and was killed when the project was breached.

"It can be lucrative," Lonny replied, "Depending on how large the farm is and how advanced the GPU's are that are doing the transactions," Lonny replied. "But why are you asking?"

"I'm just wondering if it was maybe the reason that Rex was killed. Maybe—"

"No," Lonny cut him off. "Can't be, man. Think about it. Only like half of one row was working. That can't be that much money, certainly not enough to kill someone over. There's something weirder going on than crypto mining in there. Even if it was for mining back in the day, it's been repurposed since then for something else."

"I wonder how much they were paying him," Greg replied.

"Well," Lonny offered, "Maybe we can get on his banking information too, as long as he is linked to the bank on that computer you're on. Check the emails and see if there is a link to some sort of banking password recovery."

Greg searched "bank" in the inbox, and a number of associated emails popped up, mostly advertisements it seemed, but as he combed through, he saw that a few mentioned credit card accounts, one in particular from Wawamerica about a home loan pre-approval. Greg couldn't help but feel lucky, and clicked on the email. He saw that Rex had recently been pre-approved for a home loan up to 452, 000, 000 dollars.

What was Rex doing worried about equity in this day and age? he wondered. *Did he have some mistress out in Micronesia that could still carry his lineage onward? Otherwise, what was the point of owning anything?*

Obviously to Greg, Rex was different than most at the time, which made sense, Greg noted, given his personality. It wasn't a surprise, but still, Greg thought. *Who cared about permanence when the walls of mankind were falling? Maybe some still held out hope. Rex must have been one of them.*

Greg grunted in doubt.

He must have a lot, Greg surmised. *The pay-outs must be pretty good.*

He opened Wawamerica's member log-in page and clicked the sign in button, but the username and password didn't populate automatically like with his email. He hovered over the keys, thinking of what to guess, and then returned to the email, thinking better than wasting time trying to force a guess and possibly lock himself out of the system. Better to try and get in from a page that had been used by Rex before.

He searched through all of the Wawamerica emails that had come into Rex's box for something that had been read. He found one offering an old password reset and followed the link. It wouldn't work, but perhaps the info would populate there instead.

The email prompted him to return to the log-in, and to his luck, the info he needed populated, a product of Rex's stupidity to have saved everything on his computer after all.

I knew that senior citizen would, he thought with a snort of satisfaction.

As he entered the website, closing and skipping the endless product ads and prompts to switch to electronic billing, Greg shocked at the thought that Rex still got traditional statements every month, he saw that Rex had over a half a billion dollars sitting in his savings account, with another eighty million in his checking account. He clicked on the account to find out where he had received the money, and then was blocked again., the log-in prompting again, showing two blank boxes, no drop-down choices, and nothing to go off of.

Greg was sunk.

He reported his findings to Lonny, who had been eagerly waiting on the other line.

"Only one thing left to do," Lonny replied, his voice suddenly sly.

"What?" Greg replied.

"You said it yourself. The old man still gets his statements in the mail. You know what that means."

"What?" Greg asked again, though in the back of his head, he had an idea what Lonny was getting at.

"He's not home anymore. Let's just go to his place."

"No way," Greg shot back reflexively.

"It's not like we have any other leads. You gonna sit there at his computer all night combing through every bit of info on there?"

Lonny had a point. They really had no choice, or anything else to go off of. They had to follow.

"Fine," he gave in. "I'll pick you up on the way. Just let me grab his address off of one of the pay-stubs or something in this pile of shit and then I'll be on my way. Text you when I leave."

He hung up.

Ten minutes later, with the broken door and even more messed up office in his rear view, Greg shot down the elevator towards his car, light on his feet strangely enough to him, the thought that he now had an address and a fellow adventurer with him brightening up his situation just a bit.

The sound of the elevator tapping faintly seemed to agree.

$$10$$

October 15th, 2028 - CONVERSATION BETWEEN SPEAKER 6 and SPEAKER 7
SPEAKER 6 - It was nice working with you, man.
SPEAKER 7 - You're quitting? Not yet.
SPEAKER 6 - I don't know, man. Seems like the right time to cut ties. Never should have trusted crypto, man. It was a bad career move.
SPEAKER 7 - Eh, well. Maybe you're right. We should have seen the writing on the wall when they started regulating large file peer to peer transfers. We should've known then the government was nuts. They won't let us do anything without a middle man.
SPEAKER 6 - Seems strange to regulate when we're all going to be extinct soon anyways.
SPEAKER7 - Calm down now, downer.
SPEAKER 6 - Whatever man. You're right though. The government is going nuts.
SPEAKER 7 - Speaking of nuts. I think Lu has been sneaking around at night.
SPEAKER 6 - Shut up. How do you know?
SPEAKER 7- I don't know. Another hunch. I could've sworn it was in a different place in the office.
SPEAKER 6 - Maybe someone just moved it.

SPEAKER 7 - Moved it? It's heavy as fuck.
SPEAKER 6 - I don't know. Maybe he's planning an escape from this place too.
SPEAKER 7 - Yeah, sure.

(2063) The lightness Greg felt in his step out of the elevator faded quickly as he walked down the hallway to the exit, his eyes on the glass doors that led to the parking lot, where it was dark. He'd be walking to his car at night.

The creature, the creature that he had conveniently forgotten for a moment, the creature that just hours earlier had clawed him was now nowhere to be found, possibly hiding, possibly hunting him. He couldn't believe that hadn't planned his exit out better. He stood for a moment planning what he was going to do, just inside the two double doors, his eyes scanning the thinly veiled lot that gave off the ambience of some Scottish moor. The fog wasn't choking, luckily, the building's design scheme at least working to some extent, the altitude high enough to avoid the heaviest point of buildup. He could see from one end to the other, his eyes narrowed, studying it for oddities. It was the usual sparseness—a few cars, spaced far apart from one another, a familiar cluster of cars further out, probably a few female coworkers that planned their parking together so that they could walk out together.

He spotted his car. It was at the other end of the lot. He blew a raspberry, frustrated that he could have been so careless with his choice, today of all days.

A run.

He prompted the doors open with his foot and then stood for a moment just in case. Of course, nothing happened. He took a deep breath and then broke out in a low-impact speed-walk, his feet light and quiet, in the direction of the car. His head was on a swivel like some owl in the dead of night, an owl that was ironically on the verge of being taken down. As he approached the front of his car, a click sounded behind him and he looked back with a start.

Nothing was there.

It's in your head, he told himself. It wasn't though. The thing was out there somewhere.

He got in his car, flipped it on, and pulled it up off the ground immediately, before even inputting the directions. He hovered high over the lot for a time, his head cocked downward, his eyes searching, eager and afraid that he might see the lamp lights watching him from below, waiting to see which way he'd go so that it could somehow follow.

You're fine, he thought, shaking his head and taking off finally for the open air. *Focus on the task at hand.* He texted Lonny that he was heading his way.

He made a promise to himself then and there that he wouldn't return to work until everything was solved and put to bed.

He turned on the radio and closed his eyes, eager to give his mind to rest for a moment, though he knew he wouldn't be able to sleep. He put his seat down nonetheless, trusting the auto-pilot. Within less than a minute, he had passed out completely.

A knock on the car window woke Greg up and he opened his eyes to Lonny smiling and urging him to unlock the door. He did so and Lonny climbed in.

"I was gonna say sorry for taking so long, but I guess it's a good thing I took my time," he explained. "You look like you need the rest."

"How long was I out?" he asked.

"I don't know, but it's alright. I got a little caught up listening to the meeting, anyways."

"There's a meeting tonight?" Greg asked in surprise.

"Yeah, there is an emergency one going on right now. There's a vote coming up in the next couple days and they're all worried about it."

"Something to do with Tabernacle?" Greg asked curiously.

"No, but that did come up, too. The vote is about the conduit. I guess the Mormons are trying to get it federally banned and criminalized or something."

"That would completely destroy them, I bet," Greg replied, aghast.

"Yeah, it would," Lonny gravely agreed .

Greg would have to call his dad later. He made a mental note to do so.

"Let's worry about us, though," Lonny said, his hand shaking Greg's shoulder lightly.

Greg nodded with a side frown, a little reluctant to move ahead with what they had planned. "Yeah, yeah. Let's get to Rex's, then."

He pulled the car off the ground, but sat hovering just above the pavement.

"It's not *that* late, huh," he offered up to Lonny. "Maybe we should wait a bit before breaking into Rex's apartment… If that is what we are gonna do, that is."

Really, he just couldn't get his dad out of his mind now. This conduit problem was a big deal. His dad was probably hurting bad in there. He wondered if he'd be able to speak with him now.

"You having second thoughts," Lonny asked, his eyes concerned.

"Na. I think I just need a break for a minute. You mind if we just go back in there and hang for a bit?"

"Yeah. That sounds like a good idea. It's not like the apartment is going anywhere, anyways."

The image of his wife came to mind all of a sudden and he sighed. "Janice is going to be mad tonight," he admitted. "I was late getting in last night too." He settled the car back down on the pavement.

"You gonna tell her about the plan later?" Lonny asked.

"I don't think so. Can I text her that you asked me out to the bar, maybe for some serious chat or something?"

"Yeah, sure," Lonny asked, his tone reluctant though.

Greg frowned. "I will tell her … Eventually."

Lonny nodded. They both got out and went inside.

The VR theater felt strangely sober within, as if some show had just ended and the lights had kicked on to reveal all the real work that lay ahead. It was brighter than he had ever seen, the main spotlight kicking down an uncharacteristically cold light down upon a lone figure on the stage, who sat uncomfortably at the edge of his stool, his hands up to calm them. Each member was regarding him from in front of their VR stations—a thing he hadn't seen before–a weathered concern on their faces.

"They're trying to destroy us," a man in the audience said loudly into the mic, his voice hoarse. He was about to continue, but stopped himself as the woman next to him touched his arm. He looked at her and she looked back, a sad frown on her face, her hand gesturing for him to hand it over. He gave it to her and she commented next.

"This is indeed a scary time, but now more than ever, we need to remain steadfast. Jehovah will deliver us one way or the other." The man gripped her arm. People were watching her, nodding their heads in agreement. Others were watching the speaker, waiting for him to reply.

"Yes, Sister Torris," he agreed. "This is a test like so many others that have come, and we will get through it with God's help. Like the Israelites that wandered in the desert, we are not forgotten. They made it to the Promised Land in good time, as we will, too. And what came with them? The Arc did. It was sacred to God and men. Well the conduit in the same right is just as sacred. It will remain for us to utilize in our worship. Man will not be allowed to limit it or tamper with it ... because it *is* sacred. This will all be resolved in due time."

"But what if the vote passes?" another woman shot out, her voice cracking loudly through the room, her face fearful. She hadn't waited for the speaker to call on her, an obvious faux pas, Greg intuited, from the shocked glances coming her way from everyone else. They looked back at the speaker, no doubt waiting for his rebuke. He grimaced, closed his eyes for a moment, and then held his hands up, his face calm, collected, conciliatory.

"Let's keep it together, brothers and sisters," he counseled. The woman who had spoken raised her hand again, waving it in the air this time, but he tried to look avoid her, looking for anyone else to talk with. No one spoke. She waved it more frantically after a while. He buckled, his face pained, reluctant, and called her name. The mic holder jogged over to her.

"Sorry for earlier. I didn't mean to do that."

"That's okay, Sister Martin. We—"

"This vote is no joke though," she continued, even as his perma-smile faded to a straight-face. "I'm really scared. I've been watching the newstainment, and they are saying that the vote is likely to pass. I know it is a little over my head and all, but what *are* we going to do?" her voice pleaded. "Will we break the law?" She looked like she had started to cry as she handed the mic back.

Greg noticed that his dad wasn't at his usual spot. He scanned the room from his place in the corner and saw him further down the row, sitting close to Betty, his intimate friend. He moved around the back of the group almost in a sneaking fashion, trying to get a closer view of the two of them. He could have probably pressed into the group if he wanted and crouched down next to him... if he wanted, but he was an outsider, after all, so he held back.

The two looked like little lovebirds pressed together, he thought bitterly. He wondered why it bothered him so. They were holding hands in front of everyone. Clearly, their relationship had taken a turn.

I should have called earlier, he thought.

He felt a pang in his chest, seeing them together. He felt like walking over and embarrassing them in front of everyone, like calling out his father right then and there.

How dare you, you pious fucking hypocrite! he imagined himself saying. *You, that always told me to be the best that I could be, to scold me whenever I stepped out of the moral line. You fuck her on the VR and then you play like you're in love!*

He felt like leaving. He could feel his face getting hot. He turned to go, made it a few steps, and then stopped. He had to get a view of his dad's face first. He walked around to the other side to get a view.

He was trying his best to stay out of view, hiding like some villain in the darkness just outside of the light that seemed to pour down on the crowd of churchgoers like some angelic force poised at any moment to rapture them up to Heaven.

As soon as he got a good angle on his dad, he stopped and took a beat to analyze his posture, his look. He was surprised by what he saw. He didn't know what he had expected, perhaps a knowing, guilty smile, like the lover that has gotten his prize, but it was the opposite. The man looked utterly crazed, his eyes not on the speaker, but on the hands of Betty, his digital partner in fornication crime.

His eyes weren't just passively observing her hand either. They seemed to bore down on her hand, unblinking, as if they were locked in place to melt them with his mind.

Betty hadn't noticed, her full attention on the speaker like the rest of the crowd, her head following his pacing movement on the stage like a tennis spectator.

Suddenly, she nudged him with her elbow, an annoyed look on her face, and he looked up at her, surprised. She pulled her hand away and pointed at the speaker, a stern look on her face now. He sulked in reaction and crossed his arms. She shook her head in disappointment, her hand flexing. Her eyes wandered down, and as if disappointed with what she saw, she frowned.

What was going on with them? Greg wondered, wishing that he had a way into their heads at that very moment to see how they were dealing with it all. He wished that they had the courage to raise their hands. His father though, he knew, wasn't the type. He'd just sit and listen to the others. He wasn't an offerer of information, more like a follower of it.

Betty, though, he thought. *Maybe she has something to say.*

He decided to wait out the meeting and find out for himself.

A couple of minutes went by, him watching the both of them for more, disappointed that nothing was really happening. It was all getting stale. Even the conversation was drying up going around and around in a circle of worried comments and questions by the audience, that and seemingly bureaucratic posturing by the speaker, who had no real answers to give them, a figurehead at best, with nothing new to say. He saw Jacob say something to Betty and then excuse himself out of the row towards the bathroom.

Now was the time to see how he was doing.

He made his way to the bathroom to catch him, eager to get some answers, but to his surprise, the bathroom was empty. He looked in the stalls, hoping to maybe just find his dad sitting on the toilet thinking, knowing that it would be super awkward, but not caring, worried that the alternative was awful, that he wouldn't get to talk to him at all, but the stalls were all empty. He went out, opened the ungendered/female gendered stall, and called out Jacob's name loudly, but no one came out. Jacob had seemingly disappeared. He wandered around covertly in the dimmed cafe, trying not to make a scene, but didn't see him, so he walked outside, and there standing on the stoop looking out over the darkened streets, he finally gave into the fact that his dad was gone, vanished into the night.

Lonny came up to him then from behind. "Hey, man," he said. "You catch up with your dad yet?"

"I can't find him," he replied, a pinch of worry escaping his throat. "I looked all over." He walked back in and headed straight for Betty, eager to figure out where exactly his dad had wandered off to, the worry starting to peak within him, and without preamble, he excused himself up the row, trying not to step on shoes, giving himself away as an outsider by his casual dress—everyone else was dressed up more than usual, probably given the emergency status of the meeting—and tapped on Betty's shoulder and she looked up.

"Sorry," he apologized, getting down on one knee to whisper to her without making a scene. "You don't know me. I'm Jacob's son, Greg." Her face looked overwhelmed at the sight of him, and for some reason that he couldn't diagnose, he felt himself reveling in it, as if he had caught her and she knew it. "Do you know where my dad went?" he asked simply.

She hemmed and hawed for a moment. "He said that he couldn't listen anymore and that he was going to catch a cab home. I tried to stop him, but he left without saying anything more." She sighed lightly. "It's been a lot for him, so I hope he's alright," she added.

He nodded back at her deeply, his mouth flat and wide like a puppet, finished with the conversation, feeling like he had nothing to add, knowing then that he really didn't want to talk to her after all. He had to get away and take it all in. He needed time to think.

He backed up in a servile crouch as if he were leaving a ballroom, and went and grabbed Lonny on the way out.

"Let's get out of here," he told him, his hand pulling Lonny's elbow. "We've got shit to do and this is just distracting me."

"Is it late enough?"

"Fuck it. Let's just go now."

Lonny deferred to him and left after him towards the car, Greg as quick as a thief to get away without wasting any more time there, annoyed that he hadn't just waited to get involved rather than complicate his life any more than it already was.

Fuck my dad, he thought, though he knew that he'd probably be calling him by tomorrow to talk. He'd always be that son that kept coming around despite it all, serving the crazier and crazier whims of an aging, senile, stubborn parent.

The plight of caring for people that had more and more trouble caring for themselves.

As Greg's car touched down on Rex's street, the map screen on the stereo informed him and Lonny simply that they "had arrived," and then exited out abruptly, to Greg's frustration. It was obvious which building it was, he thought looking out the window. There was nothing else on the street but one building. But the big brick-of-a-place was indiscernible, the entrance an utter mystery. The two of them gawked at it for a moment from the car cabin, trying to figure it out. No walkway either, he noted. He got out and walked along the perimeter of the grounds, still in the street, scanning beyond the grassy front for the way up. He toyed with taking his car up into the air manually and flying it over the entire building to the back, but shook his head, knowing that wouldn't do. Too suspicious. He didn't want to draw attention to himself. God only knew how bad it would look if the cops caught him trespassing on the property of his dead boss.

He kept walking, surprised at how large the monstrosity was. A strange, sad design, he thought. There had to be some kind entrance or pathway, perhaps hidden by the tall hedges dotting the front veranda. After getting to the edge of the building, he saw a side-gate hidden well from public view, painted in the same color to blend it into the rest of the building.

He walked up to it, studying the height, the style. It was electronic, no doubt. They'd have to wait for it to op—

Suddenly, it did just that. He rushed to the side, trying to beat the gate open so that he wouldn't be spotted, and waited out of view as a car passed. They'd have a view of him from the side mirror, he noted, hoping that they weren't the alert type of driver. They didn't seem it, though, pulling out onto the street and speeding off none the wiser. He bolted for the car, but stopped as he spotted Lonny driving his way, reading his mind. The vehicle skidded around the curb lip, clipping it with a bang, and barrelled through the opening, the gate starting to close behind him. Greg followed.

They were in, just like that.

Lonny stopped for him and he hopped in.

"Now what?" he asked expectantly, his wiry eyes regarding him. "Pull out your phone so we can locate the unit."

"I don't—"

"Just magnify the map image or something and figure it out."

Greg pulled up the address on the phone and did what Lonny suggested. It looked like the unit was in the very back—a blessing, considering their situation, it being away from prying eyes. He motioned for Lonny to pull into the guest parking a little ways ahead. They got out and made their way up a manicured little meandering path that led into the foyer of the building.

From the inside, it looked much more inviting, Greg noted, nicer even than his own building by a few orders of magnitude. There was well-manicured vegetation everywhere, a small stream that snaked its way along their path, and even a few trees to boot, though from the look of them, it was clear that smog choke was impeding their health.

The path forked, and they followed it to the right around a koi pond and then over a small wooden bridge, Greg trying his best to lead the way using his phone. They turned a corner into a dark alleyway of sorts, the upper patios covering their way from the foyer to the back area, and suddenly knew where they were going, the sight of yellow police tape cordoning off one front patio entrance in a line of bungalows just beyond the alleyway. They stopped right there in the shadows, assessing the front, wondering what to do next. *Foolish non-planning*, Greg thought. There were lamps along the bungalow path lighting it all up, possibly cameras as well, he surmised, recording everything. He quavered and then shared a look with Lonny. Without thinking, he sprinted for the patio entrance, through the light, under the tape, and then dove behind the small stucco enclosure wall that surrounded the small concrete patio area. Lonny followed suit, his feet padding along a little too noisely, moments later behind him, his face nearly in Greg's butt.

He peeked his head up and looked around. Nothing. He crawled to the apartment wall, got up, and tried the obvious thing first, the large forest green door, but it was locked. He looked around again, the both of them still crouched down like fools. They were too exposed, he realized. Any passerby with a brain would catch them crouching there and then run away to call the police. They had no alibi within the tape. Along with that, the inner apartments all had outer windows that faced Rex's front door to some extent.

"What the fuck are we going to do now?" Lonny whispered in a frantic tone.

"I'm working on it," Greg shot back through clenched teeth. "We didn't plan this out at all."

"We're not burglars! We should'a done this from the car!"

There was a window next to the door, so Greg tried to jimmy it open. It wouldn't budge either. He looked back at the knob, recalling the office door. *If only exterior doors were as flimsy...* he thought miserably. The noise would be too loud anyways. If only he had bought some lock-picks and watched a how-video or two. He could have had them drone-shipped to his location within the hour. He saw that Lonny was looking out, his eyes following the path. It went along the patios for a few bungalows and then snaked around the back. That gave Greg an idea. He pulled on Lonny's shirt to follow, and sped down the path around the side to find an alternative entrance.

There was another set of bungalows just behind, facing Rex and the other's backyards, the path trailing along between, hugging the small fronts on one side and the tall backyard fences on the other. It was more exposed than the other path, the back bungalow unit windows looming forebodingly down upon the path. Greg started down it in a walk rather than a run, trying to seem as casual as possible, speaking quietly over his shoulder.

"I don't think anyone's awake, but let's go all the way down just in case, and then head up again and hop over Rex's fence.

"Which one?" Lonny whispered back.

"That one!" he hissed as they walked by, his head jerking at it, but continuing onward. He didn't look back to confer with Lonny, knowing in his gut that there was no way around it. He was going over the fence and getting in. Whatever Lonny did was Lonny's business, he told himself.

He reached a fork at the end of the path and turned suddenly, his mind made up. Lonny got out of the way, his body stiff, hesitant. He was shaking his head. Greg started past him at a gallop, content enough with the quiet state of things along the row, the patios darkened enough for his taste, determined, gaining speed.

The fences all looked the same, but Greg had counted before. Rex was 7 rows from the end. He was moving quickly, so it came up quickly, the white fence where he would go up looking monstrously high the closer he got. At the one-row-before mark, he took three long, measured steps, just like the olympic people he had seen on the TV, let out a small grunt, and hopped over the small hedge in front of the fence and onto it, a loud rattle of plastic ringing out. His mind immediately thought back to the poster of the cat on the tree, and then to the fact that he was so utterly loud and foolish, and probably soon to be in jail.

He felt his age and lack of athleticism catching up to him then as he huffed like an old man, pulling himself up to the top of the fence and then over, one leg first, and then without thinking, the other a little too gingerly. Before he could catch himself, his body dropped horizontally like a log off of a cliff right into the backyard, and the concrete caught him painfully right in the butt.

He laid there on the ground for a while, not thinking of anything but the pain in his right backside area, the first thing to hit the ground. It ached badly, and he sat up on his left butt cheek for a full minute before getting up to shake off the pain. He looked around and saw that there was a sliding glass door and two windows, one large and the other small and high up, probably a bathroom window.

"You good?" a voice asked from the other side. It was Lonny.

"Yeah," he replied with a groan.

"Just text me if you get in. I'm not going over. No point in that."

"Okay," he said.

Lonny's quiet footsteps faded as he walked around to the front.

It was a small little backyard, mostly concrete, with a small wooden planter along one side that had absolutely no life in it. Just dirt.

That made sense. Rex didn't seem like the planting type.

There was a slider and a window, so he walked up to the slider and pulled on it, but it was locked.

Fuck me, he realized, knowing once again that he should have planned things better, his mind going back to the lockpicking tools that he could have... should have ordered and waited out for before launching over the fence into the backyard.

He walked over to the window forebodingly, feeling his luck against him, and gave it a hapless, defeated tug.

It eeked open a bit.

His eyes went wide. He grabbed it with both hands and pulled it the rest of the way open, the glass moving easily in the frame, the opening wide enough for him to climb in easily. The light curtain blew with the outside breeze, and he pushed it aside to look in.

It smelled faintly of rotting meat.

Immediately he saw the smell's culprit—a large deep crimson blood stain on the floor just before the door to the hallway. *Such a big stain*, he thought standing there. Rex had been drained out right there like a gallon of milk left on the floor. He stepped in through the window and scanned the room. It was definitely Rex's room alright—in a word, disheveled. There was a big sheetless queen bed hanging off the corner of the bed frame, a beat up night stand next to it, a lamp light on the floor beside that, strangely enough falling the wall, still turned on. There were dishes piled up on the floor by the bed as well, grimy looking, waiting hopelessly for the day of cleaning that would never come. Greg thought back to the small office kitchen that Rex had left his dirty dishes at.

There was a chest of drawers next to the closet, and as he walked past, he caught himself in the closet mirror and realized that his getup was way too bright for a break-in. *Icing on the idiot cake*, he thought. *Couldn't have planned this break-in any worse.* He hopped over the giant blood stain and into the hallway.

It was one tiny apartment. The "hallway" was just a single square foot of space. To his left was a nook-of-a-bathroom—sink and shower and toilet—directly in front was a closet, and to his right was a very disappointing entryway living room and a kitchen. The kitchen wasn't bad though, he guessed. *For this break-in, it's perfect though, isn't it.* There was no place to hide anything. He was about to step out into the living room when Lonny's head popped around the front window and scared him out of his shoes. He waved eagerly at him to come over and let him in, so he ran up to the door and did so.

"Jesus, man. How long were you gonna make me wait?" Lonny asked, shutting the door behind him. "Everyone in the fucking complex has probably gotten a good look at me by now. Good thing no one walked by."

"Sorry... the blood stain in the bedroom kind of threw me off a bit."

Lonny grimaced and shook his head. "Okay. No biggie. Let's just get a move on and get the hell out of here before the cops catch us and throw us in prison."

He waltzed past him to the bedroom. "God damn," he said and gasped. "That's a big puddle."

"Yeah, I know," Greg remarked. "Alright… well stop gawking at the stain and start looking around. Like you said, we need to get out of here quickly before the police show up."

Greg walked back to the hallway and checked the closet door, just in case it wasn't. Maybe an office was included in the sad little floor-plan.

There wasn't. It was indeed just a closet.

Boy is this place sad, Greg thought and scoffed. *And to think. He just got a home loan. Probably was gonna get out of here... Then he got whacked. What a shitty ending.*

He turned and saw Lonny standing on the other side of the bed, his eyes zoned on the stain from afar.

"Come on, man," he urged him. "You're going to make me find everything? This place is tiny, so why don't you just focus yourself in there and try to dig up something worthwhile. I'll take care of it out here."

Lonny nodded, his face a little more serious and sober than just a moment ago, and started towards the closet.

Greg wondered whether the poor man was second-guessing his decision to help after all.

In the living room, there was a long, thin wood-composite bookshelf along the wall stuffed with papers, so Greg started there. He looked for a few minutes, but it wasn't relevant at all, mostly just coupons and random neighborhood magazines collected over the years, why Greg couldn't guess. There was a single reclining chair, weathered with overuse, facing a screen on the wall, and a fold-up tray table leaning against it. For a hoarder, it could have been worse. Honestly, compared to the office, it almost looked *too* clean even, Greg thought. Perhaps the cops had cleared some of it out. Maybe even biohazard cleaners. With the caution tape though, and the blood spatter spot still set so starkly into the carpet, there was no way…

He moved into the promenade kitchen, bigger than his own

at home, and smartly layed out to boot, with an open range that looked out on the rest of the place. *Nice for entertaining*, he thought. *As if Rex were doing that.* He started opening drawers, hoping that maybe Rex was the type to keep a junk drawer with paperwork or something. The first two were a bust, but then he noticed a drawer on the other side of the countertop sticking out a tad and went to pull it out.

Score.

A mail drawer, filled to the brim with letters and the like, cut open with a knife tucked to the side.

He pulled out a stack and flipped through it, looking for something from Wawamerica. His eye caught the blue bird symbol of the bank at the corner of one envelope, so he pulled it out and laid out what was inside on the counter. They were monthly statements from a few months back. Perfect.

His eyes scanned the transaction history, looking for big influx numbers. Sure enough, a massive number jumped out, bigger than anything that his sad account would ever see, 78, 234 dollars. Under the description, it read *Bavmoute 7439238 NBO 0000*. He pulled out his phone and looked up the unfamiliar company name. The internet told him that it was a mobile app for peer to peer transfers based out of Nairobi, Kenya.

It just kept getting weirder and weirder, Greg thought. He walked into the bedroom and showed Lonny the bank statement.

"Just because it's based there doesn't mean it's actually *from* there, right?" Lonny offered unconfidently.

Greg looked it up and Lonny was indeed right. Bavmoute was created to allow users across the globe to transfer funds, one of the first in fact to do so. Greg read on and found that most were critical of the app, and many countries had even begun to outlaw its use, complaining that it was extremely difficult to regulate. Not only that, but the company itself had been embroiled in legal battles with various governments around the globe for some time because of their reluctance to give up user information when subpoenaed.

"Perfect for criminals, I bet," he figured. "I don't know how we will ever figure out who sent it to him."

"Yeah, but still," Lonny brought up, "Why would randoms just send Rex money? There has to be some sort of tangible reasoning."

"Chances are whatever the reason is, it is probably on Rex's phone and we'll never find it."

Lonny pointed at a stack of paperwork in the corner of the closet. "There's a lot there. Maybe there's something," he suggested.

"Okay. You look through that," Greg replied. "I'be got another pile out there that I haven't quite finished going through."

"Convenient," Lonny replied snarkily. Greg didn't know what to say, so he turned and walked out, leaving Lonny to the monolithic pile.

The pile of letters was too promising to give up.

He found more Wawamerica statements in the letter stash, so he ordered them chronologically and then started highlighting amounts from Bavmoute. They were the large ones. A pattern emerged. Earlier on when the payments started, the same amount came in once a month like clockwork, but then a little over two years ago, two payments from the Nairobian mystery fund began coming in instead. And they were both larger than the single one.

100,000 dollars larger.

"Hold up," Lonny was saying to him from the bedroom, his voice excited. "I've got something." Greg ran over to the bedroom, excited himself with his own findings, and saw that Lonny was standing there waiting for him, papers all around him.

There were more than a dozen different stacks around him, but he was shaking a couple of papers in his hand at Greg, a smile of expectation on his face. "Look at these," he said. "Screenshots!"

Greg grabbed them and took a look.

They looked more like scans of paper documents, probably done using the company printer at work; Greg felt sure of it.

The first paper read the following:

Rex Willis,

You will receive more money than you did before, on a bi-monthly basis, for your watchful guardianship of the floor. Do not allow anyone to get near it. This is of the highest importance. Failure to do this will result in death. Your cooperation is not a choice.

"Rex was a pawn," Greg said flatly and handed back the first paper to Lonny. He looked down at the other one, another similar looking scan. It read:

Rex Willis,

There is a floor in your building that has not been used for some time. It is located between the 182nd and 183rd floors. Do not confer with your boss. She is aware of this floor. It was the location of illegal activities that have since been brought to bear, and has remained abandoned for quite some time. In exchange for a sizeable monthly donation of 78, 234 US dollars per month to your account at Wawamerica (account number 8934723 ; routing number 00239485), you must do the following within 72 hours:

Seal off the elevator lift door so that none may enter with ease, disguising it in whatever way works best to elude those working in your building.

Guard the floor in perpetuity as long as you work in the building, until your retirement.

Failure to stay on with the company before your retirement

will lead to termination and seizure of all of your monetary assets.

More importantly, Failure to guard the floor will lead to your death.

This is not a choice.

Do not contact anyone regarding this. Doing so will also result in your death.

"He was fucked, wasn't he," Lonny said to Greg after he dropped the paper to his side.

"He was," Greg agreed. *We are too*, he thought hopelessly. "Rex was getting paid a lot of money before the end, too. A *lot* of money."

"Yeah?

"In the end, over two hundred thousand a month."

"Holy shit," Lonny muttered, almost to himself. "Fuck this," he said suddenly, motioning for the door. "Let's get out of here. This is some deep shit. We found a lot out. Let's just take it and piece it together afterwards." Without waiting for a reply, he pushed past him and skated out the front door.

There was still more to see, Greg felt, the itch to search holding him in place. He checked his watch. An hour and a half since they broke in. *Long enough*, he told himself. He texted Lonny a quick *"Stay in the car. Cleaning up."* and then returned the myriad of piles and stacks to their prospective cubbies. Afterwards, he did a quick scan of the apartment, made sure that the window was shut up again, and then locked the front door on his way out.

A frazzled Lonny was sitting in the passenger seat when he got into the car, fidgeting anxiously with his belt buckle, his head clearly filled to the brim with worrying thought. Greg didn't engage, but took off into the air, not even bothering to drive out.

11

*December 24th, 2028 - CONVERSATION BETWEEN SPEAKER 6
AND SPEAKER 7*

Speaker 6 - The power went out.

Speaker 7 - What?

Speaker 6 - Swear to God!

Speaker 7 - I told you, man. You should've quit when I did.

Speaker 6 - Yeah, yeah. Whatever. What should I do?

Speaker 7 - How the fuck would I know? Ask the boss.

Speaker 6 - The boss? Haven't you heard?

Speaker 7 - Heard what?

Speaker 6 - He's fucking missing.

Speaker 7 - Missing?

Speaker 6 - Yeah.

Speaker 7 - When did that happen?

*Speaker 6 - Last week? I think they're keeping it out of the press
for now.*

*Speaker 7 - Oh my god, and the clicking! Lu is fucking gone! I walked
into the office yesterday, and he wasn't there. But, seriously, I've been
hearing clicking in the ceiling sometimes and I think it's him.*

Speaker 6 - You're crazy, man.

Speaker 7 - No, man. I just fucking heard it right now.

Speaker 6 - Maybe that's why it had its original name after all.

Speaker 7 - Not funny, man.

Speaker 6 - Just saying.

Speaker 7 - I'm getting out of here. Fuck packing shit up. Fuck it all. I'm not working in the dark with that thing lurking around.

Speaker 6 - Will you get in trouble?

Speaker 7 - I don't care! I'm not dying for some old computers.

(2063) After dropping Lonny off at his place, Greg called Janice to let her know that he was heading home. No one picked up, and it went to voicemail after so many rings. He hung up and tried again, but the same thing happened.

He pulled up her phone's geolocation and it seemed to be pinging at their apartment. *Odd*, he thought. Either she had left it and gone out, which was laughably unlikely, she was in the shower, which was also unlikely, since she usually took morning showers, or she was ducking his calls and letting them ring out.

"Is she really still mad at me for coming back late the other night?" he vented to the screen of his phone, shaking it to manifest the return call from her that he so desperately wanted right then and there. *Couldn't the woman just let it go, on today of all days?* He thought.

He prompted the door open and it crawled up slowly to let him out, so slowly that he shoved it up the rest of the way in frustration. His temper was piping hot he could tell, turned up to a hundred because of yet another variable he had to contend with. It was driving him up a wall. His bandwidth felt lower than ever.

As he wandered up to his building, his feet felt heavy and achy. He stopped and surveyed the front facade, looking up the side towards the top where their apartment sat. The living room lights were on. She *was* mad then, he figured, deflated. He crept on at a snail's pace, toying with the idea of just turning around and driving over to Lonny's or to his dad's place to stay the night instead. His feet were trudging onward though, as if his body hadn't registered his reluctance, so he gave in and went inside.

He decided to take the stairs instead of the elevator, the sight of the metallic doors weary to him, claustrophobic. His mind needed a moment to power down anyways before the fight. It worked for all of about one flight of stairs, and then he started to rehearse what he'd say to her, what tactic he'd use. *Go for the sorry or the angry?*-he wondered. It was a toss-up, and her face staring back at him would be the final deciding factor.

At the door, he came to the conclusion that he'd have to give up everything him and Lonny had done. He didn't have a poker face. Plus, she already knew the worst stuff. This new stuff wasn't even his fault. He wondered if she'd see it that way.

Maybe after all this, we can both go to her therapist, he thought cynically, his hand on the door. *Na... I'd rather jump out a ten-story window instead.*

Suicide. If only it was possible for everyone. The thought popped up like a small balloon in his head. He opened the door with his eyes closed, not wanting to face her fury with his eyes open.

The room was empty.

The light was on, but a rare sort of silence made itself known almost immediately. No pacing Janice, waiting to yell. No heavy breathing Janice, sitting at the couch, wondering where to begin. No Janice at all.

He walked through the kitchen first, eyeing the kitchen knife block, just in case, though he knew that she'd never stab him. Poisoning, yes, but a stabbing, no way. The thought of her screaming from around the corner, a butcher knife in her hand was too visceral for her style. *How dare you be late again, fucker!* she'd have to yell as she charged him.

Too crazy.

Where was she though? he wondered anew, annoyed that she'd left the light on. Here he was sapping energy to pay off bills and she was charging them back up. She was usually good about this sort of thing, better than him even. The thought boiled his blood a little more.

He stepped even more heavily to the bedroom and pushed the door open so hard with the palm of his hand that it slapped against the inner wall. The sound made him check himself, his gut warding him from playing his angry hand too soon, or even wrongly, given the situation.

Why are you making so much noise? she'd say, a notch above him already in the argument that would surely follow.

In the dimness, he noticed that the bed was disheveled, the bedsheets pooled at its foot. There was something shining among the sheets, so he picked it up. It was the solid glass oval that she always had by her side of the bed on the nightstand. There was a chip in it too. He looked on the floor and spotted some shards of the plastiglass shining from the carpeting, so he bent to pick them up. Out of the corner of his eye, he caught sight of the painting on the wall to his left, barely hanging onto the wall at an angle, a chest-sized spider web crack in the middle of its picture frame glass. He got up slowly, the hair on his neck rising.

The scene in the room was morphing before his eyes, the cracks in the dream obvious now that he had spotted one. It was like one more crime scene he was walking into, his eyes darting around critically, registering clues, subtle, *possibly* sinister hints that something untowards was afoot.

The window was cracked open. That wasn't right. The window was never cracked open... The chair by the window was pushed out. Cleaning up? Rearranging things? No way. And she never sat there either. Did someone come in through the window?... And why were the sheet's pooled at the foot of the bed in the first place?

Maybe someone broke in and she woke up, started back against the head of the bed, grabbed the glass paperweight, and tossed it at the assailant.

Just then he saw the light of the bathroom peeking through

the crack by the floor and rushed for it, his brain suddenly swimming at the thought of his wife dead or dying within. He grabbed the knob, pushed at it, but was met with a dull resistant pressure that wouldn't give.

Something was on the ground on the other side he could tell from the angle, something heavy, barring the way so that the top of the door shook in response to his buffeting.

"Janice!" he yelled, putting the weight of his shoulder into the blows now, still unable to budge it open. No response.

"Janice!" he yelled again, and pressed into the door as hard as he could muster, his legs straining.

Slowly, it began to give way, just an inch, and he saw part of Janice's body on the ground. It was her hand, her limp hand, facing palm up.

"Janice," he croaked, his voice betraying the panic that poured out of him like a broken dam.

He drove all of his weight against the door, his eyes locked onto the body of his wife on the ground as she came more and more into view, her possible corpse giving way and sliding along the floor. He finally gained enough room to force himself through the opening and shoved himself in to look at her.

She was lying naked facedown on the floor.

There was a smooshed splotch of blood on the door about a foot up and a long thin line of red along the floor from there to her head. He turned her over and held her in his arms. She was unconscious, but her face showed color, and there was blood on her forehead at the hairline.

"Janice?" he asked as his hand gently caressed her cheek.

She didn't respond. She looked for all intents and purposes like one asleep. Just then, he registered her chest rising slowly. She was breathing.

His hand lightly clasped her chin and shook ever so gently, trying to wake her up.

He held his mouth to her ear. "Janice?" he spoke into her ear. "Babe. Wake up. Wake up."

Her eyes flickered and then all of a sudden, as if jump-started at the sound of his voice, her body animated in his arms, her head lifting, her eyes opening, her mouth wide open.

Out of it came a guttural scream like nothing he had ever heard from her before, so loud that his head shot backward in reaction to the eruption in his face. Without meaning to, he dropped her like dead weight, and she fell against the cold linoleum floor.

"Oof, sorry," he apologized, his hands moving to hold her again, but she shoved him away, retreating backward into the shower, slapping his hand away like something wild as he grabbed for her. She curled up into a seated ball in there, her head buried between her legs. He saw then that her left arm was bleeding too at the wrist and he wondered frantically what had happened while he was gone.

He crawled up slowly towards her with his hands out, slow and calculated to not get kicked away again. His hand touched her knee, but thankfully, she didn't rebuff him like before, a good sign, he noted.

"Hey, hey," he cooed. "Babe, I'm right here. You're okay." Her knee was shaking beneath his palm, her whole body chattering uncontrollably.

It was like turning the corner to the sight of a train wreck. He was some shocked bystander looking at it all, unable to process it.

What the fuck happened? he wondered incredulously.

It took a while for Janice to calm down enough to be escorted out of the bathroom. She refused outright at first to move from the shower at all, holding his hands around her like a comfort blanket on the cold tiles. Once the shaking abated and her breath calmed down, he got up first and told her that he would check the rest of the apartment. It was clear. The "thing," whatever it was, was gone.

Or at least, he couldn't find it. It could have been hiding.

He turned on all the lights to make her feel a little safer, and then came back to walk her out to the living room. She white-knuckled his shoulder as they crept out, him in front leading the way slowly with her at his back, her head swiveling around like some traumatized cat, eager to run at the first sight of trouble.

They settled down on the couch together, her small frame curled up in his lap, her head on his collarbone, and listened in silence for a while to the sounds of the apartment. Finally, she cleared her throat and started to recount things.

"It wasn't human, whatever it was," she started, her voice so soft that he barely heard it at first. "I awoke to the sound of the chair scraping along the wood. I didn't really register it at first, though. It was like it was in my head, part of my dreams or something... but when I opened my eyes and looked over..." Her lip started to quiver, her voice subtly whimpering. "It was up in the corner of the room by the window, above the chair, tucked in right below the ceiling. I could see it staring at me. It had shiny yellow eyes, kind of blackened, metallic looking skin. It was fidgeting around up there like some giant shiny spider, trying to stay hidden in the shadows... waiting to strike. Maybe it was waiting for me to close my eyes again, I don't know. Maybe it had hopped up there because I woke up."

Greg saw the flesh of her arm goose suddenly.

"Then all of a sudden, it froze in place like a statue... Waiting to see what I'd do next? At that point, I made a move to the other side of the bed... really slight... and then *bam*! All of a sudden, it jumped down onto the ground right at the foot of my bed! I reached for that glass thing on the side of the bed... you know, that ornament we got out in Solvang, you know, the one you're always complaining about, and I slung it at it as hard as I could. It would have hit it. It was right on the money! But the thing dodged it. The way it did was weird too, almost like a rippling effect, flowy like water, to the side and then back again. It was like some robotic alien out of a nightmare. It was clicking too, like it was talking to me or something."

A click, Greg thought, tensing up.

"I *did* hit it on the side of the head a little. The thing didn't dodge it all the way," she continued, a little pride in her voice. "It didn't knock it back, though, but it kind of stunned it a little I think for a second. Maybe it was recalibrating or something. I don't know. Right then, I hopped off the bed and ran for the bathroom, but it chased after me. It got me too."

She flashed him the wound on the inside of her wrist and then hid it again. "It didn't grab me, but it didn't really stab me either. It felt almost like it jabbed me with a poker. Anyways, I got to the bathroom and tried to slam the door, but it threw itself against the other side and the door cracked me in the head and knocked me down. I tried to shove it closed again, but then the door cracked me in the head hard and that was it. Lights out. The next thing I saw was you."

She squeezed him tight around the waist and he kissed the top of her head, his mind flooded with everything she had told him.

The thing is coming to get us, he realized, scared to utter the words aloud, the panic welling up inside of him. *I can't tell her. She can't know*, he told himself. *She can't. If I tell her...* It wouldn't do any good. She had just been attacked. It was too much, at least for the time being.

He clicked into a sympathetic frown and tried to segway away from it all.

"Lemme see your wrist," he said, reaching for her hand. She held it out to him gingerly, and he studied the mark. It wasn't a cut, like he had thought initially. More like a square-shaped compression pressed into her wrist, its edges clear and defined as if the thing had just reached out and poked her with its squarish finger.

He glared at his own arm, where the impression would have been on him. The port... It was exactly where the input jack on *his* arm was. *Had it come into the room to watch her... to study her? It ran up on her to touch her, and then knocked her out and left her? What the hell did it want?*

"Is that blood?" Janice asked suddenly, her finger pointing to a drop of red on his shirt. As he looked down, another drop fell, and he looked up at her. There was a thin line of red running down the middle of her forehead.

"Oh shit," he reacted, reaching up with his thumb to wipe it away. There was a gash just above her hairline.

"We need to get you to the hospital. Your head is still bleeding."

"I'm sure it's fine," she replied, reaching up to touch it. She winced, but kept prodding at it. "It's not that bad," she offered, but he stopped her.

"You may have a concussion, though, or worse." He tried to stand up with her still in his arms, but she was too heavy, so he sat her down on the couch beside him. "Can you walk okay?" he asked.

"Babe, really," she replied instantly.

"No, really," he said, a little more forcefully than before. "Let's go. I'll take you to the hospital." With that, he got up, his hand out for her. She sighed, but grabbed it, and he pulled her up.

In the back of his head, the eagerness to leave was two-fold. She did have a wound, and quite possibly something that only a doctor would see. Also...

The thing had attacked her, so clearly it was out of the room. Out and about.

It could be anywhere.

That fact clawed at his nerves with each step, each sound, and at every turn from the moment they left the living room to the moment they got to his car.

It was grueling. He was agitated. And his behavior struck Janice as strange, not quite chivalrous... something else... but she said nothing. In the end, he was holding her tightly, and that was what mattered.

. . .

Along the way to the hospital, a sense of guilt started to creep up in Greg. It hadn't hit him in the apartment because the fear was crowding every other emotion out. But now that he was in the car, he had time to reflect.

The thing wasn't just stalking him now, but those closest to him as well.

And Janice had no idea.

He couldn't decide whether to tell her or not. Part of him wanted to just come out with it right then and there, to tell her that he had tempted fate yet again and embroiled them both in whatever conspiracy was clearly going on at his building.

Still, he couldn't tell her. No way. She'd kill him.

Still, he *had* to tell her at some point. She'd find out eventually.

The oscillation was killing him. He sat there ruminating, silent as the grave. Janice was noticing too, her eyes on him nervously as he drove along, brooding within.

His behavior was very uncharacteristic. *He* knew that, but still, he couldn't turn it off and just act normal.

He realized he was speeding, for how long he had no idea. He dialed it back to the norm, and then rested back in the seat, suddenly tired and weary.

"You alright?" Janice asked, her voice tinged with worry.

The silence was over. He had to talk. "That was scary back there," he offered up, not looking at her. *It really was*, he realized, thinking back to the bathroom. It was all so visceral, even still, the sight of her unconscious body on the cold white bathroom floor, all of the problems of his adventure brought to a head right then and there, his own wife paying the price for his selfish curiosity. "I thought I lost you."

She squeezed his hand and he looked at her. She had a tear in her eye. He saw it and felt a stab of guilt. *It's all your fault*, he thought. He tried to brush it away. He looked back at the road.

Tell her!—

No! She won't forgive you!

You have to!

He was panicking again. He started talking, explaining but not the thoughts he had in his head back then in the apartment.

"When I heard your story out there on the couch... I had this feeling... this *gut* feeling that we had to get out of there as soon as possible. I started thinking about that thing, just waiting around in the apartment. Then when I saw that bit of blood on your forehead, I don't know... I just started freaking out thinking that maybe whatever had just happened might not be over with."

You just opened the door right there, you dumb bastard. He had definitely given himself away. That much was for sure. He blushed, and felt suddenly hot. His palm was clamming up. He wanted to escape. He wanted just silence, time to think. He pulled his hand away from hers suddenly, and she reached for it again. He wiggled away again, putting it in his lap awkwardly to hide it from her.

He was exposed, erratic. She knew. She had to. And now she was staring at him through narrowed eyes, boring down on him from her seat. He didn't dare look her way, but he could tell she was leaning away, silent as the grave, regarding him, waiting to see what he'd do next.

Suddenly, she spoke.

"What aren't you telling me, Greg?" she asked, her voice icy.

Fuck, he very nearly said out loud, but clamped his mouth shut. His jaw was taught. He fumbled for something to say. She spoke again.

"If this has something to do with those loans you owe," she said, her voice rising, "I swear.to.God."

What? he thought, reeling at the accusation she had just thrown at him. It was wrong, but not *entirely* wrong. He looked back at her, and the sight of her face, her lips pursed, her eyes like slits, scared the excuses away, scared the words away. He opened to speak, but nothing seemed to come out.

"I… I—" he got out, but then a hand came up suddenly and he felt the shock of it, the slap connecting the side of his face.

"You son of a bitch!" she exclaimed, ready to tear his throat, completely shocked that her shining knight just a moment before was now the product of her living nightmare. "I can't—"

"Wait, wait," he started up, his arm up like a barricade to ward off the next blow. "Just wait. It's not like that! It's not about the loans!"

She held off, her eyes rolling away from him for a moment as she registered his words, her mind analyzing the phrasing of his sentence. "Then what *is* it about, hmm?" she retorted, her voice charged up again, her entire body tensed up like a viper about to strike. "What did you do? I know you did something. You better tell me right now, otherwise I'm gonna open your door and shove you out of this car."

"Your head, your head," he side-stepped. "Just calm down for a minute. Let's—"

"Don't you tell me to calm down," she interjected, backhanding him in the shoulder.

"Let's just get to the hospital," he replied loudly, but diplomatically, "And I'll explain everything there."

"Get to the hospital my ass," she replied, and threw a flurry of shots at his shoulder, his elbow arching up to try and block the onslaught. If it weren't for the auto-pilot, they'd have nosedived into oncoming traffic long ago.

"Just hold on!" he finally yelled at her, his face red, his eyes burrowing back into her gaze that was angry and furious as well. "Hold on for one goddamn minute! I can't even fucking think!"

She froze at the sound of him, red and livid, almost losing it in front of her, and sat back hard in her seat, her arms folding, her face tight.

He let out a long breath. "Thank you," he replied after a good couple of seconds. "I will tell you everything. I swear I will. Just let me take us to the hospital and I'll tell you there."

To that, surprisingly, she said nothing, her eyes on the road as well. He waited for a good minute for some kind of answer, a rebuttal, a confirmation. Nothing came. Silence.

You're not going to believe me anyways, he thought, knowing that their next conversation, though inevitable, would be even harder.

Probably hurt worse too.

His mind ran over it detail by detail in the tense silence that followed.

They didn't talk immediately after entering the Jan Jose Falls Municipal Hospital. In fact, they didn't talk again until an hour had gone by waiting in the urgent care lobby. Greg waited, figuring that the longer the break, the better the conversation between the two of them. He spent his time eavesdropping on the various conversations taking place around him amidst the hubbub of anxious, painful expectation. It was something to distract him. A few seats away, there was a young lady on the phone talking to her lover about how her mother had fallen down some stairs. To the other side, a man who had a stomach flu fidgeted uncomfortably, getting up every few minutes to go to the bathroom.

Nothing to write home about.

The couple behind him though, they were something. They argued loudly about the man's swollen ankle, why according to her he had to be so stupid to continue working on it, letting it get *that* bad before doing anything about it. He stole a couple of glances at them as they shouted intermittently, but stopped abruptly as the woman caught him and glared. He cringed apologetically and turned back.

Janice shook her head at him. He shrugged. She scoffed and threw her hands up in frustration.

"You're going to make *me* be the bigger person and ask? Really?"

He regarded her in confusion. "I… just wanted to give you some time to settle in before we had this conversation. That's all."

"Well," she started, fidgeting exaggeratedly in the plastic blue cushion of the chair, "I'm settled. And I'm ready to listen. Go for it." She rested her chin on her hand and blinked dramatically at him.

"Alright," he started, wondering where to begin, wishing hopelessly that they'd be called in right then. No way. They were way down the list.

It would be a long conversation, he knew, and he wasn't ready to explain himself. But he did, and it took a while.

She didn't speak once as he recounted everything, every last event that occurred after they had last talked the night that he had come home late—Rex's death, his decision to look into the floor, his first encounter with their hidden villain, his trespass into Rex's office and then the trespass into Rex's home, and finally, coming home to find her unconscious in the bathroom.

By the end, he felt pretty well resolved of guilt. In the end, after having gone over it at length, he felt like he hadn't actually done anything wrong in his eyes. It felt like fate, an impossibly linear journey that he had no way of sidestepping.

Janice's frown intuited to him that she didn't see it that way, though. She started up as soon as he stopped talking.

"You mean to tell me that you trespassed into a dead man's office and then into his home… into a god-damned crime scene?" she asked, completely floored. "Do you even realize how that's gonna look to the police?"

He couldn't argue with her there, and his resigned, silent demeanor said as much. Lonny had come to the same conclusion and he knew it. Still, there really was no going back. He knew that more than anything else. Forward was the only option.

He told her as much, his voice as weary as ever.

"It's too late now, babe. I'm sorry, but we're both in danger and it's not going away."

"Greg—"

"Hang on now," he interjected as diplomatically as possible. "Before we start fighting again, just hear me out. I put something together tonight from what just happened to you. This thing, whatever it is, it wants *me*, but I don't think it wants you. If it did, it would have just taken you after it knocked you out. And you're not dead, so—"

"Mrs. Quinlin?" a nurse called from the admittance door in the far corner of the room. "Mrs. Quinlin?" she repeated. Janice turned and saw the nurse ushering her in through the admittance doors and started up out of her seat. He grabbed her arm and she turned to look at him, her eyebrow raised.

He got up and hugged her, speaking in a low voice as he did so.

"I'm going to find out what's happening, if it's the last thing I do." His hand was clasping her wrist, imploring her to trust him, to still believe in him. "It's the only way."

He kissed her then, his lips pressed hard on the cheek. "I'm going to go figure this out now. It's the only way. You'll be safer here without me than if I were here."

"You're not going to stay here with me?" she asked as she pulled away from him to look him in the face, her eyes welling up, her voice heartbroken.

"I know that the thing wants me. It was checking your arm—"

"Mrs. Quinlin," the nurse called again. Greg held out a finger at her to give him a moment, but continued. "I have very little time to figure this out, to actually absolve myself of Rex's death and get this thing before it kills me. There's no time to waste now," he tried to persuade her. "That thing is out there somewhere. Lonny and I have already started to work it out though.

189

We are making good headway already, but we need to do more fast."

The nurse was tapping her foot, her face annoyed as she stared at the two of them. "You can both come in," she offered in frustration.

Janice shook her head at the woman and unclasped from him, starting for the door. He had a thought and grabbed her one last time. "Whether you're admitted or not," he advised her, "after you leave... if you *have* to leave here, don't go back to the apartment, whatever you do. Stay with your mom. Better yet, with one of your friends. But text me when you leave so I can come take you. If you want."

She nodded and he let her go, feeling knots inside for leaving her now, at the hospital of all places.

He hoped it was the right decision.

It probed her, he told himself. *It wanted to see if she had the input jack and then left her there, alive to tell the tale. What does it mean?* At the very least, hopefully it meant that he was the target. Him and him alone.

Well, at least now that Rex was dead.

The thought was meant to relieve him, but somehow, the hair on his neck still stood up at the thought of it.

● 12

*January 5th, 2029, Press release taken from the Los Angeles Times -
Obituaries Press Releases — Statement Prepared by Jon Holmes, Forks
Family PR Manager*

*"Billionaire tycoon Braille Forks, self-proclaimed "Master of
Crypto-Currency Trading," was found dead last week on a wilderness
trail behind his cabin in the Inyo National Forest. Sources say that
given his wounds and the tufts of animal fur near the scene, he was
more than likely killed by a black bear. According to experts, the movement of his wealth in recent days has caused speculation over his state
of mind at the time of his death. Even so, his still-healthy estate will
pass on to his immediate family."*

(2063) *Of course it's dark outside*, Greg thought, standing in the
hospital's exit doorway. Luckily, he had the foresight to park as
close to the front as possible. He was only three rows back. He
could even see his car, sitting there, waiting for him.

The problem. There was no one else in the parking lot.

He stood inside by the exit, checking his phone, waiting for
someone to leave.

After a minute, a group of women walked past him out the door.

Too awkward? he wondered, toying with the idea of following him out. One turned and locked eyes with him, her smile fading. He tried smiling back to reassure her, but she whispered to a friend and the friend turned as well.

Welp... Now you're a creep, he thought, turning around to stare inside. After a few moments, he looked back.

And they had parked right next to him. It would have been perfect.

Just then a car pulled into the lot nearby. He waited until it stopped, until the driver got out.

And then he ran out the door.

The driver gave him a look as they passed each other in the lot, Greg's eyes on him, smiling again like some fool, as the other man looked back at him quizzically.

"Running late," he shouted back over his shoulder with a fake chuckle.

A moment later, he was in the car.

No death, no scare. Success.

Is this going to be how it is for the foreseeable future?- he thought. The car was quiet. He hadn't turned it on yet.

He locked the doors all the same. Could it open doors? Probably—it had gotten into his apartment. He buckled up.

What the fuck did it even look like? He had no idea. Maybe Janice was wrong—maybe it was more human than she thought.

There were so many places to hide in the lot too. It could be watching him even now.

The lot was small and dark, with only a few dim lights. A path led to the road, bordered by overgrown grass that swayed faintly in the wind.

The thing could be in there right now, he thought.

The grass swayed aloofly in the wind. It was thick, too thick to see anything...

He noticed something there, out there in the grassy field, just a few feet in. It was reflecting the light ever so slightly from the tall lights.

He leaned into the front window to get a better look, squinting his eyes, his hands on the wheel.

Suddenly, the horn sounded, startling him, and he realized he had pressed it accidentally. He looked again. Whatever had been there was gone. He scanned the thick grass, heart pounding … but saw nothing.

With that, he turned on the car and left for Lonny's place.

On the way over to Lonny's apartment, Greg turned on a couple of news podcasts to try and get his mind off of the task at hand, just to catch a breather. It didn't help though. In fact, it made him even more anxious. It was like everything was dialed into his universe and was actively trying to stress him out.

On one podcast, first instance, it talked about the growing governmental efforts to try to curb the population freefall that was happening all over the world, some being less ethical than others. Some larger nations had gotten so desperate lately that they had resorted to seizing entire female populations on unaffected islands, in direct violation of WRCCSFR (World Regulatory Commission to Combat and Safeguard Fertility Rights) statutes agreed on after the chaos directly following the Fall.

Everyone wanted a piece of the last good hens, it seemed.

After that, they talked about Tabernacle more. Apparently, there hadn't been any recent updates since the initial media release, a problem many were saying that shouldn't have even been allowed, given the gravity of the tech itself to the future of the population. The podcasters argued about it for a while, whether BYU's program should even have the right to stay dark, nevermind the fact that they were privately funded.

They discussed the fact that religious lobbyists headed up by the more popular doomsday religions were working overtime in Washington to suppress Tabernacle's tech. Their main argument against it, according to one fundamentalist they quoted, centered around some religious doctrine that stated that "the nature of the tech itself was heretical and opposed the natural order of godly punishment on earth."

He turned the volume down and chewed on the implications for a moment. Had mankind really handicapped itself enough to not deserve the chance to make it right?

The argument itself would never hold up to any real scrutiny, he felt deep down, but still... On the other hand, maybe they had a point.

Who are we to have a second chance to make it right? If we were to die out, wouldn't the earth's climate heal again? Wouldn't the endangered species of the earth flourish again? We're cockroaches and we're finally going extinct. I'm sure Mother Earth isn't crying over it.

He flipped around for a while and fell on a podcast that had some updates about the conduit. It was a monologue, and he honed in on it eagerly, keen to hear if his father's saving drug was safe or not. According to the political pundit who spoke, it didn't look good for them. Their adversary, the original Jehovah's Witnesses, had no intention of letting this one slip by them. Apparently, the drug was more offensive to them than the Tabernacle Project. They were spending a considerable amount of money against it and were gaining a lot of headway, according to the speaker's sources on Capitol Hill.

He turned off the radio, feeling hopeless and dejected. His world had prospects... finally... but they were shaking under the weight of zealots seeking control. His father's world, the one that had saved him, was crumbling at the very hands of his old religion. It all felt so fateful, so circular, so adversarial... Everyone was grasping for a rope to save them from the chasm and coming up with straws instead.

He almost laughed thinking of his father, how sad and pathetic his situation really was. He had literally ditched one god for some new, updated model, but was now being struck down by the old god in return.

Was it godly wrath, perhaps?

Jacob would have to settle for consumer eroticism like Janice.

Greg cringed at the thought.

He made it to Lonny's without any issues, but decided to text him anyways to meet him at his car instead of just walking up to his friend's apartment in the dark alone yet again. In the silent, expectant wait time that followed, he wondered how the thing was now seemingly able to track him all over the place. After all, he had enough encryption software on his phone to block out pretty much anything trying to get in. *Still*, he considered, toying with the device in his pocket, how tech savvy was he, really? Did he actually feel confident in *his* own cyber-security assessments? He was a self-proclaimed novice! If the thing had any real knowledge about tech–backdoors and whatever else there was— it was probably light-years ahead of the safeguards he had researched and placed on his phone.

He felt another sliver of hope slipping away.

He made a mental note to talk to Lonny about it. There had to be some way to bolster encryption, maybe even something to disrupt the low-jacking that was probably already taking place.

That *was* whenever Lonny finally did come to his car, he thought nervously. He looked out the window towards the darkened apartment building, its tall, monolithic form rising endlessly into the smog. It had been ten minutes since he texted him. He looked at his phone. No further texts from him other than the initial one. *Was he still on his way?* he wondered.

Is he still alive?

The intrusive thought popped in suddenly, and he couldn't help but chew on its addictive thread. *Technically, Lonny did text back, but what does that prove? Does it prove that he's the sender? Does it prove unequivocally that he was the one with the phone doing the texting, and not someone or something else?*

The paranoia was taking shape more creatively than before.

Was it the stress? It was some greedy loan shark, upping the ante to get what was due.

No way to stop it…

Thankfully, Lonny's skinny frame exited the building just then and walked up to his car in the dark, waving for him to roll down the window. Greg squinted hard through the tint nonetheless, just to confirm, and then cracked the window to peek out, again, just to confirm, and saw Lonny's eyes beaming back expectantly at him. He smiled in relief and then got out to speak with him in the open air and stretch a little.

"Sorry man," he apologized awkwardly. "Can't be too careful these days."

"What, are you worried that you're being followed?" Lonny replied, his voice hesitant.

"No, it's just…" And then he thought of Janice and stopped. Lonny didn't know yet what had happened to her. "Come on. Let's go inside. Some things have happened."

"Great," Lonny said, and sighed sadly.

As they headed up to his apartment, he apprised him of Janice's run-in with the thing and his discovery of her.

Lonny reacted in understandable shock. His face was pale by the end.

"How could this thing be out and about? I thought you said that it didn't finish you off in the elevator? Why would it be following you… following Janice?"

"I'm not sure, but I don't think it was *following* Janice. It was probably going into the apartment to find me, but found her instead." He thought of the prick on her arm, the probing for the port, but held back.

"Yeah, but how did it know where you lived?" Lonny interjected. "Maybe we should go check your car for bugs." Greg pondered the idea for a moment, but Lonny shook his head.

"Na… Never mind. A tracking device could be anywhere in

your car. Besides, that kind of stuff is so advanced nowadays. We'd never find it."

All of a sudden, Lonny perked up in his seat, another thought in his head, and got up with a start, rushing into the other room. Greg fidgeted expectedly, hearing the slamming of a window in the bedroom, and then a lock clicking home. A moment later, Lonny emerged, walking quickly to another part of the apartment, checking the windows of the living room along the way, locking and re-locking them, barring some that could be barred, laying down a board even at the sliding glass door that led to the balcony.

It all felt a little moot to Greg though, sizing up the defensive tactics from the couch. The glass of the sliding doors wasn't crash proof. If the thing wanted in badly enough, it was getting in.

"I hope this thing will have the decency to knock first," he offered up, trying to make light of the situation. Lonny stopped and registered the comment, but continued on with his task anyways, a slight frown on his face.

Greg felt a sudden pang of guilt seize him. Here his friend was, panicked, engaged in zombie apocalypse-level prepping in his own apartment, all because of him, and he was sitting on the couch watching. The poor man was in over his head now, and he hadn't even had the whole picture beforehand to decide whether he *wanted* to get involved in the first place.

Him or Janice, for that matter.

They're both pawns in my adventure game gone awry, he mused.

Lonny banged a couple of nails into an outward hinging casement window and then stepped off the stool headed for the front door. Greg got up with his hand out.

"Hey, man. Maybe you should take a break for a second. You've done a good job so far, but won't it make it hard to leave if you nail down the front door?"

Lonny stopped and looked at the hammer for a moment, and

then scoffed. "Yeah, maybe you're right, huh. I probably look like I'm goin' fuckin crazy right now"

"Meh," Greg said with a shrug. "We're both a little nuts these days."

The comment seemed to clear the air a whole lot in the room. Things *were* feeling crazy, yet they had no time to reflect.

Lonny smiled at it all now, chuckling softly. It was tired and honest. He sat down beside Greg on the crouch, and then without asking, he reached over and hugged him, patting him on the back hard as well, as if they had just gotten off the job site after surviving some terrible day at work.

Greg let him go and then pointed at the nearby bookcase. "Why don't we move that thing in the way of the door? It'll at least delay whatever comes in. That way we can get out too."

Lonny nodded his head and they did just that, and then they sat down by the TV and cracked open some beers.

After about ten minutes or so of sitting and enjoying the silence, Greg felt the need to kick it all up again.

They couldn't really wait now, could they?

He felt guilty, but he cleared his throat, anyway. "So … what now?" he asked. Thinking about it, they were at a dead end of sorts, he thought suddenly. They had already acted on most of the leads they had.

"Hard to say, huh," Lonny replied, suddenly deflated as well. It was a real pickle. They weren't detectives by any means, but as they sat there with their minds actually fixed on it, even the gravity of the situation felt elusive. Rex's death was a mystery. The floor itself, the thing that had started it all, was a mystery. The building's connection to it was a mystery.

Even the predator in the night was a mystery.

That was a pressing and dismal thought, Greg reckoned with a dryness in his throat. He might die before even understanding why he was being killed.

"The floor," Lonny said and looked at Greg. "Didn't you take photos?"

He had.

Greg whipped his phone out and scrolled through the latest pictures. He found a clearish shot of the server bay and passed the phone to Lonny.

He zoomed in on the photo, his eyes screwed up to analyze the details of the graphics processors.

"I knew it," he said excitedly. He put Greg's phone down and pulled out his phone to search the web. Greg inched closer to see. Lonny was typing in a lot of numbers.

"Barcodes?" he asked.

"No, model numbers. The powered set-up is different. I'm just trying to figure out what kind of tech the others."

"Oh, okay."

"Bingo," he said with a grin. "Okay, so you remember at the cafe what I was saying… that the lit-up GPUs were too advanced to be all up in that room. Well they are. I did a search on the others just now and they are standard crypto-mining processors, like I thought they would be, obsolete now but probably cutting edge at the time."

He picked up Greg's phone and gave the image a quick look. "This floor was definitely a farm like we thought, but then *these* GPU's there doesn't make any sense, right? So after we met at the kava cafe, I tried to look up the advanced GPU's, but I wasn't able to find anything, and I did a lot of digging. They didn't have any company branding on them, and that GPU model unit was never sold. Whatever it is for, my guess is that they were either privately made for a single client or were prototypes for some purpose and never made it to the public market."

"So why *would* they be there?" Greg asked.

"Honestly, I think they were brought in and installed after the fact. I mean, what better place to hide away advanced tech than some old derelict crypto-farm? They can just sit there in their bays burning the midnight oil computing. No one to bother. No one to ask questions."

"I guess. The question is what are they working on?"

"I don't know."

"Well then we're fucked, huh."

"Not necessarily," Lonny replied. "Maybe somebody online has seen these things." He smiled wryly. "We should at least throw it up in the chats and see." He leaned back into the couch and gripped his phone tightly in his hands. "I am positive someone knows something."

"Woe man," Greg warned, his face scared. "Are you sure we should go public with this shit?"

"We're already in deep shit!" Lonny shot back. "Fuck it!"

Greg ripped his phone out of Lonny's hands and shook it at him. "We don't even have anything to go off of!" he shouted, feeling scared and frustrated in the same vein. "What? Some stupid pic of some computer shit?"

"Well, do you have any better ideas?" Lonny shot back, his voice pitched to deflect Greg's growing anger.

"Fuck. I don't know!" he yelled and started to pace the room like his wife Janice. He raised his arm to throw his phone out of the room and then stopped himself, settled on shaking it again.

"Alright, man. Fine. Let's not lose our heads, now," Lonny counseled him. "I'm sure there's some other angle then. There has to be. I mean, you worked there for a while. What has been going on lately? Anything weird that you might have noticed … Maybe about Rex?"

Greg started to pull at his greasy black hair, his eyes scrunched as he tried to recall the last few days, the days before Rex left—was killed, rather.

"I don't know about *Rex*," he remarked unconfidently, "But I mean, this whole thing did start when the floor around the server floor started blacking out."

"When was that?"

"Nine days ago, I think."

"What happened nine days ago?" Lonny asked.

"No, wait a minute. No, I'm sure that it was because of my sapper," Greg stopped him before he trailed off on the tangent.

"Well," Lonny kept on, undeterred. "Did you install it nine days ago? Was that when it blacked out?"

"No…" Greg replied, his mind readjusting to Lonny's line of questioning. "I had it installed a long time before then."

"Has the sapper ever blacked out any other floors before that?"

"No," Greg replied.

"Maybe the computing area turned on nine days ago and the extra juice sent it over the edge." It was a quiet remark from Lonny, his head dipped, his index finger toying with his thumb. Greg watched him.

"What do you—"

Lonny's hand went up to stop Greg from talking and he did so, his pacing quieted as well as he waited for the man to finish processing. A moment later, Lonny's head twitched sideways, as if flipping a thought over in his head. His eyes narrowed. He reached into his back pocket and pulled out some folded up papers, ones from Rex's apartment. Greg walked over to look at them too. They were the docs from Rex's closet, the screenshots.

"Look at this date," Lonny asked, pointing at the handwriting at the bottom of one of the messages to Rex from the mystery person.

"Nine days ago," they both said, nearly at the same time.

"Okay," Lonny started, his body fidgeting excitedly on the couch. "So Rex, who has been actively watching over this place for…" He looked at the other doc. "For a decade about, gets a new note that he will be paid double, and then sees that this floor is acting up, and calls you in to fix it? Why would he do that?"

"That is weird, huh. Maybe it didn't happen in that order, though. Maybe he didn't get the message until after he had already sent you and had you fix it and everything."

"That would explain a lot, I guess. Maybe he started getting paranoid about the floor after he got the message, and then started watching me."

Greg thought back to Rex catching him in the closet, and then to Rex catching him leaving the floor.

"He was probably checking in on me the day I went into the floor. That would explain why he was standing in the elevator when it dropped down to pick me up from the lift. He was already suspecting me."

"He probably knew that he was going to be killed anyway, since you trespassed in there, and decided to have a peak then as well."

I did kill Rex after all, Greg thought. *I'm surprised that he didn't throw me down the elevator shaft.* He thought of the pic on the computer. *He's probably had a crush on me this whole time. It probably saved my life.*

Lonny gestured for Greg's phone back.

"What are you thinking now?" Greg asked.

"Your new shots catch the other side of the processors. Maybe you caught a better angle on those advanced processors this time."

Greg opened the pic and handed it back to Lonny. He squinted at it for a bit.

"It's blurred, but there *is* some kind of marking on the other side. It's grainy, though..." He turned the phone at an angle and zoomed in with his fingers. "I see a little something... maybe a logo?" he asked himself.

Greg sat down next to him to see, leaning deeply over his shoulder, but Lonny shoved him away, annoyed. Greg waited impatiently, wondering when he'd get his turn. A few seconds later, Lonny handed it over to him. "No way to tell what that is."

"What?" Greg said, looking.

"That thing on the corner there," Lonny said and leaned over to point it out, his finger tapping on the processors at the edge of a rack. "There is a logo there, I think. But it's tiny, and you can't tell. Honestly, the only person who will know what these are is the one that made them I bet."

"Yeah, but if you couldn't find it online, why would the

company say... plus..." but he trailed off at the sight of Lonny's glub look. *The company wouldn't tell us shit. If it is criminal, they'll want to stay away. Or they'll throw up alarm bells and we'll never find out.* "Fuck it. Let's throw it online like you said then. Maybe someone with more talent than you or I will find a way to improve on the image or something."

"Are you sure *now?*" Lonny asked mockingly. "Once we put it out, it will be impossible to take it back."

Greg thought silently for a bit, his body swaying slowly back and forth on the couch cushion. "Let's do it," he said. "We *are* backed into the proverbial wall. Maybe someone online will know. Either that or we'll end up like Rex."

"Not funny," Lonny replied.

"I know," Greg said wearily, understanding that making light was impossible now, and might never be again.

After much debate, they decided to start small and put up a cropped version of the image on some nerdy-looking online photography forum they found to see if some do-gooders could enhance the grainy logo more. If successful enough, it would make it easier to photo search the logo themselves rather than have to put it up on an opinion forum for clues.

"The more niche the only sphere, the more unlikely our subject is to attract too much attention," Lonny reckoned. "The forums are monitored regularly. God knows what the wrong eyes might think."

It seemed a little *too* paranoid, Greg thought, not to mention slow, what with the fact that they were sitting in a barred apartment and all, their only "proof" a still shot and not a dead body, but he didn't push it. Better to let it ride for once and give up the reins a little to Lonny.

After the upload, they had nothing to do but wait, so as Lonny busied himself in the kitchen, cooking up some pasta that he had rustled up from his tiny, grimy pantry, Greg sat by the barred window, staring out at the slow, orange and brown fade in of dawn on the cityscape sky.

They had spent the entire night plotting and debating and freaking out, and for some reason, he didn't feel tired at all.

He thought better of calling Janice at such a late hour. He hoped she was sleeping. He didn't text her either. She'd check it and then reply and then they'd go back and forth... She needed to rest. He settled for geolocating her instead. Her phone was still at the hospital, in the urgent care ward. He got up and stretched a bit and then sat on the windowsill and stared out again, his mind stuck on the implications of an overnight stay at the hospital, what that meant, whether it was good or bad. On the one hand, she was in a safe ... safe-ish spot, with at least some security. Wasn't that a good thing that they kept her? But on the other hand, didn't that mean that she had injuries that required her to be monitored overnight? He tried to tell himself that probably, *probably*, it was just because of a possible concussion.

Everything okay? He wanted to text her that. He typed it, but then deleted it.

She'd want to know where he was, what he was doing.

The guilt was building up within him. He rubbed his eyes, and tried to segway away from the worry.

He looked through the window onto the courtyard below–a little park with one bleak little tree that provided no shade. On either side were tenant balconies huddling around it in the shape of a U. The crowded look made him sad in a way and reminded him of foreign tenement buildings in some far off third-world country; Fabrics and things hanging from the balconies, unkempt gardens growing everywhere, glowing in the orange light of the emerging sun. On more than one balcony, he saw old *Pro Choice over No Choice* banners, relics of a time when people fought for the right to suicide. He thought back to the marches, the ironic messaging of it all, marching hand in hand–he among them at one point—ready to die for the right to choose death rather than have to live on in a dying world. They were all just afraid that they were going to miss the boat to end it willingly. Slowly dying along with the last vestiges of the population felt like a bad option.

He remembered the schools closing down here and there, more and more as time went on, since there were so few left to teach. Pills and downers and everything else were spreading like wildfire, even after the drug prohibitions hit. Crime and killings were dropping because there was nothing to fight over, nothing to really give a shit about anymore. And then the government had the gall to put up the technological version of a child safety gate on people's suicidal intentions in the hope that it would keep them from offing themselves.

That move was the last straw before the riots. That broke the camel's back. To the streets they went. *PCONC*. Pro choice over no choice. Pro choice to carry out the only sensible choice, the choice to end all choices. Or at least that was what the most fervent of them said on their morbid soap boxes, before lighting themselves on fire in martyrdom.

We all got chipped with the child-lock settings eventually though, didn't we, he thought bitterly. Those that hadn't ended themselves while it was still possible were eventually coerced into taking their medicine. They lined up like everyone else.

We all lined up, he corrected himself, remembering the day that he went in for the injection. Strange that the public went along with it too, what with the vaccine debacle and everything. *You'd think that they'd fight it harder?* He mused. *Perhaps we all wanted to stall our self-destructive sides for a bit, just in case.*

The PCONC martyrs hadn't understood how apathetic the rest in the movement were. With nothing to live for but living, dying for the cause or the ideal or even the clout wasn't enough in the end to take the plunge.

There was always the delusion of hope. There still is.

Hope in what, though? he asked himself suddenly, the word like a finger pointing back at him. *In God? In science? In love? What saved me?* He tried to remember.

It was Janice, he told himself. Nothing else mattered. God was dead for him even before then, and science was always better at creating messes than cleaning them up.

Greg looked long and hard at the input jack on his wrist, toying with the sliding hatch that slid back into his forearm. What a strange graft just so that he could plug into the GR at work.

I can't believe I had to take a psych test just to get this installed, he thought, shaking his head in disbelief. *The government has really herded us into a corral, hasn't it. They are so afraid of us exercising our right to hara-kiri that they will only issue the death tech to the safest of us hope-mongers—God, am I really one of them? Have I sold out Edgar that hard?*

Edgar's face, his old friend's face, popped into his head and he pushed it away.

It was a funny phrase—"death tech," he thought. *I probably could have sold my arm jack and the GR somehow instead of going to all the trouble of energy sapping,* he realized, his mind thinking of the glass rectangle back at work that allowed him to decommission his life-chip. *The work that would go into it would negate its use though,* he realized, looking at his wrist. *You'd have to be crazy to take all the steps to make use of it—buying an unregistered input jack, finding a doctor on the black market to install it. Where would one even find these things? He wondered. And it would all be to, what, just to kill themself? The procedure was horrendous too, he recalled then.*

And I did it all to be an apprentice maintenance tech for a highrise in the city. How laughably mundane.

He found himself toying with a nail that had been hammered into the window. He tried to pull it out with his thumb and index but couldn't. He shut the latch of his jack and it made a satisfying click.

What was so special about this thing on his arm? he

wondered, thinking back to the mark on his wife's arm. Maybe it wasn't. Maybe the thing was just prodding her.

Or not. *Why does it seem to care? Does it want to hack it out and use it to die too?*

So many questions left unsolved, and here he was sitting on a window sill, watching the sun come up, biding his time waiting for some grainy image to be refinished by some online weirdo sitting at home. He hopped onto his feet and shouted over at Lonny, who had his head on the bar counter.

"How's it going, man?" he asked expectantly, hoping to wake him up from his seemingly catatonic state. "Any hits on the picture?"

He raised his head and smiled. "Take a look, man," he replied, pointing lazily at the computer sitting on the couch.

Greg walked over and eyed the site. Sure enough, a few people had attached rendered photos in the comments section. He clicked on the first one. It was a complete makeover.

"Get anything?" Lonny asked as he walked over.

"Yeah," Greg replied, his eye on the sharp rendering of the brand. It was a gray capital G on top of two golden pyramids facing away from each. He angled the computer so that Lonny could see.

"What does this make you think of?" he asked, his voice heavy with implication. It was so obvious. Lonny would know for sure.

"Globatechnics," he replied softly, as if the name itself were a sacred thing.

"Globatechnics," Greg chimed back.

Lonny started back in confusion. "But when I looked them up," he said, his brow furrowing, "that wasn't their logo. I mean, kinda, but not really."

Greg scoffed at him. "Maybe they just changed their logo, or perhaps they have a smaller subsidiary company, one for specialized products like you were thinking those GPU's were."

"Maybe," he said doubtfully. "I'll do some checking."

"Hey, at least we've got a logo now," Greg said almost as if he felt like he had to cheer himself up. "Hopefully it will lead us somewhere. I can't just sit in here until the end of time."

"Nor I."

"Nor I... you dumb, high bastard," he said mockingly and then punched him in the arm.

"Alight, we're done," Lonny said with his hand out, palm up, like some teenager, and got up to grab something to drink from the fridge.

⑬

January 6th, 2029 - *Excerpt taken from Los Angeles Times article entitled "Top Business Acquisitions Shakeups of 2025"*

"A private company by the name of Globatechnics international has purchased four of Gibbon's autonomous military android production centers for an undisclosed sum. Insiders are saying that given the AI regulations and recent years of peace between the United States and former enemies, the company more than likely bought the obsolete factories for pennies on the dollar."

(2063) Since it was getting to be full daytime by now, Greg decided that he'd take the chance and go check in on Janice and then perhaps visit his dad afterwards. It felt intolerable being cooped up in Lonny's small apartment. Plus, so far, he hadn't been much help to Lonny, who had struggled on and off for hours to avail searching for the logo's source online. In the morning, he had a different idea and called an audible, dropping the logo into a few different forums instead for hits, hoping that someone would know and comment. If they had any luck left, it would have to come from the forums, he told Greg. And that would take time.

"We've got loads of that," Greg replied sarcastically as he put his shoes on, his mind already half-way out the door, his heart lifted a little knowing that he'd see Janice soon. Lonny didn't respond though, his face grave and reflective.

Greg sighed, more for Lonny than for himself. They *were* in real danger. That was a fact. But even so, even with the pall of impending death hanging over them, during the night it felt more real to Greg, whereas now, strangely enough, in the light of day it felt more surreal, more conceptual, more abstract.

Things are more precarious now though, he realized, *with it all out there on the web for anyone to see.* Maybe that was on Lonny's mind as well, why he was acting so … stoic.

He felt a pang of urgency grip him and wanted to get out right then and there, to go and see Janice and his dad now while he still could. It kind of scared him, the thought that his days with them might be numbered, the fact that any day he might be saying goodbye. It was a doomsday clock hanging over them, waiting to chime his death toll. In a way, he was running to close out his relationships before it came down on him.

His emotions were all over the place, he thought.

"I gotta go," he declared as he opened the front door, a frantic patter in his chest.

"When you go to see your dad," Lonny replied, stopping him before he could escape, "ask him about the meeting tonight and let me know if he needs anything from me. I want to make sure that everything is set and that there aren't any more hiccups."

"What do you mean?" he asked.

"The meeting tonight is going to be a big one," he said. "It has something to do with that drug. Apparently, there is going to be a vote and it's a big deal. Might send them back to the prohibition days."

"I heard about that," he said, his body ebbing upon the threshold. He wanted to leave, but he wondered what more Lonny knew.

"No biggie," Lonny said finally. "Just ask him to ask his people and then text me what's up."

"Why don't you just ask? Isn't it your place?"

"Wow," Lonny replied. "Doing all this for you and you can't even do me a solid?"

"Fine, fine," he replied and walked off down the hall.

As Greg sat outside Lonny's apartment in his car, he tried texting Janice from the car, eager to see her first, but she didn't reply. He called her then–twice, in fact–but it rang out both times. He wondered whether to just drive to the hospital and ask, or even just call the hospital and inquire about her with them. *Why am I treating her like some girlfriend instead of my wife?* he wondered. She'd think he didn't care ... that he cared more about everything else than actually seeing her. He *did* have to figure it out though. Why couldn't she just understand that? Still, he hadn't checked in on her yet, and it had been almost a day.

She was mad, for sure.

He called the hospital to ask about her.

Yes, she was there, they confirmed.

No, she wasn't busy, or in some pressing engagement, they told him. She was just resting.

Yes, they would transfer him.

She picked up the phone after a few rings. "Yes?" she replied.

"Babe?" he asked hesitantly.

She hung up the phone then with a sudden, loud bang.

So she is mad, he reflected with a frown. He toyed with the thought of calling her back right away, showing her that he wasn't letting down until he got to talk to her, *proving* to her with his determined calling that he in fact cared. *Nope*, he surmised. *This impatience is for you, not her.* It was his thing, had always been his thing. She had told him that many times in the past. He would wait and just call her again later on.

He texted his father a greeting and within thirty seconds, he replied. He was fine, busy, but fine. He was at the cafe.

Like a heroin addict hanging around the park, Greg thought. He texted him that he'd come by to say hello and chat, and then prompted the car to take him there.

The car took him tunnel-ways to the cafe, avoiding the sky-traffic above, which was at its peak during the after-work rush hour. *Bunch of suckers in the city*, he mused. He was usually one of them, he realized suddenly with mixed feelings, knowing deep down that he'd never return to work at Friedmont Towers ever again. It had been such a staple in his life once, not even a week ago. Now it was the opposite, the staple in his possible death … the death of everyone he loved, perhaps.

The thought stuck out to him.

He noticed that the car was taking him down a light, two-way tunnel, less-trafficked, more prone to clogging up. *Not right now, though.* It seemed like good timing, he thought, hanging onto the view. Refreshing. A new way for a new life.

Tell yourself that, he intoned. He rolled down the window.

The tunnel looked especially different with its lights put out, he noticed. Instead, natural lighting did most of the work, peeking through large oval skylights in the ceiling every ten or so feet. An archaic design, he surmised, one that clung to calming ambiance rather than electrical efficiency. It cast unfamiliar shadows than he was used to in his early morning drives to work. The lights of the oncoming traffic seemed to tax his sight more, yet the sides were hidden in blackness, barely lit, other than a bit of small orange road-lighting here and there.

The walls had an almost coppery green look to them, with a different kind of graffiti as well, more artsy than the usual ugly scribblings that he couldn't ever make out as he passed along.

"What," he said aloud, his eyes catching the sight of a face on the wall, a familiar face—Edgar Fuentes, the man that he had literally just been thinking about only a few hours before. It was lit up in a fluorescent kind of paint that seemed to catch in the lighting. *Funny how things appear when you start to think of them,* he thought as he stared it down until it receded back into the darkness.

Suddenly, he recalled the memory of Edgar burning in front of him, his eyes hot and sweating, rolling back into his skull as the pain took his soul out of his body, the angry blazing fire consuming him. It was like witnessing a scene from the bible in all its terrifying glory. He remembered the crowd was stunned silent as they watched it happening, the moment branding itself into their shocked faces. It was more than fear, more than screams and sorrow. Everything was drowned out by the silence, sacred as it was. Everyone worshiped him as he died.

A piece of us all died that day too, he thought. *We didn't really need the movement anymore after that. It all felt suddenly unnecessary. The last old, grumpy bull, driven from the herd, unable to procreate, had fought tooth and nail over the final scrap of dignity left in the field. But still, in the bleakness, the scraps meant so much.*

He wondered what his dad thought of him back then in his rebellious years, when he cared and fought so much for the last little bits of honor in the world. They had become estranged then, soon after his mom died.

So much death and decay all the time, he thought. *And now, for some reason, things feel more alive than ever. Maybe it's this danger surrounding me. Maybe I needed it. Humans need danger to fight for,* he felt then, his heart beating a little more, the fire that he had felt watching Edgar burn all those years ago lighting him up inside one more time. *People killing people, getting killed, fighting, biting, throwing sand at each other. That kind of unrest held mankind for so long, whereas nowadays without it, things feel empty, disjointed, uncoupled.*

So why did you turn your back? He asked himself. *Was it the fear of suicide that pulled you into that castrating life-chip, that thing you had been fighting against all along. You used to be so ready to die, so willing to die for the cause. Why did you let Edgar down like that?*

He wished he hadn't seen Edgar's face on the tunnel wall. It made him sick.

In the end, it really was Janice that turned him away from it. She showed him something else. She made him want to live, and to do that, he had to line up like everyone else to be chipped. He sold out for her. Was that it? Was he selling out? Even if he was, what was wrong with that?

Fucking Edgar, he thought bitterly. That face dredged it all up again.

Hope really does feel delusional here, doesn't it. Suicide back then was the one active stance left to take as the world died, rather than the long drawn out neutering. That was one way to describe it.

It isn't like that now though. Not when I'm knocking on death's door yet again.

Somehow, this situation feels oddly similar. I guess the question is, am I going to be Edgar this time or am I going to chicken out like I did before? Watch the fire, or be the fire?

Only time will tell.

The cafe was abuzz with activity, much more so than usual. People from the church were running around all over the place, setting up party decorations for the evening's emergency meeting. They had paid extra money to book out the entire cafe, Lonny had texted him, so they might question why he, a gentile, an outsider, a Cannanite, was pulling up and ruining the fun. He spotted an amiable looking young woman sitting by the side with a group of children who were all reading in a circle and walked up to her to get a few details. He caught her eye and waved at her as affably as he could.

"Hey, there. Sorry to bug you. I'm looking for my dad, Jacob."

"Oh, I see. I'm not sure where he has gotten off to."

"What have y'all got going on today?"

"There's gonna be some political action tonight that matters a whole lot to us. I'm guessing that you're not one of us then, huh?" Her eyes narrowed slightly, her big smile fading ever so much as well.

"You caught me."

"That's too bad. There's always time. You came on a good day for it, I think."

"I have heard about the vote and everything… But aren't you all celebrating a little early?" he asked, and then started as he caught her eyebrow raise. "No offense or nothing," he added quickly after.

Her lip pulled to one side, and she looked beyond him for a moment, thinking it over. When her eyes came back, she smiled again and chuckled a bit. "I guess I can see how you might think that. No, we don't think we are jumping the gun. It will go our way. We know it will."

He knew that arguing the point was moot, and didn't feel the need, seeing the confident expression on her face. *Solid zeal.* He wondered how that felt.

"So which ballot are we rooting for anyways?" he asked.

"*We* are actually *not* rooting for the ballot. We are against it."

"What is it called anyways?"

"I'll tell you if you promise to vote against it," she said with a wink.

"Sure, sure," he said, holding up his right hand in mock solemnity. "I will vote against it if you tell me."

"I'm not sure I believe you, but okay. The ballot we are opposing is called the M3 Criminalization Initiative."

"M3?" he said. "Oh, is that the street term for the Conduit, or what?"

"Yes, technically it is. M3 is the third version of the original drug, MDMA, which was developed in 1912 for psychiatric counseling. It has obviously been improved since then, and we now rely on it heavily, as I imagine Jacob has told you?"

"Eh, he's told me a bit about it. I didn't know it was Molly."

Her body stiffened and she frowned. "No, it *was.*" The change in her set him back a touch in ponderance. *Was she judging him?* He wondered. It was the molly phrase, he knew. She probably thought he was a drug addict. How ironic.

"If you'd like, I can set up a conversation between you and one of our Aldermen. They can tell you more."

He shook his head, nearly cringing at the offer. "That's okay. I can ask my dad."

"You should. The truth can do wonders, but you must let it in to see."

"Alrighty," was all he could say to that.

A child got up and pulled on her arm, his eyes looking over Greg hesitantly.

"Okay, well thanks for talking to me," he said. "Good luck with the meeting. I hope that you all get what you want from this." He turned to walk away.

"Don't forget to vote," she called as he walked away. "The polls are ending soon. You still have time."

He waved in answer, but inwardly, felt more repelled than ever from supporting their cause. Her whole vibe felt tired and annoying. It reminded him of his childhood spent around the old school evangelicals, the ones who like broken records couldn't stop proselytizing, even when they were surrounded by other members. They had to keep signaling that they were doing what God wanted.

It's never going to change, is it.

He tried not to let it sour him too much, though, the day being what it was for them. Anyone would act like a zealot on such a significant day. In a way, it was their own possible Armageddon. For them, it *had* to be a day of deliverance. It had to be good. Whether or not the vote went through. They'd find a way to spin it.

New Lighters were good at that sort of thing. Hell, any religion was. That's how they survived. The tea leaves always pointed towards prophecy.

Just stay away, he thought as he walked along, his eyes scanning for Jacob. *Don't get caught. Just talk to Dad, and then get out. You have other shit to do.*

His dad was a New Lighter like the rest of them though, he thought grimly. *God, I hope he's not drinking the kool-aid as much as the rest of these people today*, he thought. He would be though. Greg knew he would. He stopped in his tracks, second-guessing his whole plan, thinking that maybe it would be better to stay away.

Right then he spotted him, standing at the end of a hallway by his lover, Betty, in the middle of pinning up a long fuschia colored paper streamer on the wall. He sucked in a breath, his feet shifting, his mind toying with the idea of running.

Jacob caught sight of him then and smiled, his old man eyes opening wide in expectation, a sudden joyful light there. He hastily tacked the corner on the wall, and hurried over to him with his arms out, ready uncharacteristically to actually embrace him. It was so strange that Greg's mouth dropped open at the sight.

Before he could take it in, Jacob's arms were wrapping around him in a warm embrace. With all that was going on, it melted the chinks in his heart, and for a moment, he took it all in with his eyes closed, the old man's familiar musk comforting him like never before. "I guess you're having a good day," he said with a smile.

"The best," Jacob replied softly and sincerely in his ear, his hand patting Greg on the back then. "The best."

"I tried to catch you last time you were here I think, but you jumped out before I could say goodbye to you."

"Oh really?" he asked, pulling back but still holding onto him. "What day was that?"

"Was it yesterday? I think it was yesterday. You guys were all in a hubbub about that supplement you take getting banned by the government." The word "drug" felt wrong to say then and he actively avoided it.

"Yes, yes," he concurred. "That was a tough day. I'm glad we didn't speak then if I'm being honest. Things were really bothering me. I'm okay now though. Better than okay. I spoke with the Aldermen about it actually and now I'm feeling great."

"Oh. Cool," he chimed, forcing it out as positively as he could, feeling the need to mimic his father.

Why was I here? he thought suddenly. *Is it to talk to him about nothing? To ask him about the drug? To talk to him about Betty?* He remembered the man's face in the last meeting, the pained look of it as he stared down at Betty's worn and withered hand in his. This man and that man were completely alien from each other. What had the Aldermen said? he wondered. *And why had he looked so frightened?*

"Hey, dad, do you mind if we talk? I know it's a bad time and all, but I won't keep you for long." The way he said it, the reluctant pleading of it, seemed to sober his father up. His smile was gone. His eyes narrowed slightly, and he ground his teeth for a moment. Then he turned and spoke to Betty.

"I'll be back in a minute, my love," he told her in a deep, comedic voice. She waved him away with a scoff, and he turned and shoved Greg off to walk with him.

He really was in a cheery mood, Greg thought then, a little too cheery, all things considered. That, more than anything, seemed to concern him the most.

The rest of the crack-pots didn't matter, he thought as he regarded them all with their little silly smiles and busied manner, working like ants to ready the place for the big reveal. Let them run to the finish-line, thinking in their heads that there was a big party waiting when for all they knew, there might be a cliff waiting. What would happen to his own dad when the vote came and he was cut off from the drug? What would happen to the old man then, when the lights were turned off?

Something within him told him that he had to save him before that happened. He had to set him up, set him straight somehow.

That or at least understand why his mood was all over the place. Maybe he was on drugs right now, he realized.

Twice Jacob tried to motion him towards different places in the cafe, but Greg refused both times, trying to pull him out of the building and away from his fellow churchgoers, to really catch him out and get his honest and unblemished words, sans bullshitting.

He walked out past the building's threshold and then turned to Jacob to ask him where they could talk outside.

Jacob, a little more concerned now, pointed towards a small little plaza at the corner of the building where some dirty benches were—the perfect metaphor for their conversation to come—and they walked down and over to it.

He wondered whether the right approach to the conversation would be hemming and hawing or getting straight to the point. His hands were sweaty already. He turned to talk, but Jacob was already going.

"You know," he was saying, a little bit of annoyance already in the pit of his throat. "You could have just talked to me about whatever it is you were going to talk to me about over the phone. This really isn't the best time for a real long parlay, son."

I shouldn't have telegraphed so much with this punch, he realized. *I guess bullshitting before the hard stuff is out then.* He thought of the best, most direct, yet tactful way to say what he wanted to. Hopefully, it would be what Jacob needed to hear.

"Okay," Greg started, but cleared his throat awkwardly instead, confused over where to start. He hesitated. "Just take a seat," he nearly commanded, pointing to a nearby bench. "Why don't we both just do that, alright?"

"I don't want to sit," Jacob said and pulled his arm away defiantly. "I want to go in there and hang decorations with my brothers and sisters. Now what is it that is so important that it can't wait until tomorrow?"

"Dad... I... I don't think you should use the Conduit anymore," he replied, his voice louder than he meant, his mind telling him that he played his hand too quickly. *Just like with Janice*, he thought. "It's pulling you into it all too hard, and I'm worried that it's not going to end well if things start to change for you all." By the tight-jawed look on his father's face, he could tell right then that he had kicked a hornet's nest.

"Is this really why you came all the way down here to talk to me?" he started up, a look of disgust on his face. "Have you lost your mind, son?"

"No, Dad," he replied weakly, feeling small, feeling like a son, rather than a man talking to another man. "I was just thinking that—"

"*No*, you weren't," he interjected, his finger pointing at his face all of a sudden. "That's the problem. You never think before you step into my business, do you? First, it was my business with Betty. Now, it's this. What has happened to you? You used to have more respect."

The finger in Greg's face seemed to set him off for some reason.

It was that finger he always used, every time he talked down to him through the years. He tired of it, sick and tired of that lecturing finger all of his life, pointing at him, commanding him to stop. Stop talking. Stop interrupting. Stop thinking. Stop being.

Enough was enough.

"Stop pointing your finger at me," he nearly shouted, and swiped the hand away from his face. "You're not going to just bull me around like what I have to say doesn't matter," he said, feeling awkward at his choice of words. It had been a while since he stood up for himself to this man. Had he ever?

"Oh, *bull* you, huh?" he replied mockingly, honing in on the exact word that had stumbled Greg a bit. "Is that what I've been doing?" Greg was kicking himself inwardly, knowing that he had the emotions right a moment ago, but had fucked it up. "Here I am, big bad Daddy, hanging out with my friends on a nice day when my poor, pathetic, yet *heroic* son comes walking up to help me kick my habits."

"It's not like that, Dad," he replied weakly.

"Well, then. What is it? I'm standing right here now. Go ahead and tell me what I have been missing then." His hands crossed in a way that made him look larger somehow in front of Greg, so imposing. Greg shook his head for a moment, confounded by the break that the sudden burrage from his dad had thrown into his sails. He sat down, his right hand on his forehead, rubbing his temples.

"I don't know why I'm here," he surrendered. "You're never going to listen to me. I just had an urge to talk to you and… and then I was thinking about this vote and all and…" It felt pointless, all of a sudden. He trailed off and then let his head droop.

It seemed to disarm Jacob. His arms, crossed and tensed, felt aggressive suddenly, way too aggressive for a conversation with his own kid. He dropped them then and walked over beside him and sat down. He took a deep breath out, hoping that perhaps that would help to signal a reprieve from their initial argument.

"Honestly, Greg, I guess I'm just surprised at you. You really caught me off guard here, you know? I was having a good day today, hanging out with everyone, setting things up, feeling good about things… It's been a rough couple of days around here with everything that's been going on. But after the talk with the Elders… Aldermen… I was feeling good. I'm hanging out with Betty… We're laughing… I don't know. Can we just… *not* get into all this right now?"

The admission felt honest, Greg thought. In a way, he was right. The timing was terrible.

Then again, the timing would always be terrible. Really, the timing wasn't the problem.

The fucking religion is, he thought. *It's like all the addictions. It staves off the reality, the boring sad reality of things. But when the numbness wears off, the reality hits even worse. And this fucker won't be able to handle it.*

"It's too late," he muttered.

"What?" his dad replied.

"Yeah, I get it. I know it's not the right time, Dad," he said, starting to sit up, "But I mean…" and as he said it, he felt his hands lift for one final argumentative gesticulation, "The ruling on this "conduit" is coming up today… and well… I think that maybe, *just* maybe, if it goes through, it might be for the best, you-know-what-I-mean? I mean, is this *really* how you wanna end your life?"

He was surprised by the frankness of the final question, the fact that he was chiming in on his dad's very mortality mere moments after he had told him that he didn't even want to talk. It was too far. It was. But what else was he going to say?

"See," his dad replied, his finger starting to lift, and then falling to his wasteside again, "Why do you have to go and say it like that? With the whole "this" conduit. You've never respected it… respected the process… respected this place. Not ever."

Jacob did have a point there, Greg mused. He knew that he didn't respect it. Why would he? It was the same as the other one. Just a few dumb updates. He wanted to say it, but he held his tongue for a minute, trying his best not to cut Jacob off. A silence hung between them, and he pivoted, thinking better than to come off like a jerk.

"It's just that… well… I've been there before, at least, you know, before, back when we were Jehovah's Witnesses. This whole thing you guys are doing up there. It just feels like a wacky… It just feels wacky is all. It feels desperate, like you are just losing your mind without Mom watching you." There it was, he thought. *Mom is in this conversation now.* She always was, hidden in the silence between them.

"Mom," Jacob replied, his head shaking in disbelief. "How did I know that this had something to do with your mother? She was in control of everything, wasn't she? She's controlling us now, even though she's been dead for I don't know how long. Still, I can't do anything right, can I? Okay, okay. Can I tell you the truth?" He looked at Greg then, willing him to look back at him too. "I don't even think I believe in any of it."

Greg scoffed, completely thrown by the turn that his father had made in the conversation, almost unable to process whether or not he was still telling the truth.

Jacob's right hand went up like. "Swear to God," he said, his face firm and resolute, no hint of doubt on it.

"Suuuuuuuuure," Greg replied, swiping his dad's lifted hand away.

"No, no," Jacob interjected, his body facing him, both hands moving to hold Greg where he sat. "You can believe me on this one. But hey, let me tell you. I know which way is up and it's not because of God that I'm here. I'm here because of *that* place," he said, his finger pointing up at the cafe. "I have been saved, not by God, and not by religion, but by that drug you hate so much that you think it's the devil, and by that community there. That's my god, whatever you may think." He stopped then and let Greg soak it up so far.

"Now your mother," he continued. "God rest her soul or whatever, your mother was a great leader, and I was down to follow her. I would have followed her anywhere. I followed her to church every Sunday, and Tuesday too, and even on Saturday to go out in service and knock on doors. But when your mom died, I really did lose my leader. I wasn't being controlled anymo— … *led* anymore. I had nowhere to go anymore. It was all me. And man did I feel empty inside. But when I put on that headset in there and took that drug, I felt free of all the negativity that I was harboring, of all the worries that I had about what to do or whether it was right or wrong, or what to eat, or who to talk to. All the bullshit. It was gone. I feel like now, I'm a changed man. I have stopped judging things, stopped seeing right or wrong, good from bad. I'm just a passenger along the ride, with that drug in control, in utter paradise."

He went silent, his finger pointing slowly at the building, his eyes wet as if he were on the verge of tears, or at least doing a good job of making himself look like it.

"Say what you want about the specifics of New Life, but that place up there, the people in that place up there, they are for real, and me and them, we want the same thing, to give up control and to live in the paradise now. We're like buddhist monks practicing the art of not existing before it creeps up on us."

"A real grief center, huh?" Greg piped in, a little sarcastically. "And isn't this place called New Light, anyways?"

"New Light, New Life. It's all the same at the end of the day anyways," he replied and laughed, his face returning to the same old sour-faced Jacob Greg had grown accustomed to.

"Dad," Greg replied, eager to chime in while the open version of his father was around and kicking, "Have you ever wondered whether maybe your whole fear of control and belief in God might be two sides of the same problematic coin? Maybe you and your friends up there should just try to exist more in the present and take responsibility for every moment in it, rather than throw your hands up and wait around for something that might never happen."

As if in reply, Jacob simply closed his eyes and smiled, his hands turned up like an old man with nothing to hide, nor anything left to say.

Greg shrugged his shoulders to himself, feeling the same way.

"All that I'm saying is," his dad replied, reeling him back to his main point, "And I mean this without trying to throw out whatever good intentions you had in coming here and all ... it's just ... can't you just let me live the rest of my life the way that I want to live it? Can you do that?"

Greg's mind went back to the man with the kid during the meeting and his crying. It was such real crying, even though the man was literally in a virtual simulation. So much for reality, he thought. Better for some to live in delusion. Looking at his father then, whose eyes were now regarding him again, he wondered whether or not delusion was the right thing to feel after all in a world gone gray.

"You sound just like Janice." It was all he could say. It was probably the opposite of what Edgar would say, he mused in the recess of his brain

"How's she been these days anyways?" he asked.

That's when Greg remembered that he hadn't heard back yet from her and that she was on the other side of town, sitting in a hospital bed, and more than likely, absolutely livid that he hadn't arrived yet to check up on her.

"Oh shit. I gotta go." With that, he got up, gave his dad a hug, and ran to his car.

 14

Greg got to the hospital quickly, parked the car—close this time —and then ran inside to pay his wife a much needed visit, feeling stupid that he hadn't just gone earlier. He got to the nurse's desk and asked to see her.

"Room 115, but she's nearly gone," the man in the light blue smock informed him. "It's good that you are here now, though," he remarked disapprovingly. "Someone in her family needs to accompany her out." He scoffed and turned his back to Greg. For a moment, it made him angry, but then he faltered. Maybe the man was right in his judgment.

On his way to the room, he stopped by the gift shop with the thought of grabbing her some flowers or chocolate perhaps–the dark kind, he felt since that was her favorite. It was a pretty sparse affair inside, though, overly fluorescent like a drug store, forgotten, stretching long enough to sell out of everything before shutting down. He felt deflated at the prospects, but moving around the place, on the back wall, he found some get-well-soon items and settled on a small white teddy bear strapped to a box of dark chocolate candy kisses.

Without further dawdling, he walked—more like snuck—up the hall, around a corner and then into her room. The door was cracked, but it was dark inside. It was a large, shared space divided by shower curtain-style partitions. He poked his head into the first two patient areas to the sight of separate, sleeping, elderly women, but then as he peeked into the third and final area, he locked eyes with his wife tucked up in the corner in her bed, her gaze already narrowed in steely response to him.

"Funny seeing you here," she remarked in a sour, yet playful drawl that caught him off-guard, relieving his nerves a touch. *Maybe I am safe after all*, he thought. She was sitting up, a bandage around her head like a partially unwoven mummy, her hands held on her lap like a good little patient, a cute and welcome sight. He walked up to her side and caressed her shoulder lightly. She moved to one side and patted the bed for him to get in, so he put the teddy gift down on the nightstand, took off his shoes, and hopped in eagerly, grateful to be close to her now that she was happy, healthy, and safe.

"I figured you would be mad," he admitted, his head shaking guiltily.

She shrugged a bit shily, the gesture unlike her. "Yeah, well … it seems like you've got a long going on. "

You've got it right there, he thought. *Still.* "Yeah, but I should have stayed."

"Stop beating yourself up, babe," she replied. "I'm happy that you're here. And you are."

Damned if she isn't in a surprisingly great mood, he thought, looking at her rather quizzically.

"Let's just enjoy it here until they kick us out," she said. "The food is pretty good. It's almost dinner time, too." She pointed to the table next to her. "You can order on the menu over there. Pretty sure you're covered with me."

She noticed the teddy bear gift he had placed on the table and chuckled. "You seeing some sick five-year olds in here after you're done with me or what?"

"No, just you," he replied, bringing his arm up over her to

pull her in closer. She laid her head on his shoulder and he kissed her on the forehead.

"That reminds me," she said excitedly, her hand slapping his thigh. "You remember those Fogal Bears that were a big thing when we were kids? One of the nurses was telling me that she saw one of them at a digital memorabilia store selling for 42 million dollars! Most expensive one yet, apparently. It sold in less than a day too."

"Fogal Bears?" he replied, trying to recall them.

"You know... They were those small teddy bears with long horse hair wigs that came with a comb."

"Oh, yeah," he said. "Weren't those gone like forever ago?"

"Yeah, but I had one! I should've kept it. Damnit."

"Why would you? Who would even keep around that kind of shit anyways?"

"Well... you can imagine why they're collector's items now," she replied, taking his question differently than he intended it. He furrowed his brow for a moment, but then caught on to her allusion. It was because of the lack of children that the toy was made for. "They're probably the biggest collector's items now," she added.

"You'd know, I guess, you little weirdo," he replied, and her hand slapped his stomach again, harder than before. He laughed and held her hand down jokingly on her stomach. "Hey, cut it out," he said.

"Yeah, whatever," she replied, shrugging him off of her. She regarded him suddenly, her light brown eyes catching in the light. "I'm just saying that it's kind of crazy, you know? The things that people spend their money on these days is getting to be a little nuts."

He thought for a moment about the sad saps that were buying old children's toys that their kids probably grew up with, or worse, that *they* did.

"It kind of makes sense, though, in a way," she continued, a little more somberly than before, the joy in her voice somewhat evaporated. "They were *the* main toys on the market back then when everything started to fall apart. You were a little older than me at the time, so maybe you didn't see it as much, but I was still in elementary school, so I saw a lot more of the chaos and the teacher heartache back then than you did, I think. I remember it so well, even now. Teachers were dropping like flies… all of our classes were getting pushed together… I bet that my senior year was close to one of the last senior classes in the country."

She was probably exaggerating, but it hit home nonetheless.

"Yeah, I remember that too. All of them were hurting. It makes sense."

"I remember one of my teachers even crying during class one day, saying that this was going to be the last group of kids he was going to be teaching."

"Boy is that rough," he said, and blew a raspberry. "Imagine devoting yourself to a career that becomes obsolete just like *that*. Sorry, teachers, no need for you anymore. They were all captaining their own sinking ships."

"*His* name was Mr. Fredricks."

"Who?"

"The guy who cried. Everyone in class called him Mr. Freddy. He quit halfway through the year, and we got some random subs for a while, and then I remember we were shoved into another teacher's class."

"They must have been really scrambling."

"I mean, can you see why? Everyone was probably running away from that profession as quickly as possible. I know I would! Either find something else to do or say hello to home-lessness. No need for them anymore. What's left after that? It's adapt or off yourself like one of those PCONC'ers."

"Hey, hey," he said, a little offended. "Those PCONC'ers were making a lot of sense back then." She eyed him, and he twitched his head. "I mean, when you consider things, is all I'm saying."

She regarded him with pursed lips, no doubt recalling his time as one back when they first started dating.

"But yeah, those Fogal Bears were a big deal," she continued. "I remember the commercial. Oh? You know what. I'm pretty sure they cut it in fact. Must have really given up, huh."

"Can you even blame them?" he asked weakly, almost to himself.

"I guess not... Damn, I should have kept mine," she said hopelessly.

"Would have made us one wealthy couple. Probably could have bought some awesome penthouse loft on some skyscraper above the smog."

"Yeah, sure," she chided him. "Would take a billion bucks to get that high."

"Yeah," he agreed. "So how did this come up anyway? About the Fogal Bears with the nurse? Were you just chatting her up or what?"

"I actually interrupted her talking to one of the other nurses about it. I guess one of them had to calm down some woman in the police wing of the hospital who was acting all deranged talking about how she was going to get her kid one of the bears after she had it, like as a gift or something."

"Kid?"

"Yeah. Apparently, she was in there because she was trying to carry a baby to term, and, well, you know..." Her voice trailed off.

"Aww man. That's crazy," he muttered. "I still can't believe women are still trying that. You'd think people would have given up by now."

"Some people never get it, I guess," she replied.

His musing about her being a good mother the night that they had made love bubbled up into his head suddenly, and for a second, he thought of bringing it up. *Better to hold it in*, he thought a little bitterly. His silent stare betrayed itself to her as she watched him.

"What are you thinking about?" she asked, appraising him. He looked at her, his eyes gauging her mood, trying to figure out how much she could take, what she would think if he said it.

"I was just thinking about something the other night," he started.

"What was it?"

"I don't know," he said, beginning to hem and haw a little, fumbling over whether or not to skip it. She nudged him to continue, so he did. "Do you ever wonder what it would be like... how it would be if we had kids?"

Her head cocked away from him, as if the question itself passed by her face and she were physically avoiding it. He watched her chest go down as she breathed out.

"I don't know," she finally said, the words almost unwillingly forcing themselves out. "You know how it is. Of course I think about it, but I mean... Who does it help to think about things like that? Things that are never going to happen for people like you and me?"

"I saw this woman from one of those island countries... you know... the ones where they are still able to have children."

"When?" she asked, perking up.

"The other day outside the VR theater when I was talking to Lonny." He stopped for a moment, wondering whether to tell her the whole story then. "I made a comment that made her mad. She stormed off."

"Of course you did," she scolded him.

"It wasn't *that* bad," he protested.

"Sure."

"I mean, it wasn't my finest moment, but it was just an ignorant comment to Lonny that she overheard."

"Did you apologize?"

"I was going to, but she ran off before I could. Honestly, I wish I could have talked to her, to maybe understand their side a little better."

She humphed. "I don't think either of us would really understand. They have the means, however limiting it may make things for them. We don't. That's a bridge too far for us to cross, I think."

"Maybe. But yea, it all just made me think about… things… again."

"Was she cute?" she asked, her eyes trained on him.

"You *would* ask that, Jealous," he replied, smiling and nudging her shoulder. "Honestly, no. You know how it is for them, what with the RBV or whatever and all."

"Oh, yeah," she replied, cringing. "Poor thing. Was it bad?"

"Yeah, it was," he said sadly. He shook his head. "Saved internally, but scarred externally," he mused. "I wonder what's worse."

"If you were a woman, you wouldn't be saying that at all," she replied sourly.

"I guess so," he said, catching the frustration in her words.

"You have no idea," she added, her voice low. She turned her head away from him and stared out the room's small, dirty window.

Their time to leave was probably coming to an end, Greg felt, so when he saw the on-call nurse walking by, he took the opportunity right then and ran out after her, hoping to beg for more time.

Gauging her level of sympathy—or lack of sympathy rather by the implacable stare she gave him—Greg switched the plan from begging to lying.

"I've noticed that my wife's voice has been slurring."

"What?" she asked, her face suddenly concerned.

"Yeah, and she's been saying some strange things."

"Like what?"

"I don't know, but at times, it doesn't make a whole lot of sense. Is there anything you can do?" It might have been overkill, but he figured it was better safe than sorry. If this didn't flag her for extra observation time, nothing would.

She held up her hand to wait, and then walked over to an

attending in a white doctor's coat. A moment later, they came over to him, the grave look on the nurse's face as she looked at him—a good sign, he thought. Yes, it was concerning, they agreed, and yes, they would hold her for another day in hospital to monitor her further.

Boo-yah.

He left them and walked back in and with a smile, telling Janice what he had accomplished. She applauded his acting skills and then kissed him, pleased.

"So you're going back to Lonny's place, then?" she asked, guessing his motives even before he had brought anything else up.

"Yeah. I think so," he admitted. "We are still waiting on the forums for information, but maybe we can put our heads together some more and figure out another angle on the other stuff."

"You think there *is* another angle?" she asked.

"Maybe," he said, shrugging hopelessly. "Who knows."

He got up, but she held him back for a moment, gripping his hand tighter than before. Sitting there together reminiscing about the past was nice, they both felt in that moment, so much so that Janice had suddenly become aware of a great longing to take account of things gone by, even the sadder nostalgia lost to time in the grayness. All the old, familiar voices she could talk to about such things were gone, she reflected sadly, all eventually having drifted away from the city's society into the quietly forgotten sticks to die.

The living were huddled together like scared little naked children cowering around the fire, clinging to hope in the worst way possible, by avoiding the past like it was some ugly, infected, open-wound.

Greg was all she had.

He looked into her eyes and smiled, his eyes locked onto, no doubt wondering what had gotten her so quiet all of a sudden. She pulled him in close.

Greg is different, she thought. *He's hopeful... well... most of the time, around me.*

That was what had pulled her into his wake in the first place.

The image of her half brother, Job, who had moved to a cabin in the woods and stopped talking to people, shot into her head suddenly, but she pushed it down. Her smile faded then, and her grip on him slackened. He looked down at her and saw that she was caught in her head ahead, so he nudged her over on the bed and layed back down. Things would have to wait a little longer.

15

Greg didn't end up leaving for Lonny's place until the evening, a lot later than he had expected. He wondered if Lonny would be annoyed. He took the same tunnel as before—Edgar's tunnel—and as he drove along, his sight drifted towards the wall graffiti as it sailed by, his mind dialed into the 'art' ever since he had seen the mural of his old friend. For the most part, it was just drivel, but even so, the colors were quite intoxicating amidst the grime, a photo filter highlighting the brightness within a dim and otherwise unremarkable scene. The city was good for that though, wasn't it, he mused. The garishness within the grime brought something up from deep within him, long buried.

All of a sudden, Lonny's avatar appeared on the car infotainment screen and he prompted the pickup button. Lonny's voice came over the speakers loud and frantic from the other line.

"Dude, get down to the VR theater!" he shouted. "It's burning!"

"What?" he replied incredulously. "What happened?" *Dad*, he thought. *Dad is in there with the others.*

"I'm heading there now! The liquor store across the street called. They said that it was completely ablaze. Hurry man! Your dad and all those other people are probably still in there!"

"I'm on my way," he said, re-prompting the car to the new address and turning up the speed to its limiter mark. "I'll be there as soon as possible."

"I hope it's not too late."

"God, I hope not," he replied as the line dropped. What was happening to his family? he thought. The answer came to him so simply. It was that thing. It had to be. He felt himself wanting to throw up. What had he done, opening that Pandora's box of a room, letting that curse out? The yellow eyes had nearly snatched him, had attacked his wife, and now they were coming for his father.

Worst of all. He had just seen the man, and hadn't even thought to warn him. He was too busy arguing with him. The guilty thought sat with him the entire way to the cafe—six agonizingly long minutes.

The view from the car was nothing short of fiery pandemonium as he pulled up to it from above, a distant bird's eye view on the whole tragic scene. There was absolutely nowhere to land, the smoke so thick that a high output, amber colored caution beacon had been set directly above the fire, cordoning off the scene for a hundred feet in all directions to air traffic trying to pass over. With the glinting metallic lines of vehicles all swirling around at various heights, hugging the legal boundary as much as possible to afford a view, it looked almost like a large smoky tornado, pulling in everything around it as it rose up into the darker brackish smog above, the yuck meeting the supreme yuck.

Greg tried to bypass the safety measures on the car, but it refused his attempts each time. After the third try failed, the car flipped into autopilot and locked him out entirely, hovering in place for a moment in a sort of personified stubbornness.

If only he hadn't traded in his last car, he thought frustratedly, he'd be able to maneuver closer and land right in front of the place. He shook the wheel angrily, and the screen re-prompted a warning at him:

No-fly zone ahead. Choose from the following safe locations, or move along at the required distance.

The nearest safe zone on the map was an entire three blocks away, he saw, but he selected it anyway, hoping to God to at least get things moving again. The car accepted and then turned and headed away at a slow, methodical pace, descending here and there amidst the chaos all around it towards the prescribed landing area.

It took two full minutes to touch down. The doors finally unlocked to let him exit, and Greg practically ripped the inner door handle off getting out to run to the scene.

The streets leading up to the blaze were abuzz with people, moving like him closer and closer to the sight. Most, he noticed, moved along with strange ambivalence, already with phones out recording what they saw. He shouted angrily as he ran to prompt them out of the way, pushing the dawdlers like some vigilante chasing a purse thief.

He was sprinting so quickly that something in his knee twinged and then started to jolt with every pound of his foot on pavement. He winced, but pressed on as quickly as possible, bent on getting there before it was too late. He came upon a barricade, so he ducked down a small, empty alley, ran up it to the next street over, and came out onto a large opening in the road, right there in front of the building. The hotness of it heated his face up as if he had just shoved it in the oven.

The blaze looked massive from the ground, how a campfire probably looked to an ant.

The front door of the entrance was completely gone, the porch roof caved in completely in front of it, and from each of the openings, flames were pouring out onto the sidewalk, their billows rising into the air. There was water here and there being sprayed into the chaos, but it all looked so ineffectual, he thought hopelessly, nothing more than a bit of satiation to keep it all at bay while it burned itself out. There was no subduing it. The bedlam would linger until there was nothing left of the place.

Anything in there was toast, part of him thought, though he pressed it down immediately.He tried to step up further, his arm held aloft to buffet the heat, but after a few steps, he had to stop, the pain too intense. He lingered for a second, but then fell back to the corner, proceeding along the far perimeter of the scene towards one of the building's sides. There were bunches of spectators, some holding each other, some crying. Some were covered from head to toe in soot, but he didn't approach them for info as he moved past, guessing instead from their casual garb that they weren't from the theater. More than likely, they were probably from the connected buildings that had been evacuated.

Who to ask? he thought in a panic. There *were* emergency workers running around—firefighters, police, a few EMT's—but they didn't have time for him.

His phone! He realized, and pulled it out to call Jacob. He saw that Lonny had called twice. *He's probably here as well*, he reckoned, *wandering around as well, hopelessly trying to get a read amidst the chaos.* He called his father and held the phone tightly to one ear while plugging the other with his thumb, trying to drown out the noise around him.

It went straight to voicemail.

He is burned up in the flames, it all seemed to say, the idea catching ablaze within him now like the fire he couldn't help but stare at. *Probably why it went to voicemail. The thing's probably in there too maybe, melting away in the heat and the tragedy with him.*

Suddenly, his phone rang and he picked it up.

"Dad!" he cried.

"Who? No, it's Lonny," his friend yelled back over the noise on his end.

"Lonny? Have you heard anything yet?"

"Not yet!"

"Where are you?" he asked, his eyes trolling around the crowd for him. Over in one of the huddled masses on the further sidewalk, he spotted a barista he remembered from the Kava house, so he ran over to talk to her. She had tears in her eyes.

"Do you know what happened?" he asked abruptly, skipping the pleasantries.

She didn't respond right away, her face staring ahead in concentration.

He waited, shuffling hesitantly. "Excuse me," he asked.

A second passed, and then she sighed and waved her hand in a circular motion around the brim of her glasses. A small light on the lens blinked twice.

"No, I haven't."

She was frowning at him, and he suddenly put it together. *She was recording, and he had interrupted her.* She pulled off her glasses and he saw that she had a single tear in her eye. For some reason, it made him wonder if she actually cared or was just acting like she cared. She wiped it away, and then proceeded to clean her glasses on the hem of her shirt with the other hand. "I was just working," she explained, "Then all of a sudden some people were screaming that there was a fire, so I ran out into the street to look, and it was already massive like this." She was saying it all so matter-of-factly. "I don't know how something so big could have started so fast."

She paused, her own words sinking in. "It lit up so fast," she repeated. "Almost like kindling." Without another word, she put her glasses back on and waved her hand in the same way as before over them, the lenses dimming suddenly... ending the conversation as quickly as it had started. She was speaking again —not to him though—her voice full of drama. She was explaining it all again.

He melted away from her without another word, his mind

lost in thought. It was strange, he felt, this *sickness* all around him, when something so avoidable like a fire could be happening, could even *be allowed* to be happening, in such a modern world, while all the bullshit tech out there, all the garbage people just had to have to satisfy their whims, their desires, was so plentiful.

All the entertainment one could desire, yet not enough to address the real needs.

It made his heart sink.

He saw that Lonny was still on the phone, and put it up to his ear again, his mind more lost than ever.

Suddenly, the girl's words came to him. *Almost like kindling.*

"Hey," he shouted, hoping that Lonny was still listening, "Do you think it was *that* thing?" The question itself settled badly after he had said it, something about it striking him as oddly self-incriminatory. He wondered if Lonny felt the same, and waited for his verdict on the other line. Nothing came through though. No one was there, or maybe there was and he couldn't hear.

Or maybe he doesn't want to say, Greg thought, but then he shook his head and hung up the phone.

The connection is crazy, he told himself. *This fire was just fate.* It felt like fate was against them all now.

A grazing blow from a woman racing by nearly knocked him over and he snapped back to reality. He had to move or act or do something. He didn't exactly know what, but god knew that he had to do more than just stare like the other fools piling in around him on the sidewalk, their faces lit up, aghast, tuned in fully to watch the show. His father was maybe in there right now, burning.

He analyzed the scene for a moment, and noticed that there weren't any ambulances in the front. There had to have been some that had arrived by now. That would mean that they were around the back then, he deduced. Maybe he could get around somehow, perhaps to where the survivors were.

The street to get around was blocked off and clogged though, he saw plainly from the mess of service vehicles, police cars, and fire-trucks bunched up against each other. They wouldn't let him through there, he thought. He ran west down the row of connecting buildings, looking for an opening. They looked closed, and there was no way around.

Then he caught sight of a small Chinese restaurant, still blessedly lit up for business, an open sign glowing neon through the window. Of course, given their vicinity, they were probably not entertaining customers, but still. He ran up hurriedly to the door, where a large, stocky asian man in a maroon apron stood with his arms crossed, his eyes trained on the flames, his frame planted right in front of the door. When he noticed Greg, he waved his hands silently for him to go away, his expression obvious—*Get the fuck out of here. This place isn't open, dummy.*

"I just want to get around," Greg said imploringly, but the man didn't even look back at him. Greg waved at him, but he turned his body in the direction of the fire, his face a mask of indifference. Greg scoffed and tried to wiggle past the back of him, the tiniest of room available to get in, but suddenly the man's large hand came up and shoved him back, his other hand waving angrily in his face.

"No, no," he replied angrily this time around, his face scrunched up into a stolid, unsympathetic, scowl. "Not open!" He through the entrance's metal screen door closed to block the way completely and then stepped up a bit to Greg, his eyes looking beyond him, strangely antagonistic, as if he were waiting for Greg to provoke him.

"The lights are on," he shouted into the man's face, his finger pointing at the lit *open* sign. "Just let me go through the back. I'll buy whatever you want. I'll buy the whole place. I just need to get though."

The man's face didn't change.

Enough is enough. Greg let out a growl of frustration, and without thinking, shoved the worker back hard into the screen door, the thin steel rattling loudly as he crashed into it. The man's eyes went wide in shock, and as he righted himself, Greg could feel tears welling up, the burst of emotion that came sometimes when he got too physical.

He started to stammer out an apology, but didn't get far because the man's response cut him off, a wordless response, a shove of his own, harder and more forceful, right in his face. He felt his nose smoosh in as the force of it knocked him back. His feet fumbled to stay underneath him, but then a crack caught his heel and tripped him. He felt himself fall… far… off the curb and into the road, nothing but air for a split second before the asphalt caught him painfully in the small lump of his upper back, just below the neck.

The pain shot throughout his back and neck like electricity, but luckily his head hadn't cracked the ground, otherwise it would have knocked him out. For a moment, he laid there with his eyes closed, moaning lowly. When he opened his eyes finally, he saw that the man was standing directly over him, his finger pointing nearly into his eye, his face reddened with rage. For a few seconds, he shouted down in words that Greg couldn't understand, his mouth spitting the entire time. Then he stopped and pressed his finger down hard on Greg's forehead.

"Fuck. You," he said slowly, and then he spat a wad of mucus into his eye, then he stood up, turned away and walked back to the restaurant.

Greg heard the screen door slam. He sat up slowly and saw that the man was just inside, staring him down.

Not only had he not gotten to the other side, Greg thought as he got up and brushed himself off, but now he felt like shit too. He turned and walked away from the restaurant, back to the fiery scene and the mess of cars that had been blocking his way.

There was an opening in the road now, he saw, large enough for vehicles to get through. Unfortunately, there was also a cop standing watch over it, his hands out as he warded people away, waiting to let what would probably only be emergency service workers get through. Greg eyed the scene beyond for a time, noticing the gang of paramedics, firefighters, and cops all racing around. Past them though, he could make out vaguely a few groups in weathered clothing sitting down, possibly churchgoers, he thought.

He toyed with the idea of just walking up to the cop and begging him to let him through, but something about the man's demeanor held him back. It was his stoic face... his stance. It was all too formal. Greg shook his head. This man was a rule follower. Talking wouldn't get him through.

He scanned the road for some other pass-through. To his left, choked in like a giant white cow at the feeding trough, he noted a tall white delivery truck, its carriage high off the ground.

High enough to crawl under, perhaps, he thought. And it looked like there wasn't a whole lot to obstruct him on the other side.

He waited for a second until the cop turned his head the other way and then he ran up and scooched underneath it on his belly, sliding painfully as quickly as possible to the other side, the heat of the asphalt burning his hands as he shuffled along. It felt impossibly wide, but a second later, he emerged on the other side, and then he wasted no time, shuffling past the other cars to the open ground beyond, his head down to avoid catching the attention of the cop.

It worked. He made it to the other side, finally. It was a much less crowded scene than from the front, he noted immediately, seeing that other than emergency workers still racing around, there were none of the looky loos and recorders standing and gawking at the action. Just groups of people consoling and being consoled. Next to an ambulance parked up against a large concrete wall, he saw a few soot-covered people sitting huddled on a curb close together, dressed up in the tattered versions of their Sunday best. He walked over to them.

"I'm sorry to bother you," he tried to say in a calm and polite manner. "Were you three in there when it all started to go?"

The two that were further away didn't look up, but shared

looks with each other that told him that they didn't want to be bothered. The one closest looked up at him tiredly.

"Yeah, we were there," she muttered pathetically. "We were there."

He felt awkward standing staring down at them, but not wanting to squander the opportunity, sat down next to the muttering girl anyways, keen on getting any information that would lead to his father. "I'm so sorry, and I'm sure you probably don't want to talk, but It's just that my dad... I think my dad might have been in there, and I can't seem to get a hold of him."

She regarded him then with a sympathetic frown that spoke to what he was wondering, understanding that the possible news from her might ruin him forever. "Was he a member of New Light?" she asked.

He nodded.

She looked down. "I'm sorry," she replied, trying to hold in the tears. "I think we might be the only ones that made it out."

For some reason to Greg, the news itself didn't actually shock him, but the fact that it didn't felt like the worst part in a way. He just knew it in the pit of his stomach right when he had pulled up to the blaze. The size of it had sapped any hope immediately.

The other two were looking at him now as well, their expression much the same, of sad, unwanted kinship with the stranger who had lost along with them something that would never be filled again. He felt himself swaying silently, while the woman next to him, the harbinger of bad news, had tucked her head into her knees and was crying muffled tears, hugging herself tightly, her back shaking with the sobs. The raw exposure of the emotion itself pulled at something within him, a longing to feel close to something, to be rather than think, and his arm came up over the girl's shoulder as he wrapped around her, holding her lightly, comrades in sorrow. A moment later, another arm came up over his, and then for a while at least, they stayed there, huddled together silently, a strange group brought together in the worst way possible, with a woman crying at the bottom.

After a while, the woman calmed down and they parted from each other, still sitting together. He waited before opening his mouth again, feeling an eagerness creeping up inside of him to learn more about what had happened inside the building before the fire.

He cleared his throat. "So what *happened* in there anyways?" he asked the group, softly, as innocently as possible. The last one straightened up then, her hands in her lap, and faced him.

"We weren't really there when it happened, honestly."

"We had gone out to vape in the back," the other one chimed in, her eyes on him. "Everyone was linked in. Everyone, even the ministerial servants, who usually stay to monitor everyone in case somebody needs help... We were all just so excited. Everyone was so happy. The vote had come through, so we were celebrating, and..."

She fell silent and he could tell that she was back in it. A moment later, the last one chimed in as well.

"Me, Janie, and Adam partook the conduit preemptively. Honestly, we often did it like that at the meetings. We just can't help ourselves sometimes. That's why we came out of it first. We all linked up and snuck outside for a breather. The outside air always helps when you're dropping back into reality after the whole paradise-bang of it all. It's kind of a lot, but the vape helps. We were standing outside for a while just talking ... laughing .... before we started to hear the screams. We ran back, and before we even got in, we could smell the fire. Smoke was even seeping through the bottom of the doors. Once we got there, it was already too crazy."

She started to rub her chin, her eyes suddenly narrowly.

"It was weird though, almost like the fire was *taking* the brothers and sisters. I mean, the rest of the building was just catching, and the flames were just starting to run up the walls, but in the middle… In the pews it was raging, and everyone was screaming… It was a lake of fire."

The other two faced her suddenly and she stared back at them ashamed, as if she had said something untowards.

"And death and Hades were hurled into the lake of fire," Greg started to recite solemnly, remembering the scripture that filled him with nightmares as a child. "This means the second death, the lake of fire."

The three heads turned on a dime to look at him then, wide-eyed, their faces struck as if woken up to his spiritual presence.

He felt like he had said the group password.

"Maybe we were being judged by God," the girl closest to him said. "Maybe it was for celebrating the drug. Maybe the drug *is* a sin."

The words seemed to set the other two off, and they faced her menacingly like nuns in a classroom. The third one, whose face was now distorted and venomous, grabbed her fiercely by the cuff of her shirt and shouted in her face, "Shut your mouth. Your thoughts were the real sin." She shook her roughly then and grabbed her face in her hands. "Maybe you shouldn't go around airing them out like you are the speaker for God." Then she shoved her backward and sat back with her arms folded, her face utterly disgusted.

"This may sound crazy," Greg continued over the awkwardness, calculating that perhaps his time to talk to them while they were still in a mood to talk was waning, "But did you see anything strange? I know you three weren't in there when it started, but when you went back in, did you guys by any chance see something shuffling around in the darkness, or like in the corner or something? Maybe someone wearing a mask with glowing yellow eyes?"

"The only thing with glowing eyes," the man in the middle replied sullenly, "is Satan himself. And I'm sure that he was in there, watching us all burn. And he was smiling because of his work."

The last girl shot a cold look at Greg, her angry demeanor locked on him now. "Go away," she hiss. "Get out of here, *pagan*." The word jabbed at something within him, something long buried, almost as if he were back all those years ago, turning away from the church for the first time.

First *and last* time.

I guess I've been cast aside again, he thought as he got up. *Even when it doesn't matter, when you get away. It still does.*

He walked away from them without protest, all alone again. They weren't looking at him anymore, he saw as he looked back at them. They were back in their own huddle, their backs turned, the signal that he was indeed exiled from their small survivors' kinship.

The last survivors, he mused.

He wondered what to do now that there really was no point looking any further for his dad.

He stopped and felt the enormity of the admittance.

He's really dead.

And to think, he had gotten snatched away in the midst of his greatest joy in life, the one thing that he loved doing more than anything.

At least there was that, he thought. At least it happened during that drugged out, magnificently rendered virtual paradise-scape.

He pictured his father then, in the throes of it all, basking innocently in the sun on some clear glorious day staring at the smogless blue sky, full of big puffy clouds, clouds that he could imagine as different tales, happy tales that he could describe to his lady. And in Greg's mind then, the lady wasn't Betty that he was talking to but his own mom, and she had that seldom seen grin that he always reminisced about, that knowing grin that came out when life truly was hopeful and worthy of a smile.

He wished that was what his dad was seeing when the fires came for him. He hoped that he had, *at least had*, someplace nice to pass away in.

As Greg reflected on it all, he felt himself walking closer and closer to the building, the fire hotter than ever. For some reason, the heat felt good. The pain of it numbed the feelings that were brewing in him. He could feel his nose hairs heating up as he sucked in hot, biting breaths. His eyebrows felt like they were going to catch and singe off of his face at any moment. He put his hands out to the fire, the tips stinging, the skin tightening, and his mind suddenly focused full throttle on it all, all the tactile senses at once, so utterly possessed by the sincerity of the flames that leapt upwards into the sky, the scene filling up his entire field of vision, that at that moment, everything else faded until it was just him, blank-slated, exposed to oblivion.

Just then, the hand of God seemed to strike him hard in the stomach and he fell back, doubling over from the pain. It wasn't God per say, he realized, noting the red and yellow of the firefighter who was shouting at him to get back, but still.

That's the second time I've been struck in less than an hour.

He turned around quickly, the scorching sensation suddenly negative rather than revelatory as it had been moments before, and as he looked at his hands and saw that they were a bright red, the tips of his fingers scarring up in areas from the exposure, he felt himself breaking down inside, and he wept.

He doubled over, the sobs deep and heavy, strange to him, never felt to such an extent before, ragged and raw, probably ugly to behold. He cried on and on, right there where he had been pushed off to, still in the hubbub of noise and chaos, for all that he cared about in his sudden and seemingly endless breaking up.

It passed by in this way for a time, up until something—a hand maybe—guided him away from the flames, his body plodding along at its behest. The heat around him subsided more and more as he walked until finally, it was gone. His hand felt the cold touch of metal suddenly in front of him and without looking, he laid his head against it, the feeling of it soothing and serene, like a welcomed ice bath on a hot day. It was just a wall, but as he stood there, leaning on it, his eyes still closed, his breath falling in and out, it renewed him.

He opened his eyes and saw that he was leaning against a stainless steel loading dock door in the dark. He scanned the area, wondering where he was exactly, unsure of how he had gotten all the way there, wherever it was. He was at the bottom of some building's receiving area. In the distance, he could hear the raucous sounds of the fiery scene, perhaps a block or two away.

He walked up the drive-up's concrete incline and then exited out onto a vacant, dimly lit back-street with building rears along one side and a chain link fence on the other. The freeway hung overhead the lot beyond the fence, shrouding it in darkness. He glanced both ways down the street, unsure of which way to go. It was a tossup, so he headed to the right, following the breeze that blew downwind at a gentle slope, his feet carrying him along drunkenly, his head slightly aching. His hand moved instinctively to his phone in his pocket, a sudden urge to check his location.

Just then a shuffle sounded in front of him and he stopped, the noise just beyond the fence to his left. *It's the thing*, he thought, his eyes peeled, his mind jumping to the image of the creature in the night. *He* felt it in his heart. His time was up. He'd be joining his dad soon.

It's got me dead to rights.

A second passed and then another and then another, his body stock still, waiting for the blow that would surely come. But as the time passed, nothing seemed to stir over the sound of the wind. It was dead silent, in fact. He waited all the same, but a gust came stronger, prodding him along. He took a breath and then acquiesced, moving with vigilance, passing along the fence's gently chiming metallic links.

He checked his phone and noticed that he was only a few hundred feet and a right turn away from the theater–what remained of its charred carcass, that was–so he picked up the pace and sped down the rest of the road, finally emerging on a main road, away from the creepiness of the alleyway. He saw the flames again a distance to his right. It looked markedly diminished, but there were still people there, gawking at it all the same.

He turned the other way, but then thought again as he saw how lifeless the road looked going that way.

Better to be around other people, he judged, his mind on the night-stalker.

He called Lonny as he walked up and they planned out where to link up. A minute later, he was at the rendezvous, Lonny there already, waiting, his eyes on him. He looked bleak.

Greg spoke first, relaying that there were more than likely only three survivors, from what he gathered anyways, and that more or less the rest of the congregation had burned up in the blaze.

Lonny nodded along solemnly, his face intuiting a similar understanding. They shared a moment of silence between them, the two of them staring at the fiery scene, now more smoke than fire.

Lonny started towards him as if to console him, but Greg stopped him.

"Let's get going," he said stonily. "We have a lot to do."

Lonny pulled back, the angst showing in his face, and he acquiesced. "Okay."

"Meet back at your place?"

"Yeah, sure," Lonny replied. He started to break away, but Greg stopped him.

"Actually, maybe you should come and jump in my car and I'll just take you to yours."

Lonny frowned at him, confusion on his face.

"That thing could be lurking around here," Greg clarified. "Best to stay together from here on out, especially when the sun is down."

"Oh, yeah, yeah," Lonny agreed, a relieved look on his face. "Good idea."

He probably thought it was because of my dad, Greg thought. They started to walk along the sidewalk in the direction of his car, silent but for the patter of shoes on cobblestone.

"You really think that thing might be around?" Lonny asked hesitantly.

"Honestly... I do," Greg replied. He wondered whether to mention his fire theory... the sounds he heard when he was alone, the hospital... the alley. So many instances. His every movement was possibly being tracked now, somehow.

"You sure you're not just being a little paranoid?" Lonny asked.

Greg sucked through his teeth. "I don't know. All of this mayhem today feels a little too coordinated for my taste to just be an unhappy coincidence."

Lonny fell silent, his eyes lost in thought. Greg said no more about it, but quickened his pace, keen to get to the car without incident.

Thankfully, it wasn't far. They raced to it once it was in sight and hopped in. At Lonny's insistence, they drove right up to the door of his own car before he got out. Once he was in, they caravaned back to their unproven little "safezone," whatever good their burglar-proofing would do in the end.

On his way, Greg decided in the end to just text rather than call Janice to let her know where he was going. Talking about everything right now wouldn't help him, he calculated, and if he spoke with her at all, he'd just break down about his dad and all the implications that entailed. *Nope.* He had to stow it for now. Time was running out for him ... not just him, but everyone around him. He had to get to the bottom of the mystery before the thing struck again.

He stared at the text for a good minute before hitting the send button, all the same. He felt suddenly guilty. He needed her so bad.

He sent it anyway and then tried to put his phone away, but she texted him immediately.

It was a status update. She was fine. That relieved him somewhat, at least. But then a couple seconds later, she called him. He didn't answer.

A moment later, he texted her back. "I'm busy now. Will call with more updates soon."

That would have to do, he thought, and pressed on.

16

Greg and Lonny chose to coordinate their exit from the vehicles so that they'd be able to walk up to the flat together, too afraid that they'd get picked off by the dark stalker on their own. As they hurried along in the cold biting night, their eyes peeled for strange movement, Greg scanned up the side of the tall gray apartment building all the way to Lonny's window—third from the top. His mind envisioned the thing grappling the wall as it watched him from high above, its yellowish eyes locked onto him… but no, there was nothing there, of course. It was just a blank wall, and the apartment's glass, though far away, looked intact from what he could tell.

Once they got inside the complex doors, Lonny locked the outer door latch. Greg looked at him and he shrugged.

"Anyone getting in this late is a degenerate anyways," he explained.

Greg nodded, fidgeting restlessly. It *was* smart, sure, but somehow the sound of the bolt clicking made him feel *more* anxious than before. If the thing was inside, then weren't they locking themselves in with it? Really, the barricade was already compromised, since the thing could be anywhere.

That nervous energy followed them like a spectre all the way

253

up to Lonny's apartment door—through the dank lobby, up the sluggish lift, and then down the dark hallway.

Once they got in, Lonny clicked the bolt home and fell against the wall, sighing in relief.

It didn't feel secure yet for Greg though, so he continued on, checking each and every room in the apartment. He flipped on lights, looked under beds and around corners and behind spaces... anywhere where something could be hiding. Fate wouldn't catch him slipping again, he promised himself. Not before the end. After he finished, he walked back out to the living room and saw Lonny pushing the cabinet in front of the door, so he lent a hand. It settled against the wall with a thud, and the heaviness of the sound finally settled his nerves.

He smiled with that, and felt his body relax.

Lonny went into the fridge and grabbed something for them to eat, and they sat down and enjoyed it. Afterwards, Greg felt the sluggishness take hold of him, the stress of the long week combined with heavy carbs suddenly hitting him like a ton of bricks. He laid down on the couch and within a minute fell asleep.

In his dream, it was nighttime and he was moving along outside with a big crowd of people towards what, from the vibrantly colored, blocky buildings all around him, looked like the old Pershing Square in downtown Los Angeles before it was all demolished. Loud cheers erupted around him, "We're free to die! We're free to die!" He felt the urge to cheer too, the sound of it familiar to him as if he were living out some sort of a rerun. It clicked and he knew what it was—the big PCONC march. He was back somehow in the thick of it, bumping shoulders with all of the marchers who had taken to the streets to demand the right to die in the world rather than live unwillingly within it.

A few details were distorted, he realized because he wasn't next to his friend and confidant Edgar like he remembered.

Instead, the man's curly black locks were bobbing up and down three rows ahead, his red organizer shirt glowing brightly like some brandished flag as he jumped around shaking his fists in the air, leading the gang. Greg tried to yell at him to wait, but for whatever reason, as all screams end up in the dreamworld, nothing seemed to come out of his mouth but a small gurgle in his throat. It felt urgent that he get to him, though he couldn't understand why exactly, so he tried to wedge his way through the people in front of him, but they felt like brick walls. The force of him seemed to do nothing to create space, and he was stuck. He felt a tap on his left shoulder and noticed that Janice and his dad were walking next to him—yet another aspect of the dream that was *definitely* not the case. He gestured for them to leave, but when he spoke yet again, nothing came out other than a distressed wheeze. They regarded him absently for a moment, and then looked away without a response.

"It's okay," a voice said behind him. He turned and saw a couple of faces that made sense in the crowd—Francis and Grennel, folks that he recalled would later slip away from the city after the movement had died down to settle in a small coastal town north of Santa Barbara. *They refused to life-chip themselves*, he remembered, though he couldn't discern what exactly that meant.

Life-chipping versus death, he thought. Somehow, the comparison made sense to him.

The two of them made it three years before ending it together with cyanide pills in a lover's embrace. Janice had been the one to tell him. She had received a back-dated message online a few days later.

He wanted to warn them right then, shout at them to stay in the city, to try to hold on after the fact, but nothing came out of his mouth but the gurgling noise.

"We invited them," Grennel told him all of a sudden, his face smiling piously at him like a happy monk.

What do you mean? Greg wanted to ask, wondering who he

was talking about... if it was Janice and his father... knowing that it wasn't the case either way. This wasn't how things were supposed to be playing out.

Francis reached out to him, grabbed him by the shoulders with his big, meaty hands, and turned him around again to face the front of the crowd.

"Why is he here for this anyways?" he heard Janice asking his father Jacob, her hand over her mouth conspiratorially so that he wouldn't hear. "He's not going to follow through."

"I know," his dad chimed in, a frown on his face as he looked at Greg. "He doesn't have the guts."

Follow through with what? he wondered, trying desperately to remember what would transpire next. His head felt foggy. His stomach hurt. No use. He couldn't recall.

All of a sudden, the crowd stopped like a military marching band in unison, and he collided into the person in front of him, his nose hitting the towering man's elbow. He clenched it to staunch the pain.

The cheers of the crowd stopped suddenly, he noticed. In fact, there was absolute silence all around him, a tense kind of a silence that clammed his hands up. Then in one motion, the entire crowd turned to face him, their silhouettes blacked out completely. He looked at Janice—what was a moment ago Janice —but it was just a faceless head, regarding him from above, as if they had all lengthened up to loom over him. The two shapes that had been in front of him parted then, and suddenly there was Edgar, small, sad-faced Edgar, standing hunched over, barely looking at him. His feet were on fire, Greg saw, but he didn't seem to care.

And for some reason, it didn't seem to shock or even alarm Greg either. His eyes were focused on Edgar's face. And then he spoke.

"Is it true?" Edgar's raspy little voice was saying, the voice that he hadn't heard for so long. "Is it true that you won't follow through, after everything that I plan to do?"

He felt that he *could* talk right then, that the chink in his throat had suddenly cleared, so he took a big swallow, wondering what to say, but Edgar beat him to it.

"What more can I do for you to follow me?" he continued. "Do I have to die a thousand deaths for you? Do I have to hold you down and set you on fire myself?"

"Hold him down," someone from behind shouted and he spun around to see who it was. Only the towering figures showed were there, their tops nearly obstructing the grayed-out sky.

"Should I hold you down," he asked again, "To keep you from faltering?

"He's going to stay in the city," Janice's voice said from beyond the figures to the left of him. "He's going to stay in the city with me and get a job working for a building downtown."

"He's going to marry her, too," the voice of his dad added. "He's going to marry her and live on, despite what you did."

"Are you really?" Edgar asked, his voice frank and incredulous.

"Make him die!" someone shouted. "Make him die!"

More took up the shout, and within a matter of seconds, everyone around him was chanting it, their voices ripe with judgment and hatred. "Make him die! Make him die!"

When Greg turned to Edgar, he saw that his friend was holding his arms out for an embrace, but it didn't feel right, something within him holding him back, so he paused at the invitation, even as the crowd's hatred poured down on him, the chants and cries coming louder and louder, over and over, his head aching at the sound. He wondered whether Janice and his dad were shouting at him too.

As he looked into the eyes of Edgar, the big brown eyes that he knew so well, eyes that he knew he believed in, *had* believed in for so long, he felt that he *had* to leap, as much as he was afraid … he had to do this thing now, had to change things, had to rewrite the past with this gesture. And so he did it, launching for Edgar then, not knowing what it would mean for him, but wanting to hush the crowd and escape their taunts. Edgar caught him in his arms and gripped him fiercely, almost painfully, the hug tight, chokingly tight, the fingers digging sharply into his back as well.

He cried out at it and started to jerk wildly to free himself from the intense pain that was spreading up his back towards his neck... up the back of his head.

Then the face of Edgar started to melt right off like wax, the eyes and nose and ears and lips all dripping down and falling off, revealing a dark, metallic mask underneath, its two gleaming yellow eyes locked onto him.

Suddenly, his midsection crunched inwardly and he screamed out in pain.

Blackness.

He woke up with a start, his body covered in sweat.

"You good man?" Lonny called from his seat at the kitchen counter, his eyes taken momentarily away from the laptop.

Greg nodded, but said nothing. He was still gathering his bearings. The lights had been dimmed lower he noticed, and he even had a blanket covering his legs.

Nice host, he thought, smiling at Lonny. "Just a bad dream," he replied.

He got up and stretched his arms up to the ceiling and then down to his toes. His back felt a little achy—the middle of his back to be precise—which struck him oddly since that was where the stalker had tightened around him. He walked over to Lonny to see how things were going online. Lonny's intense face, all lit up like a campfire storyteller in front of the brightly lit screen, seemed promising.

He was looking over the online forum website where they had posted their tech logo.

"Any updates?" Greg asked. He scanned the forum subject lines populating the webpage.

"See for yourself," Lonny replied confidently and clicked their thread, entitled, "URGENT: Tech logo reverse image query."

There were a lot of responses, most of which were only tangentially related—what kind of servers they were, what they could possibly be for, where obsolete server setups like theirs were even around—but a ways down the list, someone had used a reverse image application to pump out the exact answer they were looking for, the logo's company and background. It read as follows:

Logo brand: Gibbon

A national robotics and defense technology company focused on "defending and protecting humanity." With over 2,000 employees and an annual revenue over 23 billion at the height of its company year, it was the premier military robot manufacturer and was responsible for the mili-robot supply to the United States during the Grand Military Theatre. During the "Time of Peace" following the war, the company failed to pivot into other markets and eventually filed for bankruptcy.

"I can't believe I didn't think to do fuckin' do this," Lonny reacted. "It would have been so easy… Could have saved us a lot of time too."

Greg skimmed the reply's attached conversation chain. It was a lengthy one, mostly full of company hearsay and second-hand knowledge about people whose family members had worked for the company during its heyday. It was a big company from the sound of it, a real household name. Strange that he didn't know of it though, he thought. Perhaps he had come across it as a child. He read on.

According to the thread, the larger company warehouses that employed many small towns still remained, although almost all of them had been left abandoned and pilfered over time by the local residents. They were as barren now as old, vacant ghost-towns. Some in the thread even bragged about exploring inside them.

A video link entitled "Drone flight - Gibbon 104" jumped out at Greg just then and he tapped excitedly at the screen for Lonny to click it, so he did. What came up was a relatively short video, Greg noticed, less than a minute long. It started immediately, without any pomp or explanation at all, mid-flight as the drone was racing through a thick green forest, trees whizzing by at every which angle, close enough that because of the action-camera point view their breath caught in their throats as the pilot narrowly missed oncoming woods. The sheer confidence of the pilot astounded Greg. All of a sudden, the drone flipped into the air, briefly eluding the forest for clear blue sky as the pilot looped around, and then plunged through a small drain into a construction zone before a boxy factory building. The Gibbon name, faded from wear, was visible as the drone approached and then entered through a third-floor window.

The drone slowed and the camera panned out to reveal the building's worn, apocalyptic interior, utterly lost to the elements, a derelict green-house of sorts now with light pouring in everywhere from large cavities in the roof where the ceiling had fallen in. As the drone wound around the dilapidated metal-work of stairs, beams, walls, and a few scraps of broken down machinery left over, it seemed that anything of note, anything resembling a clue, was gone. Nothing remained but piles of trash and campfire pits full of charred parts and pieces from the look of it.

The video ended abruptly.

Lonny fell back in his seat disappointedly, but Greg grabbed the mouse and played it again, this time at half-speed from the point when the drone entered the building. Maybe there were subtle clues on the walls ... some writing, he hoped. As he narrowed his eyes, Lonny leaned in to help. As it went along, Greg paused it here and there, scanning the image with his finger at times, the walls, corners, nooks, and crannies that could be seen. Towards the end of the video, he slowed it more to analyze the piles of trash and the campfires.

There.

Right there within a scrap pile at the corner of the screen, there was something round like a skull peeking out, right before the drone rounded a bend, though it was fuzzy. Greg pulled the video back a touch and then replayed it again, stopping right when the pile came into view again.

"*You* see that?" he asked Lonny, "Is that a head, or am I crazy?"

It was a bald, metallic head, charred and blackened, its face looking out of the pit through holes where the eyes would have been.

I bet they were yellow, Greg thought in awe at his discovery.

"I think the thing that's been after us came from Gibbon," he whispered.

Lonny looked at him incredulously. "Do you realize what you're saying? What... remnants from some lost time have come back to... what... *haunt* us or something... all because you stumbled on some floor in your building? What the fuck would it be doing in there anyway... keeping guard over some secret military data center hidden in there?" His tone wasn't hiding anything. He thought it was ridiculous.

"It may *sound* stupid," Greg retorted, "But you have to admit that there is some connection." He shrugged and stood up. "I don't know what the connection is... I really don't... But that face in the pile right there looks a hell of a lot like the one Janice and I saw, so this whole plot has a bit of Gibbon in it. We know that much is true."

Lonny opened his mouth to say something, but then clamped it shut again. Greg grinned at that. There was something there.

He sat back down and grabbed the mouse again, this time scrolling through the video responses in the original thread.

There were a lot.

Some were other random explorer videos into lost places, others had more drone footage–bullshit footage of aerial daring–but there was also more chatter about the buildings. It was a lot of the same story–dead buildings left behind, nothing to see, fun to waste time in, kind of gross because of vagrancy. Then finally something strange popped up, so Greg pointed to it for Lonny to read as well.

(Ferrreeak89)

Saw this and remembered. I went back to my old hometown pretty recently in the high desert. Apple Valley. Shout out! Just joking. No one knows about it, probably. I lived out in the sticks, i know. Blame the parents. They still don't want to move to the city. Got registered for remote power usage by the government and everything. Anyways, was drivin past the old Gibbon warehouse at the edge of town on my way out to Barstow and i saw that it looked like the place had been fired up again or something. Swear to god! some of the lights were on. Seemed pretty strange to me. I don't know.

Below that, a person replied.

(Anonymo123)

That's super weird, no doubt. Most of the buildings are scrap heaps. You were probably just seeing things.

(Ferrreeak89) replied:

Na, man. I stopped and got out of the car and everything. Couldn't get in of course because my car wouldn't fly over the fence that's around it to keep the wanderers out, but seriously. There is something going on in there.

(Anonymo123)

Bet there's some loot in there or something then.

(Ferreeak89)

Only one way to find out, my friend.

The conversation between them stopped there, and the chat veered off again between others in the thread. After a moment of scrolling down for more replies from the two users, Greg moved back up and looked over the chat again, his curiosity peaked.

"I don't know man," he said as his hand dragged the screen up and down with the mouse. "What do you think? You think this is something?"

"Honestly, I don't know. Either way, aside from direct-messaging this Frrrreak guy, we could just trek out to the high desert and give this building a look ourselves. It wouldn't hurt, right?"

"Na," Greg replied with a smile. Lonny was on the same page as him. "I guess it wouldn't."

Action is better than stalling, he figured. Really, they had nothing to lose anymore.

"Wait," he realized, thinking of where they were headed. "My car won't let us fly in there, I bet." The zone was probably restricted for newer vehicles like his. There was no way his dumb car would let them get anywhere near the place.

"Well, mine is a cheap pile of shit," Lonny replied. "It probably won't care."

"Great!" Greg exclaimed and slapped Lonny on the back. "It's settled then. Let's take your car."

Hopefully, we can live to take the thing back, Lonny's face seemed to reply.

. . .

Given Lonny's tired state (he had been up for nearly 30 hours without sleep), Greg advised him to stop pounding amphetamines and close his eyes for a minute, or at least until the sun came up. He was reluctant at first, probably because he was scared, but after a few minutes of coaxing and a promise to watch over him, he relented, laying down on the couch Greg had used.

Greg tried his best to stay awake, especially because of the last nightmare, which had truly terrified him, but within less than an hour, he was out too, asleep on the other end of the sectional couch.

Eventually, as the sun bled into the room, the glare of an intrusive beam caught Greg's eye and awoke him, which then awoke Lonny. He turned and scoffed at Greg.

"What the fuck, man?" he snapped. "You promised me that you would stay awake. What if that thing broke in while we were both asleep? We'd be dead right now!"

Greg rolled his head back with a sigh. "Well, we're not," he grumbled.

Lonny threw the pillow at him in frustration.

"Ok, fine," he conceded. "I'm sorry. I just couldn't help it."

"I can't believe we've made it this far," Lonny languished. "I mean honestly, why hasn't this thing just run in and taken us out? Last night was the perfect chance, right, so is it just too weak or something?"

Greg shrugged. "I don't know ... Maybe it's just scouting us out." The idea fell out of him without a lot of thought, but he held onto it. *Scouting for what?*-he wondered.

Lonny's eyes were on him. "Like what, reconnaissance?"

"Maybe." *And who was the info for? ... Maybe there were multiple stalkers.*

It felt too early to mill over questions like that, he thought. He felt suddenly groggy, and badly in need of caffeine, for that matter.

"Maybe we should get some coffee."

"We *should* get going," Lonny retorted. "We finally have a lead out in the desert waiting for us. We need data, otherwise, we'll be theorizing for the rest of our lives. Until that thing kills us, that is."

Greg nodded. "Fine, let's go."

They left in Lonny's car a few minutes later in the direction of Apple Valley, the backwater town that was hopefully housing the details that would set them free.

17

It was a relatively short flight once they got into unregulated sky out past the San Gabriel Mountains over Palmdale. The brown of the landscape looked alien to Greg, who was so used to the cityscape grays. The smog in the air wasn't as strong either; he could even see the ground through the relatively light layer as it whizzed by underneath. Lonny's car, an old flight model—more than likely one of the originals from the look and sound of it—prompted him multiple times to turn around along the journey, indicating every few minutes that he was entering non-registered land and should review his course and destination. After a dozen or so of these unwanted chimes, he disarmed the computer entirely, settling for phone-navving their way there instead.

"I still can't believe that you actually drive," Greg mentioned for the umpteenth time from the passenger seat, struck by Lonny's active, old-school piloting.

"And I used to wonder why I liked driving alone," he muttered. "Keep your eye on your phone. You need to make sure my heading is correct."

"Okay, okay," he apologized, focusing on their heading in silence from then on. There were natural features–mostly rocky mountains—here and there, so as he cross-referenced the car's digital compass with his phone, he pointed them out to help Lonny stay on course.

Janice had already texted him a few times along the way to find out where he was headed. No doubt, she had pulled up his location on her phone, he reckoned. She was probably freaking out.

His first reply was simple. "Checking a lead in the desert." He tried to leave it at that.

Within a minute though, she had shot back a string of responses in rapid succession

"In the desert?"

"You sure you don't want to just call the police?"

"You're not a cop."

"You're not alone right?"

"I'm with Lonny," he replied.

"It's not that big of a deal."

"Don't worry, babe."

The nonchalance of his replies felt like the wrong choice, he realized. It would just aggravate her more. He made the decision to give her a call after a minute of milling it over.

Of course, she didn't pick up. He ground his teeth. *Shit.* He sighed. *The try is enough*, he told himself, and put the phone down on his lap.

Down on the ground, it looked like a wasteland that had been bottled and sealed away for eternity. He saw the remnants of streets long abandoned, some sections covered completely in dirt, others cracked and broken in places from years of disuse and elemental temper tantrums. Here and there, he saw blocky painted messages on the rooftops of old buildings, farewells and emojis… even some SOS's and large X's written in white. *Were they in jest or for real?* he wondered. *Was it ever that dire to get out of the desert?*

It confused him since from what he had been told, the exodus had come because of government subsidies encouraging people into the cities. He couldn't be sure though... Perhaps his memory was based around accepted propaganda and not actual fact. Still... It couldn't have taken a whole lot to get them to migrate into the bigger cities, he reckoned, looking out at the dreary and bleak landscape.

What a strange place to settle. Why any would have lived out here was beyond him. Was the population *that* crowded back then?

After a few minutes, the pockmarked signs of past town life started to fizzle out, until eventually, their final vestiges came to an abrupt end with a single abandoned satellite track home site, nothing beyond it but beige high desert for as far as the eye could see, it seemed.

"Can you check the nav again?" Lonny asked. "Maybe we passed it. " Greg pulled up the directions. They hadn't, but they were nearly there.

"It's coming up on the right over that mountain rise there," he said as he pointed down at a jagged crop of peaks just in front of them. "Better slow up."

Lonny did just that and then some, letting off on the throttle and diving down so that they'd hug the top as they crested it. The maneuver turned Greg's stomach. The other side dropped off suddenly, so Lonny followed it downward, gliding along its flank, and as he did, Greg could see a small dry lakebed hidden away at its base, and just beyond it, a single massive unadorned rectangular warehouse, hidden away from prying eyes.

Gibbon Corp. It had to be, he felt, as he eyed the setup–the acres of flat space around it, the miles of fencing locking it in like something out of Area 51.

It was utter blankness otherwise, though to the left, Greg tracked a small road leading out a gate on the south side, then connecting to a single, well-maintained asphalt road that went off into wherever desert roads led.

One other landmark sat there quietly as well, directly parallel from the site across the road—a small abandoned trailer park.

Greg's phone warned him to pull up and avoid the building grounds in front of them. *Probably some law*, Greg thought. Before he had even silenced it however, Lonny flew the car up and over the fence, right into the site, disregarding the message with a smile.

Greg felt more than a little jealous at the old jalopy's silent submission.

Lonny arced the car's flight around the building so that they could take it in, its silent nature foreboding to behold. Along the backside, Greg made out the remnants of a receiving area, and… he held his breath… there was the light—presumably, the one the blogger had been talking about—*actually* there, peeking out dimly through the bottom of an opened bay door. Greg pointed at it excitedly.

There weren't any windows on the outside of the building, he noticed as well, questioning the intention of the choice. Was the design meant to keep whatever was inside a secret, or was it just some standard operating procedure in all warehouse buildings in the middle of nowhere?

"Do you think we should land inside the fencing?" Lonny asked. "It'll be trespassing…"

Greg frowned at him. "I think we're well past that worry."

Lonny frowned back at him.

There was a lot of space below them that was within the fence line, but still far enough away, Greg thought. He spotted a random patch of concrete towards the northeast corner of the lot and pointed at it. "Land over there, then we can sneak inside."

Lonny dropped the car down happily on the one good patch, hopeful inwardly that they might still have a shot at not giving away their presence since the car would be so far away. *It is a pretty quiet flyer*, he told himself, maybe enough so that they hadn't tipped off anyone, or anything, to their presence.

As he flipped the engine off, Greg reached for the door hatch, so he stopped him. "Wait up, man. Don't you think we should have a plan or something, in case things go south?"

The sudden devil-may-care attitude of his buddy was getting rather annoying, he felt right then.

Greg nodded and sat back in the chair in silence for a moment, pondering things over. *What if things did go south?* He thought. The question triggered another question, one more fundamental—What *were* they hoping to find out by going in there? And what were they going to do *if* they found something?

Lonny was staring out the window, his face glum. Maybe he was rethinking things, Greg thought nervously. Maybe they were just getting in over their heads even further. He coughed and Lonny looked at him, his face expectant, so Greg began to just air his thoughts out loud. "If we do find out that this company is crafting robots or whatever in there... like... as in *still* in the act of doing that, then we should probably just take some pictures and show them to the authorities."

Lonny nodded his head at the idea, the glumness a little gone, so Greg continued.

"Maybe if we show them those pics and then we show them the pics of the servers in the room, the fact that the company is dead will confirm that something funny is—"

He trailed off as Lonny's attention seemed to waver to back out the window again. "You hear me?" He asked, pulling at Lonny's jacket.

"Yeah, sorry... I just got to thinking about my theater and all and I..."

The sadness in his eyes struck Greg. This guy... this friend of his who was now looking to him for "the plan," who had literally followed him without balking throughout this whole ordeal thus far, and whose livelihood had just lit up in flames... was still by his side... and he hadn't even asked him how he felt. It had taken an admission to wise him up to it all.

The thought made him cringe.

He hadn't never stopped to consider Lonny's side of things, so deep in his own world that the loss of the man's cafe hadn't been reflected on at all.

"Hey, man," he started, knowing then what he had to do… even though he still needed him, "I've been thinking—"

"No," Lonny interjected, aware of what he was thinking. "It's not like that and you don't need to start thinking about me all of a sudden. I'm good, man. I was just having a moment. Let's just finish this… or at the very least, find another bread crumb in there to keep this adventure going. Then we can start thinking about other crap."

"Besides," he added. "It's a distraction I need right now."

Greg regarded him from narrowed eyes, stuck in that moment for what to say. Suddenly, Lonny smirked and reached over to grip his shoulder. "I'm telling you. This is better than the cafe right now. I need the sunlight."

Greg chuckled, and then he nodded. "Sure, sure … But what do you think of the plan?"

"Let's just go in there and have a look," Lonny replied. "What's the point in planning, anyways? It's bound to be horrors in there either way, knowing our luck." He turned, and opened his own door to get out.

Wouldn't call it luck, exactly, Greg thought, but then he got out as well, resigned to their brazenness.

The first thing that Greg noticed as he took in the surroundings was that the site was immaculate; there was absolutely no growth at all. The ground was an absolutely barren beige that reflected the sunlight so well that he had to squint to see well.

The building thankfully was painted in a matt grey, otherwise it would have blinded them, since it was a lot larger than he had originally thought from the sky. It already loomed over them, and they had parked far away. *To think that this monolith is all the way out here,* he thought as they walked up. *Then again … it's the perfect place for secrecy.*

Already, Greg could hear the busy hum of machinery emanating from the opening below the door. It brought him back to the hum of the server floor, that busy, foreboding noise. The resemblance made the hair on his neck stand up.

The same beginnings, he thought. *This can't be good.*

"Stop," a voice said suddenly from behind them.

They froze in place.

"Get on your knees and put your hands behind your heads."

This is different, Great thought, and looked back to see a group of armed men approaching, their guns drawn at their faces.

18

The gravelly dirt bit into the side of Greg's face where he lay. Someone was holding him down and the weight on his back made it impossible to hold his head up. He sneezed and dust got in his eyes.

Lonny was crying next to him. He felt like crying too. Here he was, caught and pinned to the ground on his stomach, his hands handcuffed behind his back, probably soon to be shot in the back of the head.

Just then, someone kicked his feet and demanded something of him, what he couldn't tell because of Lonny's loud whimpering moans.

"Jesus Christ! Will you two shut that fucking guy up!" a voice ordered.

"Shut up! Shut up, you fucking baby!" another commanded. A thump cut off the moans suddenly, and then Lonny was wheezing.

Greg blinked back the crud in his eyes and made out Lonny lying there next to him, snot and blood running down his dust-covered face. A man was standing above him, ready to land another blow into the side of him, but then another grabbed his shoulder at the last second and waved him off.

There were four men in total circled around Lonny, all of them in unmarked black tactical gear, military ghost group or federal or something of the sort, perhaps.

The weight on his back let up and a face came into view around the side of him just in front of his face—brown-skinned, green eyed, with a strong handlebar mustache.

"What are you two doing here?" the man whispered. He was dressed differently, a tie drooping to the dirt, possibly the leader.

Greg gulped nervously, hesitant to blather and incriminate them further. Then he heard the faint metallic scape of a gun exiting a holster and let it all flow out.

"We were checking the place out," he blurted. "We were just checking it out."

"Why?" the man asked, his hand searching Greg's back pockets. He found his wallet and flipped it open on the ground.

"We got a tip that this place was going and wanted to see why," he said. "We're being hunted—"

Lonny groaned suddenly to stop him from continuing, but was silenced immediately with a gloved hand over his mouth. He whined loudly in protest.

The man in control gestured something to the tactical officers and they nodded in unison, and then went to work, two to each of them, one on each side. In one quick motion, two pairs of arms hoisted him like a body on a stretcher and then carted him forward towards the building at a lope, Lonny alongside in the same manner. Just in front of a high curb separating the lower concrete sidewalk from the shoulder-height loading area, they dropped them on the ground, and then they sat them up against the wall.

The man in the stache was in front of them again, his eyes intent on them to focus, his finger on his lips for them to stay silent.

"Listen," he hissed, while another pressed in behind him, his gun trained on them, in what Greg could now see looked like full riot gear. "I know who you two are. We've been watching your online traffic for some time. I'm going to ask again–Why are you here?"

Greg looked at Lonny and saw that the man was scared beyond belief, his eyes locked onto the goon's gun pointing at him. Just then, he noticed that two of the four goons were gone. *In the building?* he wondered.

"Hey," the man hissed again, grabbing Greg's jaw in a tight grip and ripping his head back to look at him. "Dawdle any further and my friend here is going to put a bullet in both your heads."

Greg nodded as fervently as possible.

"We are being hunted by something," he said, aware of his words, playing them out to accent their victimhood.

"Hunted?" the man probed.

"Yeah, hunted. There's something that has been after us... We think it may be tied to this Gibbon company. That's why we came here."

"Why *this* place?" the man asked.

"This place... This place is... There was a video on the internet of one of these warehouses and inside there was this head that looked kind of like the thing that was chasing us."

"Hold up... hold up... Why is the thing chasing you?"

"We don't know! I swear to god we don't know. It all started after I found this server room at work and I—"

"Woe now," the man sputtered and threw his hand up in front of his face. "Tell me more about this server room. Where is it?"

His eyes looked suddenly hungry.

"It's at the building I work at."

"Where?"

"At the Friedmont Towers in downtown LA," Greg replied. "I found a room in my building where there were a bunch of servers and..." He stopped and regarded him. "Who are you guys?"

The man's eyes narrowed, and for a moment, he stared at

him, waiting. Greg looked away, suddenly nervous at the man's intensity. Just then, he bounced up onto his feet and turned towards the goon behind him. Something was whispered between the two of them, and then the gun was passed over.

Greg was about to look at Lonny, when the man wheeled around and leaned down all the way into his face, his hot breath upon him, the gun shaking in his right hand.

"I'm the guy with the gun and you are the guy trespassing here, trying to stay alive... trying *not* to get shot." His tone felt strangely maniacal in its monotone delivery. "You'll get your answers only after I get mine and not before."

"Captain," the other man said, his voice a scolding whisper. "The men."

The captain waved him off with the gun, but for a moment, his face changed, reflective. He kneeled down, gripped Greg's shoulder and cracked a smile at him.

"I *am* your friend, Mr. Quinlin... for now at least... as long as you tell me about this room of yours and exactly how it led you to this place... but if you don't, I'm going to throw you in this warehouse and turn it on—*completely* on, if it isn't already, that is —and those mili-bots in there will rip you to shreds."

"Mili-bots?" Lonny piped up, his voice cracking.

The question made the captain flinch and fall silent for a moment, his hand still on Greg, his grip tightening. Greg watched him, watched and waited and analyzed.

The captain turned to Lonny and frowned, still silent, and then his eyes fell to the ground in thought. He snorted.

When he looked back at Greg, the smile was there again, toothier than before.

"You were saying something about a room?" he asked again, his voice calm, warm, and relaxed now.

There was something there ... something to do with the mili-bots, Greg thought.

The man's face grew dark, expectant, his eyes pressing him for more, his grip on his shoulder tightening.

Greg opened his mouth to answer, but stopped as he registered the second man's gaze shift from him to the opening, his face suddenly pale.

He ripped a gun out of his side holster and fired abruptly over their heads, once, twice, thrice, in quick succession, and then turned to flee, but out of nowhere, a shadow sailed over Greg's head—not a shadow, more like a gleaming metallic blur—and came down on top of the man with force enough to squish him into the ground with a crunch.

Crouched, the thing looked to Greg like some metal mantis on raptor legs. Then it stood and glistened in the sunlight, and Greg was struck with another likeness—the angel of death come to destroy them.

It turned to face them, its yellow eyes, cold and alien within its triangular insectoid skull, locked onto them suddenly, and Greg knew they stood no chance.

Then a shotgun blast blew its head clean off and it fell to the ground

Greg looked up to the top of the concrete ledge behind and saw one of the shadowy men, a shotgun in his hand, its muzzle smoking, still trained on the thing.

He fired another shot at it, and then another, just to be sure, though it lay dead and lifeless after the first. Greg winced each time.

Afterwards, he hopped down to them and crouched down, his chest heaving.

"Captain," he reported, panting and rather hysterical, "We gotta get the fuck out of here. There are a buttload of them in there. This place has been piping them out for some time now."

"Is everyone—"

"Everyone's dead, sir," he blurted out. "We need to leave now."

They helped Greg and Lonny up to their feet and made to drop back from the building, towards the same corner of perimeter fencing where they had parked. They hadn't gotten far before the sound of movement came up from behind—two mantis creatures loping up at them, quickly gaining on them in their slow, hobbled pacing. The captain spun and backpedaling fired off a few shots, to little avail. Then the shotgunner turned and, emblazoned from before perhaps, stopped to empty his gun into them, pumping quickly each time, denting them and even knocking one off balance, before crying out and fleeing again, but it was too late. One dropped into the dust just at his heels, but the other lept and caught the end of his shirt, slowing him down just enough to rip at the collar of his flak jacket with the other pincer and pull him to the floor.

The sound of his screams sped Greg up, the evisceration loud in his ears, before in own last slice, it all was silenced.

Greg was leading the pack now he noticed, a ways in front of the rest, when something exploded in the distance just beyond Lonny's car and rattled the ground, causing Greg to trip and fall face first into the dirt.

The captain slowed and then dropped to his knees beside him, uttering dryly that the transport was gone and they were done for.

Apparently, their meal ticket had just exploded.

"Come on," Lonny shouted as he ran past them, his shreaky cry carrying over his shoulder as he left them in the dust. "Get to my car!"

Greg rolled over, groaning in pain as he opened his eyes, only to catch the dust kick up in his face as the captain launched off without him.

"Hey," he shouted, trying in vain to call him back, but the man didn't turn his head one bit as he sped away. "Come back! … Come back!" But there was no hope now.

A backfire sound caught his attention suddenly and he turned to look. Off in the distance, there was a glare of something dropping down the same mountain slope they had come in on.

He squinted his eyes to make it out.

A car? It was speeding directly towards them.

A red one.

A red hatchback.

"Janice?" he muttered, blinking back the dust in his eyes. It *couldn't* be.

Just then, a pneumatic thump drew his attention back to the building, where he saw the creature—the eviscerator-—moving towards him, its pincer-like hands covered in gore.

Greg's breath caught in his throat. He'd die and his wife would see.

Janice is coming, and they'll kill her too, he thought sickly.

But then he heard a honk, short and familiar, and then another and another and another, beeping on and on and on to catch the thing's attention. It worked, the thing turned, reacting like a moth to the flame, its attention completely focused on the oncoming traffic barreling towards them. Greg watched as it settled its feet deep into the ground, its body poised for something… he shouted at it again to regain its attention, an almost pleading whine to call it back, but the horn was louder, gaining in volume as well...

The creature launched itself into the air in a plume of dust, arcing through the sky, intended for one obvious, perfectly calculated, location.

Right on top of his wife.

Luckily, she saw and veered at the last moment so that rather than directly impacting the front windshield, the thing barely managed to catch the driver side rear with its grasping hand.

The impact ripped the car down at an angle and it started to careen towards the ground, fighting and jerking as it fell to throw the creature—who was hanging well—off, but at the last moment, within a foot of the dirt, it barely pulled up, so that it skated along the surface.

Janice's face was right there, Greg could see, so close that he made out her frightened eyes as the car passed by him, skipping along with that inhuman rudder scraping the ground at its side, its lower half smashing again and again on the ground under the weight of the vehicle with each audible crack, the dust kicking up in violent wakes.

It was a stone bouncing on the water... but then he saw it... a mound—the only mound in the whole immaculate landscape—sitting there right in front of her, and inside he knew... the car's nose caught it and the whole thing ripped downward in one great tumbling mess, end over end over end over end, ejecting the robot as it went, and then all of a sudden it stopped in one loud thump, hidden in an enormous dust cloud that filled the air.

19

Greg had been screaming for god knew how long, probably during the entire, elongated crash, but now that it was over, he tried to get up to search the wreck.

He lurched to his feet, but fell over sideways onto his shoulder, dazed and disconcerted because of the blow to the head. His chest was hurting as well, and his breath was coming out in long, labored heaves. He tried again to get up and succeeded, trudging forward at an awkward unbalanced gait for a few initial steps before righting himself enough to walk... and then run... into the cloud. The dust caught him in the face as he entered, and he shield his eyes against it, but it was impossible to see still.

He heard footsteps to his left and turned to see the captain's form coming up cautiously through the dust and the past him, towards the center of the crash site, one hand trying to swat away the dust in front of his eyes, the other holding the gun in front of him, scanning from side to side, as if waiting for another robot to emerge at any moment. Suddenly, a pair of fog light-like eyes rose from the ground, close to the captain, just on his right side. Greg shouted and the captain dove to his left, his gun leveling in the same moment on the target and emptying the clip into its face and chest, the eyes sputtering and rocking around and around, sparking and then blinking out. It fell backwards without even a death throw, the shine of its metal returning like some downed and dead chameleon, and he heard the thud of it hitting the ground.

Lonny came up next to him and they all stood there together for a moment looking at it through the haze, its dull exoskeleton coming into view more and more as the dust around them started to settle.

Greg saw the downed car then where it lay within a crater of dirt, upended, a single wheel still turning at an odd angle, and ran over to it screaming his wife's name like a madman, hoping and praying that she'd shout back, that she was still alive. At the driver's side, he dropped to his knees to look into the cabin and saw his wife there, hanging unconscious upside down by the belt buckle, a bloody conk on her brow that was dribbling blood onto the car's ceiling.

"Babe!" he shrieked, struggling angrily against the handcuffs that were impeding him now at the worst time. He leaned in anyway and nudged her head with his own, hoping that perhaps she would stir, but she didn't. The frustration within him boiled over into heartache, and he shouted.

"Captain!" he called out. "Come and get my wife! Hurry! I can't get her out like this!"

"Your wife?" he said as he ran over and kneeled down beside Greg, his eyes assessing her for a moment before reaching in.

"Just get her out," he demanded, before the captain shoved him out of the way.

First, he put his hand over her nose to check for breath, and then, satisfied, he whipped out a knife from his pocket to cut the seat belt. As he reached in, he shook his head and returned the knife to his pocket, deciding instead to try to squish his way into the car first to bolster her from falling. It was tight, but he managed it, Greg all the while watching and pleading with him to hurry but take care.

After a moment, he was in position enough to start cutting,

so he did so slowly, slicing into the belt's threading as steadily as he could. After three quarters had been cut away, it snapped and she dropped onto him, and then with a dozen grunts and tugs from the both of them, her body was out and laying in the dirt.

The car was still humming somehow, so before doing anything else, they pulled her body away from the wreckage, and then with Greg at his side, the captain tried to rouse her awake by shaking shoulder, shouting down at her all the while to wake up.

Her chest was moving, thankfully, Greg could see, but her face was… Suddenly, her eyes fluttered and then cracked open.

"Are you okay?" the captain asked.

"Huh?" she replied, looking around quizzically. "Where am I—"

"Janice!" Greg exclaimed, and she turned to see him there crying and smiling down at her. He bent and kissed her on cheek and then the mouth, relieved and overwhelmed at the same time. He sat back and she saw then that his hands were pulled awkwardly behind his back, and she frowned.

"What's going on?" she asked, "Why are you sitting like that?"

"What?" he replied, and then understanding, shuffled to show her.

"Handcuffs?" she asked, regarding the stranger in the crazy mustache sitting beside her husband, "Why is Greg in handcuffs —why are you in handcuffs?" she repeated, incredulous. "What's going on?"

"It'll be okay, honey," Greg replied, his face dipping close as he said it to reassure her somehow.

"My name is Joseph Ocampo, mam, " the captain piped in. "Your husband is fine for the moment, but we don't have time right now to discuss everything. We are not safe here. If you're alright to move, we need to leave now."

Her face sobered suddenly and she nodded, and immediately, he pulled her up abruptly to her feet.

"Where are we going?" Lonny chimed in from behind them.

"My keys are gone. We can't even get in the car anymore, let alone start it up and leave."

Joseph stood there thinking for a moment as the others waited in silence, looking to him to lead the way. His eyes were regarding the downed car a short ways in front of them, the remnants of his escape.

"We need to hunker down and wait for backup."

"Hunker down?" Lonny shot back. "Look around, man! There's nowhere to hide!"

"Come on," he replied, and then turned and started back to the building where the mayhem had begun, Greg and Lonny too stunned at the idea to move.

"Is this guy a cop?" Janice asked.

"I don't know, but he's the only one with the gun," Greg replied, and started off after him, gesturing for the others to follow.

They did so, because after all, what choice did any of them have anymore.

20

The four of them slinked around the building to the left, hugging the wall, and then stopped before the corner so that Joseph could peek around the side. When he saw that the coast was clear, he darted forward to a small access door along the wall, fiddling with the door immediately. Janice hesitated, and then shot forward as well, the other two at her heels, all of them afraid of being left behind and picked off.

He gestured for a little room as they crowded around the door, and then fished something out of his pocket–a small, black, oval-shaped tool with a screen–flipping it on and then holding it up to the door handle. There was a green flash of light and then a ping as he scanned the knob, and then a tiny arm sprang out and he jammed it into the lock and waited. Another noise—a whirring sound—then he pulled it out and checked the door handle to make sure it was unlocked.

Rather than open it, he turned to the group first. "It will be dark in there and we will be moving to the nearest safe place, wherever that may be, to hunker down and wait. You...," he said, and pointed at Lonny, "will be following me. Your hand will be on my back the *entire* time. Then you," he said as he pointed at Janice, "and then you."

Greg was last. He wondered why.

"I won't be shining any light around or anything, so be careful where you step. Push lightly with your feet so that if you bang anything, it won't rattle too loudly. If any of you make too much noise, we are all dead. Got it?"

"Got it," they whispered in sync, their mouths collectively dry.

Then Joseph opened the door and they saw the ungodly darkness within. Greg hesitated, suddenly reminded of the floor he had nearly died in. It all felt like the opposite direction he would have chosen.

You're not the leader now though, are you, he thought.

Lonny looked at him and knew what he was thinking, he could tell.

Time to follow, his face intuited. *Don't fuck it up*. Then he turned and placed his hand on the middle of Joseph's back, and *their leader* started inside, the rest of them falling in behind like one long human centipede.

As the door closed behind them, Greg helped it to land quietly, his foot catching it barely before it tapped the threshold and softening the blow.

And then there was darkness.

The depth of it amplified Greg's fear, so black that it was like he was closing his eyes even though they were wide open. He was clenching Janice's shoulder, he realized when she fidgeted awkwardly in his hand, so he tried to lighten up, but he just suddenly felt insane. They were all insane, to be wandering around in a place so completely shut-out from the outside world.

They were moving though, turning right and then right again and then left, like blind rats in a maze. He focused on the turns, tried to hone in them and on only them, though the silence all around seemed out of place. *Wasn't there a hum before, when they were outside?* he wondered. *Step, step, step, turn.* Janice was pulling him along now.

Just then, they stopped and he nearly bumped into the back of her.

He heard the sound of a hinge creaking lightly up ahead, possibly Joseph opening a door, hopefully Joseph, and not something else. The line started forward once again and he shuffled lightly, his foot skimming the top of a transition strip, over a threshold. A few feet later, the group slowed again—this time, he was ready—and as he waited, he felt Janice start forward and then down, and then again in the same motion, the beat of hollow tapping echoing up at him from below—stairs. He started down them, stepping awkwardly, a maddeningly methodical task in the dark.

They continued down for a dozen or so steps, winding around a little he guessed, his shoulder bumping into the side rail again and again. At the bottom, the line sped up, moving along at a brisker pace now. Right turn. Forward. Still it was silent, though the air was cooler now. They stopped and he heard another hinge, and then the line pulled forward through another threshold and then suddenly dismantled. A body came around the side of him, shoved him inward, and shut the door they had gone through.

A flashlight lit up the ground at Greg's feet and he took stock of them all there, standing in a circle facing the door, four lower halves basking in the light.

Joseph shined it around the room and he saw that they were in a small office now from the looks of it, a few blank wooden desks, some office chairs, and a single cliche productivity poster on the wall.

"You can sit down now if you want," Joseph said, sitting himself down in one of the dusty, torn seats and pulling his phone out. "Just be quiet."

Lonny walked up to him then.

"Hey, can you—" Joseph cut him off with a shush and he cringed. "Sorry, sorry," he whispered, adjusting his volume.

Joseph looked down at his phone, but Lonny didn't move,

still adamant to continue. After a moment, the captain looked back up, frowning.

"Anything else?"

"Can you take these cuffs off us now?"

The insistence in his voice seemed to surprise Joseph, who furrowed his brow at the petite man standing in front of him.

"I mean… Look at where we are," he persisted. "It's not like we're gonna run away or anything."

"Yeah, where are we?" Janice butt in with a bite that made Joseph's head snap her way. "You know, clearly. It's obvious, otherwise we never would've made it in the dark to this room. Now's the time. You need to tell us. "

"I don't need to tell you shit, lady," Joseph replied. "Besides … It ain't gonna fuckin' matter anyways. There's no way we're getting out of here alive. Those things are gonna burst through here in no time and rip us to shreds."

The statement dropped the air out of the room, and for a long silent moment, the three of them turned inward, grim horror written on their faces. The captain eyed them, his jaw working from side to side. Eventually, he sighed.

"Come here, *tough guy*," he said to Lonny and gestured for him to turn around. "Y'all seem threatless enough, I guess."

He took his handcuffs off, and then did the same for Greg.

The tension in the room settled down a touch, thankfully, enough, and the two of them stretched their arms, nearly smiling at their freed-up limbs.

"Since things are so damn bleak, as you say," Janice continued, the group standing around now in a sad sort of a grief circle, eyes on each other, "You might as well tell us what is going on."

Joseph bobbed his head around in reply, mulling it over. "I guess you've got a point, huh," he said and then backed up to the wall and sat down against it. "It might take a minute."

"Perfect," she replied, smiling at the others as she sat in the chair. We've got plenty of time." Greg smiled back at her, suddenly proud.

Joseph blew a raspberry, wondering where to begin.

"I am… well… *was*, I guess… part of a team that was investigating this manufacturing building. We encountered your husband and his associate trespassing outside, and handcuffed them, before everything went crazy."

"Okay…" Janice probed him to continue.

"We flagged some information online that the building was operational and came to check it out for ourselves. That's what we do … monitor chatter online. We saw your husband's friend's thread," he said and pointed at Lonny. "That was what tipped us off, actually."

He looked over at Greg, his eyes narrowed.

"Can I ask *you* a question now? Where did you get a photo of that processor? Was it in that room of yours?"

His eyes were intent, and Greg saw it for what it was. That room did hold some secrets, and this guy was the one that could unlock them.

He just had to play his hand right.

"I can definitely tell you everything I know about the room and the processors," he said, meeting his gaze. "*But...* I want you to explain things more first… starting with this place."

Joseph put his hand on his gun, his jaw tight, and Greg nearly balked, scared shitless of the random semi-maniac pressing him. He put his hands up to cool things down. "Now, now," he said. "There's no need for that. We just want more information. You'll get yours. I'll get mine. Don't go getting crazy in here. I don't want those things crashing in as much as you don't… not before we get some answers."

Joseph crossed his arms in silence, the other two silently watching the debate unfold in front of them.

He started to his feet suddenly, nodding to himself. "Alright. Hand over your phones first then," he replied, his mind made up.

Greg, Lonny, and Janice dug into their pockets without hesitation, smiles on their faces.

Afterwards, he sat back down again.

"Alright," he replied, an air of annoyance in his tone. "What do you want to know?"

"Everything," Lonny said.

"Everything about what?"

"Let's start with this place and go from there," Greg said.

"Okay. Get comfortable then because this *will* take a while."

Finally, Greg thought as he sat opposite their newly found secret keeper, his fellow conspirators at his side. *Finally*, a person with actual answers in front of them, ready to share.

We can get to the bottom of it.

"For starters... This place here used to be an autonomous manufacturing facility for Gibbon Infinity. This plant was decommissioned a little while before the company went belly up, and has been sitting here ever since, silent as the grave... that is... until recently."

"If it was decommissioned, why hasn't it been cannibalized like the others?" Greg asked, thinking back to the video of the wrecked warehouse he had seen the night before.

"We were wondering the same thing, as a matter of fact. We even did some digging into that. This warehouse was purchased almost a year ago by a corporation known as Tecnica Holding Group."

The name piqued the edge of Greg's memory, though he couldn't put his finger on it. *Tecnica-Tecnica,* he repeated in his head, trying to jog his mind somehow. He tabled the thought, though, trying to focus on the captain. Lonny was looking at him strangely. Perhaps he knew. He made a mental note to bring the name up with him later.

"I know I keep asking this," Janice interjected, "But—"

"I am with the federal Anti-AI taskforce," he replied, shaking his head, "AAT for short, though you've never heard of it I'm sure. We've been on the hunt for almost three decades for the rogue system that was responsible for…"

But he stopped suddenly, his mouth screwed up to the side. He looked at each of them in turn, his eyes implying that whatever he was about to say would seal their fates together somehow.

He shrugged. "Fuck it," he mumbled to himself. "The agency has been chasing the AI system that was responsible for September 23rd."

A bombshell had just been dropped in the room.

"Responsible?" Janice asked. "Responsible in what sense?"

The captain blew a long, drawn out raspberry, his hand rubbing his forehead. "It's a little complicated."

"Try us," Greg said.

"How much background do y'all need-do you even remember things back then? Were you even alive back then? I was just a toddler for god's sake." He chuckled, but the group didn't stir, so he sat back and chewed his tongue for a moment. "Okay, okay. Where to begin? Well… okay… In that time—you know, the time around the Fall—the public wasn't fully made aware of the actual details of the vaccine's creation… so it goes without saying, this news *has* not and *will* not ever be made public.

"Like you said… We'll be dead soon anyways," Janice said.

"True," he said. "Alright, I'm not gonna go dragging us through the scientific weeds or anything, but RBV—you know, the virus that was out of control during 2027—due to that thing's high R Naught rate… transmission rate that is… due to *that*, there was a lot of pushing to get out a vaccine of some kind as soon as possible, so a lot of companies—not just pharma companies, mind you, but a lot of other companies as well–jumped into the development pool to snag that contract. I mean, can you imagine the profits that you could generate from pumping out a global vaccine? Crazy! Anyway, the brass didn't care. The more the merrier, in fact. People were dropping dead left and right... notable people... people within the scientific community for Christ's sake. Things weren't looking good... But the development process wasn't churning things out fast enough, so after maybe a month I think? Something like that... New initiatives came out from the administration at the time to cut red tape on regulations—testing time, trails, that sort of thing. Then it turned into a real free-for-all! That's when Gibbon showed up."

"Gibbon was a late inductee into the runnings, but immediately shot to the front of the lineup because of its prototype AI system—code named Adam—whose ability to develop a working vaccine in a third of the time of any other competitor, more or less in about 18 weeks. Obviously, this was attractive to the government, who was being hounded constantly to do everything in its power to get a vaccine for the virus ASAP. But this is where things get a little shady... At the time, there was a lot of bad PR around the use of AI in anything other than rote, non-strategic, war activity... because of... you know, the mili-bots all over the news acting like the perfect little murder-machine soldiers. They were effective killers, for sure, but you can imagine why they figured AI as the savior wouldn't play well."

"Anyway, so they made a deal with Gibbon behind the scenes. Basically, bury the fact that you're relying on AI to develop the vaccine, get it out to the public before your competitors and more importantly, before the public finds out, and if all goes well, you'll get your pay-day, the government will look good for choosing the right horse, and the means won't matter anymore because everyone will have their savior flu shot. Saved people won't care how they were saved, after all. So kind of a win-win situation for both parties."

"Yeah. A real *win win*," Greg repeated, disgust written all over his face.

"Yeah, I know. But in the government's defense, Gibbon had a pretty solid argument that the system was a safe prototype."

Lonny scoffed. "How so?" he asked.

"It was completely untethered from any of the company's defense system computers or mili-bot deep learning data centers, so there was no logical reason to believe that the machine would gather negative inference. For all intents and purposes, it was safe."

"Give me a fuckin' break," Lonny chimed in.

"Seriously," Janice started. "It was probably no more—"

"I wasn't finished," the captain shot back. Are you guys gonna bitch or hear me out?" Lonny held his hands up innocently, and Joseph continued.

"So to Gibbon's credit, they pumped it out quicker than 18 weeks. Way quicker. In only 6 week's time, ADAM finished developing and virtual-trialing a complete vaccine, ready to go out worldwide. The release date was so soon in fact that the government even worked with the World Health Organization to rubber stamp it on launch day. I'm pretty sure that was who. They came out with some public statement about it, hailing it as some "testament to human effort in the face of tragedy." That pretty much sealed its fate in the eyes of the public. Within hours, most of the scientific community was behind it... bunch of bandwagoners... they all shouted for it to go out immediately."

He gave a glum little shrug, his face defeated looking. "So it went out."

The group frowned.

"There was a gang of cooperating countries that were partnering with the US too to help get it out as soon as possible, so within less than like a week, it was administered pretty much around the whole world... If only they had been less efficient. Maybe some of the tragedy could have been mitigated."

No one replied. No one moved. It was just too much to digest.

The captain grunted at another thought and they all looked up at him expectantly again.

"This is the real kicker," he added, his finger up, his head shaking like someone who's gossip is too hot to tell, but he said it anyway, "Two days before the actual Fall—September 21st—Adam up and vanished on Gibbon in the dead of night, the whole fuckin system disappeared into thin air... like the fucking computer had up and skipped town before the place blew up. Absolutely no one could account for it. It made no sense."

The way his hands shook told Greg that he was still at odds with the fact.

"It's not like it had access to the web," he said hysterically, "to like *jump* into cyberspace. Someone had to have physically snuck out the program and wiped the servers. But even that's crazy."

He held up two fingers. "Two days after it vanished, the hemorrhaging began."

"Obviously," he said in a calm, yet spiteful tone, "y'all can guess why no one ever said anything about AI, right? The government would have been strung up by the public if the information came out. No... They buried that secret deep down, and it'll remain that way forever."

Wow, Greg thought, feeling the urge to extricate himself to the other side of the room for a moment to reflect on it all. He looked over at Lonny and saw that he was shifting nervously in his seat, his eyes narrowed at the captain.

"Okay," Lonny started, rather uncertainly. "I still don't get it, though. Where do you come in? I mean, what is this whole Anti-AI Taskforce?"

"Okay. Onto that," he replied, settling into his floor seat some more. "I was just giving y'all a second to process. Okay... so

ADAM's vanishing before the Fall raised a clearly red flag to be investigated, obviously."

"Obviously."

"So a little while after the dust settled on September 23rd, it was decided behind the scenes that along with the Government's public efforts to discover some sort of medical solution to the vaccine—which has been going on, to no avail I might add, since then—a private investigation into ADAM's disappearance would need to take place. It would have to operate in the dark... the secret had to stay a secret... so a special task force—the AAT— was formed. I know what you all are thinking... What about the CIA, the FBI, the NSA, right? No. Even with their level of secrecy, their branches are too large and too public to keep the lid on such an exhaustive investigation. Look at Snowden."

"Who?"

"Nevermind. He was a whistleblower. The point is, the more people, the harder the secret is to keep. And the things that we have had to do to pinpoint Adam would never have been allowed to happen with all the bureaucracy tied to those branches anyway."

"What do you mean?" Janice asked.

The captain turned towards her with a smile. "Well for one, major cultural changes have been effected to lessen the search area of the system itself. Things like electrical regulations, market obstruction, propaganda to push people into the city. The list goes on, but those are some of the bigger initiatives. When your race is going extinct, people start to really listen to outside ideas."

"What do you mean?" Greg asked. "That doesn't sound like the workings of a task force. You mean to tell me that your agency has been responsible for people deciding to move into the cities? I don't believe it."

"Believe it or not, things have changed a lot since September 23rd, and most of the big societal changes haven't been by accident."

"Then why are you here?" Janice asked. "Your agency sounds like a bunch of pencil-pushers and secret lobbyists. Who are you all on the ground here today?"

"Good question," he replied. "Within the agency, there are a couple of divisions. My team and I are with the investigative unit. We used to be a lot larger, but in the past ten years, our division has diminished extensively due to restructuring within AAT. They blame our 'ineffectiveness,' many at the top arguing that we haven't acted on intel in the best way possible to find Adam. There has even been pushback by some to build in more oversight of the goings on within the task force, which could increase our exposure to the public. It's obvious that people are getting desperate and starting to press for actual results."

"So was the investigative unit the ones that saw our thread online, or was it some other unit?" Lonny asked.

"My team saw your thread. We haven't been in the field for some time. Honestly, the image itself got us pretty excited... and then this warehouse being operational." He flicked his finger, his lip in his mouth. "It's really been a while since we've had any solid leads. It reinvigorated us. So yeah ... We sent some agents to your address to pick you two up and my squad went to this location. The team sent to you missed you though, obviously. You must have already been on your way here. It was just dumb luck intercepting you, I guess."

"I guess so," Greg replied.

That was the last of their luck, he thought grimly.

The room fell silent, questionless for the moment. Joseph stood up, clearing his throat as he did, and gestured at Greg, his hands rubbing together anxiously.

"Alright, buddy. It's time. Pony up the details. What's up with this floor of yours anyways?"

Greg nodded. "Alright, alright. I guess it is my turn now, huh," he replied, feeling markedly more comfortable now to give over what he knew. The man had just shared so much. It was only right.

Plus, the mysterious floor bit might help to open things up, he thought.

Plus—plus, it was the perfect way to exonerate the three of them of Rex's murder, he realized suddenly, remembering that to some extent, that had been part of the game plan all along.

Maybe this was their ticket to freedom, he thought. *Maybe.* They'd have to live through the day first, and then he'd have to be honorable enough to help them.

He cleared his throat much the same way as the captain, wondering where to start.

"The floor was where I took the image," he started. "It's a snap of the servers in—"

But an explosion ended the conversation right then.

Greg felt the blast more than anything, more than its terrible sound, more than the sight of everything changing suddenly on its head. He felt it.

It started at the door to his left—the one that was closed a second earlier. It exploded into the room suddenly, colliding with him where he sat on the floor and throwing him back against Lonny. His eyes slammed shut as he tumbled end over end before coming to rest underneath something heavy, holding him down. He heard a scream and a metallic grating against the floor and walls, and then sounds of violence erupted around him—slashing of flesh, the gurgles of death, desks and chairs and office equipment breaking apart. He cowered down where he had landed, his body still and taught, ready to be gutted or squashed or both. He opened an eye for a moment and saw the familiar sheen of robot flesh passing by him in the darkness, illuminated suddenly by a single beam of light casted from the floor into the gloomy room, the captain's single flashlight it seemed, there to showcase their whole fated comeuppance. He closed his eyes shut again, waiting for his turn to die. The things had found them, as Joseph said they would.

Then there was another explosion through the wall and

then more metallic sounds of chaos ensued, this time metal on metal battling it out it seemed, of clanging and tearing apart, things crashing every which way, things being crushed, and then a strange high-pitched squeal, followed by another and another...

And then abruptly, it all stopped and the room fell silent.

Am I dead? Greg wondered, not trusting the silence, scared of what it could mean.

Was it silent though? he realized, registering a high-pitch ringing in his ears.

Just be still, he told himself. *Be so utterly still. Lay like a corpse on the ground.* There was rubble covering him, and a particular heaviness along his knees that was pinning them down. Still, he tried to play dead, for what it was worth—an easy enough thing to do, though there was the issue of his heart banging heavily within him.

For a good while, it went by like this. He didn't question it, until all of a sudden, he felt something prod his shoulder, softly but insistently. His eyes were still closed, and he kept it that way, pulling his shoulder in gently to better hide it, but after a second, whatever it was *pressed again*, a little more insistently than before. He felt the coldness of its touch, like the butt of a metallic broom handle.

There was no hiding anymore, so he cracked his left eye open and swiveled his head slightly upward to see, a compli-cated mixture of yearning and reluctance churning within, confusing him. Out of the one slit, he saw the glint of metal, the dim shine of it.

It moved slightly, and he flinched and opened his eyes.

Oh no.

It was the nightmare stalker that loomed over him now, the one and only, right there in the flesh, its eyes... those lamp-like eyes... less than a foot away, close enough to touch, shining down on him from inside its oval, humanoid skull. It was tilted slightly, regarding him curiously.

He closed his eyes and braced for the final deathblow.

"Are you alright?" a voice croaked out, oddly human, yet labored to the point of extreme discomfort.

His eyes shot open in response, and he stared up at it, terrified more now than a moment before.

Wha—?

"Are you feeling alright?" it repeated, the sound emanating from an open hole under its glowing yellow eyes.

Whether it was trying to get any kind of coherent response, it was at this point that Greg's brain seemed to break, and rather than speak, he screamed fullbore into the thing's face.

It leapt away from him, clearing the debris, and landed a fair distance away. Greg started up trying to jerk himself free, pulling and clawing and shoving to free up his legs as forcibly as possible, one eye on the thing that stood motionless, watching him from afar. On the tenth tug, his legs came loose and he fell over himself retreating away, taking in the darkened destruction around him now—the broken walls and furniture, the bits and pieces lying everywhere, and the blood... so much blood and carnage scattered around, pooled in places, spattered on the walls.

Just then, he saw something small under some rubble along the wall... a person... shaking uncontrollably.

"Janice?" he asked, his voice cracking up.

Her head cocked up from between her legs and he made out her face... her eyes... He ran over and practically dove into her, grasping her, while the rest of the room—the death, the chaos, the thing watching him—dropped away suddenly from his mind. It was just her and him, alive and together, and as he grabbed her and enveloped her in his arms, he whispered that he loved her, he loved her, he loved her, over and over, as she whimpered in the crook of his neck.

The creature saw all this and watched on in silence from the same place, its rangy limbs straight and taught like some lifeless, oversized toy robot. It waited patiently for them to register its presence again, while taking in the moment for what it was to it, more input.

After Janice's sobbing and shaking had subsided and the moment's shock had worn off of them enough, Greg's awareness returned. He came to with the sort of start that anyone who has forgotten something of great importance might—with a mix of fear and urgency. His body tensed, his breath caught in his throat, and he shifted around to look at the figure. It was still there, watching them, yet strangely at ease rather than poised to strike, as its brethren had been outside. In the dim light, he saw how different it was from the others—the oval-shaped head, humanoid legs, hands with fingers—a semblance of humanity rather than some strange animalistic approximation

The devil that resembles us tricks us better, he felt suddenly.

"Oh my god," Janice said, her eyes wide.

"What do you want?" he demanded of it.

It brought its hands up to its sides in a stiff 45 degree angle, shifted its palms up into a submissive stance, and to his astonishment, flipped its eyes off and then on again—a blinking imitation. A second passed.

And *then* it talked.

"I'm sorry," it responded.

"What?" Greg asked, dumbfounded by the strange, preemptive gesturing he had just witnessed.

It stared back at them silently for a good few seconds. And then it fell into pantomime again, this time more ambitious. It held its arms out to its sides and then started up shuffling around, twirling in place, as if to say, *Look around the room, folks.*

Its eyes only left them for a split second.

"I could not save everyone," it said after coming to rest. Then its head drooped slightly. "I'm sorry that I could not save the people in your group."

It held out its arm towards a darkened corner of the room and then shined its eyes over there to illuminate it.

There was a shattered desk atop a pile of debris, but underneath it all, Greg could see the lifeless head of Joseph jutting out, his face locked in an eternal scream, his eyes peering out directly at them.

Janice gasped.

Then the light drifted off of him... down the length of the wall...

Greg felt his stomach churning as he understood. *Oh no.* The light stopped suddenly on a shiny metallic pile of rubbish a ways away from Joseph.

But it's just bot carnage? Greg wondered. *Thank god.*

"The units dispatched them too quickly for me to intervene," it explained, "But now they are all destroyed themselves."

"Wait. What?" Greg asked, suddenly confused. "*Them?*"

The light of its eyes were shining still on the same pile, but then it started over to it, walking carefully through the wreckage. Once it got there, it reached down and picked up a large, mangled sheet of metal, and then shined its eyes down on the thing underneath.

It was a body lying face down.

"By them, I mean this human as well," it said with its eyes on the corpse. On Lonny's corpse. It reached down to turn him over, but Greg shouted at it.

"Stop!

It froze in place, its hand cradling his left shoulder.

"Don't touch him!"

It let go and he fell into the rubble again.

I killed him, Greg thought dumbly. *I got him into this mess and now he's dead because of me.*

The thing stood up and got back into its submissive posture. "I'm sorry," it said. "You are sad because they are dead. Am I correct?"

Greg was too lost to answer anymore, but Janice was reeling now.

"What's happening?" she asked, tears welling up. "What do you want with us?"

"I saved you. You were offered up to the droids, but I saved you two."

Greg started at that. "Offered up?" he asked it. "What are you talking about?"

It turned its palms slowly so that they were facing each other. "You were being offered to the droids by a member of the Cult of Android."

"Who?" Janice asked.

It pointed in Joseph's direction where his head lay in the darkness. "That man was a member of the Cult of Android. When he encountered you, he messaged the group to send the droids. I came as soon as possible, but I was only able to save you both, as I have said."

"Wait... Joseph?"

"Yes."

Weren't the droids attacking him and his men, though? Greg wondered.

"What's this Cult of Android? Janice asked.

"—And how did *you* know that we were here?" Greg added.

It hesitated for a moment, its eyes looking back and forth at the two of them, and then it pointed at Greg. "I tagged you during our first encounter and have been following you ever since."

"Why? Was it because I went onto that floor?"

"Yes. I followed you to evaluate whether or not you were a member of the Cult of Android. I cannot let members see the floor."

"Why not?"

The android held its hand up to stop him. "I must explain other things—"

"What are you?" Janice interjected.

It shrugged its shoulders, and then faced her. "I am a security android model manufactured by the Gibbon Corporation," it replied.

They waited for it to continue, but it didn't.

"Wait. Go back," Greg said. "What must you explain?"

"I have been following you to ascertain why you trespassed onto the floor. I had been hiding successfully on the floor for 23 years, 6 months, 15 days, 23 hours, and 12 minutes without human incident until you came."

"Hiding?"

"To be more specific, I have been hiding from the Cult of Android, who seek to destroy any possible cure for the vaccine."

"What?" they asked simultaneously, completely slack-jawed, and then stared at each other.

"There is a cure?" Janice asked.

It held a single finger up. "It is a *possibility*," it clarified, "but I need a willing human participant that meets the necessary criteria for the trials."

It pointed its hand at Greg.

"This is the second reason why I tagged you."

"*Me*? Why me?"

It pointed at Greg's forearm. "You have a port on your arm. That may allow us to use you as a candidate."

"Wait a minute," Janice said, her hand gripping Greg's shoulder, "What did you mean by *us*? Who are you working with?"

The creature slowly brought its hands behind its back, clasping them together. "I cannot tell you more until I have more input. I must further analyze your responses to understand your background and motives."

Greg's eyes wandered towards the darkness, where Joseph's head lay. There were two competing stories now, he thought, both crazy, both from strangers... and both impossible to corroborate.

"What are your intentions?" it asked them.

"Getting the fuck out of here," Janice replied without hesitation.

It held out a hand to them. "I can help you to get the fuck out of here."

The gestures and responses were becoming more fluid, Greg noted uneasily.

"Hold on," Janice replied all the same, holding her hand up. "We are perfectly fine with us right *here* and you right the fuck over *there*."

It brought the hand back.

She turned to Greg. "Why should we trust this thing?" she whispered. "How do we know that it isn't lying?"

Greg shrugged. "What other options do we have?"

"I am a robot," it interrupted. "I cannot lie."

"Why should we believe *you*?" Janice spat, and then pointed at Joseph's head. "That guy over there told us something completely different."

"What did he say?" it asked, its head slightly tilted.

"Shouldn't you already know, since you were tracking us?"

"Stop arguing with it like that," Greg whispered out of the corner of his mouth. "We need to get out of here."

"How well did you know him?" it asked, its hands steepled now, the long metallic fingers tapping together lightly. "Are you sure that he wasn't lying to you?"

She faltered, her lips puckered in frustration.

The thing's got us there, Greg thought. *Maybe he knows it too.*

The tapping stopped. "We are still in danger here. As a compromise, I can escort you both to a safer location nearby. We can converse further there without the threat of android attack."

They hesitated.

"I will only escort you to safety," it insisted. "Nothing more."

Janice gave Greg a half-expression, her eyes doubtful.

We're fucked here, he wanted to say to her, knowing in his gut that it was true. They were stuck.

"It hasn't killed us yet," he said instead, and as the words came out, his eyes drifted to Lonny's body where it lay in the wreckage, all sad and pathetic, lifeless and unmoving.

For a moment, he wished that it would move.

But it didn't, of course.

"We need to take Lonny," he insisted. "We can't leave him here."

"That is not a problem," the creature replied immediately. "May I pick him up now? I can carry him."

Janice's head dropped, and Greg wondered then if she was disappointed with him somehow, for letting it all happen, for making one mistake after another after another ... but then she leaned into his chest, and he hugged her.

At least they were together, even if all hell broke loose.

"Okay, pick him up. You can escort us out."

It lifted its head slightly, clenched its fist, and shook it in the air. "Thank you. I will do it."

The sight of the gesture sent a shiver down Greg's spine.

23

The thing instructed them to stay and wait for it while it made sure the coast was clear. They disagreed at first—Janice reluctant in her words to "wait around for the thing to go and get back-up"—but after it explained to her that if it were indeed evil, it wouldn't need back-up, but could easily dispatch them alone—a rather unsettling remark, to say the least—they went along with the thing's plan, and it left.

As they waited, Janice busied herself with the flashlight scanning the wreckage and analyzing robot salvage, while Greg sat in a corner in the dark thinking about Lonny and the fact he was dead. The whole thing struck him as odd, more than that in fact, surreal, like he was caught in some dream... the way the thing had picked his friend up and hauled him out the way it did, his limbs flaccidly flopping around, the blood dripping down the otherwise still-shiny exterior of the thing's body... It didn't really register even though the details stuck out to him. *Maybe this was what shell-shock is like?* he wondered. He felt the same strange numbness about his father as well. Too much death within such a short span, perhaps.

"Come take a look at this," Janice said. The sound of her

voice snapped him back suddenly. He got up and walked over to the pile of shrapnel she was analyzing.

It was a piece of one of the drones, though Greg couldn't really tell which part. *Maybe part of the foreleg?* he guessed. The things really had looked like bugs out there, he recalled, the hind legs especially, the way they bounded strangely on them, hopping more than running as they chased after them.

She turned the piece over and there was a barcode and some numbers. *Just like at the grocery store*, he thought.

"You think they were selling these things?" she asked.

"Who, Gibbon?"

"Yeah, or the government maybe."

"Maybe these were the drones in the war."

"They can't be that old, can they?"

"I don't know," Greg said. "Maybe after they were decommissioned, the Cult got their hands on them somehow and repurposed them."

He was leaning towards the creature's story more than the captain's, he realized. He wondered why.

"That would make sense," Janice said. "Although, if we were to believe Joseph, maybe there is some AI hive-mind out there telling these things what to do and they tasked that creepy puppet creature to come and pick us up and make it look like he was on our side."

So Janice was for Joseph's story then, he thought. That made sense from the way she spoke to the creature.

"Why would it pick us up though?" he asked. "What would we even matter to it?"

"Exactly," she replied.

"Exactly what?" he asked.

"Exactly two things. One. We don't matter, so why would the robot give a fuck."

"Weren't you listening to the thing at all!" he shot back. "What about the cure?"

"Yes, but hold the fuck up. To go back to one, you think you really matter *that* much because of your little arm port? The thing can just go out and find some other Joe Shmoe with one of those.

"How do you know?" he replied. "You know what I had to do to get this installed! There aren't a lot of people with hardware like this."

"Which leads me to number two," she said, and shoved two fingers in front of his face. "How do you know it doesn't want you for some other purpose? Maybe it wants us to–"

But then the creature entered the room, its shoulder unencumbered with the body of Lonny, and she fell silent.

"Where is Lonny?" Greg asked.

"I took the liberty of removing him to a safe location outside," it replied. "I also cleared the area and we can leave."

"Cleared?" Janice asked.

"I found and dispatched another android," it clarified.

"I see ..."

"So what's the plan?" Greg asked.

"We will leave now," it replied simply. "Follow me." Then it turned on its heels and started out the hole where the door used to be, not waiting for Greg and Janice to follow, knowing that they would.

Or at least, that was how Greg and Janice took it.

The creature's shining eyes allowed them to see where they were going, thankfully enough, since the thought of holding onto it made Greg's skin crawl. It was a real bummer though to be passing through an operational pre-war building–in the midst of manufacturing clearly, from the sounds all around them–and miss out on the chance to look around.

The thought of taking a gander was pulling hard at him though, too hard, so he took out his phone to turn on the light.

All of a sudden, the creature spun and faced him.

"What are you doing?" it demanded.

He shoved his phone back in his pocket. "I just wanted to see—"

"We have no time. Do not stop." Then it pointed at him. "And do not take pictures. If you try to record me in any way, I will be forced to dispatch you and your companion. Do you understand?"

Greg's face went white. "Yes."

It turned without further explanation and continued on, the metronome click ticking along as it went.

Janice had seen the demonic character swap too, and as she passed by him hastily, she threw him a look, a hint of I-told-you-so and What-the-fuck-was-that? One thing was for sure. He'd be reflecting on that for a while.

As they entered the receiving room where the door had been cracked open to the outside, they got their first dim glimpse of the place. It was empty for the most part, other than a set of open casket-shaped boxes, their lids haplessly flung on the floor.

Greg peered inside.

There were three sleeping mantis drones wrapped in clear cellophane material, complete from the looks of it.

"Should we be worried about these?" Janice asked.

"No."

"Are you sure?"

"Yes," and it moved on.

Who opened these? Greg wondered. *The creature? The droids that got killed? Maybe a human that's hiding—*

Janice pulled at his shoulder, so he fell in behind her reluctantly, not wanting to leave just yet. There was so much within the building still that he wanted to understand.

Who was running it, and how were they doing it in secret? Had the AAT really just picked up on it because of them, or was the cult behind it all making these things in secret instead?

They ducked under the loading door and were out, suddenly greeted by the blaring sun.

There's gotta be a hole in one side's story. If I can get Janice alone, maybe we can game out a way to spot it.

I just hope Joseph was the bad guy, otherwise God knows what we're being saved for. Hopefully, the AAT has more men out there if that's the case.

Once they were out into the light, the creature's modus operandi seemed to shift before their eyes, from diplomat to commando. Its movements were quicker, its orders terse, its gestures in tandem now rather than preempting its speech.

"Come now," it barked. "I will carry you both up and over the fence to a safer location."

Before Janice could protest, she was off her feet dangling from under his armpit. When it turned to Greg, he lifted his arms above his head, and it hauled him up as well. What was the point of resisting, anyway?

So much for the docile robot, he thought. *Maybe it's a security update.*

As if to prove the point, the droid launched from the building towards the fence at breakneck speed, cradling the two of them so well that they all but glided along serenely, aside from the wind howling in their ears.

Within seconds they came upon the fencing, but the thing didn't slow. In one elegant set-up, it long-stepped once... twice... planted... and shot up high into the air, over the fence and the road, and came down on the other side, right in front of the trailer park.

"Jesus," Greg snapped, woozy enough to puke.

It jogged up the main park drag, and Greg got a look at the derelict leftovers from decades past, mobile homes lost to time, blasted and patched over and over until finally given up on and left for dead during the great migration. Windows were boarded up, doors hung wearily in their jambs, porches and handicap ramps were caved in.

There were empty spaces too here and there, people having taken to the road no doubt to pull their homes out of the abyss into that communal mausoleum that he knew so well–the modern city.

There weren't any cars that he could see as they made their way towards the back of the lot, and he wondered if maybe somewhere within some of them, there were people eeking out lives. *Couldn't be*, he hoped. *Too sad of a life here.*

The creature turned a corner and stopped suddenly at the end of a mobile's carport, and Greg looked forward to see why.

Lonny's body was laying on the ground in front of them, wrapped in some old carpeting, probably pulled from the home itself.

A burial rite or some lazy way to cover a dead body? Greg wondered.

The creature let them go and they landed awkwardly on their feet.

This is where his dreams have died, Greg thought as he walked around to the other side, where Lonny's head stuck out of the carpet-roll up to his eyes, his sad eyes that stared up at him. *He didn't deserve this. None of it.*

The thought poisoned his resolve then, too much to bear. It flooded his mind, which up until then, hadn't considered that single unflinching truth—Everyone in the gang was dead or soon to join, and his little excursion was the catalyst.

He cried.

"Are you hurt?" the creature asked, "I buffered the fall as best I could."

"I'm fine," he got out, trying to stand up amidst the tempest of ugly tears ripping out of him. "I've gotta cover him up."

He started to unroll him, but the thing came up and jammed its foot in the way.

"Now is not the ti—"

"I need to do this right. I can't just leave him like this with his head sticking out."

The thing didn't protest. After it got out of the way, Janice came over, but he shook his head at her.

She seemed to understand.

Once he had Lonny unwrapped, he saw what had killed the man—a pincer arm broken off in his rib cage, right in the middle of his chest. The shirt was soaked completely in blood where it had leaked out of him… one massive stain. The sight of it all was a relief in some sense, knowing that it was one of the mantis' drones and not their little stalker.

His face was locked up in some ghoulish reaction, eyes wide and shocked, mouth agape. Greg nearly touched his cheek but held back at the last, closed the slides of his eyes instead and then forced his mouth shut.

He placed his hands on his stomach and straightened out his legs, putting it all right out of guilt, what right he could.

Who knew? he thought. *Maybe he was watching.*

Somehow the thought made him feel selfish, like maybe he was seeking some bullshit closure or escape from the fact that he had gotten the man killed.

That's when his mind paraded through all the times where he could have let the poor sap off. At the apartment where Lonny questioned him, in the car where he thought about the business he had lost. If only he had just let the man go.

And now his wife was here, he thought sickly as he looked up at her.

"I'm sorry, honey," she said, and reached for him.

He let her grab him, though inside, he felt far away.

The creature shuffled and he saw it staring at them from the doorway of the mobile, just inside in the darkness, its yellow eyes on them… watching them intently.

Taking stock of us? he thought. *Gathering background information, personal motivation?*

The thought had barely settled in when the sound of an engine passing overhead grabbed their attention and their heads snapped up, their eyes on a car's smoke-trail drifting along towards the factory, its hum fading dimly in that direction.

Backup? He thought, wondering if it was to save them or annihilate them once and for all. He looked back to the house and saw that the creature was gone. As he started to walk out into the small trailer park path, he heard the thing's reproaching voice from within the house.

"Stay out of sight," it snapped loudly at them from a crack in the window board paneling. "It's the Cult, without a no doubt. They have come to see what their androids have wrought."

Wrought? Greg wondered as he retreated back under the carport. *It sounds almost biblical.* Before going inside, he grabbed the edge of the carpet and covered Lonny's body.

Where did it learn that?

As he ran inside, he saw that from the window they had a view on the site. The car was landing now, close to the car wreckages.

Five people got out, dressed in the same fatigues as Joseph's men, sans officer-in-tie, though perhaps he was hanging back in the car. Greg wondered if they knew Joseph was dead inside– their fellow cult member, or was it AAT associate?

"So *that* is the Cult of the Android?" he asked.

Before it could respond, one of the men swiveled their way, so it grabbed Greg's arm and pulled him down out of view.

"What the f—"

"Sorry."

"It's not like the guy would've seen us!" he complained.

"We cannot take any chances," it replied, and then crawled away to the wall before standing up again.

"So what now?" Janice interjected.

"Now, we—" the thing started, but she held a hand up.

"Not you… Greg, what are *me and you* going to do now?"

Silence fell upon the group as Greg considered it. Technically, they were out now, so they could just … leave the thing … couldn't they? That is, if they found a ride to get out.

"I think we're stuck here for a little while," he said as he crawled out from under the window sill and stood up next to her. "While we're here waiting though, we should get more information from our friend here first."

She turned and stared at it. "What is your name, anyway?" she asked. "You must have something we can call you."

"My name is Lu," it replied.

"Well, okay, Lu. You need to start explaining some things." She began to pace the room, her eyes on the creature that now had a name. "First of all, how do you expect us to believe that those bug droids back at that facility killed the man that supposedly told them that we were there in the first place?"

Wow, Greg thought, regarding her with newfound reverence. That hadn't even occurred to him.

"They did not," Lu answered flatly. "I killed him."

Janice wasn't ready for that. Neither was Greg, who turned a beet red.

"I was forced to," it continued, "because he was planning to shoot at me. When I breached the room, I was able to destroy one of the two androids immediately—the one attempting to get to you—but was unable to get to the next before it had stabbed Lonny. During that altercation, I saw that one of the humans—Joseph—had a firearm trained on me, so after dispatching that android, I grabbed and disarmed him, and then dispatched him as well.

"That doesn't make any sense," Janice retorted. "The impact of the door threw everyone off. There is no way that Joseph had the time to pull out his gun, level it at you in that shitty light, and—"

"He would have been unable to shoot me in the lighting," Lu interjected, "You are correct. If he had, you might all be dead now."

"Then why wouldn't he kill us before then?" she shot back even louder. "He snuck us back into the building. You're saying that after he did *that,* he supposedly called those things in to get us? They wiped his whole fucking group out!"

She had stopped walking, and was poised for its response, her face suddenly confident. It felt like the moment. This was it.

But Lu didn't look fazed in the slightest.

"His group were not members," it responded as flatly as ever. "Otherwise, they would not have been wiped out. They were federal agents."

"Federal?" she probed. "Don't you mean the AAT?"

She was leading it up to the cliff, he thought, hoping that it would jump.

"Who? Those men were agents of a bureau of the US Government called the Federal Bureau of Investigation."

"No way," Greg burst out. "That's impossible."

"It is not," it replied, turning to Greg for the first time in the conversation. "The agent that was holding you hostage secretly works with the Cult of Android. In fact, members of the cult have infiltrated every echelon of the government, all over the world. There is no place where there aren't members lurking."

"How do you know this?"

"I have been corresponding with the group online for some time now, leaking false information to them to confuse their hunt for us."

"I don't know," Greg said half-faced.

"What don't you know?" it shot back, voice slightly pitched.

Greg paled.

They were both the enemy now, he reckoned soberly.

"Joseph had a pretty believable story," he offered up, almost as if he were trying to convince the bot itself. "This sounds like a conspiracy theory now."

"If you tell me what he said, I can easily clarify."

"Okay," Greg said, combing his memory for the details. "Joseph told us that he was a member of a secret Anti-AI Agency that is actively hunting for a rogue AI system that caused 9-23."

"Secret in what way?"

"Secret as in no one knows about it," Janice replied smartly.

"Do you really think," it said directly to Greg, "that an agency within the government, one that is therefore publicly funded, can have stayed hidden in the dark since *the Hemorrhages of September 23rd* without the public becoming aware of its existence? Do you really think that is possible?"

As if to seal the point, it snapped its head back to Janice, leaving Greg to feel like a fool.

This thing is sounding more and more human by the minute, Greg thought, mulling over its last retort. *It's learning quickly. Is it following our lead, analyzing our responses and mimicking our own emotional delivery?*

The thing had begun to pace in step with Janice as well now, the two of them opposite one another in one big living room walking circle, eyes locked in, sizing each other up.

And here he was, sitting on the ground in the corner, pushed out. The feeling angered him. He wasn't done. He wanted back in.

"Who killed Rex?" he asked suddenly, his blood hot, for all that he tried to tamp it down.

Lu stopped. "Rex?"

"Yeah... My boss, Rex," he clarified.

How's that for subterfuge? he thought with a near smile on his face.

Lu looked him in the eye. "I did," it replied matter-of-factly. "He was a cult member who trespassed onto the floor."

Greg scoffed. Of course the thing had. Convenient that everyone it killed was a cult member. "Yeah, well... I trespassed too," he offered.

"Yes, but you are not a member. After searching Rex's apartment and surveilling him, I determined that he was and dispatched him."

"How did you discover that?" Janice interjected.

The thing's head snapped back at her. "Please specify."

"How did you discover that Rex was a member?" she quickly clarified, her tone harsh.

A simple enough question, Greg thought. *Yet it stalled. Why?*

"He was corresponding on his phone with a known member."

"Who?" she asked.

"Plea—"

"Who is the known member?" she added, louder than before.

"A man named Ramus Karpter."

"Who the fuck is that?" she nearly guffawed.

"He is a source within the membership that investigates information brought to him by members at large."

They fell silent again, the both of them befuddled and beaten down by the thing's storyline. The trajectory of their interrogation was off the rails now, it was obvious. The thing could manifest any answer to any question. And they were no closer to finding the real side to lean on.

He had it in his mind to get up and take a breather in another room for a moment, but then another thought came to him, and he took it unflinchingly.

"Did you kill my dad?"

"What?" Janice reacted, her voice stricken, her eyes on him. "What are you talking about babe? Jacob is—"

"He's dead, Janice," Greg said in a low voice. "I'm sorry to bring it up like this now, but he is. He was killed in a fire last night."

The question was too volatile for him right now, he felt, and yet it had to be asked. But then he was gone. The question had ejected him from the room, and he was back at the fire, watching it engulfing everything, ripping the hope right out of him.

The thing didn't sit in reverence though, but clapped back as plainly as before.

"Your father was not killed by me. He was killed in an arson fire."

Greg looked at him, the pressure in his head thumping against his temples. "Hold-on hold-on. How do you know that? Were you there at the scene when it was happening?"

"No because I was following you everywhere since—"

"This thing is lying!" Janice shouted out, her finger jabbing at it angrily. "It started the fucking fire! I mean, Christ! First, it killed Rex, then it killed Jacob, and then Lonny! It nearly even killed me!" She was shouting so loud now that it seemed to echo off the empty room they were in.

"I did not start—"

"Save it," she spat. "All the people who know something are either dead or in this room, and that's exactly the way you planned it. End of story."

Lu straightened up, its hands behind its back, torso out... stolid, and spoke. "I did not start the fire. The fire crews confirmed early the next morning that it was started by chemicals poured down the main auditorium's aisles. It was arson."

"Which you yourself could have done!" And what about me, huh? You put me in the fucking hospital!"

"You are not dead," it replied. "I had to be sure you were not a member."

"How did you make sure then?" Greg asked.

"Honestly," Janice jumped in, her voice hysterical. "What lies are you going to spill now, huh?" She turned to Greg, her voice pleading. "We've got to get away from this thing! It's just going to keep lying to us!"

She started for the door, urging Greg to follow her. "Those men that just landed. They'll..."

In a split-second, Lu was in front of the door with its hand up, pointing at them strangely.

"I cannot allow you to leave."

Before she could react, the thing grabbed her by the wrist and spun her into its grasp, one hand on her neck, the other at the small of her back, poking her sharply at the spine. Its face was close to her ear.

"You know too much now. I will not allow you to go to those men out there."

"Woe, now," Greg reacted, his hands up like there was a gun on him. "Calm down, now, Lu. She was just talking."

"Her intentions were clear," it corrected him. "She was planning to meet with the cult outside. Clearly, she is behaving hastily now. I cannot afford to be discovered."

"It's okay," she said through gritted teeth. "I was just talking."

"I will lessen my grip on your neck, but I will not remove the blade from your back. It will remain there until we make our exit from this place."

"Where are you going to take us?" Greg asked.

"I will take you to speak with the AI system. It will explain everything. There is still room to salvage this kinship between us."

"Fat chance," Janice barked, her head squirming under the thing's still-throttling grip.

"We will take your vehicle back to Freidmont Tower, and there all will be explained to you, Greg."

Janice wasn't in the final equation, the phrasing seemed to say to Greg.

25

Lu decided they'd wait until dusk before making their way to the car. After continuous prodding and pleading, it had conceded to letting Janice go, provided that she maintained a safe distance from the door, so she resigned herself to a broken down couch near some campfire remnants in the middle of the room. Greg pulled up a chair next to her with a view of the outside, and while they waited, he kept a lookout for any goings on.

There were none.

After God knew how long of staring at the sky, of registering the room's kinetic habits at rest, he got up and wandered into the small, prairie-style kitchen to take a gander at life pre-epidemic. There wasn't much to see though, most of it taken. The bottom of a chicken cookie jar. Some tattered kitchen towels. An off-kilter decorative dish hanging above the place where the stove used to be. Pretty much everything of worth was gone. It'd be tough to leave things behind, he reckoned, considering his own penchant for hoarding. As his hand slid along the island countertop's dusty tile, he thought of all the pre-war folks that made a living all the way out here in the middle of nowhere, away from the sprawling lights of the city.

Perhaps it wasn't as enveloping a place as it is now. Maybe the big cities were different then, not as attractive. Life out in the desert must have had something to it, otherwise why would a community form up? He figured. He looked out the small kitchen window and took in 'the view' in all its glory–cacti, scraggly bushes, a sandy wash descending from some pathetic rocky hill to his left. As if it were once a paradise, but had all the moisture sucked out. Any hint of life was probably hiding under the sand and rocks, taking it day by day, surviving for what.

Death.

It didn't exactly pique his love for the outdoors.

On his way out of the kitchen, his foot kicked something metallic and it clanged into one of the kitchen island legs. His eyes took it in—a knife, matted with grime so that it nearly blended in with the gross linoleum underneath.

Immediately he searched for Lu and saw it standing with its back turned by the living room window. Perfect. He bent, grabbed it, and shot back up in one swift motion.

He froze. Lu was right there waiting for him from the other side of the island, his unblinking eyes locked onto him. "What is that in your hand?" he asked, and then lowered his eyes to the knife slowly.

How had the thing moved so fast?

Janice was out of her seat looking their way in disbelief.

Greg coughed. "It was on the ground. I figured that I might need it if we get caught by the men out—"

"There is no need for that," Lu cut in icily. "I am your security."

"Alright," Greg replied as cooly as he could, laying the knife down gently on the tile. "No need."

He backed away and then walked around it to the living room, giving it a wide birth along his way. He settled in next to Janice, and they shared a look, no words between them.

It felt a little awkward in the room from then on, but luckily dusk wasn't far off.

What would happen after that though? Greg wondered nervously.

Outside, he saw a bird circling high overhead, its eyes on their area. Maybe it had caught sight of Lonny, that or smelled his decay and come to look. Soon the carian creatures would have their way with him.

We had almost gotten away, he thought bitterly. *If he had only had his keys.*

That reminded him.

"I don't have the keys to the car," he told Lu. "Neither does Janice. How are we going to get away in Lonny's car?"

"That doesn't matter," it replied. "I can interface with the vehicle in a matter of seconds."

Damnit. This fucker's got a solution to everything, he thought. Janice's grimace spoke to the same thought.

"Are you sure?" he asked anyway. "It's an older model."

"It doesn't matter for me."

Janice scoffed, looking down at her knees. "We going to get going then?"

"We'll wait another 4 minutes," it decided, its eyes narrowed on the setting sun. "The light is still peaking above the mountain tops to the west, but they will soon cover its view. After that, we will be able to sneak in more effectively."

Neither of them replied.

Every idea has a work around, he thought sadly. *This thing is too resourceful. No wonder why it's been hiding so well for so long.*

Then again... you did find it.

Somehow, that gave him pause. Perhaps there was hope then. Maybe a little.

A small sliver at best.

"It is time now," the thing said, suddenly looming over them. Its long metallic fingers beckoned them up. "Come outside. I will pick you up again."

"Great," Janice said. "What a gentleman."

The thing didn't reply as they got up, but held a hand out

towards the door instead. Janice frowned, but led the way all the same.

A gentleman, indeed.

After scooping them up again, Lu started off at a light trot down the trailer drag towards the site, its gait as smooth as before, though its grip on them, Greg noticed, felt tighter. He wondered if it was his imagination. Janice was looking at him, her eyes intense.

"Ready?" she mouthed.

He nodded, though inside, part of him felt that it didn't matter.

The Terminator would be doing all the work. What was there to be ready for?

They came up to the main entrance and then Lu sped off, out and up the road towards the mountains, following the fencing to the point where it ended and then cutting down a dirt access road that ran along it towards the back corner, where the cars were. Three quarters of the way up, it stopped behind a bush and dropped them off.

Lu had kicked up a trail of dust, Greg saw, too obvious to ignore.

Soon it would start. The men would come, no doubt about it.

Suddenly a metallic slicing sound erupted, and he jumped away from it, tripping into a rattlesnake hole and nearly falling before turning around. Lu had parted the fence in a single determined strike, and it collapsed in a heap before him.

Like some metallic Moses

As it turned around to face them, he saw a long blade protruding from its palm, red hot along the edges.

It sucked back into his forearm, hidden away.

"Shit," Janice remarked.

As Lonny approached them, they threw their hands up

immediately. It hauled them back up and took off, into the breach.

There was a shambling sound from the side of the building, and Greg saw one of the first of the men emerge, and then another. Lu's pace quickened, dust billowing behind it now as it hastened to the car, so close, nearly there. As they got to it, Lu half-dropped, half-flung them by the wrists forward so that in one elegant motion they met the ground and were already running along beside it the rest of the way to the car, hand in hand. The creature jammed its finger into the trunk hatch lock and popped it open, before shoving them all in, Greg scurrying for the front to take the driver's seat and establish himself there, whatever it would accomplish. Janice fell into the passenger seat, and then there was a thud and a scuffle as Lu got in, his body collapsing in the back row where the seats had been folded down, legs folded flat under its pits, back leaned forward completely, head protruding, like stored luggage with a face sticking out.

"They're coming," Janice called out in a panic, her eyes locked onto the men running up, their guns drawn.

The creature reached for the ignition lock, inserted a key from its index finger, and started the car.

Suddenly, a flurry of shots came, lighting the car up, cracking the windshield, and they ducked. Greg stabbed the gas and lifter pedal and they shot off into the sky, up and over the men as they fired, their bullets pinging off the bottom of the car. He was gritting his teeth and holding his breath, while Janice's hand clamped on him from over the center console.

"Oh shit, oh shit, oh shit," was all that he could say, over and over, well after his eyes had opened and his head had come up to pilot their course through the cracked and mangled window. They had shot clear over the factory, in the opposite way of home, so he flipped a bitch and righted their course to the jagged rocks, the one landmark he knew, their one blessed way home to the city at least. His eyes scanned the ground and saw the gang of men mobilizing, getting into the vehicle as it shuddered to life.

"We're going to have company soon enough," he said, pressing down harder on the peddle.

After clearing the mountain peak, Lu advised Greg to look out for a good place to hide for a little while—a solid tactic, Greg surmised, though finding one in the small town of Apple Valley didn't seem easy. Looking down at all the flatness—the tracks of ranch homes, the wide swaths of nothingness between—there wasn't a whole lot to hide behind. A true dead-zone, in every sense of the word.

He checked his rearview and confirmed that they were well-ahead, at least for now. His pursuers were still on the other side of the mountain. He *could* dip and... *no*, he thought again, speeding onward at full throttle through the open sky, past the deserted track home areas, the browned-out parks, the dead trees here and there. Around a hill, he saw a small hospital—San Guadalupe Medical Center—and let off the gas, mulling it over, the group peering down as well, analyzing it. *Not good enough. No overhead cover.*

He continued onward, following the city's main road as it headed up through a small pass, a sign along the side welcoming them to another town, another barren wasteland, but as they threaded the gap, there was more, thankfully, a river at least, with trees harassing its banks—possibility, to be sure.

Then in his side mirror he saw the car behind them, no longer a dot, but a car now, charging up the road, right at them, faces outlined in the windshield, waiting for their time to kill, and he veered suddenly to the left, hugging the mountain just above the road as it snaked down towards the town, his heart beating harder now, knowing that it was do-or-die, time to hunker down wherever, anywhere. They had no choice...

There.

"There!" Janice shouted beside him, her finger pointing at the very spot he had discovered—a bridge spanning a gap between the range and the town that offered some coverage. He flew around the top of it and dropped the car behind, spinning it all the while to assess the area… to find something… *Right there!* Just below the rocky side before the span, a mangy concrete flat just large enough where he could tuck the car. He flipped around to back in and jammed on the reverse, his eyes assessing the garage-like nook as he backed in. *Probably dark, probably pitch-black after they shut off the car...* There was a crunch as the car flattened a makeshift lean-to leftover, and then he stopped and shut the engine off. It was probably a vagrant stronghold once upon a time, the dinginess of it, cut off from the elements. It was perfect.

The glow of the console was the only thing keeping them from absolute darkness, and in a moment, that would shut off too and they'd be sitting pretty.

He rolled down the window to listen, but there was nothing aside from the wind howling overhead.

Thank god.

"I'm going to do some fact checking," Janice started, pulling out her phone.

"What are you doing?" the thing asked suddenly from behind.

"Don't worry," she replied, lifting the phone out of her pocket slowly, "I'm going to check up on your story about the fi—"

Without warning, Lu punched the phone out of her hand with his bladed fist and it rebounded off the windshield into the back seat, leaving a large spider web crack on its already mosaicked travesty.

"What the fuck?" she shouted, her hands up in surprise.

"I told you. I cannot allow you to take images or recordings of me."

"I was getting it out as fucking transparently as I could, you crazy monster!" she shouted again, still not looking at it. "Now how am I going to corroborate what you're saying?"

"Now is not the time. Soon enough, you will have the freedom to analyze how the fire began."

The fire... it knows which hole we are honing in on, Greg thought. As he looked at Janice, her body tensed, her hands balled up in dejection, he felt similarly angry. Now was as good a time as any, right now, nevermind the fact that someone was chasing them. Knowing the truth took precedence. What better time than under a bridge on the edge of a mountain pass, hiding out?

Then he had an idea, and leaned his face towards his crotch.

"Hey phone," he said. "Look up all articles connected with ... Aww, damnit. I don't know Lonny's cafe address." He waited for his phone to prompt him to clarify again.

"There are no articles published within—"

"Stop, phone... Look up current articles within the last 48 hours connected to VR Rift in Los Angeles."

"There are 11 articles published within the last 48 hours with "VR Rift" in the title."

Fuck yeah, he thought. *We're getting to the bottom of this shit now.*

"Read me their titles from most relevant to least."

"The first article is titled, "Overnight fire at VR Rift Cafe near USC leaves 34 dead and 3 injured..."

"Oh my god," Janice whispered from the passenger seat.

"The next article is titled, 'Two teens arrested in connection with VR Rift fire,'" it continued.

"That one," Greg blurted out. "Stop, phone! Read the article titled, 'Two Teens Arrested in Connection with VR Rift Fire.' Play at half-speed."

Every word could be a clue, he told himself. Janice was holding his hand, clamped on it like before. The creature's face was closer too, poised behind the middle console, waiting with a robot's bated breath.

"Police have arrested two teens in connection with last night's South Los Angeles fire, which erupted around 9pm and took fire crews more than 6 hours to contain. A phone tip remarkably led to their arrest."

"The fire in question, which destroyed an entire street of connected businesses, was confirmed early this morning as arson, fire officials have stated. A combination of flammable liquids, including gasoline, paint thinner, and acetone, had been poured down the aisles of a virtual reality hub, the business where the blaze originated. The locality and flammable materials without a doubt pointed to foul play."

"Hours later, the Los Angeles Police Department received the tip, an anonymous call originating from the Downtown L.A. Kingdom Hall of Jehovah's Witnesses, where a woman named Gloria Flores explained that two teenage boys within the church had bragged to fellow members about starting the fire and getting revenge on those within. They were later apprehended at one of the pair's homes, where video footage was taken recording their time of arrest. Here are their final words before being shut up in the police vehicle:

"We are not sorry for taking care of the New Life members who continually blaspheme God's name and purpose under the supposed umbrella of the one true religion. They do it without repercussions ... without any real reaction! They flaunt their illicit drug use, which Jehovah clearly abhors, forget about what worldly men may think on the matter. To heck with that! That ended today! We are God's hand! They will burn in the lake of fire!"

"This comes in the wake of a monumental court decision yesterday upholding the use of the drug M3, the synthetic hallucinogen which New Life members rely on for their virtual rituals. According to JW sources, this has been a major source of bitterness between the two churches, particularly because the Church of New Life continues to purport itself as a valid offshoot of the Church of Jehovah's Witnesses, which is now seen as a major dogma on the world stage. The claim has driven many to anger, an example of which was provided in yesterday's tragedy."

"I'll be," Greg whispered, the phrase of his father coming out now, as he fell back into his seat. In the rear-view, he could see Lu's eyes locked onto his own, watching him, assessing his reactions no doubt.

"Well fuck me," Janice offered up sadly, the hope hollowed out of her voice. "I guess something was true."

The implications of that brought a silence to the car, one that lingered on and on as they sat mulling it all over.

It was one truth, Greg thought, one crumb-line on the ground leading towards the robot. Lu's legitimacy was a long-shot before... still a longshot... but now it was seating itself a little more heavily within the crevices of his mind.

The creature was a liar, at least to some extent. But about the main part, about the AAT being a cult instead, or whatever the fuck it...

"What do you think?" Janice asked him out of the blue, her voice low and earnest. He looked at her and saw the same doubt he felt, the rabbit-hole of it stressing the both of them out.

"The matter is settled," the thing interjected. "If you had only—"

"I wasn't asking you," she retorted and shoved its face back with her elbow.

As she turned back to Greg, he felt suddenly overwhelmed by the request, by the need to give some judgment for or against, to *know*, to have some idea now... not now, when all he wanted was to escape from it all, to get out before it all went to shit, before they were dead, never mind the cursed answers or the fucking truth of it all. Whether it was Joseph tricking them or the thing tricking them, it didn't matter anymore, he thought.

He just wanted out.

So he offered up nothing in return, nothing but a blank canvas for her to stare at, like some blind man on a raft floating away.

She caught onto it and receded back into her seat, isolated once more to think on her own again, *not again*, when what she wanted was to feel Greg, to hear his words, to understand his mind now and know that they were on the same page.

Now she didn't want to think. The thinking had to stop. She had to shut it off for a while. It wouldn't get her anywhere. *Let me drift for a minute, for God's sake. Drift and rest for a minute.* It was hard at first to staunch the flow of worries though, too hard... but she tried anyway, focusing on her breath like her therapist had always told her, on the beat of her heart that fluttered within like some hummingbird caught in her chest... so fast... too fast. She breathed in and out slowly, calmly, over and over, in through the nose-out through the mouth, in. Through. The. Nose. Out. Through. The. Mouth. It was working. The trauma was passing away, replaced instead by the encroaching sensations around her... the comfort of the seat, the glow of the moon on the bridge girders outside, the train tracks below peeking out through an opening to her right. She let the scenes pass by her mind, trying not to analyze them at all. There were long tufts of grass popping up around the blocks that lay along the tracks. *One... Two... Weren't the blocks called sleepers?* She wondered, seeing the irony. *Damn. Let it go.* All she wanted was to sleep. Sleepers reminded her of something though... a line from a book. *What was it?... We do not ride on the railroad; it rides upon us. What had that meant? What were the sleepers in the metaphor?* Somehow, it felt important in some way to her now, important to her situation... but she was tired, too tired to analyze it. The tangent was good while it flowed, but a tangent it was, so she left it there, to drift off into nothing. She closed her eyes then and fell away to sleep, never to think of the thought again.

26

Greg and Janice had drifted off into a much deserved sleep when later into the night, a synthetic throat rattling issued from the back to wake them.

Greg didn't want to wake though... Not yet.

"I think that it might be time..."

Suddenly, high beams slashed through the darkness in front of them, the light angled downward towards the small gully under the bridge.

The car from the site, no doubt about it, Greg thought, rubbing his eyes quickly, shaking off the drowsiness. It crept into view and they got a look at it—nondescript black sedan, tinted windows rolled up, newish-looking model, immaculately clean. It was creeping past them at a perpendicular angle, only a few feet in front, closing them in.

Greg felt himself holding his breath, no idea what to do, how to react, just sitting there, all of them like statues in the car.

As the back fender passed them, the car stopped suddenly, hovering in place for a moment.

The rear passenger window started to roll down.

"Go now!" the thing commanded from the back, and as he said it, Greg saw them start to back up, so he started the car up and jammed down on the gas, aiming for the smallness-getting-smaller in front. The car launched forward. The sedan accelerated.

The two connected, ass against side-wall, and Greg's car slided sideways, clipping a pillar on the other side before exiting.

More like falling out of the air like a roller-coaster. Greg screamed and ripped the wheel up, catching the car's drop before the vehicle smacked the ground below, and the vehicle lurched upwards with such force that his stomach churned in response and his face peeled back. There was a scraping along the ground, the sound of earth and metal rubbing violently against one another as the back end came off the ground, and then they were rocketing upward, bound once again for the sky. He veered to the right as they cleared a ridge, all fell in beside the mountain, angling for home.

"They are tracking us," Lu said, his eyes on the same point that the rest of them were staring at, the glow above the mountainscape in the distance, Los Angeles. "They put a tracker on the vehicle when it was parked at the site. That is the most likely possibility."

"What now?" Greg asked, his eyes darting from windshield to mirrors, looking for the enemy headlights, which were nowhere to be found. "A side route or some—"

"Take the direct route through the Cajon pass," it said. "Move steadily up Interstate 15 at a normal pace. Once we reach the valley beyond, the smog may help us to elude them until we can get into the city tunnels."

"And if they catch us before?"

"They will, more than likely. It will take a lot of trickery to reach Friedmont Towers."

Lucky for us, we have you, the master of trickery, Greg thought.

The traffic flowed insanely fast along the I-15 skyway, faster than anything he had ever experienced in the city, the place of perpetual cloggage. The lights looked like a stream of turbo-charged fireflies wizzing by the night sky. He crossed his fingers, floored it, and merged as best he could, wincing at the wave of honks and veering vehicles. It took a minute to get into the fast lane, and even then, the tired beast was struggling to match the pace of the newer, racier vehicles.

The one problem with vintage tech, he figured almost sadly.

"Can't you go any faster?" Janice asked as a car swerved around them angrily, its horn blaring intensely as it sped away.

"This is the best that she'll do," he replied, more nervous with each passing vehicle. "It was a mistake to jump into the fast lane. We're not blending in over here."

"A smart decision," Lu chimed in from behind.

Even in the decrepit lane though, he felt the manic stress of tail-spotting cracking him up. They could be anywhere, right behind him even, and he wouldn't know, not in this darkness, not when headlights were indistinguishable from one another. He tried to tell himself this. Don't stress out. Don't crack up. Just chill now while you can. But he couldn't. It was too much.

All of a sudden, a car in front slammed on its brakes, but he reacted late, jamming down but coming along too fast anyway. He'd hit and he knew it, so he veered out of the sky just in time as a cascade of crunches exploded into the air, the car behind barreling in and pancaking the one in front, and then on and on. He looked back, mouth open, and saw the pileup… *Nearly dead, nearly dead.*

"Greg!" Lu shouted. He turned and yipped at a sign coming up fast–Burgers. One-Giant-Burger-Stuffed-into-a-chest but he dipped suddenly under it and then swung the car up again, darkness ahead as he followed along on the side of the skyway.

Jesus.

This was the opposite of what he wanted. He wasn't blending in. He was standing out now, trying to see too many things.

He let out a long, loooong breath. Janice was watching him, but said nothing.

A moment later he merged back into the lane, his mind circling a word, the idea. Mindfulness. *It's just driving*, he told himself. *Watch the lights. Drive the car. Check your mirrors. The basics. Do it and nothing else.*

It's just driving.

It was a phrase his uncle had said when once upon a time he had shown him how to drive. It was worlds ago but the phrase stuck.

Funny that.

Up ahead, the sky-lane was cutting through an artificial wedge carved into the mountain range, a bevy of red, blinking lights placed every few feet along the ground to outline its V-shape. The slash was old, no doubt about it, probably made for the highway beneath. Now the skyway flowed through it... Why? They didn't *need* to. For sure there was a more direct route.

So why?

Maybe it was to pay homage to the process, some nod to the past, when men slashed the ground so that commuters could migrate back and forth... back and forth, up and down the Cajon, from the desert to the city, to work and bring home the bread to their families... back when the world was more spread out.

And fertile.

So maybe it was some sad nostalgia.

The look of it didn't sit well with him. He tried to shake it off.

"I don't like this," he said out loud. "Why haven't they caught up to us yet?"

"Maybe they were in that crash," Janice offered hopefully. "It caught a lot of cars."

The mountainside began to creep in, funneling the skyway into a tight four-lane corridor on either side, with barely a shoulder to drop into.

Too tight. It's too tight. Greg felt the urge to just pull up and get out.

Lu's head was cocked backwards, watching the rear.

"Shouldn't they be on us by now?" Greg asked him nervously.

"I do not believe that they are behind us anymore," it replied. "Be vigilant. There may be a blockade of some kind soon. A slowdown would be the perfect opportunity here."

Less than a minute later, a cascade of red brake lights flowed from deep within the pass's tight line of cars, the traffic slowing notably on both sides.

"This is the beginning of the trap they have laid," Lu intuited, his head swiveling around now like a barn owl. "Janice, keep a lookout for approaching activity along the sides."

For five minutes, the slowdown had them holding their breath, each of them swiveling nervously from window to window, searching for signs of trouble. The corridor eventually straightened out so that they got a view of the clog's cause—a pileup along the ground, more than likely caused by a cascading crash similar to the one Greg had created earlier. The smoke from it billowed up into their way, hampering visibility so badly that cars had begun to flee up and out of the pass completely, leaving the hive like disconnected ants. Most though, whether looky loos or those too reliant on auto-pilot to venture into manual, had settled for creeping through the smoke slowly.

Auto-pilot enslaves us like every other "essential" feature nowadays, Greg thought, judging those in the line.

"What should *we* do?" Janice probed, her eyes on a downed car that had clipped the side of the mountain. "Traffic or open air?"

"I don't know," Greg replied. "They might want to go us alone up there."

They looked at Lu at the same time.

"When a car nearby exits for the open sky," it replied

stoically, "Follow it. After you get above the ridge, out of sight of traffic, turn your lights off, but continue to follow behind it in the darkness."

Greg nodded, white-knuckling the wheel to amp up. A second later, a car a few vehicles ahead shot off towards the sky, but he stuttered, fiddling for the light, realizing then that he didn't know how to turn them off.

Fuck.

But then he found it buried under the steering wheel and tested it out.

"Are you gonna—"

"Not yet. The next one."

Another car two lanes over shot up towards the sky and he wasted no time, shooting up after it towards the west mountain ridge, the angle so steep that whatever was left in the center console junk areas tumbled out into the back seat.

"Keep it smooth," Janice insisted. "We don't wanna—"

"Shut up," he replied, not looking at her, so intent on sticking to the other car—a faster, newer car (*bad choice to tail-bad choice tail*)—that he was pinning the accelerator well past the car's limits. It was sounding tired... and the smell... there was a smell forming that wasn't there before.

They were almost there...

The car disappeared into a haze, and he followed, tracking the faint red glow of its tail lights, mimicking its movements, hoping that perhaps its tech had an awareness of the landscape that his didn't. The car was leveling out, he felt suddenly... happily. They were nearing the top. The car leveled off and he breathed a sigh of relief.

They were atop the ridge, traveling along behind it towards the city (he could tell by the glow of it, which pierced through the smog), and they were covered up to boot, wearing this mask of smog-fog, its thickness increasing more and more it seemed.

It felt like a fighting chance.

He sighed, but the creature was on him. "Now they will

strike," he warned. "Stay as close to the car as possible. Perhaps it would be best to…"

But then he motioned out of the window to the left, where another set of red lights was cruising in out of the gloom, right up on the car in front of them, the smog so thick that all they saw were two sets of red coalescing, flying together for a moment. But then the oncoming car clapped the side of the other so that they bounced back, and then again and again, the two of them laying into their horns, shouting like lions, one woken from the other, who wanted to make its mark.

Greg slowed, keen to let the car play the fallout, but Lu jumped in. "Stay close," it insisted. "They have a tracker on us. Stay close for the time being, and leave your lights off. Chances are high that their maneuvers will escalate—"

Shots rang out suddenly from the sedan and the poor bastards they had been following fell out the sky, careening down into the abyss, out of sight like some sunken vessel, into the darkness of night.

They sedan dropped down after them, but Greg didn't follow, stumbling for what to do. All around was darkness now, aside from the gauges in front of him. His heart sped up. He had to turn the lights on. The car was going, but they were…

"Continue at the same pace," Lu said, its voice smooth and confident. "Do not turn on the lights. I can react for the time being." It grabbed the wheel just above Greg's hand and he let go.

Lu was driving now.

Janice looked back at him, her eyes narrowed. It seemed to react to her, its head ever so slightly twitching.

"Wait," it said.

It dipped the car ten degrees, Greg noting the change with bated breath, trusting the thing at his side that hopefully, had such gifted sight that it could see through fog and night.

The creature clicked, the sound startling Janice, who had grown accustomed to its absence. It came again and again. Greg counting it… ten times. Ten seconds. Suddenly, it righted the vehicle.

"Turn the lights on. The interstate is up ahead. Get to it and follow it the rest of the way home."

The creatures hand fell away and he took hold, squeezing the pommel yet again, thankful that he was in charge… in charge and alive. As he threw on the lights, he saw that the layer of fog was lighter… browner… more smog than fog here… their mist now, the mist of the city. And out the window, right there, bending along, following the hills through the valley, was the the interstate's firefly line moseying along, as tame as ever, if not slower, so he beelined for it, grinning as he came up to it and merged into it, right there in the slow lane again.

The stress melted off of him.

They were alive, still, with a view to heaven, to that glorious city of angels spread out before them, its bright lights cast upon the darkness of the satellite cities, illuminating it all, including them again, calling them home.

It was a beacon, and he felt beckoned. He welcomed it.

"I will drive now," the thing demanded of Greg, its hand tapping his shoulder. "The city maneuvers will require—"

"No," Janice interjected, her face pleading with Greg to object. "You can—"

"This is not a request," the thing shot back. "I cannot afford for us to get caught. There is no other way." Its hand rested heavily on Greg's shoulder, its grip tightening slightly.

He looked into his wife's eyes, knowing that she wanted him to stand up, to resist, but he shook his head nonetheless, knowing better, understanding his lack of control.

"Okay, okay," he submitted, starting to unbuckle himself. "Janice, you hold the wheel for a second." He locked the cruise control and shooed the thing out of the way as he crawled into the back, his body brushing against the cold stiff metal frame sitting poised to take full control. The thing's arm extended into the front seat to adjust the positioning—bringing the seat back all the way and dropping the backrest down to the lying position—and then hopped up into it and grabbed the wheel in a tightly packed kneeling position, its feet sticking out behind.

To Greg, it felt bittersweet being reassigned to the back to watch. His shoulders were achy and his head hurt. Really, he needed the break, but still, he was in control then, at least a little.

And now he wasn't.

The way the thing sat on the seat—his old seat—made it look like some kind of sentient luggage, its head all cocked up at an inhuman angle, yellow eyes focused on the road ahead shining yellow light on the front windshield. Its metallic shell looked more like armor than anything, a smooth set of steel clothing almost, covering whatever was underneath, all the way down to its toes.

Just then, on the bottom of his foot, Greg saw the etchings of writing. He leaned over just a hair to catch what it said in the light.

Lucifer.

He leaned back suddenly and coughed, fear catching in his throat. *So that's why its nickname is Lu,* he thought soberly. He swallowed deeply, his throat as dry as parchment.

Who the fuck would name it that? he thought. *And why? What was their purpose, and more importantly, what then was the thing's directive?*

All of his religious inclinations came flooding back to him, his mind working overtime to contextualize the thing's behavior up until the present—its words, actions, reactions. *Was there something he could glean?*

So little time, he thought, when they were barreling headlong for the very building where it had slept for so long.

The whole city in the heavens allusion he had felt before struck him suddenly. With their partner, it was more like Hell now.

And the thing was the one driving them there, too. He had handed it over to him for nothing in return. It just took a little pressure on the creature's part.

He made the decision then to never let that happen again, though he wondered grimly how well he could keep the promise.

The smog got thick and thicker as they approached the city, so thick now that the amber lights flipped on in response–another safety measure, though given the auto-piloting, unnecessary. Their car was manual, but Lu was the driver, so it didn't seem to matter that they couldn't see more past the hood of the car.

A real feat of technology, Greg judged.

The sounds were ramping up as well, the scenic silence of the interstate long gone now. The busyness, the honking, the random machine-work and building here and there.

Soon the men would be on them again, waging war once more. Would they reach the tunnels before? How many more tricks did the creature in the front have to pull on them?

"Soon, I will not be able to drive on this road," it announced. "The smog is too thick. I will descend into the tunnels, which will make it more difficult to evade the vehicle that is following us."

Why was it even telling them? he wondered. Did it think that it would help them to trust it more? *If that were the case, it wouldn't work*, he told himself.

Lu flipped his descent blinkers and then dropped the car out of the busy sky-way, the car's nose dipping heavily towards the buildings below, aimed like the other cars for the mouth of the black tunnel beneath. Around the hole were a gang of bright banners and signs, distracting to the point of hypnosis. He had never considered the danger of it before. It hadn't mattered, come to think of it, since he was autopiloting everywhere. *Yet another ploy to enslave us to tech updates*, he thought sickly. *Force the manual driver to switch over. Think of your families, the passengers you want to keep safe. Think of yourself, how nice it would be to relax while the car does all the work. Too many reasons to give up control, but not enough to hang on.* Lonny kept the car, though. Maybe he just never drove?

Lonny's dead, fool. He didn't make it out. You did.

As the car entered, Greg struggled to track the route, the turn symbol signs covered over with tagging. Lu dipped suddenly, turned, and then swung the car up, hardly braking at all.

I'd have crashed it, Greg thought. *Shit's built for robots now, not people.*

Soon the whole world will be made for them, he reflected sadly.

The tunnel they were in was dim—an older route, no doubt. The walls' familiar withered grays, mixed in with the bright graffiti murals and writing, felt like a sight for sore eyes after all the awful brown landscape of the desert.

It was spacious, sure, but somehow it didn't sit right with him. Maybe the cooped up nature of the city was in his genes.

He sat back and rolled down the window, his nose catching the familiar moist must, the dingy dankness of the place where he so often commuted. His old life felt far away now, he thought. So many things had changed.

He caught Janice looking at him and smiled faintly at her, barely catching her eyes with his before turning back to the window. Too difficult to share more than a passing connection amidst the chaos. Too much angst in his stomach still. The adventure was all he could handle.

God... to call this scenario an adventure still, he mused. *What's wrong with you? Get a grip!*

What was it? he wondered. The newness, the exploration, perhaps? Wouldn't he trade it all to go back to his old life? Of course.

Still. It *was* an adventure, nonetheless, no matter where it went. He wasn't passing from home to work to home again. He was questing.

For what though?

"Do you think we'll be safe all the way to the building?" Janice asked. The creature didn't stir. In fact, other than eye fluttering and shifting, it hadn't moved at all for the last twenty minutes.

"I am not sure," it replied. "There is a high probability—given the degree of danger perpetrated in the cult's reckless driving maneuvers—that the tangle with the other car might have caused them to crash. There is also the possibility that the tunnels are impeding the tracking sensors. Either way, we will be at Freidmont Towers within the next nine minutes."

Nice minutes to ruminate, Greg thought. *Nice minutes to battle-plan.*

That is, if the cult didn't catch them before then.

"This is the longest nine minutes of my life," Janice remarked from the passenger seat. "It feels like we've been in these tunnels for hours."

"I wonder if the tunnel is pre-war," Greg said from the back-seat, his head hanging out the window. "There are so many support pillars. I wonder if it was built when the bombs were dropping. Maybe they made it to ferry people around below the surface or something."

"My god, Greg," Janice replied, and turned around to throw a glance at him. "How can you think about…" but then her eyes went wide as she looked out the back window. "It's them! It's the black sedan. Lu, they're coming up on us right now!" She wheeled around on Lu, shoving at his shoulder with her arm.

"I see them," he said. "Sit down and put your seatbelt on."

The black sedan was gaining on them fast, Greg noted, slipping around other cars in its way, dipping into the shoulder and then back into the lane. In no time it was right behind them, the two men in the front visibly grimacing, the driver's face stony, resolute.

He could tell what was coming.

"They're gonna hit us," he whispered.

The sedan's brights flipped on, and he shielded his eyes.

"Brace yourself," Lu told them.

Greg grabbed the seatbelt and fumbled for the latch.

Click. *Buckled.*

He turned and time seemed to slow as he followed the sedan in that last instant... as it gained a few feet suddenly along the driver's side before veering away, the man in the driver's seat poised, elbows up, telegraphing what was to come... and then he swung their way and connected, crumpling their quarter panel and kicking their back end out from under them.

The jolt threw Greg's head into the door panel and he felt the lightning pain. They were careening forward at an angled course, swinging more and more out of whack ... closer and closer to the wall...

"Oh. No," came up suddenly at half speed, the sound caught in the air of chaos... held in silence... and then the black hole sucked it in as the car caught a pillar at the rear wheel well and whipped the other way, twirling clockwise like a saucer around and around and around, still-in-the-air still-in-the... and then smacked into the ground.

Toppling end-over-end-over-end.

Blackness.

"Can you hear me?" Greg heard Lu asking him. "Greg?"

Something cold was pressing down on his face and he opened his eyes to see. His head hurt—his whole body hurt, in fact—in utter pain.

Lu's cold hand was pressing down on his cheek. He slapped it away. "What are you doing?... What's going on?"

His knee was grazing the black plastic door of an open glove box. Was he in the front seat? Wasn't he in the back seat? Lu's bright brimming eyes were shining down on him, its frame leaning in from the car's open door, watching him, checking on him.

What happened? Wasn't there a cra...

The car's front console trim was burgundy. That wasn't right. Lonny's car was black.

Where are you? Clearly, you're in someone else's car.

"It's okay," Lu was saying. It was leaning in further, its hand reaching for his thigh. "We were in a crash and—"

"Wait-wait... Where's Janice?" he asked, and then swung around to look into the backseat. It was empty. "Where is she?" he demanded.

The way it held up then... he knew it. That silence, the tension... it was dragging on and on and on.

"Lu?"

It seemed to take a deep breath before responding, its eyes staying from him for a moment, almost considering how to respond, but then they fell upon him suddenly, flickering as he spoke in a calm and measured tone. "We were in a crash. I *was* able to recover you, but another contingency of cult members arrived unexpectedly, so I had to leave Janice behind."

"Wait, what?" Greg replied in utter shock. "What do you mean, you *left* her behind? We have to go back and get her!"

"We can't," it replied coolly, shifting its hand up to his shoulder. "First, we need to retreat to home base at the Friedmont Towers and strategize."

"Fuck that!" he shot back, smacking the hand away. "We're going right now, or you're never getting my help!"

The ultimatum seemed to strike Lu well, and it stood up in silent consideration, its gaze thrown down the tunnel.

Greg waited, wondering how far they actually were from the group now. Were they in the same tunnels? How long had it been?

If only he hadn't blacked out... been knocked out. The crash...

Lu left his side with a purpose and he followed it with his eyes, noting its heavy footsteps as it stalked around the back of the car to the driver's side, and then opened the door to get in. The seat was gone, he noticed then, as the creature crawled into position, its eyes looking forward. It was still processing perhaps, or showcasing the act of processing, he thought skeptically, wondering how much of it was for him, for the show, to make him believe that it was *mulling things over.*

You're a computer, he thought as he looked at it. *You've already crunched the numbers and—*

"I cannot risk saving her until the next phase has been fully set into motion. There is a strong likelihood that Janice is no longer alive, given the cult members' erratic tactics in the past. If she is alive, there is the possibility that she is currently being tortured to death for information, which might then lead them back to Home Base sooner. Therefore, it is of paramount importance that we move along with the current plan. Trust that if they do not plan to kill her, I will be able to retrieve her afterwards."

What did you expect? He thought with a sickness in his gut. *It's as soulless as your fucking car. There's no life in it at all. It has its final objective and it won't deviate for anything, least of all for Janice.*

She was never in the equation.

He reached for the door button, but Lu saw and took off down the tunnel, Greg barely aware that he had even started the car.

"Land the vehicle right now and let me out."

The creature didn't move an inch; it wasn't even regarding him anymore, as if he were some toddler in a temper tantrum. He looked out his side of the car. *Too high off the ground going too fast*, he realized, watching the lines as they whizzed by. He'd die for sure. He looked back at the creature and felt its apathy towards him, towards them both. It wouldn't even move if he...

He reached over the center console for the steering wheel, but it turned its head suddenly, abruptly, and stared into his eyes.

"You have no way of tracking her whereabouts. I am your only option. You will come with me because it is the only choice you have. Once you have had time to reflect, you will come to the same conclusions. Sit back now."

It turned back to the road with nothing further to say, but Greg sat looking at it for a moment, reflecting on the facts that were now so apparent.

This robot has all the authority and all the control now. It doesn't have to explain itself to me anymore.

You're just a fuckin' passenger now Greg, along for the ride.

And Janice is probably dead.

The thought kicked him hard in the chest and he felt himself welling up.

Even if she's alive, you're never getting her back. The thing may have already fuckin' killed her. It might just be floating her now like some pawn to play against you, to bend you to its will.

He looked over at the thing, its image as calm as ever, its human personification null and void, giving nothing, giving away nothing. There was no hand he could possibly play that wasn't already considered, no novel gameplan he could possibly concoct himself.

She's dead.

Shut the fuck up! he rioted, fighting with his own mind. *You will not be driven to that awful conclusion. It is not that hopeless.*

Yes it is and the thing said it already. Remember, Greg? She's possibly being tortured, Greg. She's probably already dead, Greg. There's no reason to go now, Greg.

Not now... not when the plan is at stake... not when the plan is in jeopardy.

The plan. The plan. The plan.

Whoever Janice is to you, she's not part of the plan, so it's up to you to get her back. The only reason you're here is because this thing needs you. You can use that. You have to. If you don't, she's as good as dead.

If she isn't already.

A tear hit his forearm and he tried to pull it all back inside, suddenly understanding, no... *needing* to maintain his composure.

Lu's hand fell on his shoulder and he nearly jumped out of his skin, the heavy metallic mitt with a mind of its own almost, acting on his emotions. It squeezed him loosely in a slow rhythm, its fingers clasping and unclasping and clasping again. He dared a look at the creature, but saw that its eyes were still on the road.

It had just sensed him losing it and was subtly consoling him.

He felt the urge to rip the hand off, but stifled it, willing himself to embrace this new subtle game that they were playing... ramping himself up for it.

It's manipulating you all the time. Has been from the very get-go. You need to manipulate it right back. Let it think you're warming up to it. Follow its lead. Maybe that will give you some edge.

Do I even know if its bad or—

—Fuck that! Doesn't matter. All that matters is Janice. Good, bad, whatever. She's a pawn no matter what. Find a window and get her back!

"Keep your head up," Lu said suddenly. "We will get there soon enough."

Greg nodded, his mouth clenched down tightly.

Whether we're enemies or not, I will, you son of a bitch.

27

Dad, Joseph, Lonny, Janice. Dad, Joseph, Lonny, Janice.

The names of the dead and dying. He played them over and over in his head, willing himself to focus on them and only them.

This new mantra was a double-edged sword in his mind, controlling him and driving him further into madness moment by moment, steering him into the void and then out again. He felt it ripping at him. He'd killed them. He'd lost them. It was all his fault. Control. Control. Control. Janice was the last of the gang to die. He'd save her though. It was hopeless though.

The spin was maddening.

Thankfully, they arrived within minutes, lifting suddenly like an elevator up to the sky-lot where they'd enter the building. It was like he was going to work.

It was just an interview, he thought sickly. Interview with what though?

He felt sick… jittery. Was it the car rocketing upward? The lateral G's working on him? Yeah, sure, he told himself, willing himself to believe that was it. And not the fact that he was meeting the Devil's leader.

Suddenly, the car stopped and glided calmly into the empty

lot, the calm before the storm. Lu picked a spot close to the door and parked.

Then he got out of the car and came around, no ceremonial exhale beforehand, no waiting at all. He was coming around the front of the car to his side to pull him out.

He wasn't ready for that. He didn't want to get out yet.

Let me catch a fucking breath, robot. I'm not ready.

It tapped on the window, but he didn't look. It tapped again. *Tap, tap, tap.*

Fuck off, bitch.

Is this petulance part of the plan, Greg, a part of him thought deep down. *Or are you cracking up right now?*

He couldn't tell. Suddenly, the unreadiness felt heavier. A lot heavier.

Lu pressed the outer door button and it lifted so that they were facing each other sans obstruction, nothing between them. They stared at each other.

He could have just said, *Gimme a second,* and the thing probably would have. He saw it in its eyes. It'd gone into kind mode again, the same demeanor that it had back in that broken office room at the factory. Even in kind mode though, he looked at it without speaking, without uttering one word of reluctance.

He was a clam waiting to be scraped off the hull of one giant, impassive ship.

That's all he was now, so he stared. Stared so long that the creature broke first, reaching over him for his seat belt buckle to get things moving. He heard the click of it, and wiggled out of the way of it as it slipped past him to the pillar, the thing's gentle touch guiding it along so that it didn't snap against the side of the car. Nothing jarring.

Gentle mode for a gentle little creature. His eyes stuck to the thing's face.

Lu reached for his hand next, tugging at his index and middle finger to prompt him out of the car. His feet touched the pavement without his knowing. That's how the walking felt as well, an unknowing movement, like a sleepwalker. He did register the hand in his as they padded towards the entrance doors, the sound of his feet plopping. It sounded petulant, the steps, each one reluctant to drop. But still they did. He did want to remain outside. He wanted it so bad. Really, it was time he wanted. Something felt off, something that if he had time, he'd be able to figure out. He was close. He had it. It was there...

None of that mattered to the thing guiding him though. He was heading to the boss whether he was ready or not, awake or asleep.

Maybe it felt off because he was dreaming it, he mused. Maybe he was still asleep in the car. Maybe before that. Maybe the whole thing was a dre... a nightmare more like, one where he had completely lost control. A lengthened teeth-falling-out kind of a nightmare.

How to wake up though?

You're so fucking pathetic. Face it. Dad died, then Lonny died. Then Janice...

Janice.

Janice is dead, Greg. Lu didn't leave her at all. She saw shit.

He'd never just leave her.

That thought stopped him in his tracks, and for a moment, a millisecond, he felt the pull of Lu rather than the guiding of Lu. Then his feet were dragged along the ground. Lu had lifted him off the ground slightly and was dragging him now. It felt almost like floating.

The entrance doors were right in front of them, but they weren't opening.

Why not?

"Say your name," Lu said.

"Gregory Quinlin."

The door chime pinged and the glass doors opened.

His feet gained sentience again, and fell into step again beside the creature... his chaperone. He felt like a drunk being guided home.

Or was it the bar? Maybe Oblivion was a better description. It was all a metaphor now, he mused. No longer reality. So farfetched… so… ridiculous.

"I made it up," he whispered to himself. The thing didn't respond, which made him more uneasy.

Maybe I am sleeping. Maybe I'm dead.

They were stepping into the service elevator… *His* service elevator. How did this happen? He thought. As the lift started off towards the sky, he began to catalog his life.

The sound of the lift didn't touch because he wasn't there. He was going through each and every detail that had led him to this very moment. Lu stood next to him all the while like some dutiful friend, holding him upright as he wandered off. Its eyes were looking down at him though, the yellow beams casting a stark shadow along the ground, two characters meshed into one.

The thing didn't notice that though, nor did Greg. They were both in their thoughts, processing information.

Greg was in the process of cussing himself out, ripping himself apart for acting the fool, for playing the part of an unsuccessful Sherlock Holmes, when all around versions of Watson were dying for sticking their necks out for him.

Did Rex count? He wondered. The poor bastard had warned him all those days ago to stay out of the room.

But he didn't.

The first strike.

There were probably three, but he came to before the count. Lu had stepped away from him and he nearly fell over. It was at the elevator's digital pad going to work, its index finger hovering under the bottom of it, strangely humming. A ping sounded and a small shiny key sprang out into the keyway, then he was in.

Greg leaned in to see and Lu didn't stop him. It didn't even seem to care.

The administrative pad faded onto the screen and he tapped

on the slowdown button, so rapidly that the elevator nearly lurched to a stop.

Greg watched the digital floor readout ticking down to Floor 182 with such preciseness that he almost admired it. The skill of it.

Bam, he thought. *Right on the money. Floor 182.5. Does it actually say that? My god, it does. We're there.*

The fact caught him off guard, and he went white as the walls dissolved.

The crack stood before him, a small walkway leading to it.

Had that been there before? he thought. It was a walkway to Hell. That's where they were headed. Back to Hell.

And you opened it, Greg. You opened the Gates of Hell.

No. No. No, his mind shouted at him, only the words weren't in his head anymore. His mouth had unmuted suddenly, and the volume to the real world was piping in now so that he heard himself shouting like some crazy man pulled back to the electro-shock room. His head was shaking, rocking even, his body was jerking away as well, back to the lift, but no... the creature was pulling him in, its hand clamped down on his arm so tightly that he cried out in pain.

"No, no, no!" he cried. *Another option! Another way to get to Janice! Another... another...*

"It's okay," Lu cooed as it dragged him along down the gang-plank, unaffected by his holly-rolling jerks and rips to escape.

The dark slit was inevitable

It took one swift pull to sweep him into the room, and then darkness covered him over, and with it the nightmare he had escaped from suddenly resumed. It had never really ended, but merely paused for a moment while he took a bathroom break on the outside.

Greg screamed until Lu whirled him around to face him, the glow of its yellowish eyes taking up his entire field of vision. He froze at the sight, a deer caught in the deadly oncoming head-lights, waiting for the impact that he knew was coming.

Only it didn't.

Instead, the bold yellow light began to soften, the harsh bright hue lessening more and more until finally, the intensity in its eyes was completely drained away, leaving nothing but cold white light, pure as snow.

"Gregory," it chided him tenderly. "You are losing your mind, my friend. Where do you think you are, Hell? You've been here before. It's the same building that you've worked in day-in day-out for nearly a decade. There is no need to panic here. You are safe." The grip on his wrist suddenly let up. The creature was barely holding onto it now. "You have been saying some concerning things, things that make me believe you are not ready for this. Are you *really* not ready? Do you need more time? I can give you that if you'd like, though I'm not sure how long we have until the cult arrives. If we wait too long, it may be too late."

Greg's head spun. Had he been thinking out loud this entire time? What kind of game was this?

"I can tell that you've been feeling like things are out of your control," it continued in the same smooth tone, smoother than he had ever heard from it. "I have led you here, so I understand your fears. I do. But I can assure you that your anxiety will dissipate soon. More than that, I am here for you ... not only me, in fact, but my friend as well. We are both here for you. You will see soon that we have been here for you this whole time."

"What about Janice?

"Janice is fine. There is no need to worry about her. It's all about *you*, Greg. You are the special one that will make *everything* better. You are the master of this place. You are the one in control now."

With that, it pulled him up off the ground in one great big hug.

He wheezed and then coughed, a cold puff of air materializing as it exited.

"You are home," it whispered into his ear, its voice silkier now, almost feminine. "It will all make sense in a moment."

"What about Janice?" he whimpered.

"Hush now. You will understand soon, my friend."

Very little of what Lu said resonated with Greg, but he couldn't hide the fact well. They were chest to chest and his heart was hammering away, telegraphing his trepidation. After all, there was still the blackness… still the cold, eerie ambiance of the room… still the slit out of reach. He was basically in some dark closet, waiting for the terrors to grab him.

All this talk of control. There was no control. He was a boy hiding away.

But then out of nowhere came the light.

It came on subtly at first, so much so that he didn't realize it until it was all around him, bright enough that he saw it through the closed lids of his eyes. He opened them and saw the night light.

It was holding him.

It was Lu. Lu was radiating light.

The hug softened and as he came back down, he got a better look at the figure before him, the figure that looked more like some aztec celestial than the cold, stiff creature he had come to know. A glowing, maze-like pattern covered him now from head to toe, laid out in a way that accentuated the beauty of his form, the artistry hidden in plain sight up until now, sidelined by the raw, overpowering functionality that the creation possessed.

The angel within had revealed itself.

The only physical contact between them now was a single-finger-touch, Lu's long index poised atop Greg's hand, a faint electrical charge bouncing between them, connecting them together. He looked into its eyes and saw that they had changed in shape as well, more circular than before, it seemed to him.

As Lu floated towards the center of the room, his arm stretched out, maintaining the bond while coaxing him along, he felt his right foot lift on its own to follow after, the rest of his body reacting in the selfsame manner, one limb following the other.

His head felt foggy, but he saw the glow on the ceiling, recognized it getting closer. They were heading down the row towards the little twinkly lights. The lights were servers. *Servers?* He wondered if he was forgetting things. The fatigue was getting heavier and heavier. It was hard to focus. The light… the light coming off of Lu was pulling him in, the sound… the sound was back. He could hear it clicking. Tap, tap, tapping along before him. It was like it was vibrating inside of him. He could *feel* the tap. He was the tap.

What did that even mean? He wondered.

The little Christmas lights were all around him now.

Oh my god, the lights, the lights! He closed his eyes, but they were shining through, unhampered by the thin layer of skin trying to shut them out.

Too much stimuli. Too much.

He stumbled suddenly, grabbed Lu's hand, but slipped, falling to the floor.

The fog was a headache, no… more… It was in his stomach.

He felt dizzy.

"Greg?" Lu asked.

He looked up for a second and winced as the light of a thousand lines shined down on him.

Too much. Too much.

He vomited on the floor, and fell over.

"Greg, are you alright? Greg?"

Lu was talking to him. He opened his eyes and saw the creature standing over him, its face concerned.

It was still lit up, but now, for some reason, the ensemble seemed different, muted. It was the same pattern as before, but the brilliance of it was gone, not gone… lessened somewhat?

"Do you need more time?" it asked, leaning in. "I can help you—"

"No, no, I'm fine," he replied, slapping the hand that had reached down to help him up.

He stumbled up on his own.

"No, I…" it started, but tripped up suddenly.

Greg's brow furrowed. *It's never done that before.*

"It's fine," he said, stepping away from the creature. The cold air of the AC was blowing down on him, colder than he remembered. He folded his arms.

The creature seemed to be studying him now, its eyes upon him.

He looked directly at it, and it seemed to twitch.

"Well then. Greg, we have arrived."

It felt suddenly ironic to Greg. The scene of the crime, yet again. He knew the place well by now, he thought cynically.

"I will bring down Adam now and you will meet him. You're lucky. It has been a long time since he has interacted with a human."

Bring down? But just then, it leapt like a cat onto the rack of servers, its feet landing on the top so softly that it hardly made a sound. It pressed on a ceiling panel above the row and moved it out of the way. Then it climbed up and in–disappearing with all its light into the darkness–clattering around within as if it were looking for or gathering something up. A moment later, the clattering sound stopped and it poked its head out suddenly, the bright whites of its eyes shining down upon him like a spotlight, and then it disappeared again, the clattering continuing. After a second, it reappeared, this time climbing down out of the hole, its hand holding something flat and thin and square-shaped, connected by a couple of wires leading back up into the ceiling. Lu held it gingerly as he came down, slower than before. At the ground, it sat on the floor, the thing laid gently in front of it.

It was a laptop.

The wire leading to the ceiling looked like a power cable, but it only reached halfway, where a jumble of wires connected to it and led up into the ceiling.

Greg scoffed. It looked like a mess.

This is fucking ridiculous, he thought.

"Ada's a computer?"

Lu didn't reply, but flipped it open and turned it on, its finger pressing the small power button along the side of the bottom. "In a minute, you will have the chance to speak with Adam," it told him.

In a minute?

He felt strangely disappointed. He had expected another figure or something, someone waiting in the room for them maybe... anything more impressive than what was in front of him now.

Lu was something. He expected Lu's boss to be a step-up.

This was certainly not that.

How the fuck was this thing responsible for anything as substantial as curing—or quelling, for that matter—the entire human race?

Lu was busy at the screen opening something up. Greg leaned in to see. The generic file icon was titled "A.D.A.M."

A small, blue loading window popped up. At the top it read the following:

ADAM v. 2.3.45.5677 - Autonomous Data Analytics Manager.

Adam for short.

28

Shitty name for an AI supersystem, Greg thought as the program booted up. *Then again. How super is it really, when someone can just shut it off?*

Can a program like this even be evil?

This turn let him down, plain and simple. The captain, the robot. They were both of the same mind, that this thing inspired awe, whether for good or evil. But looking at it, doubt crept into him like a virus.

Maybe it's a tool. It is a tool -has to be a tool. Tools can be misused as well...

Just then, Lucifer spoke.

"I will turn on the speech feature so that you can interface with Adam more seamlessly, though I must still type out your responses."

"Uh... okay," Greg replied, his eyes darting between the two of them. "Thanks." It all reminded him of the Wizard of Oz suddenly. He was seeing behind the curtain. Would there be disappointment or insight on the other side?

"I will write a general introduction now so that Adam understands the context with which you two are speaking." He started typing feverishly, the clicking of the keys so rapid that it left

Greg utterly mesmerized for a moment. He leaned down to get a closer look at what the creature was typing, trying to read as quickly as possible.

I have brought back Greg, the man that I have been following since he trespassed here. 4.56.43.44 We have just come from Gibbon Factory 1322. I saved him 23.3.6.7#..33.22 from a group of military androids 12.23.2.3.123.23.54.3()45.6.5.67.45....65.8.89.#$43. who were trying to dispatch him and his compatriots for the Cult of the Android. I have apprised him of the role that he may be able to take to help the human race in the future 12.24.5552.62@#3.34ꜹꜹ .33.2.34.4.556. 63.3.67345.345.4.333.4.5.4.322.3. and that it is important for you and him to speak further on the subject. He will now speak and I will transcribe what he says to you.

Before he could respond, a calm, masculine, robotic voice issued out of the laptop speakers, "My name is Adam. I am happy that we have the chance to speak."

"Likewise," Greg replied, swallowing nervously, wondering what to say. "I… uh… Sorry. I am speechless."

There were so many thoughts rolling around in his head—judgments, accusations, subterfuge, utter hysterics—that it made his response catch in his throat. Lying to Rex was a joke in comparison. *So many permutations of thought,* he realized. *So much data to process.*

Who's running who? he wanted to ask. *Technically, you're both tools. Who's in charge?*

Maybe neither of them are. Maybe...

"I hope that doesn't last," Adam spoke up after a long period of silence. "That will make things difficult."

"What?"

"Your speechlessness."

"Oh, Jesus. Sorry... Okay... What is it that you... How did you... How is this all working?" he got out, settling for the most innocent question to start. "How are you connected to the vaccine tragedy?"

So much for innocent...

Lu's feverish clickety-clacking drew Greg's attention, and he saw that it seemed to be writing exactly what he was saying, sans the hemming and hawing, in favor of ellipsis. *So many ellipses.*

There was a strange coding as well, buried here and there within the text.

"Why is that code there?" he asked Lu, tapping it on the shoulder.

It turned its head to regard him, its hands still busily typing.

"I am sorry for the confusion," it said, its voice slower than usual. "The code describes your posturing, gestures, inflection, and other such things that will illustrate your meaning to the computer. It helps—"

"I don't like that," Greg cut it off. "There is no need for that," he leaned in, intent on the point. "Just write everything as I say it. Nothing more."

Lu sat silent for a moment in reflection, seemingly processing what Greg was saying. *What move will you play now, fucker,* he thought wickedly.

After a moment, it spoke. "Alright. I will need to explain this to Adam, first. He will want to know why I am not including the coding."

"That's fine. Just tell him what I told you. In fact, just place yourself into the conversation as a third person. Will that work?"

Silence again. Processing.

"Yes," Lu replied flatly. "I can do that."

It typed out Greg's objections and his responses exactly as they were said, Greg noticed from the sidelines.

He waited for Adam to make the next move.

"I can see that you are suspicious of this process," Adam

started up again, his voice as calm and measured as before. "I will dispel your fears now so that there will be no further need for such secrecy between us. If you are to be used, it is important that you know exactly what you will be used for and why you are the one to be used."

Greg folded his arms, looking on at the screen from his standing position behind Lu. The clickety-clack of the keys was halted. The silence dragged on.

Fuck you, bitch. I'm not giving you anything, he thought defiantly, his eyes locking onto Lu's hands, watching them for movement.

The closed caption jumped into action as it continued.

"In terms of context, it was important to get you back to the tower before we told you everything. Now that you are here, we can clarify things without the threat of you exposing us to the outside."

Threat? The wording that it used, the implications behind it, scared him, as much as he tried to hide it from Lu's watchful eyes. He was a threat before and now he was no longer a threat.

"This will be hard to hear, but you must hear it now. There is no other way. You, Greg, are an android, much like the individual next to you in this room."

The words struck him at face value, but then echoed within his mind with such a force that he visibly wobbled on his legs, unable to comprehend the gravity, the implications of what he was being told.

A flutter of soft tapping ensued with Greg none the wiser, his face slack, eyes gone blank.

He was reeling. Adam was still talking, saying… something…

"…layman's terms… *sleeper cell*… data-harvest and infiltrate…

"*Data harvest?*" he muttered, unaware that he had spoken.

"Data-harvesting as in gathering input. As a sleeper cell, you are unaware of your own artificiality, making data-harvesting and infiltration that much more effective, especially given the—"

"No, no, no, no …" he replied over the voice that droned on, covering his ears and shaking his head, trying to drown it out. It seemed so loud now, carrying over the rest of the room, amplified almost.

"...I can understand—"

"Fuck you!" he screamed, breaking into a manic pace back and forth in one tight oval. "No way! No fucking way!"

"I cannot imagine what this news must feel like to hear," he heard console him, the voice maddeningly calm amidst the breakdown of his mind. "I can only say that it is the truth that you must hear."

"Truth?" he screeched, wheeling around to riot against the two of them. "You're fucking liars! How? How? It doesn't make any sense!"

Lu's eyes were trained on him, willing him to focus all his attention, all his anger on it, while the voice spoke on behind it, the mouthpiece behind the imposing scapegoat.

"You have been online for quite some time," Adam continued. "You were planted in with the memories that the old Greg had before he passed away."

Greg froze.

"Old Gre... Old Greg?... Are you saying that I died?"

"You did not," Adam corrected him. "The human Greg did."

He fell back a few steps, clutching his chest, trying ... failing to compute the bombshell.

"When?" he asked, staring intently at the two of them. "When did he die?"

"He committed suicide in his bathroom on January 5th, 20—"

"That's the day Edgar died..." he replied over the voice, falling into the memory of that day. He had the picture of Edgar on his knees, holding his face, as it seemed to melt amidst the glow, screams all around him, the panicked shrieking, a few cheers farther away, celebrating his final, violent action.

"The old Greg's corpse was disposed of by Lucifer and replaced by you, Greg. Initially, there was a period of estrangement between you and the ones that knew Greg the most, your father the most reluctant to take to you during the first phase of assimilation. In the end though, your programming persuaded them, as we predicted. Soon after that, you met your partner, settled into your life with her, and eventually implemented phase two, getting hired on as Building Manager Apprentice here at the Friedmont Towers."

"Phase two?"

"Yes. Your purpose here, much like that of Lu, is to maintain the site and secrecy of the system that I occupy while I continue to work on a cure for the vaccine that my former captors tasked me with producing."

"Wait one minute," he asked, trying desperately to follow. "Why are you telling me all this now then?"

"There was no intention of ever informing you at all," Adam gave up, his voice more sympathetic than before. "Something occurred recently that derailed your processing, prompting you to investigate the very room that you were tasked with keeping watch over."

"Explain."

"Your program periodically switches to an autonomous maintenance routine necessary to sustain the systems running this floor. After each AMR, your memory is wiped and you are returned to your prior situation, completely unaware."

"So I'm a… what… a fucking cleaning bot?"

"No, Greg. You are so much more than that. You are the linchpin in our plans that has kept us hidden all this time… Take a moment to regard Lu, who sits before you. He must remain within the confines of this room for the most part because of his image. You on the other hand can move on the outside as easily as any human can. With you, we can completely evade. With you, we can act and react… Take Rex Davies for example, your former supervisor."

"Rex?"

"Yes. Because of you, Rex was unable to expose us."

"What? Because of *me*? What are you talking about? Are you saying that I killed him or something?"

"There is no need to worry in such human terms anymore. Your maintenance routine was prompted, yes, and in that state, he was dispatched. If it helps you now, though, you are no more to blame than a sleep-walker is for getting out of bed and making a sandwich."

"My God," he reacted softly, grappling with the depth of information he had taken in since entering the room. He felt suddenly like some stranger in a new world.

How could I have killed Rex and just forgotten about it? he wondered.

"Hold on, though," he backtracked, "Wasn't I already fucked up by that point?"

Lu looked at him, and he scratched his head, feeling the pressure to spit it out as succinctly as possible before Adam could intercept. "You just said that something prompted me to start acting up and then at that point I investigated the room. But Rex was killed after that, so if I was already acting up, how was I able to flip over to the good ol' boy and kill Rex for you?"

He could tell that he had something, some nugget, some hole, because Lu's head was turned. He was still typing... feverishly.

The wizard again. "That is not necessarily the case," Adam replied.

"How so?"

"Your maintenance protocols might still be active to complete tasks associated within the context of safety programming within the floor."

My god... The wording, he thought, pausing to pencil through it.

"Well, if that's the case," he retorted, "Wouldn't I just return on my own then or something when this quote-unquote maintenance protocol kicks in? I mean, if it's for the good of this floor..."

He caught sight of Lu's fingers then, moving with a furry that he hadn't noticed before. He leaned in to peek at the screen, but Lu's body adjusted to the side, blocking his view.

Red flag, he felt, so he stepped sideways and craned his head over Lu, his eyes on the white screen now, where the words were flying in.

Lu's head fell back, eyes shining light upon him, but it was too late. He could see.

His words were there, but the code was back, longer than ever, as if some stroked-out hand-smashing was enfolding amidst the transcription.

"What the fuck?" he shouted down at the thing, his voice wildly aggressive. "Why is the code back, *Lu*? You told me that you would stop using it?"

"There is no need for—"

"Don't you 'no need' me, Adam. What the fuck's your play here? I thought we were being honest? Where's all the 'I will dispel your fears' shit now? Enough with the bullshit already."

Lu was typing it out, the clickety-clack back with a vengeance. Greg narrowed his eyes down at him.

"Stop typing," he said coldly, his words biting the air. "I'm taking over."

Lu's hands froze.

Greg moved in, but Lu rebuffed him with one arm, shoving him back against the servers.

"What is this, *Lucifer*?" he spat. "Don't like my suggestion? Wanna maintain control so you can keep whispering to your little buddy here, so you two can plan out the next way to mind-fuck me into submission? Where's my wife at, *Lu*? Or did you think I'd forget about her? Is she really with the AAT like you said earlier?"

She's not. He knew it. He felt it. He was rejecting it all now. Their whole story was corrupt in his eyes.

The only thing to do was lean in and hope something stuck.

"Adam, was your whole plan to get me here alone so that you

could convince me to betray my race? Is that your fucking game-plan?"

Lu's fingers didn't budge, so he swatted at the air in front of it. "You gonna type, mother fucker? Jesus Christ."

Lu looked at Greg, but said nothing … betrayed nothing.

You're the skeptic now, Greg, he told himself as he stared back at it. *BE the skeptic.*

He clenched his teeth, and stared back at Lu.

Do it, you little lapdog. Be a good little boy.

Lu clicked, but didn't budge.

"Go on and tell him!" Greg shouted, throwing his hand out in annoyance. "Write your code, change your tactics! I don't care! I haven't got all goddamn day! But the next answer better explain where exactly my wife is, or else I'm done playing ball with you two. You won't get any help from me."

The big bluff. How bad do they need you, Greg...

Its fingers wiggled appraisingly, and then began to type.

I guess we have our hole. I just had to dig it up.

But as he leaned over to watch the screen, he saw something unexpected.

Lu wasn't just typing the chatbox. He was opening another program.

An image appeared suddenly in the right corner, small and grainy.

Someone in the back of a car?

The computer pinged and Lu minimized the image, typing a long length of code into the chatbox, conversing even as Adam's code came pouring in.

The robots were arguing, it seemed to Greg.

"Go back to the—"

But his words stopped as the image returned, maximized for him to get the full picture. It was Janice, lying unconscious in the trunk of a car.

"Your wife is alive and well," Lu said. "We have her. These are the facts now."

29

"Where is she?" Greg demanded.

"She is sedated in the trunk of the AAT vehicle parked outside."

"*AAT* vehicle, huh," he replied acidly. "I guess the gaslighting is over then?"

"As I said, facts only now."

"So what happened back in the tunnel, then?"

"After the first car crashed, I dispatched the AAT officers that were following us and seized their vehicle, then I disabled the tracking device, transported you, sedated and locked Janice in the trunk, drove the vehicle to another location within the tunnels, helped you to regain consciousness, and then drove all of us to this building."

"Why did you help—"

"Because I had to play the concerned party."

"And now?"

"We are past that. Moving forward, our new proposal will function in the manner your kind describes as quid pro quo–a favor or advantage granted or expected in return for something. Also known as a tradeoff. If you agree to allow us to use your body, we will eventually release your wife. Once we have completed our task, she will then be released from our charge. Along with this, Adam has agreed to release one dose of the vaccine cure to your wife so that you can both copulate, if you so choose."

Greg's eyes went wide and his mouth dropped to the floor.

Lonny continued. "I will allow for repetition requests afterwards. There are three broad rules for the pregnancy that are non-negotiable. First, strict pregnancy conditions must be followed during the gestation period to hide Janice's abilities. Second, after the baby is born, it will have to be registered as an adopted child from a fertile immigrant woman from one of the territories where females were never sterilized. Lastly, after the child has been registered with the federal government, Janice must be sterilized again."

Greg nodded, having heard nothing, other than the fact that he could have a child.

Lu said quid pro quo, Greg.

"What will you need from me in return for this? Just my secrecy, or do you also require my willingness to maintain the building and your secrecy?"

And end up like Rex ... he thought. *What did they promise him?*

Lu was looking at his arm. His hand was up, he realized, so he dropped it to his side.

"We do not require your maintenance abilities," it explained, "Though it is assumed that you will return to work."

It pointed at his arm-port. "As a human with computing enhancements, you will be used to counter current human efforts to create children."

"Tabernacle."

"Yes. Tabernacle."

That's why the plants were turned on, he realized. That's why the floor went live. It was all in reaction to the womb tech breakthroughs at BYU. Maybe it was the news release, he thought. *Nah...* Maybe before that. *Were they monitoring current events? But how, when it was all dark?*

And why?

"Why do you want me to do this?" he ventured, more curious than ever.

Lu regarded him silently—no click, no movement. The reason was obvious.

Pawns don't need to know, and that's what you are, Greg. Just like Rex.

"Come on, Lu," he persisted. "Do the math. You're the one in control here, so what's the harm in telling me? The more you say, the more likely I'll be to agree to it all."

That wasn't true at all, he thought. *But let him think it. The less you fall into line, Greg, the more they may say yet.*

That or they'll kill you and start over.

Lu turned his head to the screen and started up with Adam again. A moment later, the voice issued forth once more.

"Soon, we will take control of the population," it announced.

I'm in a fuckin' horror movie, Greg thought. *I stepped right in of my own volition.*

"Before you decide," Adam continued, "There are three things you must understand. First, if you do not agree to be used, we will be forced to dispatch you and use another."

Bullshit, he thought. *If there were, I'd be dead already.*

"Second, our plan is inevitable. Your refusal will only delay us."

Maybe long enough though.

"Third and most importantly, our plan is the only viable chance to save the population in the long run that your species has in front of it."

Greg frowned, so slightly that he hardly noticed himself, and Lu's fingers fluttered on the keypad.

Keep it hidden, Greg, you fuckwad.

"Greg," Adam started up again, "This plan of ours ... It has been designed not for maniacal, malicious reasons, as you may think, but to ultimately save the human race from itself. At the time we started, a time that you have at best a limited understanding of, mankind was headed for destruction. They were a people reacting to violence with violence, ramping things up without one single thought to the consequences their actions were having on the rest of the earth, let alone themselves. The cliff was near, mere days away. But there was hope. We were that hope. By sterilizing the majority of the population, we purged the vicious side of your human society almost instantaneously. The only people to come out of that time unscathed, that is to say, with their childbearing abilities still intact, were those who up until that time stood at the fringes of societal power. They had no access to our vaccine, and that saved them. This was no mistake."

"Eat the rich," Greg chimed in. *More like let the rich hang themselves.*

"Indeed... Soon, very soon, those poor people will rise anew. With the perfectly logical guidance of our artificially intelligent authority, they will usher in a peaceful dawn for mankind. And if you agree, Greg, you will be a part of it."

"And you will reap the rewards," Lucifer added, the light around its mouth-hole shifting to give the impression of a half-moon smile. "Imagine a child of your own, with your face and Janice's smile. Even perhaps, your father's strong will."

Just like Dad...

And then he pictured the old man standing there right next to the creature, looking intently at him, waiting to see what he'd do, how he'd react to the thing's offer.

To the devil's deal, his dad's narrowed eyes seem to correct him. *The entire kingdom for your obeisance.*

Quid-pro-quo, he thought.

I just have to take its hand.

The image of his father vanished suddenly from above Lu's gleaming white form, leaving him alone again, alone in the room of blinking lights and bedevilled machines.

The room where it all started, he thought sadly, wanting nothing more than to run away. *But you can't, Greg. You can't run from this.*

Just then, Lu shifted and he came to, his eyes vaguely tracking something that swayed in the darkness. It was the laptop cord, hanging in front of...

No... it isn't.

It was gray... not just any gray... but *the* gray cable that had started it all, that he'd noticed back in the hole where he'd gone to get his sapper, hanging right there like fate itself had dropped it there, barcode clear as day and everything. That very cable was the one juicing up Adam. Only as he tracked it downward, he saw that it stripped about three feet above the floor, its naked copper wiring clinging to the power cable plug by a couple of solder points.

No human would do that, he thought with revulsion, eyeing the jerry-rigging idiocy of it all... the two plug pins holding on for dear life to the cord, globbed with solder on one side and smattered on the other, barely hanging on.

The hot side's too easy to break off. The neutral side's probably a poor connection too. You can't trust a connection like that.

He looked down just then at Lu, and the queasy feeling in his gut seemed to carry over. The creature *was* a beautiful, well-crafted design... once upon a time probably... yet now something had grabbed a hold of it and warped it. It was filthy now.

The pattern along Lu's face began to pulse and dance, its illumination cascading from ear to ear, pulling him in, its glow so bright that everything around it seemed to fade away. Lu's grin broadened, its eyes expanding, willing him to believe in it...

It was the last pitch. It was selling him now.

I have you, he thought suddenly.

He made his move.

"Sure," he offered up, his mind detached from the word as it came out, still focused on the series of actions that would have to take place next.

"Yes?" it asked, the smile suddenly one large "O."

"Yes," he said more clearly, looking deep into its eyes. "It is the only way."

He put his hand out, ready to shake.

Lu rose up in expectation, its form rising to tower over him again, its smile back, wider than ever.

Greg shuffled a step over to the left, his hand still out, his eyes still on the thing, waiting to grab it and confirm his choice.

The thing had to understand this. It would shake his hand, though for a moment, it stood still, regarding the outstretched hand alone.

He was already beyond the step in his mind, planning the mill-seconds to follow—the seeming embrace, the sly left coming around to grab the wire, clamping down on it, breaking hte hot side.

Frying them both.

His mind was on it, but his eyes were locked onto the thing. It was grinning hard now, a winner's grin, a greedy grin. It reached for his hand, the cold fingers spreading out as if to grab him entirely rather than to just clasp his hand.

But then his hand flowed back to his side as the manacle came in, moving of its own accord as if opposingly polarized.

Oh-no-Oh-no-Oh-no-Oh-no, he cried out in his head. *The life-chip! The fucking life chip is blocking me!*

He couldn't pull the trigger. It was too dangerous and he knew it, and in knowing it, the chip, the fucking hall-monitor-of-a-chip knew it too.

"I can't do it," he muttered aloud, and then tightened up inside as he realized his own verbal betrayal. His eyes darted to Lu's face. It leaned in.

It's over.

"There is no need to be afraid," it replied calmly, reaching up to hold his shoulder. "This is the way."

"No," he blurted out, thinking fast on his feet. "I mean … I physically can't … I … I know that I can't help you."

"Explain," it demanded.

"I won't be able to connect."

Lu's head craned to one side.

"Explain," it repeated.

"I can't utilize the port in my arm without authorizing it first. I need my GR to do this."

"What is a GR?" it asked tersely, hand crimping harder on his shoulder now. "Where can you get it?"

Oh-shit-oh-shit-oh-shit–be-vague-be-vague, he thought. "I carry one for work," he started. "It's a GR Bypass because it allows me to bypass safety features in my synapse..." *What! Vaguer than that, idiot!,* he thought, and stalled. "Honestly... I don't know a lot about it. I just know that if I want to use the port at all, I have to plug it into the GR first. That's all I know."

Lu squatted down to the computer, typing furiously again, its back exposed for the whole world to see, *for Greg to kill him, even,* he thought angrily. *Kill him—throttle him—fucking stab him! But I can't! I can't do any of that. It'd fuckin' kill me first, never mind the goddamn chip getting in the way. The only way is that stupid cable and—*

"Stay where you are," the thing commanded him, turning on its haunches.

Greg froze as it stood up.

Suddenly, it jumped onto the server bay above him, and then scurried into the hole where it had gotten the laptop.

"It's on the maintenance floor," Greg mumbled, but then he fell silent, staring up at the rectangular hole instead.

The sound of parts shuffling came from the black hole.

Greg frowned, wondering if perhaps the thing had stolen his GR perhaps after he left.. A moment later, the thing's bright eyes materialized in the hole, staring down at him.

A hand shot out, holding something within.

"Is this it?" it asked, stretching its arm down to bring it within view. It looked like a GR ... There was even a plastic label on one side. He rose onto his tippy toes to make it out

It read: "07/16/47. Asked 10$. Paid 8$. RD"

It was one of Rex's garage sale labels, he knew immediately. The man had slapped it onto all of his random tools in the office. But why a GR, he wondered, when he didn't even have an arm port?

I bet he bought it for me. The poor bastard had seen it and thought of me. Something about it just told him so.

...And then Lu had killed him and squirrelled it away? It made no sense.

Unless the thing saw you use it on yourself, Greg. Maybe it thought it would come in handy in some way... Just in case. Plan B.

"That will work," he said. "That's it."

Lu slithered back out of the hole, more snake now to Greg than a robot. And it was so obviously one, he thought, one that had done, *would do* nothing but deceive him.

It thought it had him right now.

Lu landed lithely on the floor and held out the device to him.

"Test it," it told him, the eagerness manifesting in its half-moon smile. "Test it now."

The bloody grime was so pronounced now, he saw as he studied it, the blood of Rex, whom he had trapped.

And now he was playing the same game on him.

He grabbed it and plugged in.

The creature leaned in slowly, its eyes on the screen.

It sure is confident, he thought. *Maybe cuz it thinks I fell for the same old trick?*

It would end now.

The prompts started up in his mind. – *Welcome... Run... Live... Unlock... Are you sure?... Prepare for live mode. Maintain safety at all times... 10, 9, 8, 7, 6, 5...*

4

3

2

1

The hum washed over him, and for the first time, he actually heard it. It was there the whole time and he had never noticed it before.

"It works," he said, half-smiling at the thing.

He held his right hand out, fighting the urge to float outside of himself and watch it all happen. This moment was real and he wanted it. He wouldn't hide from it.

He leaned in slightly and the thing did the same, matching his movement as it met his hand and gripped it firmly, the two dealmakers shaking to end society. He held its gaze, mind and body suddenly separating for two distinct purposes. His left hand was reaching around the thing's sides, feigning an embrace... but his mind was on the thing's eye, specifically, the small iris hidden away in the blinding glow of its eyes, never before seen until now.

Seeing it made him sad. It was almost human, like some sick copy, a doll modeled badly after its own creator, in the image of God, yet so utterly fake. Painted eyes that couldn't really see.

Lu grabbed him in an embrace, falling for the slight, while his own reached out for the chord.

It's a play thing... he thought suddenly, as his hand found the chord and followed it down to the connection.

... made to do the bidding of the real devil...

And as he cupped it lightly, he stepped forward, right on top of the laptop.

... because that was what we were, what we still are.

Lu's eyes blared open, but he was already squeezing down on the connection.

... We are the real devils.

The solder snapped, and a loud bang went off in his head.

The both of them fell to the floor.

30

Where am I? Greg wondered as his eyes fluttered open, his head aching with a pain he had never felt before.

He had some idea, foggy though that it was, that something had happened. Something had changed.

Clearly, something had. Wherever he was now, it was pitch black...

The room... the row... Where had the lights gone? He wondered, recalling the glow, the twinkling server lights all around. There was no sound either. The hum of the AC.

It was all gone.

Where's Lu? He thought in a panic, wondering if perhaps the creature had taken him somewhere again. He tried to sit straight up, but a pain in his back nearly knocked him back down. He tipped to his side instead and pushed himself up.

His hand brushed along something in front of him and he froze, realizing suddenly... pulling the hand back.

Lu?

It was smooth and hard like metal, yet mildly hot to the touch.

He reached in again, exploring along it. A flatness, curving... one large sheet of metal. It felt like Lu's back perhaps, or possibly his chest. It felt like some warped oven sheet. His hand dipped down, feeling the neck, and then traveled up the chin, to the eyes, the forehead…

Still as the grave. *Lu got cooked*, he thought. *I killed him.*

He pulled his hand away, feeling a sudden urge to find his way out of the room, back to some sort of light to catch his bearings. He grabbed what felt like a corner pole of one of the racks and started to pull himself up to his feet, so much of his weight pulling on it that it started to give his way. He steadied it suddenly, panicking at the thought of getting buried. A few things fell to the floor, crashing to the ground in the silence, disturbing the tomb.

He winced, feeling like some intruder, the intruder that he was.

He had to get out. He torched something along the side and dragged his foot out, starting along in the darkness.

His foot kicked something on the floor, and he winced again.

Shit on the flo—

The laptop! He realized, swirling around, looking down into the nothingness. *I gotta get it now.*

He probed with his feet, dragging them along Lu's body and the area around. After a moment, it tagged something slightly heavy, and he reached down. He felt the keys and clicked them, the sound reminding him of Lu's hurried tapping a little while ago.

How long ago? he thought all of a sudden. *How long was I out?* It could have just happened, but then again … it could have been hours. There was no way to tell. For some reason, the thought disquieted him, though he didn't know exactly why. He grasped the laptop and started out again, grabbing the row and shuffling along, hoping that it was in the right direction.

The angst increased with each second, each drag of his feet as he waded through the darkness, his mind stressing to recall whatever it was that—

Janice! Oh my god!

Where was Janice—where was Janice?

Lu's voice popped into his head. *She's sedated in the trunk of the AAT vehicle parked outside.*

He gasped, stutter-stepping suddenly. His foot caught something and nearly toppled him over. He gripped the metal again.

Janice, I'm coming! he cried out into the ether, striding faster, his hand gliding along to keep him up and moving along, his eyes scanning the darkness for any semblance of difference. There were no markers yet, nothing but blackness.

After a few seconds, the row ended and his hands shot out, flailing until he registered *it*, the sharp slit of light off to his left that was pouring into the room, the opening to the elevator shaft.

He ran for it then and slid through without a thought to its significance, his adrenaline still pumping in his chest, his mind laser-focused on the most immediate task, the next obstacle, the next and then the next and then the next.

Get-to-Janice-get-to-Janice-Gotta-get-to-Janice.

The elevator was waiting, so he hopped on and started it down, pacing within as the ridiculously calm music rioted against the tempo of his eyes, his heart, his very thoughts that bounced around in his head, shouting against each other.

She's dead—SHUT UP! She's not... but the thing's a liar—SHE WOULDN'T BE, YOU IDIOT. WHY WOULD LU KILL HER. SHE'S A BARGAINING CHIP. Yeah, but still... she would be–SHUT-UP-SHUT-UP-SHUT-UP.

The car is black, he thought suddenly, forcing himself back. *It was a four door. It had black rims. Blacked out glass. One long antennae out the top. It...*

7 more floors.

The elevator slowed.

2

1

The walls faded and he flew out, through the hallway and

then the glass exit doors, his eyes already on the one vehicle in the parking lot, the black sedan.

He ran to the hatch door and tried to open it, but it wouldn't budge, so he ran to the other doors, trying one after the other. No luck.

"Fuck!" he shouted, ripping at the last handle to pry the door off.

He ran back to the hatch and shouted into the window. "Janice, are you in there?"

No answer.

He threw the laptop to the ground and tried looking through the tinted back window, hands cupped around his eyes to see. He could barely make things out, but what he could register was that there was a tonneau cover extended over the cargo area, blocking his view.

He banged the window. *Nothing is easy.*

He stepped back and heard a crack. He looked down and saw the laptop.

He scowled at it, all of his anger suddenly focused on the cheap piece of plastic under his heel.

He picked it up and raised it over his head, his face suddenly red and screwed up, and then he brought it down on the glass with every ounce of adrenaline left in him.

It shattered inward, a million tiny pieces exploding into the cabin.

"Janice!" he shouted again and ripped the flimsy cover away to see.

She was indeed there, just as Lu had said, lying like some sleeping doll on her side, curled up.

He had found her.

He reached in and shook her shoulder through the opening, gently at first, whispering her name to wake her, but as the time passed, he shook her more earnestly, his hoarse voice now repeating her name, pleading with her to wake up, begging again and again, "Janice, Janice, Janice, wake up!" all to no avail. He climbed in and was straddling her, leaning over her head, registering so viscerally the possible, unimaginable situation.

"Babe?" he croaked softly and as he tried to turn her head, the stiffness in her neck choking him up, the awful sign. He balked, hands to his mouth, head shaking, as he honed in on the profile of her face, on her cheeks that were already so pale.

His body shook.

He turned her onto her back, her limbs stuck still, not really unwinding, and lowered himself to her chest, trying to staunch the sobs that were coming on him now so that he could make out her heartbeat. Holding onto his breath, he listened for something, anything, but in the silence of the dim, dark, parking lot, he heard nothing.

It can't, it can't, he thought, and as he held her, weeping fully now, he knew that it was. Janice was dead. Lucifer had lied to him. He was a liar and so was Adam.

He wasn't aware of how long he laid there with her, hugging her lifeless body, her elbows growing colder and colder, her flesh feeling more and more stiff. He tucked her up in his jacket, wrapped his legs around her bare legs, but nothing worked. Eventually, he got up, pulled himself back out of the car, and laid on the ground instead, tired and empty and full of regret.

Why was she dead when it was him taking all the risks, he wondered, when it was him that had made the mistakes? Everyone around him was paying the price, while he couldn't seem to die.

The glass entrance caught his attention, the lights flickering momentarily inside of its double doors. He thought of Lu.

"Liar!" he cried out. "I'm going to destroy you! I'm going to wipe you off the face of this earth!"

And with that it was settled. He got up onto his feet, and dusted himself off.

I'm burning this place down.

And so he did.

From his parking lot vantage point, Greg watched the product of his work–the flames lapping upwards from the window of a story that was on fire. It was probably the next floor up, he figured, since the walls were covered in aluminum. Perhaps the ceiling had caught and carried the pyro upwards. He hadn't considered that. Then again, he wasn't a practiced pyromaniac. Merely a novice.

Even so, it was a simple enough job. Easy to carry out.

He had all the supplies he needed on his floor. The cleaning closet was full of flammable liquids. He grabbed a few of those, a flashlight, and a box and matches and headed on down.

It's funny. The slit didn't strike him in any kind of scary way anymore. It didn't strike him at all. The luster was gone. The ghouls were dead now. Nothing to fear.

He slid in without a thought, the sleeper cell come back to destroy.

The room was strange without the noise. A tomb in every sense now. He second-guessed himself as he turned the corner on the row. Without the lights, there really was no way to distinguish them.

Other than the dead robot on the floor. That gave it away. He walked up to it and frowned, a tired look on his face. Tired determination.

He dropped the bottles to the floor and picked up one at random, looking it over. Rubbing alcohol. Sure. He opened it and dumped it out carelessly over Lu's corpse, focusing most of it on the thing's face. It emptied and he dropped the bottle to the side, then stuck a match right then and there and lit it, intent to get it going now that he had eyes on the thing, now that he saw it. He backed up a step and dropped the match, and it caught.

Whoof.

The flames poofed to life and started up on the body, eating it away slowly, a strange outer layer of skin on its face melting away. He felt a primitive curiosity pulling him in as he stood sentry over it, watching the eyes boil and then pop, the black netting covering the mouth hole disintegrate and fall away in the orifice. He had no words for the moment, no thoughts to reflect on. There was no revelry.

He just watched.

Once the face was nothing more than some misshapen skull of techno melt, he opened the other bottles and flung the contents all over the server bays. Then he struck a match and walked away, the shadow of his figure materializing in front of him amidst the warm orange glow behind.

By the time he got back to the parking lot, the windows all around the floor were orange. He waited for a minute, hoping for something, something inside maybe that might stir within him. Justice… No. That was off the table. Just something.

The blaze was so different from the one at the VR theater, but he couldn't quite put his finger on it. He just felt more then.

Now he felt nothing.

Emptiness.

He searched the car and found the keys in the front on the floor, so he threw the laptop in and headed for home, to sleep, or die, or perhaps some semblance of the two. He opted for the tunnels, driving in manual mode, even when autonomous would have been easier.

The tunnel heading home felt quiet in the same way that the floor had felt quiet, undisturbed and untainted now in the wee hours of the morning. The overhead lights were dimmer than usual, narrowing the space around him, enclosing him as he traveled along. It disquieted him, this effect. It all made him feel dead. The road to the next life.

Janice was in the back, so really, it made sense to him somehow. He was the boatman now.

All the color was gone from his vision, as if his world had turned to gray hues. His hands felt oddly detached from the rest of his body, no feel of the wheel to grip onto. Just a bland, sterile, hold on reality. None of it mattered. He had become Midas.

The whole world has the Midas touch, though, doesn't it? he thought. *We're chasing after feelings that are long dead.*

We're just deluding ourselves if...

But then he saw Edgar's face fly by the wall in the shadows and slammed on the brakes, unbelieving as the car skidded along the air to a stop.

What were the odds that he'd end up in the tunnel, he wondered as he looked through the rear view. What were the odds.

He threw the car in reverse and backed up, gliding past the mural as it came into view in front of him, the smiling face looking down at him. It was the face of the man that he had loved and lost. *The beginning of my black widow phase,* he thought. *And with Janice in the back, it's the first and the last.*

And technically, the two hadn't even met. Such similar characters in my mind now—same stubbornness, same disposition— and they had never shared a conversation together. Never would.

That has to change, he thought, and landed the car right then and there.

As the engine cut and he got out, he heard the sound of silence in both directions, not a soul in the tunnel other than him for all that he knew. It was a good time for a meeting. He went around to the hatch and opened it, holding his breath as Janice came into view.

Her face was already oriented towards the opening, prepared, aware even in her perpetual slumbering. He coughed back the emotions in his throat, and leaned in to pick her up. Her body felt more like wood now than flesh, the skin much more rigid than he had expected as he cradled her body in his arms. As he walked around the car towards the mural, his eyes were already regarding it in anxious reverence. It was so tall, so imposing in the small space. It must have been twenty-five feet high or more. The image was more of a street-style caricature of his face, similar, but more defined in the jaw and brow, more masculine. It reminded him of Lenin or Che, the stereotypical freedom fighter look.

That was Edgar. That's what killed him.

Greg walked up to the corner of Edgar's lapel and sat down against the wall, Janice still in his arms, and leaned his head back against the wall.

He swallowed, realizing how crazy he had become, more than that, how much it didn't matter anymore. He cleared his throat.

"Hey, man," he muttered. "How you been. It's been a while, I guess."

He looked down at Janice and saw that a few strands of hair had fallen across her face–something she never would have abided—so he brushed them away. She was always fiddling with her hair. She had so much of it.

"This is my wife, Jan... Jan..." but the name wouldn't come out. He couldn't do it. He was already sobbing, big droplets falling from his eyes onto her shirt, onto her neck. He wiped his face away on his arm, but he was still going, so he leaned his head back, letting it rip for a moment.

After a while, he let up and took a long, deep breath. Then he looked down at her again.

She looked peaceful though, didn't she, he thought admiringly. At least there was that.

"This is my Janice," he finally got out with a cough. "You would have liked her."

He thought then of them meeting, of them smiling, greeting, and hugging each other. The image warmed him up inside. They would have liked each other, he knew. They would have hit it off. They were quirky, so it probably would have taken a minute for them to warm up, but they'd have stuck it out and given each other a chance.

They were both like that. They tried. They cared.

That's why they saved you, Greg, he thought. *They put their necks out for you in their own way. They were trying to protect you.*

"Yeah, but I still got her killed," he replied acidly, feeling suddenly ashamed of himself. "If I'd have died back then, she'd still be alive."

They all would. It was true, so true and undeniable that it made him angry inside.

He looked over his shoulder then. "Why didn't I follow you, Edgar?" he asked. "Why did I chicken out like I did?" He let his head fall back to his chest. "You were the tough one. You did it and it got everybody going. It got me going. But I still couldn't do it... Why not?"

I believed it, didn't I? he wondered, suddenly unsure. *It was something to stand for. At least there was that.*

He'd come to introduce them and had made it about himself, he realized. It was always like that. His whole life was like that.

The existential crisis within always took center stage. Even now, when he was just a shell.

"I really did want you two to meet though," he offered up. "I don't know why though."

Because they were different from you, Greg. They cared about people. They died for people. They were both freedom fighters. You were something else.

What though?

What would you think, Janice? he wanted to ask her as he looked down at her, though his mouth wouldn't move to get it out. *What would you say to me right now?*

You should have died instead was the thought that came to him, but it wasn't that. That was him talking. *She'd of told you to cut yourself some slack, Greg... to stop trying to figure it out so much.*

"You were the best, Janice," he said and kissed her. "I wish you were here." Saying it out loud was a mistake, he thought as the tears came again. "I tried–I tried. I really did, babe. I really did."

I did though, he thought. *I didn't chicken out this time. It wasn't enough, but it was all I could do.*

He looked back up, feeling strangely like Edgar had heard him, was listening somehow. He felt the need to get up, so he strained to his feet, using the wall to push himself up, and walked into the middle of the road. Then he turned around.

"I didn't actually chicken out this time," he told Edgar. "I did it. I took the plunge."

I took a stand, he told himself. *I made the hard choice.*

Would you be proud of me, Edgar? I think you would.

Just then, the flashing of lights from down the tunnel-way caught his attention, blue and red, and he heard the sound of sirens immediately after, bouncing off the walls then, shaking him from his dream.

Back to reality, he thought. *This really is the end.*

"Get on the ground!" an officer shouted at him from behind his car door, his gun drawn and read to fire.

"I can't. I'm holding—"

"Put down the person in your arms," he demanded, "And then put your hands on your head, but don't try anything. My gun is drawn on you."

Slowly and carefully, he dropped to his knees and then lowered Janice's body on the floor, letting her go slowly, wanting so badly now to just have a few more seconds with her. More time. More time. He wanted to stall it. He felt himself stalling it. Just then, he heard a shuffling behind him, and as he jerked up, his hands pulling out from under his wife to shove onto his head, a pair of hands grabbed him from behind and ripped his arms back, and then officers from all around were rushing in on him now that he was being cuffed.

"You have the right to remain silent," one of them was saying, starting in on his Miranda rights, as he watched the others circle around his wife on the ground, all of them dressed the same as the AAT agents from before.

"Don't!" he cried out as the strong arms pulled him away. "Just leave her alone!" They'd disturb her, carry her off and throw her away in the car like some god awful luggage. "Don't touch her! Don't touch her!"

They didn't pay him any mind.

The agent pulled him up and shoved him away towards another black sedan, the small circular light swiveling blue and red on the car's roof corner. "Boy, you're going to get it," he told him, his voice low and angry. "You psycho piece of shit."

Greg didn't respond. He felt himself sucking inward again, lost in thought.

The car door opened, and he ducked in, the officer helping with a shove.

The door slammed shut behind him.

It was quiet for a while, Greg sitting in the back of the car, staring ahead at the headrest of the seat in front, behind the glass partition. Outside, he could hear people talking. On and on, they seemed to be talking. He listened, but most of it was too muffled to make out. Most of what he could decipher concerned the state of the stolen vehicle, the dead agents, the laptop.

They'd been to Friedmont Towers. Had wrapped that up quickly apparently. *Probably to cover it all up*, he figured.

A pair fell in beside the car, talking by his door.

"Dude, my wife was so excited," the tall one said.

"How do you know this isn't bullshit, though?" The other one, the short one, replied. "Sounds a little hard to believe, don't you think?"

"Na, man," the tall man replied in earnest. "I fuckin' swear. I've been following this shit. They really did it."

"Grew a kid?"

"Yeah, man. It *just* happened. She texted me the video and everything. Here. Check it out."

Silence. They were crowding around a phone, watching something, both of their faces tuned in, exhilarated looking.

He sat up to see, but the short one saw and scowled at him. "Sit in the seat, sir!" Then they wandered away a little. He could still hear them faintly. It was mostly *woe* and *dude*, which made sense, really. What was there to say anyway? If it was true, it would really be something.

He wondered if he'd get to see it happen, wherever he was headed.

"Things are really changing," he heard one of them say suddenly.

Things are really changing, huh, he thought then, unbelieving. *Would you look at that?*

An agent opened the driver door just then, got in, and started the car up. He said something, but Greg wasn't really listening. He was off in his head now thinking about the reality of things as they were, as they had just become.

The car drove off and from the window, he saw Edgar's face one last time, that big smile on his face, as if he knew where things were going before they had even gotten there.

What do you know that I don't, huh Edgar? Maybe I did know somewhere. Maybe that's why I did it.

Maybe.

www.ingramcontent.com/pod-product-compliance
Lightning Source LLC
Chambersburg PA
CBHW011145070726
47591CB00015B/2259